RUNNING WITH THE PACK

OTHER BOOKS BY EKATERINA SEDIA

The Alchemy of Stone
Bewere the Night (edited; forthcoming)
The House of Discarded Dreams (forthcoming)
Paper Cities: An Anthology of Urban Fantasy (edited)
The Secret History of Moscow

RUNNING WITH THE PACK

EDITED BY EKATERINA SEDIA

PRIME BOOKS

RUNNING WITH THE PACK

Prime Books
www.prime-books.com

For more information, contact Prime Books:
prime@prime-books.com

ISBN: 978-1-60701-219-1

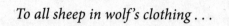

To all sheep in wolf's clothing . . .

TABLE OF CONTENTS

INTRODUCTION

There's a view of werewolves (espoused even on the back cover of this volume) as an expression of the animal and the dark in the usually suppressed and mild-mannered civilized person; we like to think of ourselves as beasts, our wild instincts kept in check only by a thin veneer of social necessity. This fantasy is a persistent and appealing one: a jacketed executive by day, but the moment the full moon breaks through the clouds, watch out! There will be claws and fur and blood and howling.

But is this view accurate? I'd like to propose that it is not. In our natural state, humans are large, hairless apes who run well and live in groups. We are not predators—we are prey, something many romantically-minded individuals discover (one assumes, to their chagrin) while trying to survive in the wilderness, communing with nature, and engaging in other solitary pursuits in areas inhabited by large meat-eaters. Wolves and large cats are predators; we are their food.

And this, I think, is really the crux of the matter: werewolves are not the expression of our own wildness, but the longing to be like those who hunt us, the desire to become the predator. In that sense, the entirety of human civilization, our conquest and subjugation of the world, can be seen through such a lens. Being prey is embarrassing and undignified, it exposes our soft chewy insides, and who likes that? So we dominate and posture, and pretend that we are wolves inside of ape suits, rather than just . . . well, apes.

Then again, all of this is conjecture. If you look at the diversity of the stories presented here, the familiar tropes twisted in interesting ways, you'll see that lycanthropy is much more than a simple urge to be an animal—it can be a metaphor or a joke, a tale of extinction or a new beginning, a disease or a blessing. So why don't you sit back, crack the book open, and indulge in the fantasies of being a predator?

Ekaterina Sedia
January 2010
New Jersey

WILD RIDE

CARRIE VAUGHN

———◆———

Just once, he wouldn't use a condom. What could happen? But it hadn't been just once. It could have been any one of the half-dozen men he'd drifted between over the last two years. His wild years, he thought of them now. He'd been so stupid. They all had said, just once, trust me. T.J., young and eager, had wanted so very much to please them.

"I'm sorry," the guy at the clinic said, handing T.J. some photocopied pages. "You have options. It's not a death sentence like in the old days. But you'll have to watch yourself. Your health is more important than ever now. And you have to be careful—"

"Yeah, thanks," T.J. said, standing before the counselor had finished his spiel.

"Remember, there's always help—"

T.J. walked out, crumpling the pages in his hand.

Engines purred, sputtered, grumbled, clacked like insects, and growled like bears. Motorbikes raced up the course, catching air over hills, leaning into curves, biting into the earth with treaded tires, kicking up clods, giving the air a smell like chalk and gasoline. Hundreds more idled, revved, tested, waited. Thousands of people milled, riders in fitted jackets of every color, mechanics in coveralls, women bursting out of too-small tank tops, and most people in T-shirts and jeans. T.J. loved it here. Bikes made sense. Machines could be fixed, their problems could be solved, and they didn't judge.

He supposed he ought to get in touch with his partners. Figure out which one had passed the disease onto him, and who he might have passed it on to. Easier said than done. They'd been flings; he didn't have phone numbers.

"Look it, here he comes." Mitch, Gary Maddox's stout good-natured assistant, shook T.J.'s arm in excitement.

Gary's heat was starting. T.J. looked for Gary's colors, the red-and-blue jacket and dark blue helmet. He liked to think he could pick out his bike's growl over all the others. T.J. had spent the morning fine-tuning the engine, which had never sounded better.

They'd come up to one of the hills overlooking the track to watch the race. T.J. wanted to lose himself in this world, just for another day. He wanted to put off thinking about anything else for as long as possible.

The starting gate slammed down, and the dozen bikes rocketed from the starting line, engines running high and smooth. Gary pulled out in front early, like he usually did. Get in front, stay in front, don't let anyone else mess up his ride. Some guys liked messing with the rest of the field, playing mind games and causing trouble. Gary just wanted to win, and T.J. admired that.

Mitch jumped and whooped with the rest of the crowd, cheering the riders on. T.J. just watched. Another rider's bike, toward the back, was spitting puffs of black smoke. Something wrong there. Everyone else seemed to be going steady. Gary might as well have been floating an inch above the dirt. That was exactly how it was supposed to be—making it look easy.

"Ho-*leee!*" Mitch let out a cry and the crowd let out a gasp as they all saw one of the riders go down.

T.J. could tell it was going to happen right before it did, the way the rider—in the middle of the pack to the outside—took the turn a little too sharply to make up time, gunned his motor a little too early, and stuck his leg out to brace—a dangerous move. His front tire caught, the bike flipped, and it might have ended there. A dozen guys dropped their bikes one way or another every day out here. But everything was set up just wrong for this guy. Momentum carried the bike into the straw bale barrier lining the track—then over, and down the steep slope on the other side. Bike and rider finally parted ways, the bike spinning in one direction, trailing parts. The rider flopped and tumbled in another direction, limp and lifeless, before coming to rest face up on a bank of dirt. The few observers who'd hiked up the steep vantage scattered in its path.

For a moment, everyone stood numb and breathless. Then the ambulance siren started up.

Yellow flags stopped the race. Mitch and T.J. stumbled down their side of the hill trying to get to the rider.

"You know who he is?"

"Alex Price," Mitch said, huffing.

"New on the circuit?"

"No, local boy. Big fish little pond kind of guy."

The rider hadn't moved since he stopped tumbling. Legs shouldn't bend the way his were bent. Blood and rips marred his clothing. T.J. and Mitch reached him first, but both held back, unwilling to touch him. T.J. studied the rider's chest, searching for the rise and fall of breath, and saw nothing. The guy had to have been pulverized. Then his hand twitched.

"Hey, buddy, don't move!" Mitch said, stumbling forward to his knees to hold the rider back.

T.J. thought he heard bones creaking, rubbing against each other as the rider shuddered, pawing the ground to find bearings. Next to Mitch, he tried to keep the rider still with a hand on his shoulder. Price flinched, as if shrugging him away, and T.J. almost let go—the guy was strong, even now. Maybe it was adrenaline.

The ambulance and EMTs arrived, and T.J. gratefully got out of the way. By then, the rider had taken off his own helmet and mask. He had brown hair a few inches long, a lean tanned face covered with sweat. He gasped for breath and winced with pain. When he moved, it was as if he'd slept wrong and cramped his muscles, not just tumbled over fifty yards at forty miles an hour.

At his side, an EMT pushed him back, slipped a breathing mask over his face, started putting a brace on his neck. The second EMT brought over a back board. Price pushed the mask away.

"I'm *fine*," he muttered.

"Lie *down*, sir, we're putting you on a board."

Grinning, Price laid back.

T.J. felt like he was watching something amazing, miraculous. He'd *seen* the crash. He'd seen plenty of crashes, even plenty that looked awful but the riders walked away from. He'd also seen some that left riders broken for life, and he'd thought this was one of those. But there was Price, awake, relaxed, like he'd only stubbed a toe.

Price rolled his eyes, caught T.J.'s gaze, and chuckled at his gaping stare. "What, you've never seen someone who's invincible?"

The EMT's shifted him to the board, secured the straps over him, and carried him off.

"Looks like he's gonna be okay," Mitch said, shrugging off his bafflement.

Invincible, T.J. thought. There wasn't any such thing.

At the track the following weekend, T.J. was tuning Gary's second bike when Mitch came up the aisle and leaned on the handlebars. "He's back. Did you hear?"

The handlebars rocked, twisting the front tire and knocking T.J.'s wrench out of his hand. He sighed. "What? Who?"

"Price, Alex Price. He's totally okay."

"How is that even possible?" T.J. said. "You saw that crash. He should have been smashed to pieces."

"Who knows? Guys walk away from the craziest shit." Mitch went to the cab and pulled a beer out of the cooler.

It was true, anything was possible, Price might have fallen just right, so he didn't break and the bike didn't crush him. Every crash looked horrible, like it should tear the riders to ribbons, and most of the time no one was hurt worse than cuts and bruises. In fact, how many people even looked forward to the crashes, the spike of adrenaline and sense of horror, watching tragedy unfold? But something here didn't track.

T.J. tossed the wrench in the tool box, closed and locked and lid, and set out to find Price.

Today was just practice runs; the atmosphere at the track was laid back and workmanlike. Not like race days, which were like carnivals. He went up one aisle of trucks and trailers, down the next, not sure what he was looking for—if he was local, Price probably didn't ride for a team, and wouldn't have sponsors with logos all over a fancy trailer. He'd have a plain homespun rig. His jacket had been black and red; T.J. looked for that.

Turned out, all he had to do was find the mob of people. T.J. worked his way to the edge of the crowd that had gathered to hear Price tell the story. This couldn't have been the first time he told it.

"I just tucked in and let it happen," Price said, a smile drawing in his audience. He gave an "awe, shucks" shrug and accepted their adoration.

T.J. wanted to hate the guy. Not sure why. He wasn't quite his type. Or maybe it was the matter of survival. Price had survived, and T.J. wanted to. Arms crossed, looking skeptical, he stood off to the side.

Price looked friendly enough, smiling with people and shaking all the hands offered to him, but he also seemed twitchy. He kept glancing over his shoulder, like he was looking for a way out. T.J. worked his way forward as the crowd dispersed, until they were nearly alone.

"Can I talk to you privately?" T.J. said.

"Hey, I remember you," Price said. "You helped, right after the crash. Thanks, man."

T.J. found himself wanting to glance away. "I just want to talk for a second."

"Come on, I'll get you a beer."

Price led him to the front part of the trailer, which was set up as a break area—lawn chairs, a cooler, a portable grill. From the cooler he pulled out a couple of bottles of a microbrew—the good stuff—and popped off the caps by hand. Absently, T.J. wiped the damp bottle on the hem of his T-shirt.

"What's the problem?" Price asked.

T.J. wondered if he really came across that nervous, that transparent. He was trying to be steady. "The crash last week. What really happened?"

Price shrugged. "You were there. You saw the whole thing."

T.J. shook his head. "Yeah. I saw it. You shouldn't be standing here— your legs were smashed, your whole body twisted up. Everyone else can write it off and say you were lucky, but I'm not buying it. What really happened?"

He expected Price to deny it, to wave him away and tell him he was crazy. But the guy just looked at him, a funny smile playing on his lips. "Why do you want to know? Why so worked up over it?"

So much for playing it cool. "I need help."

"And why do you think I can help you? What makes you think I can just hand over my good luck?"

He was right. T.J.'s own panic had gotten the better of him, and he'd gone grasping at soap bubbles. Whatever he'd seen on the day of the crash had been his own wishful thinking. He'd wanted to see the impossible.

"You're right. I'm sorry. Never mind." Ducking to hide his blush, he turned away, looking for a place to set his untasted beer before he fled.

"Kid, wait a minute," Price called him back, and T.J. stopped. "What's your name?"

"T.J."

"What would you say if I told you you're right?"

"About what?"

"I'm invincible. I can't be killed. Not by a little old crash, anyway. Now—what are you looking to get saved from? What are you so scared of?"

Now that he'd said it, T.J. didn't believe him. Price was making fun of him. And how much worse would it be if T.J. actually told him? He turned to leave again.

"Hey. Seriously. What's wrong? Why are you so scared of dying that you need me?"

T.J. took a long draw on the beer, then said, "I just tested positive for HIV." It was the first time he'd said it out loud. It almost hurt.

"Rough," Price said.

"Yeah." T.J. kicked his toe in the dirt. And what did he expect Price say to him? What could anyone say? Nothing.

"Hey," Price said, and once again T.J. had to turn back, obeying the command in his voice. "What are you willing to do to turn that around? You willing to become a monster?"

"You talk to some people, I already am," T.J. said, putting on a lopsided smile.

"You know about the Dustbowl?"

"Yeah."

"Stop by tonight, seven or seven-thirty. If you're really sure."

"Sure about what?" he asked.

"Just show up and I'll explain it all." He walked away, past the trailer to the cab of the truck. Meeting over.

It seemed like an obvious trap—he'd show up and walk into a beating. The Dustbowl was one of the bars up the road; some of the riders liked to hang out there. Not Gary—he was serious about riding and didn't feel much of a need to show how tough he was off the track. T.J. had stayed away; the place had an uncomfortable vibe to it, a little too edgy, though it was hard to tell if the atmosphere was just for show. He preferred drinking at one of the larger bars, where he didn't stand out so much.

He didn't know whether to believe there really was something different about Price, something that had saved him from the awful wreck, or if Price was making fun of him. He could check it out. Just step in and step back out again if he didn't like the look of the place. Make sure Mitch knew where he was going in case something happened and he vanished.

That would solve his problems real quick, wouldn't it?

He hitched a ride with some friends of Mitch who were on their way into town. T.J. must have sounded convincing when he said he was meeting somebody and that everything was okay. The sun was close to setting, washing out the sky to a pale yellow, and summer heat radiated off the dusty earth. The air was hot, sticky, making his breath catch.

The Dustbowl was part of a row of simple wooden buildings set up to look like an old-west street, but without disguising the modern shingles, windows, and neon beer signs. At one end was a barbeque place that T.J. had heard was pretty mediocre but cheap. The place smelled like overcooked pork, which made his stomach turn.

Walking into the bar alone, he felt like an idiot. Not just a loser, but a loser looking for trouble. The bullies would be drawn to him. He had to shake off the feeling—if he looked scared, of course he'd get picked on. He straightened, rounded his shoulders, and took a deep breath to relax. He had to look at ease, like he belonged.

Feeling a little more settled in his skin—he tried to convince himself that everyone in the half-filled room wasn't staring at him—he went to the bar, ordered a Coke, and asked if Alex Price was here.

"He might be in back," the bartender said. "That guy's nuts—did you see his crash last week?"

"Yeah," T.J. said. "I had a front row seat. It was bad."

"And he gets up and walks away. Crazy." Shaking his head, the bartender turned away.

T.J. put his back to the bar and looked around. TV screens mounted in the corners showed baseball. Tables and chairs were scattered, without any particular order to them. A waitress in a short skirt delivered a tray of beers to a table of mechanics from the track. No sign of Price. He'd give it the time it took to finish the Coke, resisting the urge to upend it and down the whole thing in a go.

Halfway through, a woman came out a door in back and sauntered along the bar toward him. She was petite, cute, with softly curling brown hair bouncing around her shoulders and a size too small T-shirt showing off curves.

"Are you the guy looking for Alex?" she said.

"Yeah."

"Come on back, he's waiting for you." She gave him a wide smile and tipped her head to the back door.

And if that didn't look like a bad situation. . . "There a reason he can't talk to me out here?"

"Not scared, are you? Come on, you can trust me." She sidled closer, gazing up at him with half-lidded eyes and brushing a finger up his arm.

He never knew in these situations if he should tell her she was wasting her efforts, or just let her have her fun. He let it go and went with her. He was good enough in a fight—he just wouldn't let anyone get between him and the door. It would be okay.

She led him through a hallway with a concrete floor and aged walls. A swinging door on the left opened to a kitchen; doors on the right were labeled as men's and women's restrooms. At the end of the hall was a storage closet. Through there, another door opened into a huge garage—four, maybe five cars could fit inside. Nobody out front would hear him if he yelled. He tried not to be nervous.

A tall, windowless overhead door was closed and locked. A few cardboard boxes and a steel tool closet were pushed up against the walls. Right in the middle sat a steel cage, big enough to hold a lion. A dozen or so people were gathered around the cage. Alex Price stood at the head of the group, drawn straight and tall, his arms crossed.

Oh, this did not look good. T.J. turned to go back the way he'd come, hoping to make it a confident walk instead of a panicked run.

The woman grabbed his arm. "No no, wait, we're not going to hurt you." Her flirting manner was gone.

T.J. brushed himself out of her grip and put his back to the wall. She gave him space, keeping her hands raised and visible. None of the others had moved. Their gazes were curious, amused, watchful, suspicious—but not hateful. Not bloodthirsty.

Price just kept smiling. "The cage isn't for you, kid," he said. "Remember when I asked you if you're willing to become a monster?"

T.J. shook his head. "I don't understand."

"I can cure you, but it won't be easy."

"It never is," T.J. said. He met Price's gaze and held it, refusing to be scared of this guy. "I still don't understand."

"We're a pack," he said, nodding at the people gathered around him. "We've talked it over, and we can help you. But you have to really want it."

"Pack," T.J. said. "Not a gang?"

"No."

The people only looked like a group because they were standing together; they didn't look anything alike—three were women, a couple of the men were young, maybe even younger than T.J. A couple wore jeans and T-shirts, a couple looked like bikers, like Price. One guy was in a business suit, the tie loosened, his jacket over his arm. One of the women wore a skirt and blouse. They were normal—shockingly normal, considering they were standing in an empty garage behind a bar, next to a large steel cage. T.J. felt a little dizzy.

"He's not going to believe anything until we show him, Alex," the woman with the curling brown hair said.

"Believe what?" T.J. said, off balance, nearing panic again. She had a sly, smiling look in her eyes.

"You want to do it?" Price said to her.

"Yeah. Sure." She looked at T.J., then quickly grabbed his hand and squeezed it. Her skin was hot—T.J. hadn't realized that his hands were cold. She whispered, "I want to help. I really do." Then she went to the cage.

This was a cult, he thought. Some weird, freaky religious thing. They had some kind of faith healing going on. Did Price really think faith healing had saved him?

T.J. stayed because *something* had saved Price.

The woman took off her clothes, handing them to the woman in the skirt. One of the others opened the cage. Naked, she crawled in and sat on all fours, and seemed happy to do so, as the cage door was locked behind her.

"Ready, Jane?" Price said, reaching a hand into the cage. The woman licked it, quick and dog-like.

As if this couldn't get any stranger. T.J. inched toward the doorway.

"Don't go," Price said. "Wait just another minute."

The woman in the cage bowed her back and grunted. Then, she blurred. T.J. blinked and squinted, to better see what was happening. He moved closer.

Her skin had turned to fur. Her bones were melting, her face stretching. She opened her mouth and had thick, sharp teeth; that hadn't been there before. This wasn't real, this wasn't possible, it was some kind of hoax.

T.J. stumbled back, launching himself toward the door. But Price was at his side, grabbing his arms, holding him. T.J. could have sworn he'd been on the other side of the room.

"Just wait," Price said, calmly, soothing, as T.J. thrashed in his grip. "Calm down and watch."

In another minute, a wolf stood in the cage, long-legged and rangy, with a gray back and pale belly. It shook out its fur, rubbed its face on its legs, and looked out at Price. T.J. couldn't catch his breath, not even to speak.

"That's right," Price said, as if he knew the word T.J. was trying to spit out.

And that was the secret. That was how Price had survived. Because he was one of those, too. Every one of them was like her.

He tried to convince himself he wasn't afraid of them. "It's crazy. You're all crazy." He hated that his voice shook. He still pulled against Price's grip—but Price had a monster's strength.

"You're not the only one who's stood there and said so," Price said.

"So what are you saying? That's the cure? Become like that?"

"We're all invulnerable. We don't get sick. We don't get hurt. Oh, we still age, we'll all still die someday. And the silver bullet part is real. But when nobody else believes in this, what are the odds anyone's going to shoot you with a silver bullet?"

"And the full moon thing is real, too?" T.J. said, chuckling, because what else could he do?

"Yes," Price said.

"No, no," T.J. said, giving himself over to the hysteria.

Price spoke softly, steadily, like he'd given this speech before. "All you have to do is stick your hand in the cage. But you have to ask yourself: if you're not brave enough to deal with your life now, then why would you be brave enough to stick your hand in the cage? You have to be brave enough to be a monster. You think you're that brave? I'm not sure you are."

Of course he'd say it like a dare.

T.J. had spent the last few weeks in a constant state of subdued panic. Trying to adjust his identity from healthy to sick, when he didn't feel sick and didn't know what being sick even meant. And here he was being asked to do it again, change his identity, his whole being. He'd spent his whole life changing his identity, announcing it, feeling good about it, then feeling it slip out from under him again. He thought he'd done the right thing when he told his parents he was gay. They'd kicked him out, just like he'd known they would. He'd been ready for it—happy to leave, even. But from one day to the next he'd gone from closeted son to outed and independent—free, he'd thought of it then.

He went to the clinic and got tested because he'd had a raw, nagging feeling that he'd done it all wrong and was paying a price for all that freedom. From one day to the next he'd gone from healthy to not. And now, Price was offering him a chance to do it again, to change himself in the space of a minute. To an animal, a creature that shouldn't exist, with sharp teeth behind curling lips.

The wolf's eyes, golden-brown, stared at him, gleaming, eager. The woman—still flirting with him.

He could face one horror, or the other. Those were his choices. That was what he had brought on himself.

But wouldn't it be nice to be invincible, for once?

"It can't be that easy," T.J. whispered.

"No, it's not. But that's why we're here," Price said. "We'll help you."

If he asked for time to think about it, he would never come back. He stepped toward the cage.

It was going to hurt. He repeated to himself, *invincible*, and he glanced at the people gathered around him—werewolves, all of them. But none of them looked on him with anger or hate. Caution, maybe. Doubt, maybe. But he would be all right. It would be a like a shot, a needle in the arm, a vaccination against worse terrors.

Price stood behind him—to keep him from fleeing? The others gathered around, like they wanted to watch. All he had to do was reach. The wolf inside the cage whined and turned a fidgeting circle.

"You can still back out. No shame in walking out of here," Price said, whispering behind him.

It didn't look so monstrous. More like a big dog. All he had to do was reach in and scratch its ear. T.J. rested his hand on the top of the cage. The bars were smooth, cool, as if the steel had absorbed the chill from the concrete underneath.

Kneeling, T.J. slipped his hand down to the side, then pushed his arm inside. The wolf carefully put her jaws around his forearm. He clenched his hand into a fist, and by instinct he lunged away. The wolf closed her mouth on him, and her fangs broke skin.

He thrashed, pulling back, fighting against her. Bracing his feet against the bars, he pushed away. That only made his skin tear through her teeth, and she bit harder, digging in, putting her paws on him to hold him still so that her claws cut him as well as his teeth. Behind him Price grabbed hold, securing him in a bear hug, whispering.

The pain was total. He couldn't feel his hand, his arm, the wolf's gnawing, but he could feel his flesh ripping and the blood pouring off him, matting in the fur of her snout. All that infected, tainted blood.

He looked away and clamped his jaws shut, trapping air and screams behind tightly closed lips.

By the time Price pulled T.J. away from the cage, he'd passed out.

When he woke up, he was in a twin bed in what looked like a sunny guest room. The decorations—paisley bedspread, out-of-date furniture set—lacked personality. The woman who had been a wolf sat on a chair next to the bed, smiling.

He felt calm, and that seemed strange. He felt like he ought to be panicking. But he remembered days of being sick, sweating, swearing, fighting against blankets he'd been wrapped in, and cool hands holding him back, telling him he was going to be fine, everything was going to be fine. All the panic had burned out of him.

He pulled his hands out from under the sheets and looked at them. His right arm was whole, uninjured. Not even a scar. But he remembered the claws tearing, the skin parting.

He took a deep breath, pressing his head to the pillow, assaulted by smells. The sheets smelled of cotton, stabbed through with the acerbic tang of detergent—it made his eyes water. A hint of vegetation played in the air, as if a window was open and he could smell trees—not just trees, but the leaves, fruit ripening on boughs, the smell of summer. Something was cooking in another part of the house. He'd never smelled so much.

The woman, Jane, moved toward him and her scent covered him, smothered him. Her skin, the warmth of her hair, the ripeness of her clothes, a hint of sweat, a hint of breath—and more than that, something wild that he couldn't identify. This—fur, was it fur?—both made him want to run and calmed him. Inside him, a feeling he couldn't describe—an instinct, maybe—called to him. It's her, she did this.

He breathed through his mouth to cut out the smells, to try to relax.

"Good morning," she said, wearing a thin and sympathetic smile.

He tried to speak, but his dry tongue stuck. She reached to a bedside table to a glass of water, which she gave him. It helped.

"I'm sorry I hurt you," she said. "But that's why we do it like this, so the choice has to be yours. Do you understand?"

He nodded because he did. He'd had the chance to walk away. He almost had. He wondered if he was going to regret not walking away.

"How do you feel?" she said.

"This is strange."

She laughed. "If that's all you have to say about it, you're doing very well."

Her laughter was comforting. With each breath he took, he felt himself grow stronger. It was like that moment just past being sick, when you still remembered the illness but had moved past it.

"I'm starving," he said—the hunger felt amazing. He wanted to eat, to keep eating, rip into his food, tear with his claws—

And that was odd.

He winced.

"Oh, Alex was right bringing you in," Jane said. "You're going to do just fine."

He hoped she was right.

On his first full moon, on a windswept plain in the hills of central California, he screamed and couldn't stop as his body broke and changed, shifting from skin and reason to fur and instinct. The scream turned into a howl, and the dozen others of the pack joined in, and the howls turned into a song. They taught him to run on four legs, to smell and listen and sense, to hunt, and that if he didn't fight the change didn't hurt as much. In the morning, the wolves slept and returned to their human forms, but they remained a pack, sleeping together, skin to skin, family and invincible. They taught him how to keep the animal locked inside until the next full moon, despite the song that called to him, the euphoria of four legs on a moonlit night. He'd never felt so powerful, not even when he left home.

He'd called Mitch and told him that he'd been sick with the flu and was staying with a friend. When he returned, the track had changed.

It had become brilliant, textured, nuanced. The dust in the air was chalk, sand, earth, and rubber. The exhaust was oil, plastic, smoke and fire. And the crowd—a hundred different people and all their moods, scents, and noises. A dozen bikes were on the track; each engine had a slightly different sound. He sneezed at first, his nose on fire, before he learned to filter, and his ears burned before he figured out how to block the chaos. He didn't need to take it all in, he only had to focus on what was in front of him. But he could take it all in, whenever he wanted.

The world had changed. Terrifying and brilliant, all of it.

Alex had given T.J. a ride. Before T.J. left the truck, Alex touched his arm, calming him. The animal inside him that had been ready to tuck his tail and run settled.

"You going to be okay?" Alex said.

"Yeah," T.J. said, breathing slowly as he'd been taught, settling the creature down.

"I'm here if you need anything. Don't wait until you get into trouble. Come find me first," he said.

If the pack was a new family, then Alex was its father, leader, master. That was another thing T.J. hadn't expected. He'd never really had a father-figure to turn to.

Over the last week he'd learned what the price for invincibility was: learning to pass. Moving among people, thinking all the time how easy it would be to rip into them and feast, imagining their blood on his tongue but never being able to taste. Because if he tried it—if any of them ever actually lost control—the others would rip his heart out. That was how they'd stayed secret for centuries: never let the humans know they were there.

So he worked on Gary's bikes and thought about the engine, belts, carburetor, and transmission, and remembered that the people around him were his friends and didn't deserve to die by a wolf's claws. He wanted to keep his old life. It was worth working to keep. That was the trick, Alex and Jane taught him. You can keep your old life. It won't be the same, but it'll still be there.

And he'd actually get to live to enjoy it, now. It was a relief. Made him want to howl.

Something fell on him, knocking the wrench out of his hand. He sprang to his feet, hands clenched, turning to snarl at whoever had done it, interrupted him—*attacked*. Then he closed his eyes and took a deep breath.

Mitch was waving him over. A dirty rag lay on the ground next to the wrench, that was all that had hit him.

"Gary's last race is up, you coming to watch?" Mitch said.

His wolf settled. T.J. put away his tools and followed Mitch to the straw bales ringing the track.

"You okay? You seem a little jumpy lately," Mitch asked.

He didn't know the half of it. "I'm okay. I probably need more sleep."

"Don't we all," Mitch said.

It gave him a sense of déjà vu, watching Gary and Alex ride in the same race. This time, though, the PA system was too loud, the crowd of spectators pressed too close, and he didn't know who to watch, Gary or Alex. Gary was his friend, the guy who paid him under the table to keep his bikes running, who'd given him a break when T.J. needed one so desperately. But Alex was . . . something else entirely. Something bigger than T.J. had words for. Alex was the way he felt howling at the full moon.

The crowd buzzed, because this was Alex's first race after the spectacular crash. It had only been a few weeks, but it seemed much longer, months or years ago. Gary won the race; Alex didn't crash again. The incident faded from memory in that moment, but T.J. realized he saw the crash as a turning point—it had changed his life.

Last race. Gary was moving to the pro circuit, to a track out east, and had asked T.J. to come with him. The three of them made a good team. It was a huge opportunity, to go from scraping by as a bush league mechanic to working for a team with a real shot. But a weight seemed to tie him down. Like a collar and leash.

He and Mitch raced to the finish line to meet up with Gary. This was another of T.J.'s favorite things about the track, racing, bikes, and the crowds gathering after the race, offering congratulations and condolences, dissecting what had happened, arguing, handing out cold beers and drinking as they wheeled bikes back to their trailers. This had been the last race of the day; the party spilled onto the track. Someone blasted AC/DC on a radio, and people started dancing.

Gary lounged back on the seat of his bike, enjoying the attention he was getting. T.J. found himself drifting toward Alex. To an observer, it would have looked like the natural movement of the crowd, people circling, clusters gathering and breaking apart. But T.J. had Alex's black jacket in the corner of his eye, and even amid all the sweat, dirt, spilled gas and oil, he could smell the animal fire of another werewolf. A pack should stay together. Alex, helmet in the crook of his arm, caught his gaze and smiled.

"Good race," T.J. said, as he might have said even if they hadn't been werewolves, and Alex the alpha of his pack.

Feeling nervous and awkward—his wolf was prowling, and T.J. suddenly wanted to be out of there—he started to drift back to Gary and Mitch. He wanted to be near his human friends.

Alex stopped him with a hand on his arm that sent a flush over him. Staticky, warm, asexual, comfortable. He could rub his face across the man's coat. The feeling could get addictive.

But he held himself apart and tried to slow his breathing.

"Gary's leaving. He asked me to go with him."

"You can't do that, you know," Alex said. "Your family is here. Stay, come work for me," Alex said.

And how would he tell Mitch and Gary? "I like Gary," T.J. said. "He's been good to me. He's a good rider."

"I'm a good rider."

T.J. certainly wasn't going to argue with that. Shaking his head, he started to walk away.

"T.J."

He struggled. He had two voices, and both wanted to speak. But his wolf side was slinking, hoping for Alex's acceptance. "I don't have to do what you say."

"You sure about that?"

If he didn't walk away now, he'd never be able to. It was like that last dinner at home—if he didn't say it now, he never would, and then he'd curl up and disappear. So he turned and walked away, even though some sharp instinct wanted to drag him back. Claws scraped down the inside of his skin; he tried to ignore it.

Back with Mitch and Gary, rolling the bike to Gary's trailer, he started to relax.

"Saw you talking to Price," Mitch said. "I didn't think he swung your direction." He was teasing but amiable. T.J. gave him a searing look.

Gary and Mitch left, and T.J. stayed behind. The circuit was over, racing done for the season, and the track settled into a lethargic rhythm of local practice. Guys screwing around on backyard bikes. T.J. scrounged up mechanic jobs when he could, and worked cheap. Alex rented him the guest room in the outbuilding behind his rural ranch house—the room where he'd woken into his new life. Just until he got back on his feet. Whenever that was. Months passed.

He drank at the Dustbowl with the rest of the pack, spent full moon nights with his new family, and that was the life that stretched before him now. But at least he was healthy.

No, truth spoke back at him—he'd traded one disease for another.

He'd taken a shower and was lying on the narrow bed, not thinking of anything in particular, when Alex knocked on the door. He could tell it was Alex by the knock, by the way he breathed.

"We're leaving for the Dustbowl."

Part of T.J. sprang up, like a retriever wagging its tail and grinning. Another part of him wanted to growl. He didn't feel much like socializing. "I think I'm going to stay in tonight."

"I think you ought to come along."

Alex's commands never sounded like commands. They were requests, suggestions. Strong recommendations. He spoke like a parent who always had your best interests at heart.

T.J. started to give in. It was his wolf side, he told himself. The wolf wanted to make Alex happy so the pack would stay whole, and safe.

But he wondered what would happen if he said no.

He sat up. "I don't really feel like it."

Sure enough, the door slammed open, rattling the whole frame of the shack. T.J. flinched, then scrambled back when Alex came at him. He tripped over the bed, ended up on his back, with the alpha werewolf lunging on top of him, pinning his shoulders, breathing on his neck.

T.J. lay as still as he could while gasping for breath. He kept his head back, throat exposed, hardly understanding what was happening—his body seemed to be reacting without him, showing the necessary submission so that Alex wouldn't hurt him. He flushed with shame, because he thought he'd have been able to fight back.

Alex got up without a word and stalked out of the room. T.J. moved more slowly, but followed just the same.

T.J. sat in the corner, away from the others, staring out, turning over thoughts that weren't his. He could run or he could fight. And what happened to safety? To peace? All he had to do was sit back and take it. Not argue. Not rock the boat, not stick his neck out.

He couldn't stop staring, which in the body language of these creatures meant a challenge. He dropped his gaze to the bottle of beer he hadn't been drinking.

Jane pulled a chair next to his and sat, then leaned on his shoulder, rubbing her head against his neck, stroking his arms. Trying to calm him, make him feel better.

"You know I'm gay, right?" he said.

Pouting, she looked at him. "We just want you to be happy. We want you to feel like you belong. You do, don't you?"

He closed his eyes. "I don't know."

"It doesn't matter as long as you're safe, right? You know if anyone came through here and gave you trouble, Alex would go after them, right?"

He almost laughed. Like she knew anything about it. "That isn't the point."

He'd raised his voice without realizing it, glaring at her so that she leaned away, a spark of animal flashing in her eyes. Heavy boots stepping across the floor inevitably followed, along with a wave of musk and anger, as Alex came to stand beside Jane. It was the two of them, bad cop and good cop, keeping the pack in line. Like they were one big happy family.

T.J. should have gone with Gary.

He stood, putting himself at eye level with Alex—also a sign of challenge. "I'm leaving," he said. Alex frowned. His mouth had been open to speak, but T.J. had done it first. The rest of the pack was here—they'd fallen silent and gathered around, the happy family. T.J. recognized a gang when he saw one.

Alex laughed—condescending, mocking. As if T.J. were a child. As far as their wolf sides were concerned, he supposed he was. He thought back to Alex throwing him to the floor, felt that anger again, and tamped it down tight. The alpha was trying to get a rise out of him, goad him into some stupid attack so he could smack him right back down. T.J. wouldn't let him. All he had to do was stare.

"You'll be on your own," Alex said. "You won't like that. You'll never make it."

T.J.'s mouth widened in a grin that showed teeth. He shouldn't taunt Alex. He ought to just roll over on his belly like the others. But he shook his head.

"I've done it before," he said. "I can do it again."

And the wolf rose up, standing in place of the scared kid he used to be.

They could all jump him. He looked at the door and tried not to think of it, pushing all his other senses—ears, nose, even the soles of his feet—out, trying to guess when the rest of them would attack. He'd run. That was his plan.

"You don't really want to leave," Alex said, still with the laugh hiding in his voice.

T.J. looked around at all of them, meeting each person's gaze. The others looked away. They'd all come here by accident, through werewolf attacks, or by design—recruited and brought to the cage. T.J., on the other hand, had come to them alone, and he could leave that way. Maybe they didn't mind it here, but one of these days, T.J. would fight back. Maybe he'd win against Alex and become the alpha of this pack. Maybe he'd lose, and Alex would kill him. But they could all see that fight coming.

Which was maybe why they let him walk out the door without another argument. And rather than feeling afraid, T.J. felt like he'd won a battle.

He hadn't been brave enough to live out his old life. But he'd been brave enough to stick his hand in that cage.

Before he left the area, he had one more thing to do. Just to be sure.

A different guy was working at the clinic, which was just as well. "Have you ever had an HIV test before?" the staffer said.

"Yeah. Here, in fact. About eight months ago."

"Oh? What was the result? Is there a reason you're back? Let me look it up."

T.J. gave the guy his name, and he looked it up. Found the two positives, and T.J. wanted to snarl at him for the look of pity he showed.

"Sir," he said kindly—condescendingly. "With a result like this you should have come back sooner for counseling. There's a lot of help available—"

"The results were wrong," T.J. said. "I want another test. Please."

He relented and took T.J. into the exam room, went through the ritual, drew the blood, and asked T.J. to wait. The previous times, it had taken a half an hour or so. The guy came back on schedule, wearing a baffled expression.

"It's negative," the staffer said.

T.J. exalted, a howl growing in his chest.

The staffer shook his head. "I don't understand. I've seen false positives—but two false positives in a row? That's so unlikely."

"I knew it," T.J. said. "I knew it was wrong."

He gave the guy a smile that showed teeth and walked out.

SIDE-EFFECTS MAY INCLUDE

STEVE DUFFY

◆

24-HOUR DENTIST said the sign, in Mandarin and English. Hayden tried to put out of his mind that awful old joke of his father's, when's your appointment, *tooth-hurtee*, and stepped inside. Though it was close on midnight, the streets were still bustling, tangy with exhaust fumes and the smell of the all-night noodle stalls. Inside the frosted-glass and brushed-metal reception area it was air conditioned and monastically quiet. The nurse who answered the buzzer installed him in a futuristic bucket chair, discreetly indicating the selection of reading matter spread on a nearby coffee table. Running, for the hundredth time that day, his tongue along the edges of his teeth, Hayden noticed with little or no surprise that among the magazines was the very issue of *Scientific American* he'd been reading on the plane, back at the start of it all.

"MIRACLE" CHINESE DENTAL TREATMENT TO UNDERGO TRIALS IN WEST, announced the headline. Trapped in mid-flight hiatus, equidistant between London and Hong Kong, Hayden had been leafing through the magazine like the diligent sci-tech rep he tried to be, on the lookout for snappy, comprehensible articles free of algebra or chemical symbols. Medicine wasn't his area, so what drew him to this piece? Simply that long-distance plane travel often tended to set his teeth on edge, start up aches and twinges in his back fillings. Something to do with the cabin pressure, he wasn't quite sure. Did it matter that his crowns had been fitted at ground level, where the PSI would be different? Perhaps the whole thing was psychosomatic, a displacement of some unconscious phobia to do with long-distance air travel. There wasn't really anyone he could ask: no one he knew seemed to suffer the same problem. Unconsciously, Hayden stroked his jaw as he read on past the headline.

According to the text, scientists from the University of Hong Kong —using a groundbreaking mixture of ancient Chinese herbal lore and cutting-edge stem cell procedures—had come up with a paradigm shift in the treatment of dental problems. Initial trials of the new medication, a simple rub-in gel, had exceeded all expectations, and already there was said to be a flourishing black market as small pirate gene-tech labs churned out their own bootleg versions of the remedy. A side-bar explained the science part. The genes which controlled first and second dentitions in the human—milk teeth through wisdom teeth—had been identified several years previously, in the wave of slipstream discoveries subsequent to the Y2K breakthrough on the human genome. The Hong Kong scientists, experts in the field of transgenics, had concentrated their efforts on the so-called genetic switches which . . . Here Hayden paused, distracted by a slowly increasing sense of no longer subliminal apprehension.

He'd been grinding his teeth, ever so slightly, as he read. He knew this was something he did, not just in his sleep but when concentrating; both his girlfriend and his dentist had told him so. Now, if he clicked his top molars against his lower, he could feel . . . what *was* that? He tongued around furtively inside his mouth, inserting a finger once he was sure no-one was looking in his direction. There, just at the back . . . oh, great. Of course. Naturally. Six weeks on business in the Far East, and a wisdom tooth cracked clean down the middle.

It had been the Bombay mix back in the departure lounge, he recollected glumly; no doubt about it. He distinctly remembered chomping down on the bulletlike roasted chickpea as his flight had been called, that suspicious splintering feeling he'd put to the back of his mind amidst all the check-in anxiety . . . that was the culprit, all right. Super. He didn't even like Bombay mix that much. Maybe he could sue Heathrow for the cost of the treatment.

Dismally he manipulated the injured tooth back and forth, feeling the broken surfaces grind together like shattered crockery. The tactful, near-subliminal voice of the flight attendant at his shoulder made him pull out his finger with an audible plop. "Have you got any painkillers?" Hayden asked, knowing in advance what the answer would be. Regretfully, the attendant explained the airline's strict policy with regard to passenger medications. Hayden nodded despondently, and stared out of the window at the cumulus clouds below. They looked like brilliant white molars in the cerulean gums of some unimaginably huge sky-troll.

The first actual sensations of pain had kicked in just prior to landing, after some four hours of incessant fiddling (tongue and fingertip) and an ill-advised glass of ice-cold mineral water. On the shuttle in from the airport his cheek had begun to puff out; once in his hotel room he'd hooked open his mouth in front of the bathroom mirror, fearing the worst. And finding it, in spades. Hard up against the gum-line there was a lump roughly the size and colour of a cherry tomato. It was hurting so badly, Hayden suspected it might actually be throbbing, visibly and palpably. Fully aware of what a stupid idea it would be, he inserted both index fingers, bracketed the swelling, and squeezed experimentally. The resultant right-hook of pain sent him staggering back from the mirror, cursing and whimpering through a mouthful of abscess and hurt.

In this way Hayden spent most of his first night in Hong Kong: alternately checking out the site of the damage in the mirror and pressed against the window in search of distraction. The waxing moon rose over the Island, soared across the tops of the skyscrapers and plunged into the fuzzy sink of light pollution above the western districts. Hayden followed its progress like a wounded timber wolf, baying with each pulsing wave of toothache, the pain as relentless and regular as the jets that slid across the night sky, heading for Lantau and the International Airport.

He was up in plenty of time for his nine o'clock at Chen 2000 Industries. Unfortunately, between the sleeplessness and the jet lag, he looked like a homeless man who'd sneaked in off the street to panhandle cash in the atrium. With some difficulty—everyone at Chen 2000 spoke excellent English, but he was starting to sound more and more like the Elephant Man—he went through his sales pitch, careful not to let his molars clash as he spoke. Suffice it to say that the case for fast-surface gate conductors from England could have been better put. On the way out he tried to make a joke of it all, pointing ruefully to his swollen cheek, and was rewarded with polite nods and smiles from the junior executives assigned to see him off the premises. Their smooth uncaring faces had showed marginally more interest in his PowerPoint slides and sales patter.

If the first night had been bad, then the second had been raw torture. As part of his duties, he'd been obliged to attend a banquet in the company of several important clients. Torn between not eating, which he understood would be disrespectful to the local culture, and eating, which he knew would probably end in tears, he'd chosen the latter, and had gingerly inserted a dressed tiger prawn into the opposite side of his mouth from the shattered tooth. Even before the chopsticks had cleared his lips the magnitude of his mistake became apparent. The hot hoi sin had sluiced around his tender mouth and gone straight to the root of the infection, where it had cut clean through the various analgesic treatments he'd been able to score from the pharmacy next door to the hotel. Like a dental probe wielded by some Nazi Doctor Death, the chili sauce skewered straight into the flaming abscess. The pain that ran up the outraged nerve nearly split his head in two.

His involuntary moan of anguish had turned heads all around the table. Passing it off as a cough hadn't really helped, since even the slightest movement of his head was by now enough to make it feel as if his jaw was about to crack apart. Desperately, he'd searched the platters spread out before him for something—anything—he could reasonably appear to be eating (his plan was to nibble round the edges, and to smuggle the rest of it into his napkin), but whatever wasn't marinaded in chilli appeared to be crispy and/or chewy, and neither option was feasible for Hayden in his current predicament. He'd spent the evening with one hand clamped to his jaw, as if trying to suppress the mother of all belches. From time to time a more than usually vile blast of pain would cause him to make a squashy razzing noise like an electrical buzzer under water, which he suspected was unacceptable in any social context the world over.

Somehow, he'd got back to the hotel. Things were starting to fray around the edges by this time, though no matter how much he drank the numbing edge of the alcohol never quite kicked in. It was the pain that was blurring things; that, and the killer sleeplessness. He'd made yet another raid on the nearby pharmacy, triple-dosed on everything (ignoring the compendious lists of contraindications in the packaging), then retired for another night of horrors.

Sleep was out of the question: he was unable to set his head down on the pillow, not even on the nominally good side. The ache oscillated between thumping pressure and piercing intensity, and by daybreak he'd felt so wretched that even the transition from one variety of pain to another—throb to stab—seemed like a relief of sorts. A grey-faced zombie leered back at him from the mirror. Was it possible, thought Hayden with the feverish, lachrymose wretchedness of a small child, for someone's *entire head* to go septic?

The next day he didn't even want to think about it. Don't go there. And the night? Well, the *night*—

"Sir?" The nurse materialised at his side. "Dr. Pang will see you now." Hayden nodded cautiously, and followed her through the translucent screens, carrying with him the copy of *Scientific American* from reception.

Dr. Pang was a neat young man in immaculate whites who projected a powerful, slightly inhuman air of professionalism. Shaking his hand, Hayden found himself wishing he'd flossed more thoroughly, changed his shirt before leaving the hotel, and generally lived a better life. To his credit, the dentist spoke excellent English and seemed genuinely concerned for his patient. *So he should at the price*, Hayden reflected ungenerously.

He settled back in a high-tech treatment chair, tilted and swivelled to the precise pitch of accessibility; the gas-cylinder hydraulics of the chair, with their all-but-imperceptible hiss at each resettling, were probably the noisiest pieces of equipment in the surgery, which otherwise resembled nothing so much as the sterile assembly room at Intel—assuming, that is, Intel were keeping on top of all the latest thinking in interior design.

"So, Mr. Hayden." Dr. Pang perched on an adjustable stool at the side of the treatment chair, leaned slightly forward after the fashion of a father-confessor. "What seems to be the problem?"

Hayden settled back, taking absent-minded pleasure in the soft creak of the leather. He stared at the suspended ceiling, the gleaming baffled louvres of the light diffusers, and wondered where to begin. "I had this toothache," he began; and then thought: *God, the toothache, yeah. What about that?* Where does pain go, when it goes? We remember the fact of its having happened: rationally, its existence is accessible to us as a memory, and all the rest of it. But does the body itself remember on some cellular level, tissue, meat and pulp? Not in the same way, or else we'd surely go crazy. Imagine if each component part of us had 24/7 sentience in its own right, equal broadcasting time, like candidates in the Presidential debate. Suppose each bone, each nerve ending, had its own hotline to the sensorium; imagine the clamour, as the body became a Grand Central of sensation, a Babel of reaction . . .

"A toothache?" Dr. Pang was waiting patiently. Hayden blinked, and tried to pick up his thread. "Er, sorry, yes. It started about a month ago, I suppose, just as I was arriving in Hong Kong."

"A month? My goodness." Dr. Pang was the picture of respectful sympathy. "Four weeks is a very long time to be in pain. Was it perhaps not so bad at first?"

"No . . . I mean yes. It was very painful." If the Eskimos have all those words for snow, supposedly, then how come extreme discomfort boils down to a single syllable? True pain is irreducible, probably; indivisible, unchanging at the root. There are modifiers, quantifiers, *stabbing* and *throbbing, acute* and *severe* and all the rest of them, but they really just serve to dress up the thing in itself: the monad constant and impregnable, the primordial principle of existence. *Ouch.* It hurts, therefore I am.

Dr. Pang's alert expressive face settled into a troubled moue. He shook his head slightly, as if in reproof. "Then you should have come to see me before now. Have you taken anything for the pain?"

Hayden felt in his pockets for the mangled remains of the various blister packs he'd picked up at the pharmacy, and handed them to Dr. Pang to be tutted over. "I was going through those a strip at a time at one point," he confessed, resettling himself in the dentist's chair. "Popping them like M&Ms. The thing was, none of them were really working."

"Of course not." Dr. Pang was shaking his head again, more in sorrow than in anger. "Over-the-counter medications such as these: you cannot expect them to deal with severe neuralgic pain. The problem must be dealt with at the root, Mr Hayden. Literally, in this case." He allowed himself an unpresumptuous smile.

"Yes . . . " Hayden was thinking. "Yes, I see that now, of course. Stupid of me, really." He rubbed a thumb experimentally along the point of his jaw. "I suppose it must have been around the third night when I just couldn't bear it any longer . . . "

Somewhere towards the witching hour, after the last of the cheap pills had worn off, he admitted to himself there was nothing for it but to seek help. He ought to have done it before, of course, but a quick status check had confirmed his worst fears: his bargain-basement traveller's insurance didn't cover emergency dental treatment. He'd have to pay for the treatment himself, and if the pricing policies of the first ten local dentists on the list he'd googled on his laptop were at all representative, even a quick backstreet extraction *sans* anaesthetic would leave a hole in his current account roughly the size of Hong Kong harbour. This trip was running on the very edge of profitability as it was: one thumping dental bill would leave him dangerously out of pocket.

Over and above that—go on, admit it—he just didn't *like* dentists. They scared him: everything about them, their white coats, their whirring drills, the lights they shone in your eyes. Their cold unblinking stares, as they leaned over you and stuck sharp metal spikes into your soft pink gums. The way they charged you an arm and a leg for the privilege of inflicting their medically sanctioned torture. Dentists? Monsters. Who else would *volunteer* for a job like that? It was a measure of the extremity of Hayden's predicament that he'd even considered going to one in the first place. Now, having come to the end of his tether, he was checking through the small-print of his freelance employment contract to see whether it might cover medical treatment. It didn't, of course: Hayden could almost hear the sniggers of the sadists in the legal department as they carefully precluded even the possibility of such a claim. Smug toothy bastards. He stuffed the contract back in his briefcase, riffled through the rest of his papers—

—and came up with the *Scientific American* he'd bought for the flight. The magazine was folded open to the last article he'd been reading, back on the plane: **"Miracle" Chinese Dental Treatment To Undergo Trials in West.** Squinting from the pain, he tried to focus on the headline; the final clause dissolved beneath his crosseyed scrutiny, leaving just four enormous words that filled the entire page, like newspaper declarations of war. **"Miracle" Chinese Dental Treatment** . . . and as he stared, those super-cautious quotes, those weasel qualifiers, seemed to dwindle all the way into transparency and pop like tiny bubbles in champagne. A miracle; Christ, yes, that was what he wanted, a bucket of that, please.

The hotel porter, once buzzed up to the room and acquainted with the contents of Hayden's wallet, was gratifyingly eager to help. Hayden handed him the copy of *Scientific American*: scanning through the article intently, he nodded from time to time, then looked up. "You want—drugs!" he announced brightly.

"No—well, sort of, yes—look, I want *medicine*." Hayden pointed to the article, then to his swollen cheek. "Medicine. For toothache."

"Medicine . . . ?" The porter (whose name was Jimmy Tsui) frowned. "You use up all your medicine already?" Only the night before, he'd pointed Hayden in the direction of the pharmacy round the corner.

"It's not strong enough," explained Hayden. "I need something *much much stronger*—do you understand?"

"Sooo . . . you want drugs?"

"Not just any drugs," insisted Hayden. "*This* drug. I want to know where in Hong Kong I can go to get some of this—look, here, this miracle Chinese dental treatment, see?" Why was everything so complicated?

Between Hayden's ravaged jaw and the magazine article, enlightenment gradually dawned on Jimmy Tsui. He jabbed a finger at the magazine and rattled off a musical burst of syllables. It might have been a brand name; it sounded pithy and to the point, *uuan-shan-dhol*. Hayden tried it out himself: "Wang-chang . . . wan-shang-dole? Is that this? The miracle thing?"

"Miracle, yes . . . " The porter nodded hard, his eyes saucer-wide in the wonderment of understanding. "You want—ask man about this?" He indicated the article, its illustration of a human head scanned by MRI into skull-like abstraction, all fangs and empty eye sockets. "Man who will sell you medicine . . . for *this*?" He pointed gingerly at Hayden's mouth.

"God, yes! Do you know anywhere I can get it? I can go up to five thousand Hong Kong, maybe seven . . . "

At long last, the porter seemed to have grasped it. "I know good doctor, yes, he got—all what you want! My shift—over, fifteen minutes! We take taxi into Mong Kok, you and me!" He tapped a finger against his nose, then laughed a trifle nervously as Hayden followed suit. Almost weeping at the prospect of relief, Hayden made to shake his hand, but the porter was already excusing himself, slipping backwards through the door in a deferential bow.

And so, soon after midnight, Hayden found himself crossing the harbour in the company of Jimmy Tsui. The taxi injected them directly into the rush and clamour of the Mong Kok strip, close by Sim City and the soaring Grand Tower. Even at this hour the bright sidewalks were chock-full of pedestrians jammed shoulder-to-shoulder, streets glittering and congested like the chutes of the *pachinko* machines in the slot parlours, all played out to a chorus of tinny chipmusic leaking from headphones and shop doorways. Above their heads neon advertisements flickered the length of Shantung Street, pulsing through the pollution layer, making rainbows on the oily tarmac underfoot. The night smelled of spent fireworks and overheated motherboards.

Jimmy tugged at his sleeve, once, twice. "Not far now! Follow me!" Hayden did his best to keep up with the porter as he dodged and shouldercharged across the road. Once he caught sight of himself in an unlit window: the surgical face-mask with which Jimmy had thoughtfully provided him—"Best you wear this—keep mouth hidden!"—made him look like the mad doctor in a Frankenstein movie. It was all in the eyes, he decided, before hastening on to follow Jimmy down a narrow entranceway between two buildings.

The walls on either side leaned in so close there was barely room for Hayden and Jimmy to walk line abreast. Optimistically, or else suicidally, a gang of kids came rollerblading at breakneck speed towards them: Hayden flattened himself against the graffitied concrete as they whizzed past, one hand raised to guard his face. Up ahead Jimmy had come to another right turn; he waited for Hayden to catch up before gesturing theatrically and exclaiming, "This Night-town! You in Night-town now!"

Night-town took the form of another, wider alley running parallel to the strip. Each of the commercial premises stripside seemed to have its corresponding—probably unlicensed—counterpart round the back: some were simple stalls of wood-strut and canvas, while others were breezeblock lean-tos built straight on to the backs of the buildings. Jury-rigged lighting run illegally off the mains lit up the bustling alley: between that and whatever moonlight could reach the concrete canyon, Hayden could just about pick his way through the detritus underfoot. Dismembered cardboard boxes blocked his way; drifts of Styrofoam packing beads, twisted snares of parcel strap, split plastic bags in the process of leaking their unguessable contents. Bedded down amongst the rubbish here and there were people lying slumped against the walls, needy or beyond need, it was impossible to tell. Whenever they passed one of these unfortunates, heads lolling anyhow, skins the colour and texture of mushrooms grown in tunnels, Jimmy would grab Hayden's arm and hurry him onwards. All the while, the ambulant dwellers of Night-town padded past on their backstreet errands, clustering briefly by each chop stall before disappearing off into the shadows.

Extractor fans heaved and whirred stale second-hand odours at them: cigarette smoke, fast food, generator fumes. Hayden pulled his mask up over his nose and pressed on after Jimmy. Which of these booths was to be their destination? This one, perhaps: the concrete box with no door stacked floor to ceiling with cans of Kirin beer? Or the one opposite: racks of old iPods and Wiis, all scorched and heat-warped, the pinstriped proprietor perched toadlike on a tiny stool in the doorway, both hands permanently hidden inside the open briefcase that lay across his knees? Maybe this one: a whole wall full of Blu-ray discs, no cases, the discs hung up on nails, their laser-etched data tracks scattering rainbow moirés of light across the faces of the teenagers who examined them.

None of these, of course. Instead, Jimmy stopped outside a plain doorway towards the end of the block, in between a dirty-looking noodle parlour and a tattooist's with screaming demon shingle. "This way," he announced proudly, "the basement!" He ushered Hayden through the door, and followed after him down a flight of concrete stairs. At the first turn there lay sprawled another of the mushroom people. Hayden stepped gingerly over him, but Jimmy administered a sharp kick in the ribs that sent the man crashing against the wall. "Filthy monkey," he spat after the unfortunate indigent as he scrambled away up the steps. He turned to Hayden. "You follow me," he urged, and pushed past him down the stairway. By the light of red emergency bulbs, they continued their descent.

Down to an open fire-door, before which Jimmy stopped and looked round, nervously it seemed. Hayden smiled encouragingly, then realised he was still wearing the face mask. "You come please," said Jimmy, holding wide the door.

The corridor beyond was disturbingly dark, lit only by a crack of greenish light that shone through a door left ajar at the further end. It didn't look like normal room-lighting; Hayden was put in mind of the luminosity of certain sea creatures, or weird electrical discharges like Saint Elmo's fire. Jimmy jogged down the corridor and gave a sharp double knock at the door, then vanished inside after signalling Hayden to wait.

Hayden heard voices through the open door, Jimmy's first of all, then that of another, much older-sounding man. After a few seconds Jimmy reappeared. He positioned himself very close to Hayden and spoke almost directly into his ear.

"Doctor has agree to see you. Make—examination! Ready in a little while."

"That's good," said Hayden uneasily. The subterranean consultant will see you now. They waited by the door, during which time Jimmy played a game of Tetris on his mobile phone. In the absence of chairs and magazines in this unorthodox waiting room, Hayden got bored; he made as if to take a look inside, but was blocked off rapidly by Jimmy. "Wait one minute!"

Frustrated, Hayden gestured with his hands at the bare corridor;

Jimmy shrugged, *I don't make the rules round here.* But even as he spoke, a guttural word of command came from inside the room, and Jimmy clapped his hands in satisfaction. Taking Hayden by the shoulders, he propelled him through the doorway. "See you outside," he said, and vanished.

What had Hayden been expecting? Something stagey and traditional, a scene from the movies: a whiff of the mysterious East. An old-fashioned apothecary's with boxes of dried frogs, incense on braziers and twirling paper lanterns; or a smoky Triad opium den, the lair of Fu Manchu. What he actually found himself in was something else again.

It was a plain concrete bunker, dank and claustrophobic, lined floor to ceiling with industrial slotted shelving. There were no light-fittings, nor were there any candles or lanterns. The only illumination came from an enormous fish-tank, which was lit partly by electric light, and partly by the eerie bioluminescence of whatever was inside it—Hayden couldn't quite make it out, and wasn't really sure he wanted to know anyway. Silhouetted against the greenly glowing tank was a figure, standing very close to the glass but facing Hayden.

He'd sounded like an elderly man, but looking at him now he could have been any age. Between the green medical cap and a face-mask like Hayden's own hardly any of his features were exposed, and over his eyes he wore tinted swimmer's goggles. The rest of his uniform consisted of a green smock and dark trousers, terminating an inch or so above his rope sandals; *old man's ankles*, noted Hayden, glad to have something to cling on to. The overall effect was deeply unsettling, and probably only a man in Hayden's sort of pain would have dreamed of going through with it. But he was desperate, and he wanted more than anything to get it over with, so he advanced a couple of steps into the room and bowed slightly.

The doctor said something brusque and croaky. Hayden thought of fetching Jimmy in to translate, then remembered that rolled up in his coat pocket was the invaluable copy of *Scientific American*. Bowing once more, he held out the magazine, indicating the article in question. The doctor made no attempt to look at it. Hayden gestured again for him to take it; this time the doctor extended a rubber-gloved hand and snatched the magazine away. He studied it for a minute, then rolled it up very tight as if wringing a chicken's neck. He stared at his patient blankly, waiting for him to acquire basic conversational Mandarin perhaps. Behind him, the air filtration unit in the tank bubbled softly.

Hayden had hoped the doctor would catch on sooner. What to do? Gingerly, he removed his face-mask, the better to articulate his wants. "Aaangh," he said, mouth wide open, finger pointing inside to the source of all his misery. "Naad toos. Agh ong." Surely the old codger could see what the matter was? "Bad tooth. That one." *Please.*

The doctor unrolled the magazine, looked from the article to the inside of Hayden's mouth and back again. He traced his finger along the text and read aloud, "Den-tee-shon . . . denteeshon?" He looked back up at Hayden. Hayden nodded his encouragement. "Denteeshon,'"the old man repeated pugnaciously. Again Hayden nodded. The doctor spread his hands wide in the universal mime for *no idea*, and threw the magazine at Hayden's feet.

Hayden scowled, then winced as his wrecked tooth yanked on its taproot of agony. How difficult was this going to be? "Look, I've got a toothache," he said, speaking slowly and emphasising words as if clarity alone would render them comprehensible to the doctor. To drive the point home, he pulled back his lips from his teeth to reveal the offending molar. "Hajg hju—" the doctor recoiled as if offended, and Hayden removed his fingers from his mouth—"Have you got any of *this stuff*?" He tapped the headline, ran his saliva-smeared finger beneath the familiar words, words that now only mocked him: **"Miracle" Chinese Dental Treatment**. The old man shrugged, and Hayden felt like picking him up, all six stone of him, and shaking him till the medication fell out. Why couldn't everyone speak English, for God's sake?

On the verge of giving up and going back to the hotel, he tried one more time. "Jimmy, the man who brought me here? He said you'd be able to get me treatment for it. Like in the magazine?" Pointing at the *Scientific American* on the floor. "He called it wan-chang something . . . wang-shan-dole?"

Behind the face-mask came a sharp hiss of indrawn breath. The doctor had understood that part, all right. Emboldened, Hayden repeated it, pointing at his tooth: "Wang-shan-dole?" He smiled, hoping at last to get the consultation properly under way.

Quaveringly, the old man pointed at him, and fired off a breathy burst of Cantonese; something fast and high and wildly inflected. It ended in *uuan-shan-dhol* and a question mark, and a finger insistently jabbed in Hayden's direction.

Hayden seized eagerly on the one thing he thought he recognised. "Wan-shan-dole," he assented, pointing at himself.

Even under his mask there was something almost comically incredulous in the doctor's attitude—*what, you?*—as he let off another volley of Cantonese, again with that magic *uuan-shan-dhol* tucked away in it. Before Hayden could agree with him, the doctor was off and rooting through his shelves.

Without turning to Hayden he kept up a running commentary out of the corner of his mouth, shaking his head and throwing in the odd *uuan-shan-dhol* for good measure. At the time, Hayden was too impatient to register subtleties, but looking back later he got the feeling the old man didn't really care to have him in the room much longer than was absolutely necessary, now he'd diagnosed the problem.

After all that fuss, it took the doctor less than a minute to come up with the goods: a pocket-sized cardboard box completely covered with small print in Pinyin and Standard Script. He held it out at arm's length; Hayden went to take it from him, and had to grab it as it fell. The old man had simply let it drop, before snatching his hand away as if afraid of catching Hayden's toothache.

Hayden turned the box round and round. "That's great," he said, hardly daring to believe he had the miracle cure in his hands at last. "Absolutely brilliant. How much do I owe you?" He took out his wallet and held it invitingly open.

The doctor, more animated and seemingly more nervous than before, scuttled forward and plucked out a few bills at random. Looking at what was left, Hayden realised he'd taken forty, fifty HK at most. The larger notes he'd withdrawn specially from the cash dispenser in the hotel lobby remained untouched. "Here," he urged, taking out one of the hundreds and waving it at him, "that's for your trouble," but the doctor wasn't having any. Backing away from Hayden, he jabbed a finger at the door and hit him with one last volley of croaky Yue dialect. Then he turned to the monster aquarium behind him. The consultation was at an end.

Slipping the cardboard box into his inside pocket, Hayden headed for the corridor. At the door he paused and tried to say goodbye: the old man turned impatiently around, lifted his face mask to reveal a flaccid maw lined with spiderish old-man's beard, and spat on the bare concrete floor at his feet. That seemed final enough: Hayden left him to his fishing.

Jimmy was practically jogging on the spot with nervous excitement. "Come on now! Time—to go!" Hayden had to hurry after him up the stairs and back outside. They barged down the alleyways to the main street, Hayden feeling oddly like a john might feel on being dismissed from some tart's parlour: surplus to requirements, something embarrassing to be got out of the way before the next punter showed up. At the taxi rank, Jimmy shook his hand for an unnaturally long time before relieving him of some of the high-denomination notes the doctor had spurned earlier. Once in the cab, Hayden couldn't wait; hands trembling ever so slightly, he reached into his pocket for the box with the medicine in it.

"So," said Dr. Pang, his face rigid in barely-concealed disapproval, "you self-medicated with this black market treatment?"

"Yes," admitted Hayden. "Yes, I did. And it worked."

"Really?" One eyebrow expressively tilted.

"Really," confirmed Hayden. "What it said in the magazine? Miracle cure? They weren't exaggerating. Like turning a switch, and the pain just wasn't there any more. One dab of the gel, and . . . wow." Unconsciously, beneath the face-mask, he smiled at the memory.

"It's never quite as simple as 'wow'," Dr. Pang informed him sternly. "There has been considerable trepidation as to possible side effects of your 'miracle treatment,' to say nothing of the ethical dimension of this new research in transgenics. Observations among the trial groups have pointed up several areas of grave concern—"

"Oh, I know," said Hayden, lying back in the chair and scratching his masked jaw ruminatively. "It's not as if there haven't been some side-effects . . . "

But who cared, if it wasn't hurting any more? Which it wasn't; he rubbed on gel from the tube, and the gel worked. It was cold going on, a snowball in the face, and within seconds you could feel it going to work, numbing, soothing; *ah*. Before he got back to the hotel he realised, with a sort of delirious disbelief, that he was pain-free. Experimentally he mouthed the words. His tooth didn't go *ow*. He said them aloud, until the taxi driver turned round. Regally, Hayden waved away his curious stare.

No pain for Hayden that night, and for the whole of the marvellous day that followed. He slept in—he slept! and it didn't hurt—he slept in late, skipping his eight-thirty the following morning in favour of a lie-in, a long hot shower, and an extra pot of coffee brought up to his room. And he drank the coffee, and his tooth didn't hurt any more. And he looked out of the window at the sun above the harbour, and no toothache. And he stuck his finger in his mouth, and the swelling had already gone down. It was fine.

The idea was that the gel would hold him till he got back to London, where his own dentist, a melancholy Welshman called Llewelyn, could deal with the tooth, cap it or drill it or yank it out. Whatever. That was one for the future, and Hayden was too busy relishing Hong Kong sans the agony. Padding across the room in bare feet, a lordly beast returning to its lair, he caught sight of himself in the mirror: his grin looked like something Jack Nicholson might sport at the winding-up of a particularly glorious orgy.

First thing on waking up, quite late in the afternoon; more gel. Mmmm. Rub it in, all nice and analgesic. And something to eat; Christ he was hungry. Big hairy lumberjack portions, now, straightaway. He started to call room service, but halfway through he changed his mind, and bounded into the shower instead. Bathed and dressed, he loped down to the lobby in search of a taxi.

By the time Hayden was disembarking at Causeway Bay all the businesses on the island were emptying out, each office block disgorging its load of commuter ants to jam up the streets below. Hayden took a deep breath and launched himself into the crowd, but his way seemed surprisingly easy; as if space were being cleared for him, somehow.

He dived into the first restaurant he saw, a gleaming twenty-first century chow-parlour which seemed to be called the Futuristic Dragon. There he ordered up plate after plate of good things, all the protein he'd been denied over the last few days. Already all of that was starting to feel like a nightmare he'd once had, years and years ago. So complete was the current absence of pain, it seemed almost ludicrous to think that only yesterday he'd been desperate, maddened, panicking like a rat in a trap . . . hah. Absolutely ludicrous. He laughed out loud; some of the other diners glanced over before hastily averting their gazes. Supremely indifferent to everything except the contents of the platter laid before him, Hayden tore in to the exquisite char sui pork.

Several meat courses and the best part of an hour later, Hayden untucked his napkin and pushed his chair back from the table. Sated for the time being, he felt like strolling some of his dinner off.

Though still busy by Western standards, the streets were appreciably less insane by the time he was stepping out in the direction of the Mid-levels. Pedestrians own the city, thought Hayden contentedly; car drivers slide through it untouched and unenlightened, subways are just burrows. Pedestrians lay claim to all the spaces; they flow through the arteries of the city and the city flows through them. As if to prove it, he took an unnecessary turn left at the next junction, following a sign that said Happy Valley. How long had it been since he'd walked anywhere just for fun?

For the next few blocks Hayden let chance determine his route. This he did by selecting, more or less at random, various passers-by, and following very close behind them, matching his stride exactly to their own, sometimes less than an arm's length away. As soon as they became aware of his presence, he would drop off, and select a new target. The fourth or fifth of his marks rumbled him almost immediately, though; they'd gone only a few paces when the man in front, a portly, respectable-looking type in a three-piece suit and, improbably, a white solar topee, suddenly became aware of Hayden's presence. He turned, saw Hayden falling back just a moment too late, and unloosed a string of indignant abuse in a hoarse high register. Along the street, people glanced in their direction, then turned, either incuriously or prudently, away. A couple of schoolgirls in pleated skirts and St. Trinian's straw boaters had seen what Hayden was up to some blocks back; smothering their laughter behind their hands, they were filming this latest altercation on their videophones. When they realised Hayden was looking at them, they screamed and ran away, *gwailo, gwailo.* With no immediate object in mind, Hayden followed them for a while.

By the time they'd vanished into some glitteringly meretricious megastore or other, he had no idea how far away from the hotel he was. His various diversions had led him uphill, which he supposed meant south and away from the harbour. Probably he was somewhere above Happy Valley by now, near Aberdeen Park perhaps, still a good few miles away from his hotel. Not that he was bothered: it was good just to walk, to stretch the muscles in his legs and fill his lungs with unprocessed air. He breathed in deep, relishing the stink of charcoal braziers and the savoury smell of street food, all the jostling aromas of a strange new city at dusk. He consulted the rising moon, and decided his hotel ought to lie in *that* direction. As he set off, three shadows subtracted themselves from the gloom of a nearby shop doorway and followed him.

Perhaps a mile later, Hayden found himself on the outskirts of some sort of public space, a closely planted grove of trees and bushes that fell away precipitately down the hillside. Beyond the topmost branches of the trees he could see the harbour down below, even pick out the landing lights of helicopters like fireflies round the cargo bays at Kai Tak. Hayden supposed he *could* waste time going round the park, or else he could just barrel right through it. Confidently—see what valorous animals we can be, when we're only free of pain?—Hayden set off along the path.

Underfoot was hard compacted sand, no slips, no trips. Even when the branches of the trees closed above his head, there was still enough moonlight for him to pick his way. (Had his night vision always been so acute? Damn, he was in good shape. Queue forms to the left, ladies.) The path wound down the hillside, till it was blocked all of a sudden by a wrought-iron gate set in a high hedge. Private property? Hayden thought not; and in any case the gate opened to his touch.

Inside was a small burial ground, very compact and quite grown-over. Small family shrines in serried ranks, with here and there a votive candle burning; white marble ghostly in the moonlight, and black tangles of bracken between the slabs. Hayden stepped into the enclosure, closing the creaky gate behind him. Somewhere in the bushes, a nightbird sang out in alarm. There were flights of steps between the terraces; in no particular hurry, Hayden sat down and lit a cigarette. Behind him, the iron gate creaked. Hayden turned round. He had company among the dead.

Now for those of you who haven't been in a fight recently (as Hayden explained to an increasingly bemused Dr. Pang), when it comes to mixing it the human male knows pretty much from the get-go how he'll behave. He'll either be emollient or abrasive, placatory or confrontational; he'll flee or fight. There's just something about the quality of the encounter that pre-determines these things—a hundred split-second decisions feeding into the adrenaline centres, instantaneous judgements based on the adversary's appearance, one's own state of preparedness, etc. And Hayden felt *good* tonight, dammit. He was enjoying his walk, and he did not appreciate being followed. And just in that moment, these simple factors outweighed any more practical considerations: the fact that there were three of them, young and lean and vicious, and that the leader was waving a flick-knife in front of him as he advanced. No matter: there was no way Hayden was just handing over his wallet and his watch and his iPhone. Not tonight, no sir.

Instead he found himself up on his feet in a curious sort of crouching pose, leaning forward on the balls of his feet, his head canted to a slight angle. The one in the front—mean-looking bastard in a leather jacket, hair flopping down across his brow—snarled and said something in Mandarin. The other two laughed. Hayden ignored them entirely, and took a few steps back, feeling with one outstretched foot for obstructions, never taking his eyes off the thug in front.

Slowly, as the muggers advanced, he was retreating down a terrace of graves, letting them come after him. Bad tactics, if he was planning to run—nowhere *to* run. However, because the terrace was so narrow, they could only come at him one at a time, single file. That was better for fighting; it nullified their numerical advantage. And that was what it would come to, he had no doubt. Everything in him was drawn tight and singing; clenched, filled with energy and ready to spring.

Again the lead badass snarled something. Very clearly—very *Englishly*—Hayden said, "Come on, then, fuckface. Fucking have a go, then." Had he been paying less attention to the advancing roughneck, and more to the quality of his consonant sounds, he might have noticed some slight occlusion on the Cs and Fs, the sort of thing you associate with the wearers of new dentures, or the chewers of sticky toffee.

Thug Number One said something over his shoulder to the other two, advancing still in Indian file behind him. They nodded, and one of them leapt down between two graves to the next lowest terrace. The other one tried to clamber up to the next highest, but lost his footing and went over with a yell, twisting his ankle in the process. Hayden knew he had to act quickly, or else his one-on-one advantage would be lost.

Instinctively, he went for the high ground. From a standing start he leapt up to the higher terrace; no sooner had his feet found balance on top of the marble tombstone than he was kicking out like Jet Li, not connecting with Thug Number One but forcing him to stumble backwards in surprise. Behind him of course, was his mate, who'd tried but failed to scale the tombstones; he was kneeling down to rub his sprained ankle. The two of them went over together in a heap, and then Hayden was on them.

The impact of his landing drove all the breath out of Thug Number One, the one on top. An agonised squeal from the bottom of the pile suggested it wasn't doing much for his clumsy mate, Goon Number Two, either, but Hayden didn't care. First things first. Before he knew it he was close in and pinning the lead mugger down, forcing his arms away from his head to expose his face. In the brilliant moonlight Hayden could see the fear in the face of the kid—more than that, he *felt* it, *tasted* it rather—and it was the fear that set off some primordial time bomb buried deep within him. Heedless of the snarl that disfigured his own features, he leaned in and bit, hard and deep and fierce.

Hayden remembered little else about the fight, to be honest; the who-did-what-to-who, the wirework and the stunts. But that feeling, when he first battened on to his opponent? The roaring, the struggling, the piteous screams and whimpers at the end; his strong and bulging jaws clamped down tight against the limited resistance of skin and flesh? The power of it . . . that he remembered well enough. And afterwards?

When the two least maimed of his muggers had scrambled away, snivelling and shrieking, he'd straightened up in amongst the gravestones, and tilted his head back to the fat enormous moon above the harbour. Never in his life had he known such transformative intensity; never before such focus and clarity. Beyond the graveyard, beneath the moon, there lay the radiant sweep of Hong Kong's harbour. Everything he could see was his, it belonged to him and him alone—and he could see *everything*. No element of it escaped his hungry gaze; not the meanest, least significant scintilla. All his.

Involuntarily, he tilted back his head and howled, howled to the echo. The nightbirds rose from the branches and broke in a panicking spiral; away down the hill, even the tamest, most domesticated dogs twitched and grumbled in their sleep, hackles rising the length of their tensed spines, muzzles peeling back to reveal mottled gums and sharp teeth.

"But the teeth—!" Dr. Pang was staring at him in amazement.

"Hang on," said Hayden mildly, and instantly the dentist closed his mouth. "I'm coming to that. Bear with me." He smiled, to convey reassurance. Dr. Pang did not smile back.

Now, those things that take place in ancient graveyards after dark, under the appreciative sanction of the bleak and vengeful ancestor spirits, may end up looking very different beneath the bland pedestrian glow of electric light. When Hayden made it back to the hotel he was jacked up with energy still—he'd run the couple of miles from the hillside park to the Mid-levels in no time, and was up for another circuit of the harbour at least—but he was also exquisitely aware of the need for caution and discretion. Given the events of the last few hours, he realised that a low profile was essential at this stage of his adventures. In his jacket pocket he'd found his old face-mask, proof against infection, ubiquitous amongst the passers-by during times of epidemic and contagion; before collecting his keycard at the desk he'd slipped it on, the better to conceal the focal point of his mysterious Shifting.

Up in his room Hayden made for the bathroom, where he used up a whole bottle of Listerine rinsing and gargling. There was a sharp brassy taste in his mouth, charged, electric, like biting down on tinfoil. When he woke very early in the predawn of the next day after a short yet intense power nap filled with strenuously incomprehensible dreams, his morning coughs and snuffles drew the clotted tang of blood from the back of his throat. Again, he spat for a long time over the washbasin, looking at himself in the backlit mirror.

He looked good, though. Didn't he? A gloomy Gus no longer, freed from toothache pain and jet lag; damn it, he was *glowing*, the way pregnant women are supposed to. Thoughtfully, Hayden squeezed a coiled blue blob of the miracle goo from its tube and applied it liberally to his gums. And another. No point in doing it by halves, was there? The gunk was menthol-cold going on—he could almost imagine his gumflesh shrinking back at its touch, which would at least account for the unusual prominence of his teeth in his grinning lean-mean-mother face. His teeth, oh yeah; warily, Hayden reviewed his exploits of the night before.

What had all *that* been about, then? The various cultural taboos governing use of the teeth while fighting were sufficiently well-established in Hayden's blokey superego to make him feel a little ambiguous about the whole affair. The only habitual biter he could remember having come across was back in school, a pale malnourished lad with more-or-less permanent pinkeye and impetigo. Nigel Tavers was his name; he used to smell of piss and stand by the radiators, and when cornered he would first of all whine, then try to kick you in the goolies, then use teeth and nails till he drew blood. Not the most admirable role model. So how, Hayden asked himself, did you square that inbred distaste for a dirty-fighter with those goings-on in the graveyard last night?

And found, without too much need for soul-searching and self-examination, the answer, or at least *an* answer. It was a knife, Hayden told himself; the bad bastard in the cemetery was waving a knife at him, with every intention of using it. This being the case, he, Hayden, a nice guy who carried no weapon, was obliged to use the implements to hand; or, in this case, to mouth. Nature's equaliser, in the face of the strong threat. No biggie.

This was true up to a point; at which Hayden stopped short, and threw himself back on the bed for a luxuriously bone-cracking stretch among the sheets. Had he been only slightly more open to self-examination, he might have gone on to consider both the nature of the attack—the damage done, the extent of the retribution—and the way it made him feel at the time. The buzz, the mega bloody buzz: he could still feel its aftermath, like the tail-end of a marathon coke binge. As it was, all he could think about was breakfast.

Naturally, only the full English would do. Hayden called room service to see if it could be fetched up now, immediately, right away; no question of waiting. When it appeared some minutes later—brought up by Jimmy Tsui, of all people—Hayden was waiting at the door like a zoo animal that hadn't been fed in a fortnight.

"How you feeling?" inquired Jimmy, wheeling the trolley through into the bedroom before Hayden could wrest it from his grip and fall on the contents there and then. "Hope your medicine is—working out?"

"It's fine," Hayden assured him through a mouthful of undercooked sausage. "Look—" pulling back his cheek to reveal the problem grinder. "Worked overnight. Amazing."

Jimmy stared at Hayden's exposed dentistry; and as he stared, his own mouth fell indecorously open. Backing up rapidly, he waved away the proffered tip, and was out of the door before Hayden could press the folded bills into his hand. His parting shot came back along the corridor: "All part of the service! Enjoy!"

Shrugging it off, Hayden returned to his breakfast. God, it was great to be able to eat like a man again, and not some toothless old dear! He bit down hard on a crispy slice of bacon, and felt with lupine pleasure the action of his teeth reducing it to pulp. Not the slightest twinge from his damaged molar; all that was in the past now. Good riddance. He had a busy day ahead of him.

Meetings, mostly, rescheduled and rejigged, clean through to half six in the evening, at which point Hayden passed on a corporate dinner with clients. He had to run an errand, he explained; which was true, so far as it went. A quick taxi ride over to Mong Kok, chop-chop, and after half an hour's wandering the strip, the right back alley and the right set of stairs. As it had been the night before last, the door at the end of the corridor was ajar.

Hayden knocked, and waited till the old man poked his head out like a hermit crab ready to defend its shell against all-comers. Before the door was slammed in his face, Hayden put his weight to it, forcing it open and sending the old man staggering back into the room. Following him inside, Hayden closed the door behind them and pulled out the package from his jacket. "More," he said, holding it up so the old man could see. "I need more."

The old man's response—a near-breathless tirade of what sounded to Hayden like every curse and swear word in the Chinese language—was pretty clearly in the negative. When Hayden asked him again, politely still, it was like standing in the way of a hosepipe of abuse. He tried cajoling him; he tried flashing his wallet, he made increasingly heated demands, but all to no avail. In the end, not knowing what else to do, Hayden ripped off his face mask. "Look!" he said, thickly, as if through a mouthful of something hard and uncomfortable. Immediately, the old man shut up.

Towards dusk he'd started to feel it, deep in the roots of his teeth. At first it had been bearable, actually not at all unpleasant: that rigid crackling sensation like popping your knuckles, only this was taking place inside his mouth, inside his jaw. Then the pressure, the constant pushing upwards, flesh and bone stretching, resettling. Probably nothing could stop it, that was the feeling he had. That was okay, though; that was fine, so long as he had some more of that blue stuff. More gel, now. Surely the old man must understand?

"You did this," said Hayden, stretching his lips wide open and showing the old man what lay concealed behind the second mask, the mask of his own skin. "You did this," advancing on him now, and the old man retreating, retreating, till he was backed up against the fish tank, yammering frantically; and then the tank tipped over and everything went flying, and the underground chamber was plunged into dark . . .

"So, anyway, I took all of the stuff he had left," explained Hayden. "That's lasted me until now, but . . . " He spread his hands and looked at Dr. Pang.

The dentist frowned. "Mr. Hayden. I have to tell you, this account of yours raises the gravest questions. The science of transgenic pharmaceuticals is still very much in its infancy; goodness knows what unauthorised, possibly toxic substances you may have received from this, this *street vendor*. I must urge you to stop self-medicating forthwith, and I shall now examine you to assess the extent of the problem. Please remove your mask."

Above the antiseptic face-mask, Hayden's eyes creased in disappointment. "Doctor," he said wheedlingly, "isn't there some way we can, you know, come to an agreement on this? You know the right people, I'm sure. Can't you get hold of some of this?" He waved his scrap of paper from the *Scientific American*. "I need it. I'd be prepared to pay."

"It would be more than my licence is worth," Dr. Pang assured him frowningly. "Now it would be best for me to examine you, to see the extent of the problem."

"It's almost full moon," said Hayden, shifting slightly upright on the chair. "It'll get worse before it gets better."

Dr. Pang stared at him. "What did you call that . . . that thing the hotel porter said to you? You repeated it to the street vendor. What was it again?"

"Wanchang dhole," said Hayden, with none of his former awkwardness. The foreign words seemed to slip more easily between his swollen lips than his birth-language. "I looked it up on the internet, afterwards."

"Then . . . you know what that means?" Dr. Pang had pushed his chair slightly back from the side of the recliner. The castors rolled silently across the gleaming tiles, till he came to a halt against the wall. No sound in all that antiseptic space except the hum of the air conditioning, a white clock ticking towards one AM, and the fast, slightly ragged breathing of the dentist.

Hayden swung his legs over the side of the chair and sat up, directly facing Dr. Pang. "Yes," he said, with difficulty. "Yes, I know what it means. But do you?" Lips parted in what might have passed for a grin, he stripped off his mask.

Dr. Pang gave an involuntary cry, and tried to get to his feet. The chair skidded sideways on its castors, and he lost his balance for a crucial second; then Hayden was upon him.

COMPARISON OF EFFICACY RATES FOR SEVEN ANTIPATHETICS AS EMPLOYED AGAINST LYCANTHROPES

MARIE BRENNAN

Abstract

This study seeks to establish a hierarchy of efficacy for various antipathetic materials and delivery mechanisms thereof as used in the extermination of lycanthropes. Pre-existing data on this issue consists solely of folkloric narratives and unsubstantiated anecdotes on Internet communities, neither of which are based upon suitable experimental trials. It is hoped that this study will be only the beginning of a proper body of scientific literature, which might be expanded to include hyena men, were-jaguars, and other therianthropes.

Definition

For the purpose of this study, a lycanthrope is a human being who physically transforms into a lupine or hybrid lupine-hominid shape, acquiring greater strength, speed, and reduced vulnerability to ordinary weapons. Available evidence indicates that this alteration is linked to the lunar cycle, though a full explication of the mechanism of transformation and its contagious nature awaits further study.

Violent aggression is not a necessary part of the definition, but seems to be either an ancillary effect of lycanthropy, or a co-morbid condition with it. Anecdotal reports of friendly lycanthropes are at present unsubstantiated.

Methodology

Numerous difficulties present themselves in any attempt to scientifically test the folklore regarding materials antipathetic to lycanthropes. Foremost among these is the lack of acceptance within the scientific community as to the existence of lycanthropy, beyond the psychiatric condition; this severely limits funding, peer review, and institutional support.

Because of this lack, it proved impossible to test antipathetics under laboratory conditions. The capture and maintenance of one caged specimen, much less several, was judged to be both dangerous and prohibitively expensive. The study therefore proceeded instead via field trials. Through the online community,[1] the investigator contacted individuals who had expressed the intention of hunting lycanthropes in the immediate future. These subjects were each provided with a different antipathetic or delivery mechanism thereof, and each expressed his or her willingness to allow the investigator to document the hunt.

In most cases, the field trials were recorded by means of head-mounted night-vision cameras, worn by the experimental subject, which streamed video wirelessly to the investigator's computer. On occasion it proved feasible to set up a stationary camera. These recordings were supplemented by the investigator's own notes, and (where possible) exit interviews with the hunters.

This research was not authorized by a Human Subjects Committee or other ethics review board.

Trial 1: argent projectile (modern)

The metallurgy of silver makes it difficult to manufacture silver bullets suitable for use in a modern firearm.[2] The investigator secured the

---

[1]   Including the websites Wolfpelt, Lunar Eclipse, and Sisterhood of the Silver Bullets.

[2]   Briggs 2005: http://www.patriciabriggs.com/books/silver/silverbullets.shtml.

use of a university metallurgy lab and the assistance of a professional firearms manufacturer to produce eighteen .357 caliber rounds,[3] or two clips for a Desert Eagle pistol.

The first subject, Hunter A, was a thirty-six-year-old male with a career in law enforcement, whose wife had recently been disemboweled by a lycanthrope. After demonstrating his firearms accuracy so as to establish a baseline for comparison, he commenced the search for his target.[4]

Lycanthrope A was discovered consuming the corpse of a small child in a dead-end urban alley. Hunter A positioned himself at the mouth of the alley, approximately thirty meters from the target, while the investigator observed from the other side of the cross-street, concealed behind a newspaper dispenser. Video data shows that Hunter A's shots exhibited 64% less accuracy than in the baseline demonstration: he had previously declared his intention to aim for the head[5], but of the six shots he fired, two flew wide to the left, three flew wide to the right, and one struck Lycanthrope A in the shoulder. Hunter A attempted to fire a seventh shot, but suffered a gun malfunction, and then was struck to the ground by the charging lycanthrope. It is notable, however, that the lycanthrope fled rather than engage in further confrontation.

Retrieval and examination of the pistol shows that the seventh round did not chamber correctly, owing to the separation of the silver point from its copper case. The decrease in accuracy may arise from multiple causes, including fear-induced operator error. It may be presumed, however, that the difficulty of casting high-quality silver bullets introduces a degree of variability which will decrease

---

[3]   Thirty rounds were produced in total; twelve were eliminated due to poor quality, which would have increased the risk of gun malfunction in the field and therefore biased the data. This production issue, however, must be considered relevant to the larger question of efficacy. (For ballistics information on this ammunition, see the appendix.)

[4]   For a full account of each subject's background, involvement in the anti-lycanthrope community, and predatory efforts, see the author's monograph Under the Full Moon: An Urban Safari Into the Biology of Lycanthropes, in preparation.

[5]   While it may lie beyond the scope of this study to make tactical evaluations of lycanthrope-hunting techniques, the investigator believes it is generally more advisable to aim for the center mass, for reasons illustrated by Hunter A's results.

performance under field conditions, even where malfunction does not occur.

The escape of Lycanthrope A unfortunately precluded the possibility of forensic examination. Six spent bullets, however—one bloodstained—were recovered from the test location; this indicates that the shot which struck the target's shoulder passed through the tissue and out the other side. The investigator observed a distinct limp and other indications of pain as the lycanthrope fled (the video camera by this time was recording the pavement), which suggests a genuine injury to the target.

Trial 2: argent projectile (archaic)
The difficulty of casting silver bullets to the exacting specifications of modern firearms suggests that archaic weapons might prove more efficacious, when the variables of performance are weighed against those of manufacture. The investigator therefore secured the assistance of a professional silversmith, who produced twelve balls suitable for use in an eighteenth-century musket.

Hunter B was a twenty-two-year-old female with experience in American Revolutionary War re-enactment, whose boyfriend vanished during a camping trip in the mountains. As with Hunter A, she demonstrated her skill with a replica period weapon before beginning her search. In this instance, the investigator remained at camp, inside an SUV with the engine running and pointed toward the road.

Video data for this trial is non-continuous, due to the problems of wireless transmission in mountainous terrain. On the third night Hunter B observed her target, Lycanthrope B, drinking water from a stream. Unfortunately, she made her observation from a hillside well beyond the range of a musket, and by the time she moved closer, Lycanthrope B had vanished. Subject and investigator therefore returned to that area the following month, and this time Hunter B met with success on the first night. She found her target howling at the moon on a bare hilltop, and the yelping end of the howl indicates that her first shot struck home, though it is not possible from the recording to determine where Lycanthrope B was wounded. The target fled, however, before Hunter B could reload her musket. No limp was discernible on this occasion, which may indicate that the lesser muzzle velocity of an archaic firearm caused the projectile to penetrate less deeply than in Trial 1. Upon returning to the hilltop in daylight, Hunter B found little sign of blood, which corroborates this speculation.

The trial could not be continued on the following night due to the disappearance of Hunter B.

Trial 3: argent shot
The investigator pursued one further solution to the difficulty of silver bullets, in the form of shot. Silver beads were obtained from a craft store, and placed in a shotgun cartridge in lieu of the customary lead shot. The firearm in this instance was a Remington 870 pump-action shotgun.

Hunter C was a fifty-seven-year-old male with over forty years of hunting experience. His six-year-old son had been fatally mauled the previous summer on Hunter C's ranch. The subject declined to undergo a formal demonstration of his marksmanship, despite explanations of its value for research, but did feed the investigator a dinner cooked from a pheasant he brought down with his shotgun.

Data from this trial consists solely of the investigator's notes, as Hunter C likewise declined use of the head-mounted camera or other video-recording equipment. On the first night of the full moon he staked a female sheep in the open ground twenty meters beyond his barn, having first cut the animal with a knife, so the scent of its blood would draw the predator. He then waited inside the open barn door, with the investigator behind a hay bale. This having produced no results, on the second night he cut the ewe's throat and staked a lamb next to her, declaring that the greater quantity and the cries of the lamb would be more effective.

Methods of luring lycanthropes are outside the scope of this study, but on that night Lycanthrope C appeared. Hunter C immediately left the concealment of the barn and began walking toward his target, firing as he went. Lycanthrope C was observed to flinch slightly at each shot, and the investigator believes the subject's aim was good, but the small quantities of silver seemed to do little more than irritate the target. Hunter C continued approaching even after running out of ammunition, dry-firing and shouting with incoherent grief, and subsequently fell victim to the lycanthrope.

The lamb was unharmed.

Trial 4: argent blade

The investigator next obtained a silver-plated bowie knife. While the lesser hardness of pure silver (as compared to carbon steel or stainless steel) would ordinarily render it unsuitable for use in a bladed weapon, the antipathetic nature of silver is hypothesized to counterbalance this deficiency.

Hunter D was a twenty-two-year-old male gang member who had lost his younger brother to a lycanthrope.[6] Although it was not possible to obtain quantitative data regarding his proficiency with the weapon, as with Hunters A and B, other informants corroborated his statement that he was the victor in four previous knife fights.

In this instance the hunt was organized as a planned encounter between Hunter D and Lycanthrope D. The investigator was therefore able to position a stationary camera on a fire escape above the agreed-upon location, in lieu of the head-mounted camera Hunter D could not wear. The ideal nature of this setup, unfortunately, was compromised when friends of Hunter D refused to allow the investigator to monitor events from a safe distance via the computer. This field trial was therefore observed at close range, with notes recorded afterward.

This ultimately proved to be only a minor limitation. Measured from the moment the combatants approached each other to the moment when Hunter D's body struck the ground, the confrontation lasted for 3.6 seconds. Hunter D thrust the knife into Lycanthrope D's side, approximately in the location where the spleen would be located in a fully human body, whereupon Lycanthrope D tore Hunter D's head

---

[6] Initially this subject was disqualified from the trial on the basis of evidence that he was merely seeking revenge against the non-lycanthropic leader of a rival gang. The alternative candidate for the fourth trial, however, revoked her permission and abandoned her hunt at the same time that new evidence came to light, supporting Hunter D's claim regarding his target. (It is regrettable that this new evidence took the form of an entire gang of lycanthropes.)

from his body.[7] While the silver does appear to have wounded the target satisfactorily—Lycanthrope D was heard to howl in pain when it removed the blade—the necessity of close approach renders this method inadvisable.

<u>Trial 5: AgNO$_3$</u>

This particular trial was suggested by Hunter E, a forty-one-year-old female with over a decade's experience as a zookeeper. The investigator observed her on a message board suggesting that lycanthropes might be hunted with tranquilizer guns. Although the efficacy of sedatives and paralytics in this context is highly dubious, the darts could be adapted to deliver other compounds.

Together with Hunter E, the investigator conducted a preliminary series of experiments with modified darts. Colloidal silver, unfortunately, showed a tendency to clog the bore of the needle. Instead two syringes of silver nitrate were prepared: one with a standard steel needle, and one with a specially-crafted silver needle.

Hunter E had suffered no personal encounter with lycanthropes, and so had no immediate target. The investigator therefore introduced her to the city district occupied by the lycanthrope gang. Together they chose a suitable target, one who appeared to be an outcast member of the pack. This target was lured to an alley by means of fresh lamb chops, obtained from a nearby butcher. A stationary camera was again positioned on a fire escape, in addition to the head-mounted camera worn by the subject. The investigator observed from a parked car nearby.

Equipped with a night scope, Hunter E sighted on the target from a distance of twenty-seven meters and fired the steel-needle syringe. This produced a confused and wary reaction from the target, but no sign of incapacity or pain. Hunter E loaded the silver-needle syringe and fired a second time, whereupon Lycanthrope E fled the scene.

Examination afterward revealed that the silver needle bent slightly

---

[7] This analysis is based on slow-motion playback of the video recording. The investigator failed to directly observe anything of value either during the confrontation or after, as safety considerations required immediate departure from the trial location.

COMPARISON OF EFFICACY RATES . . .   65

on impact, closing off the bore and preventing the silver nitrate from being expelled. Traces of blood on the tip show that it did penetrate the flesh, to a depth of approximately half a centimeter; video analysis suggests the dart fell out of Lycanthrope E's shoulder soon after contact. The steel-needle syringe appears to have bounced off the target without penetration. The efficacy of silver nitrate therefore remains unknown.

Trial 6: Sorbus aucuparia
The wood of this tree, commonly known as rowan or mountain ash, is well-documented in folklore as an antipathetic for witches, fairies, and werewolves. It is unsuitable for bullets of any sort, and the preceding trials suggested that both shot and melee weapons would be inadvisable. A trap was deemed the most appropriate delivery mechanism for the antipathetic.

By the time an appropriate quantity of material had been shipped to the investigator, a number of possible subjects had suggested themselves, all in the vicinity of Trials 4 and 5. Hunter F was a nineteen-year-old male, and the leader of one half of the surviving gang of which Hunter D had been a member. When provided with a book on survival techniques, including the crafting of pit traps, he and his companions[8] arranged twelve fire-hardened spikes of S. aucuparia inside a street-level delivery hatch to the basement of a nearby building. They then covered the opening with a tarp and sent their fastest runner, a fourteen-year-old male (henceforth called Assistant F), to lure a target toward the field site.

Hunter F declined to allow the investigator to place a stationary camera, or to equip any of the participants with head-mounted devices. It proved possible, however, for the investigator to slip one on in the moments preceding the commencement of the trial. The following data is based upon that recording.

The lure returned mixed results. Sounds issuing from outside the camera's field of view indicated that Assistant F was caught and dispatched just beyond the mouth of the alley. Another individual

---

[8]   The investigator indicated to Hunter F that the trial would be biased if multiple subjects were directly involved. He responded in language unsuited to an academic journal.

(Assistant F2, male, age unknown) ran to his aid, but reversed course almost immediately, pursued by Lycanthrope F at a range of approximately two meters. Assistant F2, a heavily-built young man, appears to have lacked the dexterity of the late Assistant F; he missed his footing on the plank bridging the pit trap and fell in. Lycanthrope F immediately attempted to change course, but skidded on wet pavement and slid over the edge. Hunter F, along with Assistants F3-F7 (all male, ages unknown) ran to the pit trap, where they began throwing objects at Lycanthrope F and stamping on its hands[9] in an attempt to make it fall. This succeeded after approximately seven seconds, but the target missed the spikes; it only cracked one, and subsequently[10] ran off into the basement.

The efficacy of S. aucuparia against lycanthropes therefore remains dubious. Against human beings, however, the spikes proved quite fatal.

Trial 7: Aconitum napellus

The role of the final antipathetic is suggested by its common name,[11] wolfsbane. The most suitable delivery mechanism would seem to be a tranquilizer dart, but the unsatisfactory results of Trial 5 ruled out this approach. The investigator considered stuffing lumps of meat with leaves of A. napellus, before concluding that the likelihood of persuading a lycanthrope to consume the meat was low. An infusion of the whole plant therefore seemed the most reliable means.

Hunter G is a twenty-four-year-old female graduate student in biology. No recording was made of the seventh trial, except for notes transcribed by the subject after the event. An infusion of A. napellus was prepared by the subject upon the arrival of Lycanthrope G[12] during

---

9   Some lycanthropes observed in this study appear to have possessed opposable thumbs, but in other cases this trait is uncertain at best. There may be variation in the wild.

10   According to a report from Assistant F6; unverified by the investigator.

11   One of many common names for the genus. Others include monkshood, aconite, blue rocket, and women's bane. No antipathetic qualities have been observed in human females—beyond the naturally-occurring cardiac poison, which is equally effective against human males.

12   Formerly known as Hunter B.

daylight hours, in the period of the waning moon. When served to Lycanthrope G in a teacup and consumed by the target, it proved fatal within nine minutes. The efficacy of A. napellus against lycanthropes in their lupine or hybrid forms is still undocumented, but the howls and snarls of Lycanthrope G suggest that it operated upon more than simply the normal human cardiac function of the target.

Conclusion and further study

All the tested antipathetics and delivery mechanisms showed flaws that mar their efficacy. (Those which failed to produce any result may be deemed inefficacious by their general unreliability.) The most harm was inflicted by the modern argent projectile, the argent blade, and A. napellus, but the former suffers from difficulty of manufacture and unreliable performance, the second requires hazardous proximity to a lycanthrope, and the latter, thus far, has only proved its use against lycanthropes in human form.

Nevertheless, it is the opinion of Hunter G, in her role as investigator, that A. napellus offers the most promising avenue for further inquiry. Another course of field trials is intended, these testing the efficacy of an infusion of A. napellus applied externally, as delivered by a high-powered water gun. Trials 4, 5, and 6 have produced an abundance of suitable research targets, many of whom have demonstrated a tendency to approach the investigator of their own accord.

It is hoped that the documentation provided by this study will encourage others to pursue the topic of lycanthropic biology. There is an urgent need for a greater understanding of the subject, particularly in the vicinity of Philadelphia.

THE BEAUTIFUL GELREESH

JEFFREY FORD

His facial fur was a swirling wonder of blond and blue with highlights the orange of a November sun. It covered every inch of his brow and cheeks, the blunt ridge of his nose, even his eyelids. When beset by a bout of overwhelming sympathy, he would twirl the thicket of longer strands that sprouted from the center of his forehead. His bright silver eyes emitted invisible beams that penetrated the most guarded demeanors of his patients and shed light upon the condition of their souls. Discovering the essence of an individual, the Gelreesh would sit quietly, staring, tapping the black enamel nails of his hirsute hands together in an incantatory rhythm that would regulate the heartbeat of his visitor to that of his own blood muscle.

"And when, may I ask, did you perceive the first inklings of your despair?" he would say with a sudden whimper.

Once his question was posed, the subject was no longer distracted by the charm of his prominent incisors. He would lick his lips once, twice, three times, with diminishing speed, adjusting the initiate's respiration and brain pulse. Then the loveliness of his pointed ears, the grace of his silk fashions would melt away, and his lucky interlocutor would have no choice but to tell the truth even if in her heart of hearts she believed herself to be lying.

"When my father left us," might be the answer.

"Let us walk, my dear," the Gelreesh would suggest.

The woman or man or child, as the case might be, would put a hand into the warm hand of the heart's physician. He would lead them through his antechamber into the hallway and out through a back entrance of his house. To walk with the Gelreesh, matching his languorous stride, was to partake in a slow, stately procession. His gentle direction would guide one down the garden path to the hole in the crumbling brick and mortar wall netted with ivy. Before leaving the confines of the wild garden, he might pluck a lily to be handed to his troubled charge.

The path through the woods snaked in great loops around stands of oak and maple. Although the garden should appear to be at the height of summer life, this adjacent stretch of forest, leading toward the sea, was forever trapped in autumn. Here, just above the murmur of the wind and just below the rustle of red and yellow leaves, the Gelreesh would methodically pose his questions designed to fan the flames of his companion's anguish. With each troubled answer, he would respond with phrases he was certain would keep that melancholic heart drenched in a black sweat. "Horrible," he would say in the whine of a dog dreaming. "My dear, that's ghastly." "How can you go on?" "If I were you I would be weeping," was one that never failed to turn the trick.

When the tears would begin to flow, he'd reach into the pocket of his loose fitting jacket of paisley design for a handkerchief stitched in vermillion, bearing the symbol of a broken heart. Handing it to his patient, he would again continue walking and the gentle interrogation would resume.

An hour might pass, even two, but there was no rush. There were so many questions to be asked and answered. Upon finally reaching the edge of the cliff that gave a view outward of the boundless ocean, the Gelreesh would release the hand of his subject and say with tender conviction, "And so, you see, this ocean must be for you a representation of the overwhelming, intractable dilemma that gnaws at your heart. You know without my telling you that there is really only one solution. You must move toward peace, to a better place."

"Yes, yes, thank you," would come the response followed by a fresh torrent of tears. The handkerchief would be employed, and then the Gelreesh would kindly ask for it back.

"The future lies ahead of you and the troubled past bites at your heels, my child."

Three steps forward and the prescription would be filled. A short flight of freedom, a moment of calm for the tortured soul and then endless rest on the rocks below surrounded by the rib cages and skulls of fellow travelers once pursued by grief and now cured.

The marvelous creature would pause and dab a tear or two from the corners of his own eyes before undressing. Then naked but for the spiral pattern of his body's fur, he would walk ten paces to the east where he kept a long rope tied at one end to the base of a mighty oak, growing at the very edge of the cliff. His descent could only be described as acrobatic, pointing to a history with the circus. When finally down among the rocks, he would find the corpse of the new immigrant to the country without care and tidily devour every trace of flesh.

Later, in the confines of his office, he would compose a letter in turquoise ink on yellow paper, assuring the loved ones of his most recent patient that she or he, seeking the solace of a warm sun and crystal sea, had booked passage for a two-year vacation on the island of Valshavar—a paradisiacal atoll strung like a bead on the necklace of the equator. *Let not the price of this journey trouble your minds, for I, understanding the exemplary nature of the individual in question have decided to pay all expenses for their escape from torment. In a year or two, when next you meet them, they will appear younger, and in their laughter you will feel the warmth of the tropical sun. With their touch, your own problems will vanish as if conjured away by island magic.* This missive would then be rolled like a scroll, tied fast with a length of green ribbon and given into the talons of a great horned owl to be delivered.

And so it was that the Gelreesh operated, from continent to continent, dispensing his exquisite pity and relieving his patients of their unnecessary mortal coils. When suspicion arose to the point where doubt began to negate his beauty in the eyes of the populace, then, by dark of night, he would flee on all fours, accompanied by the owl, deep into the deepest forest, never to be seen again in that locale. The pile of bones he'd leave behind were undeniable proof of his treachery, but the victims' families preferred to think of their loved ones stretched out beneath a palm frond canopy on the pink beach of Valshavar, being fed peeled grapes by a monkey valet. This daydream in the face of horror would deflate all attempts at organizing a search party to hunt him down.

Although he would invariably move on, setting up a practice in a new locale rich in heavy hearts and haunted minds, something of him would remain behind in the form of a question, namely, "What was The Beautiful Gelreesh?" Granted, there were no end of accounts of his illusory form—everything from that of a dashing cavalry officer with waxed mustache to the refined blond impertinence of a symphony conductor. He reminded one young woman whom he had danced with at a certain town soiree as being a blend of her father, her boss and her older brother. In fact, when notes were later compared, no two could agree on the precise details of his splendor.

He was finally captured during one of his escapes, found with his leg in a fox trap only a mile from the village he had last bestowed his pity upon. This beast in pain could not fully concentrate on creating the illusion of loveliness, and the incredulous chicken farmer who discovered him writhing in the bite of the steel jaws witnessed him shifting back and forth between suave charm and gnashing horror. The poor man was certain he had snared the devil. A special investigator was sent to handle the case. Blind and somewhat autistic, the famous detective, Gal de Gui, methodically put the entire legacy together as if it was a child's jigsaw puzzle. Of course, in the moments of interrogation by De Gui, the Gelreesh tried to catch him up with a glamorous illusion. The detective responded to this deception with a yawn. The creature later told his prison guards that De Gui's soul was blank as a white wall and perfect. De Gui's final comment on the Gelreesh was, "Put down some newspaper and give him a bone. Here is the classic case of man's best friend."

It was when the Gelreesh related his own life story to the court, eliciting pity from a people who previously desired his, that he allowed himself to appear as the hominid-canine entity that had always lurked behind his illusion. As the tears filled the eyes of the jury, his handsome visage wavered like a desert mirage and then lifted away to reveal fur and fangs. No longer were his words the mellifluous susurrations of the sympathetic therapist, but now came through as growling dog talk in a spray of spittle. Even the huge owl that sat on his shoulder in the witness stand shrank and darkened to become a grackle.

As he told it, he had been born to an aristocratic family, the name of which everyone present would have known, but he would not mention it for fear of bringing reprisals down upon them for his actions. Because of his frightening aspect at birth, his father accused his mother of bestiality. The venerable patriarch made plans to do away with his wife, but she saved him the trouble by poisoning herself with small sips of opium and an arsenic pastry of her own recipe. The strange child was named Rameau after a distant relation on the mother's side and sent to live in a newly constructed barn on the outskirts of the family estate. At the same time that the father ordered the local clergy to try to exorcise the beast out of him, there was a standing order for the caretaker to feed him nothing but raw meat. As the Gelreesh had said on the witness stand, "My father spent little time thinking about me, but when he did, the fact of my existence twisted his thinking so that it labored pointlessly at cross-purposes."

The family priest taught the young Rameau how to speak and read, so that the strange child could learn the Bible. Through this knowledge of language he was soon able to understand the holy man's philosophy, which, in brief, was that the world was a ball of shit adrift in a sea of sin and the sooner one passed to heaven the better. As the Gelreesh confessed, he took these lessons to heart, and so later in life when he helped free his patients' souls from excremental bondage, he felt he was actually doing them a great favor. It was from that bald and jowly man of God that the creature became acquainted with the power of pity.

On the other hand, the caretaker who daily brought the beef was a man of the world. He was very old and had traveled far and wide. This kindly aged vagabond would tell the young Rameau stories of far off places—islands at the equator and tundra crowded with migrating elk. One day, he told the boy about a fellow he had met in a far-off kingdom that sat along the old Silk Road to China. This remarkable fellow, Ibn Sadi was his name, had the power of persuasion. With subtle movements of his body, certain tricks of respiration in accordance with that of his audience, he could make himself invisible or appear as a beautiful woman. It was an illusion, of course, but to the viewer it seemed as real as the day. "What was his secret?" asked Rameau. The old man leaned in close to the boy's cage and whispered, "Listen to the rhythm of life and when you look, do not accept but project. Feel what the other is feeling and make what they have felt what you feel. Speak only their own desire to them in a calm, soft voice, and they will see you as beautiful as they wish themselves to be."

The Gelreesh had time, days on end, to mull over his formula for control. He worked at it and tried different variations until one day he was able to look into the soul of the priest and discover what it was—a mouse nibbling a wedge of wooden cheese. Soon after, he devised the technique of clicking together his fingernails in order to send out a hypnotic pulse, and with this welded the power of pity to the devices of the adept from the kingdom along the old Silk Road. Imagine the innate intelligence of this boy they considered a beast. A week following, he had escaped. For some reason, the priest had opened the cage and for his trouble was found by the caretaker to have been ushered into the next and better world minus the baggage of his flesh.

The jury heard the story of the Gelreesh's wanderings and the perfection of his art, how he changed his name to that of a certain brand of Mediterranean cigarettes he had enjoyed. "I wanted to help the emotionally wounded," he had said to his accusers, and all grew sympathetic, but when they vented their grief for his solitary life and saw his true form, they unanimously voted for his execution. Just prior to accepting, against his will, the thirty bullets from the rifles of the firing squad marksmen, the Gelreesh performed a spectacular display of metamorphosis, becoming, in turn, each of his executioners. Before the captain of the guard could shout the order for the deadly volley, the beautiful one became, again, himself, shouted, "I feel your pain," and begged for all in attendance to participate in devouring him completely once he was dead. This final plea went unheeded. His corpse was left to the dogs and carrion birds. His bones were later gathered and sent to the Museum of Natural Science in the city of Nethit. The grackle was released into the wild.

Once he had been disposed of and the truth had been circulated, it seemed that everyone on all continents wanted to claim some attachment to the Gelreesh. For a five year period there was no international figure more popular. My God, the stories told about him—women claimed to have had his children, men claimed they were him or his brother or at least the son of the caretaker who gave him his first clues to the protocol of persuasion. Children played Gelreesh, and the lucky tike who got to be his namesake retained for the day ultimate power in the game. An entire branch of psychotherapy had sprung up called Non-Consumptive Gelreeshia, meaning that the therapists swamped their patients with pity but had designs not on the consumption of their flesh, merely their bank accounts. There were studies written about him, novels and plays and an epic poem entitled *Monster of Pity*. The phenomenon of his popularity had given rise to a philosophical reevaluation of *Beauty*.

Gelreesh mania died out in the year of the great comet, for here was something even more spectacular for people to turn their attention to. With the promise of the end of the world, mankind had learned to pity itself. Fortunately or unfortunately, however one might see it, this spinning ball of shit, this paradisiacal Valshavar of planets, was spared for another millennium in which more startling forms of anomalous humanity might spring up and lend perspective to the mundane herd.

And now, ages hence, recent news from Nethit concerning the Gelreesh. Two years ago, an enterprising graduate student from Nethit University, having been told the legends of the beautiful one when he was a child, went in search through the basement of the museum to try to uncover the box containing the creature's remains. The catacombs that lay beneath the imposing structure are vast and the records kept as to what had been stored where have been eaten by an unusual mite that was believed to have been introduced into the environs of the museum by a mummy brought back from a glacier at the top of the world. Apparently, this termitic flea species awoke in the underground warmth and discovered its taste for paper, so that now the ledgers are filled with sheets of lace, more hole than text.

Still, the conscientious young man continued to search for over a year. His desire was to study the physiological form of this legend. Eventually, after months of exhaustive searching, he came upon a crate marked with grease pencil, **GELREESH**. Upon prying open the box, he found inside a collection of bones wrapped in a tattered garment of maroon silk. There was also a handkerchief bearing the stitched symbol of a broken heart. When he uncovered the bones, he was shocked to find the skeleton of a very large bird instead of that of a mutant human. A professor of his from the university determined upon inspection that these were indeed the remains of a great horned owl.

SKIN IN THE GAME

SAMANTHA HENDERSON

—◈—

"Hex!" Miranda waved purple fingertips over the white-bone tumble of the dice, which came up one, three, six.

Lydia, her run of fours broken, cursed her eloquently. Miranda, indifferent to charges of being a loose woman, scooped up the dice and promptly buncoed.

"Bitch!" cried Lydia, jubilant. "Give up the Bunco Bear, whore!"

From the head table a child's toy, seized hastily from Cass's daughter's room before the game began, flew through the air in a fuzzy, bright green arc. Miranda caught it, one-handed and laughing, and tucked it into her cleavage.

Sandy applauded with the rest as Miranda threw one more four and then came up twos and fives.

"Time to bunco," said Lydia as Sandy grabbed the dice for her turn, and she threw. A four, a two, and one die rolled off the table and landed near her foot: a five. She snatched it up: she could claim it was a four, take the five, or re-roll.

"It was a five," she said—the single four allowed her to continue and she wanted to seem honest at this point. She'd subbed twice for this bunco group—Cass worked at the cubicle kitty-corner to her, and started asking to come the month before last—and they needed to replace a regular who'd moved out of state. No pack of bunco bitches likes being stuck at eleven members, having a ghost at table—one player rolling for an invisible teammate.

She liked this group: you got dinner instead of just coffee and dessert and the stakes of $20 apiece made it worth her while to get creative. She felt like she had skin in this game. She expected that after tonight's game she'd be invited to join, and it was always easy to fix up things so the game got cancelled the month it was your turn to host. Volunteer for June, when the task of juggling kids fresh out of school and planning summer vacation usually resulted in a scrub, or change the date late enough that only nine or fewer could come, two ghosts being the limit of anyone's tolerance. She'd volunteer to help another hostess, bringing the main dish and gaining a reputation for helpfulness while avoiding the expense of the booze.

A single four, and another, and the dice passed to Miranda's partner. She rolled one, three, three, and before Lydia could seize the dice there was an exasperated shriek and the clang of a bell from the head table and the round was over.

Miranda's bunco was worth twenty-one points, so Sandy and Lydia stayed in the pit, while Miranda and her ex-partner, a short plump pink creature whose name Sandy couldn't recall—G-something, who sold Avon and left a few catalogs in an unobtrusive way on the kitchen table—moved on to the center table and split, finding new partners, the losers from the head table. Lydia grabbed an M&M from the bowl on the pit and waved a cocktail-ringed hand at Sandy when she made to move.

"Stay where you are, Sandy-Candy," said Lydia, plumping her rather wide butt on the seat next to her. "That chair's bad luck for me."

"Shall I keep score?" Sandy asked innocuously, reaching for the pad Miranda's partner—Gretta? No, more Brit—had left behind. Lydia nodded vaguely. No one really liked to keep score, it meant you had to concentrate on top of your dinner and a wine cooler, and the uninhibited caterwauling of yourself and your fellows.

But if you were willing to keep score, and were subtle about it, and good at misdirection, keeping score was a good way of making sure you won a few more times, at least on paper, than you really had.

Bunco is a supremely simple game requiring only the skill to toss the dice. Six rounds, sometimes twelve: roll ones, then twos, threes, and so forth. Three of a kind—ones in round one, twos in round two—is a bunco. The only possible strategy is to throw as fast as possible, because the more you roll the more the chance of getting a bunco.

There are modifications, embellishments. Mini-buncos and triple-buncos and one-two-three sequences and extra points at the head table. The buy-in can be five bucks, ten, twenty, sometimes you get dinner, sometimes you get cake. These are flash and fancy icing, the true spine and soul of the game is only this: roll the dice, bitch. All the menfolk and children had fled the premises, here are your girlfriends, and you can do no wrong here—eat and drink as you will, and talk as you will about your brother's ex and your high school friend's divorce and your jewelry business. Talk and roll the dice.

It's a game of chance, not skill, so there's not many ways you can cheat. If the game is going fast and the other three women are chatting and not paying attention you can say you got one or two more points than you did—you passed on the dice and the scorekeeper would ask what you got and you said four instead of three. No one would know. And if you were keeping score yourself it was even easier.

Sandy liked winning other people's cash, liked free food, liked even better the idea that she controlled the outcome behind the façade of a pleasant face and manner, without anyone else suspecting. She felt a friendly kind of contempt for Cass and her friends, their overpriced game, their shrieking and stretch marks. They'd do very well for her, she thought.

Sandy won the round, fair and square, and moved ahead to partner small pink Gretta—no, Gwynne! That was it. It took the head table a long time to score twenty-one; the game was long and Gwynne buncoed, but before she could seize the green bear, Tessa buncoed too, and then Gwynne got three fives, not a bunco but good for five points, and in the hilarity that resulted from that and from everyone overhearing Maggie tell Harriet-called-Harry and Mia about losing her virginity, lo these many years ago, at Disneyland, Sandy claimed six fives when she only rightly had four, winning the round for Gwynne and herself when the bell rang. Dionne tallied her points without demur but Sandy didn't see Gwynne and Lydia glance at the table and then at each other.

Sandy buncoed at the head table, getting the bear and three buncos for the price of one, then Cass buncoed and sent Sandy back to the pit, her second loss of the night. She moved quickly from pit to center table to head for the final game. She wouldn't win for having most buncos—

Tessa had that pretty much in hand, but she might score most wins if she was careful. She took the score pad automatically as she sat, letting the game draw out as it would: another long one. The chatter quieted as the last match, sixes the goal, drew out.

One more win was all she needed. The game was close: nobody would notice—Dionne rolled one six, then nothing. Sandy moved the pencil as if to give Dionne her point, but left no mark. Opposite her Miranda rolled and crapped out, and Dionne's partner Cass got one six, bringing their score to twenty. Sandy held her breath and Cass rolled again: two, five, five. They were tied, at least on paper if not in truth. Sandy rolled, saw two sixes, and whooped. That ended the round and the game and gave her nine wins; she'd won the lion's share of the pool. She grabbed the dice to roll again—might as well try for last bunco and win that pot too.

The silence struck her like a fall of bricks. The three women at her table stared at her stone faced, when they should have been shrieking and cursing at her win. She felt the grin solidify on her face and clacked the dice nervously in her hand as she stared back.

The other eight, four at one table and four in the pit, were staring at her as well. Sandy's smile faded as she looked around: there was a strange, sharp tang in the air that, more than the somber gaze of eleven other women, made her hackles rise. The scattered pencils on each table, a spill of honey-glazed peanuts from a bowl across the stained cloth of the pit, the bright green bear crumpled on the floor, a cluster of half-filled water bottles and a lone, lipstick-stained martini glass gave the impression of a room abandoned in haste, and the group of women that once belonged so intrinsically to this milieu, with their good-natured vulgarity and dull jobs and side businesses and recipes and husbands and boyfriends was gone, this predatory, alien coven in their place.

Sandy grasped the dice hard until the pointed edges bit painfully into her palm, then laid them carefully on the table. She tried a final placating smile, directed at Miranda's grim expression opposite her, then let it fade.

"I think we won. Did I make a mistake on the scoring?"

Miranda regarded her under lowering brows for a few seconds, then smiled, hugely, showing all her teeth. With a dull shock Sandy saw they were very white, and very pointed. More like a dog's teeth than a person's, she thought.

"No," said Miranda. "No, I don't think you made a mistake."

The sharp smell—a kerosene kind of smell, Sandy thought in her back brain—got stronger suddenly and she shifted backwards in her chair. The path to the front door was blocked by the two tables to her left, but the arch to the kitchen was directly behind her and on the other side, the front hallway.

But that was silly. No one was going to hurt her. Not over bunco. It wasn't that important. Not like they had skin in the game. Not like her.

Then Miranda and Cass rose; Cass's chair fell with a clatter—she ignored it, poised in a semi-crouch, just like Miranda. The way they stood, knees bent not quite right, the planes of their faces not quite right—they had changed, shifted in some indefinable way, and as she watched Sandy *saw* it: the base of Cass's nose broadened between the eyes, lips lifting from teeth that were not made the way they were before.

"I told you," growled a voice from the pit. Shel. Her partner four rounds back. They had lost, Sandy making sure it was her last loss. "I told you she cheated. Second time she subbed."

Dumb bitch, thought Sandy with useless clarity through her pooling fear. I fooled you the first game too, and you though it was sub's luck.

Miranda growled, her lips lifting, her snout—it was a snout, her face shifting, malleable as Play-Doh—extending out of her formerly placid face. Sandy scrambled backwards, tipping her chair over in front of Cass to give her a few more seconds, retreating into the kitchen and, abandoning purse and coat, making for the hallway. The blinds over the sink were up and a small part of her, seeing the moon rise over the neighbor's rooftop, understood.

It wasn't even a full moon, a blobby something somewhere between full and half, not even photogenic. Seemed like cheating to her.

Of course, that was only fair, considering.

The arch to the hallway was blocked by three looming forms—small plump Gwynne, her back humped up under a pink silk blouse, her fangs protruding over her lower lip, her petite fingers now claws.

Lydia and Shel loomed behind her, their faces molded flat and feral like Miranda's.

Sandy whirled around, her heels slipping on the linoleum. Cass's shoulders, enormous and hairy, were bursting out of her dusky purple jacket, part of the suit she wore every Monday, or when clients were in the office. Sweet, kind-of-frumpy Cass, eating yogurt every morning and heating up her Lean Cuisine at lunch. Harriet-called-Harry, who had a meeting with her fifth-grader's teacher that afternoon and was bemoaning the fact that she only came up with fantastic retorts three hours later at dinner, drooled down her T-shirt, her eyes huge and yellow.

Sandy backed into a table loaded with the dirty dishes from dinner; one tipped to the floor and spun around with a clatter of silverware. More crowded into the kitchen: Tessa, Maggie, Mia—whose ears had grown up pointed, still pierced with Cookie Lee earrings. Lexie, impossibly broad and squat. Dionne, her body still human, her face a beast's.

"Keep her in here," snarled Cass. "I just got the carpets cleaned."

Sandy backed into the cold expanse of a sliding glass door and fumbled at the latch; it was closed and locked tight. She slammed the glass, trying to break it, but glass is tougher than it looks and that only works in movies, and this wasn't a movie.

If this were a movie, you would have seen a reverse angle of the sliding glass door and a scarlet spray across it.

The kitchen was very clean by the time they were done. Everyone was always careful to help clean up.

"Did you win?" Cass's husband shifted over to make room for her. He'd taken their daughter to the movies, knowing neither of them belonged here on bunco night—not a scary movie, with blood across a window, but something with princesses, and spells, and little bit of death, suitable for a seven-year old.

"The hostess never wins," she said, pausing to listen for her child stirring again before she laid her head on his chest, looking out the bedroom window at the blobby moon, small and insignificant, risen high above the trees.

He stroked her hair. "Your friend from work—Sammy?"

"Sandy."

"Did she work out?"

Cass didn't answer at first, and his fingers, twinned in her hair, stopped.

"No," she said, finally. "She didn't fit in."

"Oh."

"Some of the others think she cheats."

"Oh." His fingers were still.

"Cheated."

He didn't say anything and after a while he began stroking her hair again, and she blinked at the moon, her eyes green, then yellow, then green.

BLENDED

C.E. MURPHY

The pack had been born savages and had, almost to a man, died that way.

Almost: almost. She had been a whelp the day the hunters came, dozens of them on their thundering black horses with the pack fleeing before them. Her mother had thrown her beneath a long-dead tree, and she'd watched dark legs flash by, dangerous broad hooves kicking up the snow.

She had seen the blood, from her hiding place. Had seen it when the hunters rode back, triumphant despite their own losses. Stripped skins still steamed in the cold, making their horses toss their heads at the scent of death. She hadn't known, then, that it was her family, her cousins and her friends, who lay strewn across saddles and stuffed into saddlebags. Not until she was much older did she come to understand what had happened. That her family had run until they could run no more, and then had turned to fight. Beasts, turning tooth and claw against the men who hunted them. Horses died; men died.

But mostly, wolves died.

Fear had held the whimpers in her throat, even when the smell of men and killing was gone. Only when the forest went black with night did she creep forward on her belly and put her nose out into the cold.

A man's big hand caught her by the scruff and hauled her into the air. She had never seen a man so close: he was huge and completely without fur except long gray crackling stuff on his head, and unlike the men on horses he wore no coverings to keep himself warm. Her tail clamped over her belly, wet with terror.

He curled his lip back, showing long teeth, though the wrinkle of his forehead was like her alpha's: hiding amusement behind more obvious exasperation. *Cubs*, that expression said, and was always followed by a pack-wide chuckle that was as much attitude of pose as vocalization. The tip of her tail relaxed from its clench to offer a tentative wag.

"Well," he said, and it was the first time she ever heard a wolf speak so, aloud and with words used by men. His voice was light, a thinness to it that said its howl would pierce the moon. "One left, of a pack. But a young one, so perhaps there's some hope you might listen." He dropped her with the carelessness of any parent weary of carrying a wriggling cub. She scrambled back to the snow's crusty surface and he crouched, brushing cold from her ears and nose. "Come, pup. We must teach you to survive."

Then he turned, and before his hand touched the snow it was a paw, and his gray grizzling hair thick fur, and his tail made a beacon for her to follow as they ran from where their pack had died.

"No *ward*?" The question cut through polite murmuring, briefly silencing it. Markéta knew already not to turn; not to admit she'd heard. It wasn't that anyone imagined the sharp words hadn't reached her. It was merely that humans, inexplicable humans, pretended rudeness and gossip didn't exist, as if by so pretending they could excuse their own bad behavior. Few of them would survive a week, within a pack. They would be cuffed, stared down, and ultimately rejected, if they played at the back-biting which was a figurative, if not literal, part of human society.

The pack had been born savage, Markéta thought dryly, but humans had taught her the real meaning of the word.

"But she is too young to be a widow . . . !" The woman—an older one, with breasts of a size to feed a litter of puppies for all that she had only two—modulated her voice this time, but it made no difference. She might have whispered, and even through the ballroom's endless echoing chatter, Markéta would have heard her. It was not a gift, the retention of hearing and scent in her human-changed form; humans stank, and covered it with perfumes that worsened the original stench. Worse, they insisted on gathering in huge packs, where their sweat and nattering voices blurred into a nauseating background.

Still, she would have humans change, not herself. She had gone far enough already in becoming as they were, a truth she was reminded of every time another woman learned her story and spread it as a bit of titillating gossip. She was *quite young*, she heard it emphasized, somewhere between seventeen and twenty-one. Old enough, certainly, to be married—but if not married, much too young to be on her own. But her guardian, if he'd ever existed, had died, leaving her to make her way as an eligible female amongst society's snapping wolves.

Markéta snorted loudly enough to cause comment, and thrust off societal grace to elbow her way out to the manor gardens. They were too tame, too controlled, but they were also as close to wilderness as she would find so long as she maintained the fiction of polite birth. She was aware—as a human woman would not be—that two men followed her, both trying harder to avoid one another than find her. One was older, in his forties at least, and the other hardly more than a whelp of her own tender years.

Which were far more tender than the gossiping women within could ever imagine. Wolves lived only a short span. It was an ancient beast indeed who saw fifteen summers. Markéta was three, breeding age to be sure, but there were almost no others of her kind left with whom to mate. The hunters had seen to that. The hunters, and her people's determination to live the free life of wild things, no matter what the cost. The memory of scent rose up, bitter, black. The hunt's leader had smelled that way, like hot tar sitting at the back of her throat. She would never escape its flavor.

"Miss Alvarez." Her name sat awkwardly on a British tongue, but she'd had no sense of how human names were put together, when she'd chosen it. She'd merely liked its sound, *Markéta Alvarez*, and had only later realized that they were not two names that the English race expected to lie cheek and jowl. She might have been Margaret Allard and satisfied them, but by then it was too late.

Its advantage was that, like everything else about her, it offered no answers, but miles of gossip-satisfying questions. She was surely not dark enough for the Mediterranean descent her last name implied, nor square-faced enough to be from north of the Danube, as her first name suggested. Her eyes were distressingly yellow—a hallmark even the change couldn't disguise—and her hair, shaggy and thick, was too many colors to be called one. *Light*, they tended to decide; she was light-haired, but sharp-featured as a Spaniard, and no one could name a family of merit whose bloodlines ran to such extraordinary lengths.

But meritous she must be, else men of various wealth and standing would hardly bother following her into the gardens. Markéta nodded to her suitor without turning his way: his scent was of more use in identifying him than sight. "Master Radcliffe. Surely you endanger my reputation by encountering me unescorted."

"Surely I'm too old and dull for anyone to think your reputation in any but the safest of hands, with me." There was not a single note of deprecation in the older man's voice; he sounded as utterly sincere as any man could. But his posture, half-glimpsed, shouted amusement, announcing he didn't for a moment believe himself. "If I were some handsome young rake, perhaps . . . "

"And now I must protest your attractiveness, sir, a boldness which is no fit thing for a lady to do."

"I should hardly ask you to belie yourself, Miss Alvarez. I have, in my time, made use of a mirror."

Now she turned to him, smiling, though his attitude would still tell her more than his face ever could. "And what does the mirror show you, Master Radcliffe? A well-dressed gentleman still possessed of a leonine head of hair, whose face bears the wisdom of a man in his prime?"

"My mirror," he said with a bow, "is not so kind."

If only his eyes were yellow, and not dark, he would be a man worth mating. Her pack leader had made that clear, as he'd taught her how to cast off the wolf and pretend at being human. There were some few of their people wise enough to put aside the beast in a world growing increasingly cruel to wolves. Some few who had become as Markéta now was, wearing sheep's clothing in a rather literal sense. Not that her ball gown was wool: it was summer and warm, but she had more often made a dress of what she would have once considered a meal than she liked to think.

It struck her for the first time, as she gazed at Master Radcliffe, that her years were limited. Even with whole seasons spent as human, she might not extend her lifetime beyond two or three times its natural length. She would be dead by thirty, and long since too old to breed by then; that was a duty that should be given over to her daughters as she aged.

Daughters she might never have, if she couldn't find a mate of her own breed. The pack leader hadn't told her what to do, should that come to pass. Die alone, without a pack and family of her own, or risk all on a human? Wolves, like humans, largely mated for life. It would be impossible to take a human mate without telling him the truth, even if she were willing to remain human and bear one cub at a time through a pregnancy that lasted most of a year, instead of a blissfully short two months.

The forest and its hunter threat sounded suddenly far more appealing than it had since the day her pack had died. A short and savage life, to be sure, but a simple one too, without the complications of society or the difficulties of cross-breeding. Some of those thoughts were perhaps reflected in her gaze, because Radcliffe stepped forward, a question in his pose.

For the first time in her own memory, Markéta stepped back, avoiding the confrontation of entanglement.

Radcliffe hesitated, surprise and disappointment marking his stance. Before she could speak, another man's voice said, "Master Radcliffe. Miss Alvarez."

Her name had a crack in it, wide as a board; her second suitor was barely a man at all. She had been introduced to him earlier in the season, at another ball so crowded his scent was indistinguishable from the masses even when they had danced. Twice, if she recalled; he was handsome enough, and struck her as a man who would spend his life doing her bidding without ever wondering why. Thomas, his name was; the young Master Alistair Thomas. His father and his fortune were of note, and those combined with his affable nature made him the apple of many a young lady's eye. It would not endear Markéta to her competition that he had come to the gardens seeking her.

She regretted her retreat from Radcliffe already, and all the more as he took a discreet step back, appointing himself the position of elder and guardian with that single move.

"Miss Alvarez," Thomas said again, then stopped, evidently flustered by her silence. Markéta curtsied toward him, letting the action take her a half-step nearer Radcliffe. The older man's posture improved very slightly—there was no room for improvement beyond that; he stood straight and tall as a youth already—and Thomas managed to falter again, even without moving or speaking.

"Master Thomas," Markéta said. "Do you find the gardens to your liking?"

"Gardens?" He blinked, as though unaware of his surroundings until she mentioned them, then rallied with a smile that understandably set hearts a-flutter. "Truly, Miss Alvarez, their beauty diminishes into nothing when such a flower as yourself stands among them. I should hate to take you from your company," he added, all polite form that had nothing of truth in it. His expression took Radcliffe in, weighed him, and dismissed him as too old and probably too poor. "But perhaps when you return to the ball you would care to dance."

He irritated her, for some reason. For dismissing Radcliffe, for intruding on the moment she and the older gentleman had shared. It would never do to scold him for his behavior, but there were other ways to make displeasure known. Markéta turned her gaze full on Radcliffe and spoke as clearly as she ever had. "I should like that very much."

Thomas was affable, perhaps, but not a fool. He stiffened and took one sharp step in retreat. "Then I shall see you inside."

Markéta nodded, a cool smile already in place as a breeze carried the scent of his tension to her. Black, tarry, thick: a familiar smell strong enough to taste, lingering at the back of her throat. Her remoteness scampered before shock and an upswell of anger. She ought not have mocked Thomas for the break in his voice, for it was hers now, shrill and unattractive: "Do you smoke, Master Thomas?"

Surprise splashed across his face. "I can't say that I do. What—"
Clarity rolled after surprise, and he bent his head to sniff at the shoulder
of his coat. "My father's tobacco. He's only just back from France, so
perhaps I'd have not smelt so strongly of it when first we met. My
apologies, Miss Alvarez, if it offends you."

"It's . . . " Markéta closed her eyes, willing away the memory scent
brought, though in truth it was her nostrils that needed closing;
vision would never offer her as much information as odors could.
A moment passed before she looked on the young man again, ready
to trust her voice. "It's an unusually pungent breed of tobacco, I
should say. I imagine I've encountered it before. Your father hunts,
perhaps?"

Delight lit Thomas's smile. "He does. Are you a hunt enthusiast,
Miss Alvarez?"

"I have an unusual interest in hunting." So softly spoken, eyes
downcast, anything to keep the words from the wild honesty they were.
It had been so long, *so long* since she had taken to four legs and chased
rabbit and deer; since she had used her senses and her body the way
they were meant to be used. And there was more besides, threat in
the softly spoken admission; threat which dull human ears couldn't be
permitted to hear.

Nor did Thomas hear it, his zeal entirely for the topic he believed
at hand. "How splendid. That is, in fact, why Father's been to France.
He hunts there; the sport here has grown weak, with the eradication of
wolves."

"Come," Radcliffe said abruptly. "There have been no wolves in
England for centuries, Thomas. Watch your tongue; you'll alarm the
lady."

"There have been a few," Thomas corrected, but without aggression.
He kept his eager eyes on Markéta, not so much as challenging Radcliffe
with his gaze. "It is the story put about that there have been none, but
there were, indeed, packs left roaming until only a few years ago. They
are startlingly canny, wolves, and seem to go to ground for years at a
time. But my family has hunted them for generations, at the throne's
behest. Here, in Scotland, in Wales, even in Ireland, and now in France
because there's nothing left to hunt in the isles."

"I do not believe it." Radcliffe huffed, and Thomas finally looked away from Markéta, patience in his bearing.

"Perhaps you would like to visit our manor, Master Radcliffe. There my father keeps pelts from all his hunts, and you will see the newest of them has hardly had time to let dust settle. He prefers the alpha male, but in his last English hunt that beast escaped him. It was old, though, and will have died since then, and he has its mate's fur instead."

"I should like to see these furs," Markéta said distantly. "If I may be so bold as to invite myself along, Masters Radcliffe, Thomas?"

Smugness rushed through Thomas's posture and scent, and the glance he threw at Radcliffe was triumph embodied. "I shall have my coach fetch you on Thursday next, if it suits?"

"That will do," Markéta whispered. "That will do very well."

She wanted so very badly to shed her human form and hunt the hunter. For almost a week she'd waited, keeping herself confined in her townhouse, because to leave was to invite temptation. Even cobbled streets and the sour wind carrying civilization's stench through the city was close enough to wilderness when she had the temptation of a hunt at hand.

It was temptation she could not risk. The thinking part of her—the part her pack leader had tried so hard to develop—recognized that. A wolf wouldn't go unnoticed in London's streets, and even if by chance it should, she dared not meet the hunter who had destroyed her family in her lupine form. His gift was killing wolves. Her only chance lay with striking as a woman.

So she paced before the windows until the servants blushed with discomfort; a well-bred young woman did not stare into the world so hungrily, as if waiting to invite it in to ravish her. As if waiting, she thought, to be loosed on it, so she might savage it. It was preposterous, playing the role of a maiden fair, dressed in soft white muslin and pointed shoes. She would have herself barefoot in red and black, the colors of blood and death, but no, no, no. She had to think, keep her mind clear; the man she went to see would be her family's murderer, and she the only one left to seek vengeance.

"Mum." The housemaid's voice stopped Markéta's stalking. She swept up her cloak, adjusting it crookedly over her shoulders and throwing off the maid's attempt to help. The girl's words followed her, their information already imparted by her arrival in the parlour: "The carriage is here, mum . . . ."

"Hold supper," Markéta commanded. "I don't know when I shall return." When, or *if*, though she would never add fear to the maid's scent by saying such a thing. The maid agreed, and Markéta was out the door to the coach before her manservant could lend a hand.

The pair of matched bays before the carriage tossed their heads and whickered uncomfortably. Markéta quenched the urge, as she always did, to put her hand beneath their noses and drive their discomfort to madness. Animals knew; they always knew. Horses shied from her, and even the most aggressive dogs snarled and backed away. Cats stood wary, one paw lifted, then disappeared into darkness. Only humans saw nothing more than the girl she presented as; only humans were so blind.

"Miss Alvarez." The coachman opened the door, but it was the man within who offered his hand to help her up. Radcliffe, not Thomas, and his expression lit with sly pleasure at her surprise. "I was so crass as to insist I be allowed to escort you, Miss Alvarez. My town house is so much nearer your home than Master Thomas's. It seemed unkind to make his man come all this way, when I was obliged to pass you regardless."

"I'm delighted. The journey will go so much more quickly with pleasant company." Markéta drew her skirts in, childishly pleased she hadn't frightened the horses after all. "Your horses are very fine."

"Thank you. My family breeds them on our country estate. It is, I'm afraid, the source of our income: gross commercial ventures in horseflesh. Are you shocked, Miss Alvarez?"

"I should think a man able to persuade a thousand pounds of beast to his will would be a firm and fair hand with a household as well. What woman would find that anything but enticing? You must have a fair stretch of land, then, Master Radcliffe." For a moment the city houses outside the window slipped away, turning in her mind's eye to pastures and rolling green hills.

"Enough," Radcliffe admitted. "My favorite stretches are the woods. We have several, some of them very old and peaceful."

"And unriddled by wolves," Markéta said softly. "How lonely for them."

"For the woods, or the wolves?" Radcliffe wondered, and when she glanced at him, lifted his eyebrows. "You disapprove of the hunt."

"I believe I said I had a peculiar interest in it, sir."

"You did, but it was my thought that the words said something entirely other than the heart felt. Forgive me my presumption. I did not mean to offend."

"No," Markéta said, softly once again. "You have not."

He put a hand over his heart, and took the topic to the pleasant inconsequentiality of the season's fine weather, but her gaze strayed to him time and again and she wondered what else he had heard, that she had not said.

Alistair Thomas greeted them with her mother's pelt in hand.

Society had rules of engagement, meaningless twitter of words like so much hurried birdsong; Markéta knew she must be participating in that, because there would be a resounding, deadly silence if she were not. She did *not* admire the pelt; that much she was certain of, because Thomas's pleasure in displaying it faltered. Radcliffe was reserved, allowing precisely what Thomas had insisted on: that it was a new fur, recently taken, and so there had indeed been wolves on England's shores more recently than he'd known. Markéta had no idea what she herself said, nor how she could say it with any degree of calm.

The fur's scent was so long gone it might never have been, but even without scent, without life, it could be no one other than her mother. The darker grey streaks above once-yellow eyes had made her fierce, and stripes of white on her muzzle had given her canines extra length to threaten both prey and ill-behaved pups with. She had been mother to the pack, and to see her reduced to a flopping length of skin turned Markéta's insides cold and hard.

"Did you join this hunt?" She barely knew her own voice, dissonance ringing through it. Worse than dissonance: *she* could hear the wolf in her voice, even if the men couldn't. It wanted to howl, and only stringent human decorum kept her from letting it loose.

Disappointment flashed over Thomas's face. "My father wouldn't have it. I was a poorer shot than I might have been, and he wouldn't risk me or the hunt on it. Three men died that day even so."

"And how many wolves?"

"Nine." Another man's voice, deeper and richer than Alistair's, broke in, and was accompanied by a clatter of footsteps on marbled stairs. Markéta startled, knowing it to be a violent reaction, but there had been nothing to her beyond her mother's fur in Alistair's hands. Only lately did she look upward, take in the echoing length of hall they'd been ushered into, its walls mounted with animal heads and its ceiling painted with scenes of the hunt. And this a town house, she thought; the country estates would be exhausting in their attention to murderous detail.

The man on the stairs was as unlike his son in form as could be, an oak to a sapling. He carried no extra weight, just size, and his chiding was good-natured. "Al, you can't intend to leave our guests in the foyer all afternoon. Forgive my son, madam, master. His enthusiasm at times overwhelms his sense. I'm Alan Thomas, Lord Thomas if you must, though too much ceremony is tedious. And you must be Miss Alvarez. Master Radcliffe. My home is yours, won't you come in?"

Radcliffe guided her forward when her own feet wouldn't take her. Her breath was lodged in her throat, stuck there by tar and blackness as Alan Thomas's scent rolled down the stairs with him. She had thought him a black devil, not fair and jovial, but the taste of blood and death clung to him without remorse. She managed a curtsy so stiff it hurt her knees, but Lord Thomas took no offense. Instead he looked her over, then threw a tobacco-stained smile toward his son.

"This is the young lady with the interest in the hunt? You could hardly have found better, Alistair. Look at her coloring, those eyes, she could be a wolf herself. Oh, Lord forgive me, I'm as rude as he is. I'm a man who speaks my thoughts, Miss Alvarez. Perhaps you won't hold it against me."

"Do you favor women who speak theirs, my lord?" Her voice was strangled in her throat, and Radcliffe, unexpectedly, put his hand at her spine, a show of—not lending strength, she thought. Of solidarity, as her mother had once stood by the pack leader.

Lord Thomas's eyes narrowed, making him suddenly wolfish himself. Not so convivial after all, for all that his gaze was the ice blue of a cub and not gold like an adult. "Would you think it fair, Miss Alvarez, if I said I'd met few women who voiced their thoughts? Whether they have none or whether society has trained restraint into them, I cannot say, but a woman of reason and consequence is a rare thing, in my view."

Her vision was not good: she saw few colors, and her focus was that of a hunter's, honing in on a single individual. But it worsened now, until Thomas stood out against a blurred background, prey for the hunting. "Then I will endeavor to impress upon you that a few of us, at least, are as capable of matching wits as any man, my lord."

"I look forward to it. So you have an interest in the hunt. Do you ride, Miss Alvarez? Can you shoot?" Lord Thomas escorted them into sitting rooms so opulent Markéta might otherwise have laughed. Crystal turned sunlight to shards of light glittering across parquet floors, and overstuffed chairs were gathered to make different sitting areas. One was by the unlit fire, but they were guided to seats overlooking the gardens. A wolf's pelt, older than her mother's, lay across one of the sofas, and Alistair tossed her mother's there with as little regard.

Markéta sat there so she would at least not have to *look* at the furs. Alistair Thomas sat beside her, casting a subtle glance of victory toward Radcliffe, who gave no signs of noticing as he settled into a chair across from them. Lord Thomas dropped into another armchair, but leaned forward, gaze avid as he awaited Markéta's answer.

"I'm afraid I'm a poor rider, my lord. Horses do not like me. And the sound of a rifle hurts my ears."

Polite doubt crawled into his expression. "How then can you be enamored of the hunt?"

"I can track." Again, Markéta barely knew her own voice. She had spent so long training the snarls and yips out of it, so long working away the growl so all that was left was a pleasant alto. But she bit off the words as though her teeth were long and sharp, and no man who called himself a hunter could mistake the challenge behind them. "What I track, I can kill. What else is there to the hunt, my lord Thomas?"

His lips peeled back from his teeth in what might have been a smile. "No one can always kill what they track, Miss Alvarez. Not even I, and I have many more years experience than you."

"Almost always," Markéta whispered, "is often enough."

Alistair shifted uncomfortably on the seat beside her. "Surely this isn't an appropriate discussion to hold with a young lady, Father."

"Oh, on the contrary." Wicked delight gleamed in Radcliffe's eyes. "I think it most fascinating. Perhaps a wager, if Miss Alvarez is willing. You have extensive gardens here, Lord Thomas. Dare you pit your tracking skills against the lady's?"

Curiosity burgeoned in Markéta's breast, distracting her from the reminders of her family's death. Lord Thomas could hardly refuse such a wager without a degree of humiliation, which Radcliffe surely knew. She knew her own reasons, certainly, for needling at Thomas, but it had not struck her that Radcliffe might have his own. Nor was there a discrete way to ask, but if they had a common goal she could at least apply more pressure to the suggestion Radcliffe had laid down.

Her smile was brief, but genuine. "A challenge," she said lightly. "How delightful. I accept."

Emotion flew across Thomas's face: chagrin and pride and a willingness to humor the poorer folk. "I cannot refuse, if our guest is so certain of herself. You must promise to forgive me if I should come out ahead in this wager, Miss Alvarez. It's ungentlemanly, but I hate to lose. I cannot make allowances for your sex."

"I wouldn't want you to, my lord. And if I should win, I trust you will be as forgiving. What shall our quarry be?"

"I've seeded wild boar on the estate." Thomas watched her carefully, and Markéta made no effort to hide the lifting of her eyebrows.

"Boar is an animal harried by packs, even packs of men, my lord. Would you dare the kill, all alone?" She would not; she was not, even in the face of vengeance, that great a fool. It had been decades and more since boar had roamed Britain freely, just as it had been so long since wolves had. Pack memory told of stolen piglets, delicious to eat, but also told of the size and speed and rage of a full-grown boar. Markéta's people were larger by some significant part than their single-aspected brethren, but boar met them weight for weight, and sometimes better than. One wolf against a boar was madness.

But one man, unarmed, was dead.

"I have a horse, a gun, and no fear of the creatures. Are you so bold, Miss Alvarez?" Thomas's smile was the wolf's again, though no wolf had such a streak of cruelty in it. That was a human trait.

"I had thought a deer, or even a game of hide and seek," Radcliffe said, dryly enough to almost hide the note of concern in his voice. "Miss Alvarez has made no pretense of tracking differently than you, my lord. She would have no horse, no gun. Surely you wouldn't pit her against a monster capable of killing a man with a single blow?"

"No," Markéta said. "Thank you for the concern, Master Radcliffe, but I believe I accept. I should like to prove to Lord Thomas that the hunt can be carried out in more than one way." This time her smile was as false as firelight was to the sun. "And prove, perhaps, that a woman can be equal to a man in many ways."

Thomas stood with a clap of his hands. "I'll have my men harry a boar from the wood, then."

"Oh, no, sir." Markéta came to her feet as well, as full of wide-eyed innocence as she could be. "Not on my behalf. I shall enter the wood myself and find my own boar. Perhaps he who returns with the kill first will be declared the winner?"

Tension flushed Lord Thomas's face, but he nodded. "And tomorrow we'll dine on the fruits of—our," he conceded graciously. "Our labor. If you would be so good as to remain with us overnight, Miss Alvarez? Master Radcliffe? I assure you, the estate can absorb you with no thought."

"It will be our pleasure." Markéta spoke for Radcliffe, thoughtlessly, but he chuckled and made a murmur of agreement. Smiling, she bobbed a curtsy. "Shall we hunt, then, my lord?"

Boars grunted and squealed, distressed by the scent of a half-forgotten predator. They were complacent, unaccustomed to being harassed by any but men on horseback, and therefore less inclined to fight than to trot heavily through the wood, grumbling without being genuinely afraid. It helped that she only wanted to direct them; one wolf was not enough to hunt a boar, but with canny foresight and enough speed, she could herd a pack.

The numbers mattered: there was the king and his mate, and a handful of half-grown piglets old enough to be both delicious and dangerous. An armed man might succeed against any one of them, but anger the lot and weapons would do little good. That was why hunters, human or otherwise, separated one from its pack.

That was why Markéta did her best to drive them all into Thomas's arms. Not just for vengeance, though that was key, but because it was good to run, to hunt and harry, to leap from one side of the offended herd to another, snapping her teeth and catching wild scents. She hadn't stretched her legs so well in months, and playing at a whole pack of wolves was work enough to keep her thoughts honed and focused wholly on the moment.

Even she was shocked when Thomas came out of the brush. He had used the wind well, staying upwards of it, while it had been to her advantage to keep the pigs downward, where their crashing and snorting might carry as well as their scent. She had been at the boars' heels, far enough back to not anger them; far enough, now, to meld into the low undergrowth and watch as panic struck hundreds of pounds of pig flesh.

The piglets broke in every direction but hers, one rushing for Thomas's horse. Its mother struck out after it, too late; hooves flashed and the smaller beast's skull collapsed. It rolled forward, dying body tangling in the horse's legs, and Thomas fired his gun as the mother boar charged at him. A single shot, and he made it count; few men might have struck the pig's eye, though her momentum carried her forward and brought the horse and rider down even as she fell.

Thomas leapt clear, the blood that spattered belonging to the horse, not himself: it was done for, belly split open by the female's bite as she died. The male, screaming fury, rushed Thomas, who flung his gun away and drew a long knife, his pigsticker spear broken by the horse's fall. There was no fear in his scent, nor could there be, should he hope to survive.

A snarl rose up in Markéta's throat. She turned it to the sky in a howl, sharp sound of warning and loss, and trotted out of the brush to let the hunter see her.

For a deadly instant surprise took him, and in that moment, so did the boar.

She had never seen one throw a man. It caught his gut easily, and turned its weight against him, flinging him a distance only aborted by the presence of an oak tree. Thomas hit it with bone-cracking force and slid down, blood turning his shirt and hands to crimson. The boar snorted, charged again, then veered away into the broken underbrush, chasing after its offspring.

The horse lay on its side, thrashing. Markéta darted around its dangerous legs, scampered back from bared teeth broader and stronger than her own. There were other predators better suited to this kill than wolves; her jaws were strong, but she had seen how big cats could strangle their prey in mere seconds. Wolves tore and shredded at haunches, only taking the throat last, when the beast was already weakened, and the horse was still too strong with fear to be called weak. Still, it deserved better than the death coming to it, and she lunged in when silence took it for a moment.

It took a long time, blood hot and sweet on her tongue. As its gasps died, she heard Thomas's increasing, and rolled her eyes, desperate to see but unwilling to release the horse and extend its death any longer. The gun was gone: Thomas had flung it well away, and was bleeding too heavily to search for it. But he was strong, and mercy shown to the horse could count against her own life.

It finally shuddered and died, strength gone from its great muscles. Markéta backed off, head lowered as she swung toward Thomas.

He was white-faced, drained of blood but not emotion; rage etched deep lines in his skin.

"What is man but a pack animal?" The words came from Markéta's throat distorted, harsh, angry; a wolf was not meant to form human speech. She changed again, staying where she was, lithe on all fours, horse blood drooling down her chin. She had abandoned her clothes before taking lupine form; they would not change with her, and she knew now she looked a wild thing, monstrous human bathed in blood.

"We are only those who chose to heed the wild, so long ago. We learned to stay away from your penned cattle, your easy sheep, your fine horses. We hunted in the wood, and ran as one, while you our brothers constricted yourselves into dull unsensing human form. We did not threaten you, hunt your children, ruin your lives, and yet you came for us. That was my *mother*!"

She forgot, in springing forward, that she was only a woman, and had no teeth to tear his throat with. Instinct older than thought judged her and made weapons of her hands, curved to dig fingers in where tooth would not do. She might not have bothered; her weight was on his belly, where the boar had seized him, and the man screamed.

It drew her up. Not from mercy, but because to talk, to threaten and to posture, was the human and not the lupine way. A wolf hunted and killed, rather than allowed its prey to linger.

A pity, then, that this man, and others like him, had obliged her live so long in their world. "My mother," she whispered again. "My family. My pack, dead for sport."

He smiled, bloody and brief. Drew breath, held it, and spat it: "*Dog*. Do you think . . . we didn't *know* . . . what we hunted? Mongrels. Monsters. Sinners. You are the last . . . in England . . . and my son will carry on the hunt in Europe!"

She ought to have been wary. Ought to have known he would carry another weapon; that a second knife could be secreted more easily than a gun. He moved faster than a dying man should, but the surge of muscle warned her. The blade glittered and she turned into it, ducking low, body transformed without a thought. The horse's neck had been massive in her jaws; his wrist was fragile, and bone shattered all too clearly beneath his scream.

She tore the sound out with a single bite, spitting away flesh she had no desire to feast on. A wolf would have taken his throat before, and never learned that he'd known what he hunted. That was worse, worse by far, than she might have imagined. She would have to leave Britain, find her brethren elsewhere and warn them.

A branch cracked, folly of human intrusion. Markéta snarled and fell back from Thomas's body, lost between knowing whether to run or to take human form and bluff. Run; she would run, away from England's shores, but first there were other men to be dealt with.

Radcliffe stood at the edge of the clearing, a gun held loosely in his hands as he stared at Thomas's body. "His father stole horses from my grandfather," he said eventually, softly, though there were no other humans nearby to hear him. "I had hoped for some satisfaction in that. Some mark of watching him embarrassed by a woman out-hunting him. I had not imagined . . . this. It is you, Markéta, is it not?" His gaze lifted to her, almost apologetic. "I saw, when you . . . when you spoke to him. When you took human form. You are a . . . "

"Wiaralde-wulf." Those words, so ancient they were made for a wolfen tongue, still hurt her throat. Markéta changed, cautiously, to her human form, to speak more easily. "A world wolf, by our own name. *Werewolf*, by yours. As old as man, and closer to the world than you now are."

"Mother of *God*." Radcliffe fell back a step, gun clutched to his chest like a woman might clutch a kerchief. "*Markéta*?"

"Please, sir." A whisper of humor bent her smile, though she could feel blood drying around it. "'Miss Alvarez.'"

He drew himself up, gun still held like a bludgeoning weapon. "You are naked in my sight, dear woman. I believe I might call you by your given name."

"Only if you intend to make me your wife." Her gaze flickered to the gun. "Will you shoot me, if I run?"

"Would you have me?" he asked at the same time. They stared at one another, Markéta still primed to run, and Radcliffe's eyes dropped to the gun he held. He cast it away with a shudder, then looked to her again. "You said to Thomas that you were the ones who chose to heed the wild. Can a man make that choice even still? Can he become . . . *wiaralde-wulf* even now?"

"Not in memory." Markéta hesitated, creeping forward a few steps. He was unarmed; she could kill him, if she must. "But in legend . . . ."

"In legend, as we tell it? Through a bite?"

"And through the tending of the wound. Why would you want it? We are hunted." Markéta spat at Thomas's body.

Radcliffe smiled faintly. "What man would want a wife capable of such astonishing feats that he could not himself achieve? Would you have me, Markéta Alvarez?"

She glanced at herself: naked, bloody, fingers caked with gore and her face and throat no doubt worse. Beneath the horror, well-enough endowed in human standards, her frame neither overwhelmed nor embarrassed by the curves she possessed. Then she lifted her gaze to Radcliffe's, watching his face and stance as she shifted to her wolf form. Scenting for his apprehension, preparing herself to face fear.

She found curiosity in his cant, and wonder, easily read as a puppy's. Eagerness, like a pup's enthusiasm for exploration, though he was a man fully grown. Caution threaded through it: he saw her as the predator she was, but extended wary trusts. Beneath it all, though, a line of confidence was struck, familiar tone seen in any pack leader. He was certain of the choice he was asking both himself and her to make.

Humans were clearly mad. Markéta changed again—she hadn't made the change so many times in a day in years, if ever—and sat staring at Radcliffe with a wolfish gaze, waiting for him to falter. Minutes dragged on, and he remained steady, until she herself looked away and gave a short sharp laugh. "Then I suppose we should find water that I might wash myself in, and my clothes, and then go to young Lord Thomas with the sad news about his father. And then I think we shall visit France, Master Radcliffe, there to further discuss our future."

"Randolf," he said absently, and offered her a hand to help her stand. "My given name is Randolf. Will you call me by it?"

Markéta froze, then laughed and put her hand in his. "Randolf. *Wolf's shield*. Did you know the meaning of your name, sir?"

He drew her upward, only smiling when she was on her feet. "I did. It bodes well, does it not?"

"If one is bound by superstition and coincidence, perhaps."

Radcliffe's eyebrows rose. "And are you?"

"I'm *wiaralde-wulf*, Master Radcliffe, a creature of superstition myself. I suppose I must then be bound by it." Her teasing faltered. "It's been a long time since I've had anyone to walk beside, Randolf. Are you certain of this?"

"I am certain," he murmured, "that there is a world awaiting us that we cannot yet imagine. Let us not disappoint it, Markéta. Let us see what discoveries lie in store."

And what future her people might find, she did not say, if there were men even now willing to embrace the *wiaralde*. There would be time enough for those thoughts in the years ahead, and she had spent so long thinking as a human did. It would be good, for a little while, to embrace the wolf.

With a smile and a loll of her tongue, she leapt forward, not to abandon, not ever to abandon, but to scout ahead of her shield until he might learn to be a wolf himself.

LOCKED DOORS

STEPHANIE BURGIS

——◆——

"My dad can't come to parent-teacher conferences on Monday," Tyler says. He keeps his voice calm and steady as he meets his English teacher's eyes. "He has to work."

Tyler is a pro at this. He can tell exactly when doubt flickers in Mrs. Jankovic's eyes and when his open, friendly expression settles it for her. There are too many eighth-graders in her class for her to chase up worries about every one of them. Too many kids in this middle school, period.

That's why Tyler's dad chose it for him.

When Tyler gets home, he hears his dad moving around in the basement—probably getting it ready for next week. Tyler scoops out some ice cream for himself and settles down at the kitchen table to do his homework early. His friend Paul is coming over later, and Tyler's dad has promised to rent them a DVD. They're hoping for *Tomb Raider*, but he's told them not to hold their breath.

Footsteps sound on the basement stairs, behind the closed door. They pause for so long that Tyler turns around to check that the industrial-strength bolt hasn't accidentally locked itself into place. He's craning around to look, vanilla ice cream still sliding down his throat, when the door bangs open.

The first thing he notices is the smell, acrid and unmistakable.

"Sorry," his dad mumbles. He averts his eyes from Tyler's shocked face, stumbles into the kitchen. He's already losing coordination, his movements shambling.

Tyler finds his voice, but it comes out as a squeak. "It's not supposed to come for a week!"

"I guess it's starting early this month." His dad shrugs, paws at the freezer, sighs heavily. "Can you get the ice cream out for me?"

Tyler shoves his chair back, hurries to the fridge. All his senses prickle as he passes close to his father. There's no visible sign yet—not unless you know how to read his dad's expression—but all his other senses can tell that the Change has begun.

Enemy, they whisper. Goosebumps crisscross his skin. *Run away.*

Dad, he tells himself, and slips between his dad's big body and the fridge. He feels his dad's uneven breathing ruffle his hair as he opens the freezer. He doesn't let himself look back or edge away. He pulls out the carton of ice cream and scoops out three dollops into a blue bowl. Only then does he allow himself to turn around.

Yellow streaks have already appeared in his father's eyes. The smell of heavy musk is growing.

How long does he have left?

The phone rings. Tyler shoves the bowl at his dad and darts for it.

"Hey, Ty." It's Paul, his voice bright and cheerful. "What movie are we gonna watch? Did we score *Tomb Raider*?"

"Sorry," Tyler says. His voice wants to quaver, but he won't let it. You can never let anyone suspect, his mother told him. That was the first rule she taught him, and the last, before she left him here alone with It. "Tonight isn't so good after all. Maybe we can do it some other time?"

Tyler has a game he plays with himself, sometimes. Times like tonight, when the heavy bolt is locked into place, but he can still hear It lurching through the basement, searching for a way out. He looks through the DVD collection on the bookcase, hums to himself to drown out the noise, and plays the Game.

The Game is this: What if Tyler's mom called on the phone right now, and he could only give her three reasons to come back? Which three would they be?

Sometimes he decides on: *I clean my own bedroom now, I got all As and Bs last quarter,* and *I'm learning how to cook.*

Sometimes, when it's been long enough since the last time It came, when his dad's just bought Tyler a new video game, or they've spent a whole evening watching dumb movies and laughing together over them, he thinks he might tell her: *Things are easier now. It's safe for you to come home. I think he's getting better.*

Better. What a joke. Something crashes downstairs. Tyler hums louder, scanning the same shelf of DVDs over and over again, trying to find one that sounds interesting right now.

It's never arrived this early in the month before.

Tonight, if Tyler's mom called, he would lie to her. He would say: *You'd better come back, or else we'll forget you. I think Dad might have already. I almost never think about you.*

He would threaten her: *If you don't come back, I'm gonna take your picture off the wall in my room and throw it away.*

And as his third reason, he would tell the biggest lie of all: *Maybe we'll decide that we don't even want you back.*

But the phone sits silent and still all night long, and Tyler falls asleep on the couch with his knees scrunched up against his chest and his hands still pressed against his ears.

"Tyler," Mrs. Jankovic says the next morning. "No homework?"

"Sorry." Tyler shrugs and slouches past her, sluggish with lack of sleep. He drops down into the seat next to Paul. "Hey."

"Hey." Paul frowns at him. "What happened last night?"

"Stuff came up." Tyler shrugs again. The movement feels heavy and slow. "My dad wasn't feeling so good." The words taste sour in his mouth.

When he looks up, he sees Mrs. Jankovic watching him.

By the time Tyler's finished with the school day, he's in a filthy mood. He stomps back into the house and throws down his backpack. In the basement, a sudden silence falls. A moment later, shuffling footsteps approach the bottom of the stairs, trying to be silent. They mount the stairs softly.

"You idiot!" Tyler yells. "I can hear you, you know! The door's locked anyway. You can't get through!"

There's a sudden rush up the staircase. A heavy body lands against the door with a thud. The thick wood holds, secured by the bolt. Tyler stares at the door, his head throbbing. A hoarse grunt of frustration sounds. Long fingernails scratch at the other side of the door.

"I was supposed to go out with Paul this afternoon," Tyler shouts at the door. "Remember? You promised you'd drive us to the mall. How stupid do you think I look now, huh? He's not even talking to me anymore! He thinks I'm blowing him off! He's going with Steve instead. They didn't even ask if I wanted to come. Which I couldn't anyway, because I have to stay here and look after stupid, stinking you!"

He swings at the door with all his strength. His foot slips on the hardwood floor, pushing him off-balance.

His fist hits the edge of the bolt. It shifts.

There's a frozen moment. Then Tyler throws himself against the door, just as the heavy body on the other side hurls itself at the wood. The bolt shifts another centimeter.

"No!" Tyler shoves the bolt with all his strength and hears it click back into locked position. He collapses, sliding down the door onto the floor. Tips his head back against the wood, breathing hard.

He hears Its heavy breathing on the other side of the door. Tyler closes his eyes.

"Please, Dad," he whispers. "Please come back soon."

Tyler was eight years old when his mother left. He came home from school one day and saw a taxi sitting outside their house. The driver sat inside, reading a newspaper. Tyler found his mother in her bedroom, folding clothes. Two suitcases lay open across her bed. Her face was pale and cold; a purple bruise mottled her jaw.

Tyler stopped in the doorway. He wanted to come closer, but something in the air held him back. "Where are you going?" he asked.

"The bolt's still locked," she said. Her voice sounded funny, flat and dry. She talked too quickly; he could barely understand her. "Your dad's coming out of it, though. You can unlock the door in just a couple hours. He'll be fine to put you to bed tonight."

"What happened to your face?" Tyler was shivering now, his arms wrapped around his chest.

She snapped the first suitcase shut. "I've put thirty cans of soup under the sink. That'll last you almost a year. You know how to heat up soup."

"I don't remember."

"Yes, you do. I've seen you do it." She snapped the second suitcase shut. "I've signed all your school forms and put them on top of the fridge."

"Where are you going?"

She took a deep breath and walked over to him. When she put her hands on his shoulders, he felt them trembling in spasms, like waves shimmering through her body. He wrapped his hands around her long, cool fingers, anchoring them against him. Her polished nails pressed into his skin through his thin T-shirt.

She said, "Listen to me. Your dad can't help what happens to him, but if anyone finds out, they'll take him away. Do you understand? They'll want to run experiments on him in some lab. They'll torture him."

"No," Tyler whispered. Tears stung his eyes. "No."

"You don't want that to happen, do you? Good boy."

She leaned forward and kissed him quickly on the top of his head. Her perfume, Winter Rose, surrounded him. When she straightened, he saw tears slipping down her cheeks. She didn't bother to wipe them away.

"Take care of yourself," she whispered.

Tyler ran after the taxi for two whole blocks. But after the third block, he lost sight of it.

And he never had the chance to ask her the question that mattered most.

On the third morning, Tyler makes two portions of scrambled eggs. *It* prefers meat, but he doesn't have any. It wasn't supposed to come until Monday, so they haven't laid in supplies, and his dad didn't have the chance to withdraw any cash for grocery shopping.

Tyler sets his portion on the kitchen table and pauses outside the basement door, taking deep breaths to calm himself.

It's usually only here for two or three days. It might even be gone by now.

But It's never come this early before, either. How can he predict anything anymore?

He presses his ear against the door. Silence. He doesn't even hear any breathing. It must be asleep, curled up in some dank corner in the dark.

Maybe It's shifted back. Maybe . . .

He unbolts the door. Waits. Silence. He turns the knob, edges the door open just a fraction of an inch.

"Dad?" he calls into the darkness, softly. "Are you—?"

It was waiting at the top of the stairs, holding Its breath.

Scrambled eggs go flying. The plate shatters against the ground. It bears Tyler down onto the tiled kitchen floor, Its yellow eyes dilated. Drool trickles onto Tyler's face as he struggles, sobbing and gagging. The rancid smell of musk envelops him.

"Dad!" he screams. "Dad, Dad, Dad—!"

It grabs his right arm. The short sleeve of Tyler's T-shirt slides to his shoulder. It sinks its sharp, crooked teeth into the soft flesh of his inner arm. Tyler cries out in pain.

Brown flecks appear in the yellow eyes.

Tyler tries to hold himself rigid through the Change, but he's sobbing convulsively now, and he can't stop. The crooked teeth embedded in his skin recede. Blood trickles down Tyler's arm. Color floods back into his father's face.

His father throws himself backward, hitting the kitchen table. Lands, shaking and breathing hard. Puts one hand to his mouth and stares at the blood that comes off his lips, onto his fingers. He looks up, his face whitening.

"Tyler," he whispers. "Oh my God. I'm so sorry. Tyler—"

He starts forward, holding out his bloody hand.

"Don't touch me!" Tyler scrambles to his feet and runs upstairs. Blood dribbles down his arm, stains his T-shirt. He locks the door behind him and throws himself onto his bed.

Through the floorboards, he hears his father crying racking, choking sobs.

Tyler lies on the bed and stares at the ceiling.

Grown-ups aren't supposed to cry.

He doesn't look at his dad on his way out to school. His dad tries to say something, but Tyler drowns out the words by humming.

He sits alone in English class. Paul and Steve are hanging out together at the back of the classroom, snorting with laughter as they play with the gross toys they found at the back of Spencer Gifts in the mall.

Tyler's arm throbs underneath his clean, long-sleeved shirt.

At the end of class, Mrs. Jankovic holds Tyler back. She waits while the other kids file out of the room. When they're finally alone, she looks at him steadily across her desk.

"Tyler," she says. "Do you need help?"

Tyler blinks. She's looking at him calmly, her hands folded on the desk.

"I can help you," she says, "but I need to know what's wrong. It's okay for you to ask for help."

Tyler opens his mouth. He tries to speak, but he can't. He puts his left hand on the cuff of his right sleeve. All he has to do is pull it up, to show her.

"Tyler?" she says.

Tyler, his father said, his voice anguished, that morning. Blood still on his lips. *I'm so sorry. Tyler—*

Tyler looks into Mrs. Jankovic's hazel eyes. He can barely breathe. He sees again the blood on his father's mouth.

The blood. He thinks about the blood.

Tears burn behind his eyes as knowledge shifts inside him.

Maybe he does know, after all, why his mother didn't take him with her when she left.

He steps back, letting go of his sleeve. "No, thank you," his voice says, with eerie politeness. "Not now."

"Are you sure? We could—"

Tyler's head shakes itself stiffly, and his legs turn him around and walk him out of the room, down the long hallway, and out of the school building.

His father is still sitting at the kitchen table, clutching a cup of coffee with both hands. He doesn't seem surprised to see Tyler back home at ten o'clock in the morning on a school day. He raises his haggard face to look at Tyler, but he doesn't speak.

"It's getting worse," Tyler tells him.

"Yes," his dad says. Just: Yes.

Tyler takes a deep, painful breath. "Is it going to happen to me?"

His father passes a hand over his eyes, wiping away a vision, or a nightmare. "I don't . . . Dear God, Tyler. I don't know."

"But Mom thought it would."

"Thought it might," his father says, his voice strained. "Only that it might."

"Whatever." Tyler's chest tightens around the knowledge.

The phone call he's been waiting for is never going to come.

He starts to turn away, but his father's voice stops him.

"Tyler," he says. "I'm so sorry. It won't happen again that way, I promise. We'll figure out some safeguard. We'll make sure you're protected. We'll—"

"I know," Tyler says. "It's all right, Dad."

The words feel funny in his mouth. False and jagged. Hurtful. Necessary.

He's never lied to his father before.

Experiments, his mother's voice reminds him. *Labs . . .*

Antidotes, Tyler tells her. *Cures.*

The phone book is upstairs, underneath his bed.

WERELOVE

LAURA ANNE GILMAN

Katya sat on her porch, and watched the street. The neighborhood had been built in the 50s, when sprawl was something you did on the sofa, and everyone had two cars and a lawn. Her house was the third in the pretty little cul-de-sac, five houses set in landscaped lots, with backyards perfect for games of touch football or Frisbee or general roughhousing—safe places for wild-tempered kids with too much energy, or teenagers counting down the days of the month, or adults who just liked to laze about in hammocks, and watch the night sky, a glass of sangria in their hands and the remains of dinner on the patio table.

Katya had raised children herself. Two boys, who had gone off and done things in the world. Max was an immigration lawyer. Leon taught grade school math and coached the local track team. Neither of them had children of their own, at least not that they told her, and she never asked why. She had no interest in being grandmotherly.

So it had been a true surprise to her when, somewhere in her sixties, the neighborhood children started coming to her with their problems.

Not the human ones, no. Only the werewolves.

Katya had come to this neighborhood when her sons were grown, had lived in the small green-painted house in the cul-de-sac for ten years. She had drawn no attention to herself, nor sought out others. But they came to her, appearing on her porch and sitting quietly, waiting for her attention. She would come out with a pitcher of lemonade, sometimes, or a thermos of coffee. They would sit on the porch, in all weather, and she would listen. And, because they were teenagers, they almost always asked variations on the same thing.

Katya gave them the truth. "Sex is for release and offspring. There is no morality to it and no immorality. Those are rules for someone else's game."

Some of them looked relieved. Some protested, swallowing the veneer of their surroundings instead of listening to their own nature.

"Sleep with them and get it over with," she told the girls. "Don't expect anything more than the moment," she told the boys. Not unkindly, not cruelly, but with age's knowledge: sex meant more to the males. It was how they marked their place, laid their scent. They were basic: hunt, kill, eat, protect. Girls looked forward, long-view. It did not matter what the pairing: the gender traits bred true. Katya was an old woman, and knew enough about nurture to give Nature her due.

Contrary to modern folklore, weres did not run in packs, did not have territories, and did not keep to their own kind. It would, she thought often, have been simpler if they did: a way to remember who they were, not losing themselves in what they pretended. Of course, that would also mean a serious bit of inbreeding, which brought its own problems. Instead they lived with humans, lived as humans, sheathing claw and tooth in handshakes and smiles, squeezing their inner selves into the brief window the Moon demanded.

But they should never forget. The danger lay in forgetting.

Not everyone felt as she did. "You should not tell them these things." A parent cornered her once in the supermarket, their carts side by side in the produce department. "You confuse them, lead them into trouble." His face had been stern, his eyes worried. Katya only shrugged; she did not invite these children onto her porch, she did not ask them to confide in her. She did not tell them anything that was not true.

"Their blood runs hot, the change confuses them, they are learning how different they are when they need to be the same, to fit in. If we are not truthful, how can we teach them?"

"Teenaged politics," the parent said with a shrug, not callous but with the casual disdain that time endows. "The change comes to us all. We all survive."

He believed that, but she knew that some did not. And there were not so many of them in this world that she could stand aside, and simply watch.

Katya had not asked for this, the sharing of confidences, the laying out of fears, but she would not shy away, either. Most of their questions were foolish ones, puppy whingings or worries. They asked, and sometimes they listened, but more often they drank her iced tea or her coffee and made their noises, and went away, not learning a thing.

She made no promises, and told them no lies. The rest was up to them.

Most of those children who came to her moved away as they became adults, looking for something new, something more. Empty-den parents moved away, and new families came, because the suburbs were kind to their folk. Katya stayed, because she had nowhere else to be, and the new children followed what had become tradition, to ask the old bitch for advice.

Once alpha, always alpha. She had not announced herself, but you could not change what you were.

The girl was no teenager, no raw and anxious child climbing her stairs. She was long and lean, the way weres were, her shoulders erect and her eyes bright and clear. Brown curls clung to the side of her head in a fashion that had been daring when Katya was her age, accentuating her nose and eyes, and her skin was dusky-smooth and unwrinkled. Her car was parked by the curb, a sedate little coupe, dark blue and brand-new.

Katya did not make her wait in the hot sun, but brought out the pitcher of iced tea, placed it on the table between their chairs, and waited.

"They say . . . you know what to do. You understand the old ways."

"They say many things." Katya poured two glasses, left one on the table and drank from hers.

"It's over. My marriage."

"I'm sorry." Katya was. She might never have chosen that path herself, but love was never to be disparaged. But she said no more. This girl was none of hers, had not grown up here; Katya had no obligation to her.

Save the girl had climbed her stairs, had lifted her throat in submission, and asked for help.

"Is he.."

"One of us? Yes."

Katya knew, then, where this would end, and felt a deep, bone-deep sorrow.

"I don't want it to be over but. . . . " The girl—woman, really—waved her hands helplessly, unable to find the words. "But it is. And I don't know how to do this."

"File for divorce?"

That got a sad, bitter laugh. "I know that. I have a lawyer. It . . . the moment I realized it wasn't going to work, I moved out, got a lawyer, told him to stay away. He didn't understand. He thought we could work it out, that I'd change back, come back to him."

She shuddered, although Katya couldn't tell if it was at the thought of going back to her ex, or the fact that she couldn't. The girl's hand shook as she lifted the iced tea to her lips. "I mean, this, the messy stuff. The inside stuff."

Katya did not nod, or make an encouraging noise. She sat in her chair, back straight, shoulders relaxed. The cane she never used lay at her feet, the wooden grain satin-smooth. Katya was old now, but she had not always been so, and she knew what would follow. The girl was seeking a reminder of what she already knew, had forgotten in her years out in the world, where people wore civilization as though it was more than a veneer.

"I want to howl my pain. I want to bite his hand when he dares touch me. I want to cuddle and tell him it's okay, I forgive him, I understand, and hear the same words from him, so we can let it go, move on. I need to move on, and I can't, because he can't and I don't know what to do."

The words fell from her mouth like well-chewed meat, soft and broken-down. Katya felt exhaustion in her bones, exhaustion and sadness growing as the words filled the air between them. Nobody had ever told this child anything, and Katya felt a growl grow in her throat. Who were her people, to have been so careless?

You cannot choose whom you love. Not human, not were. But it was safer to be human. Kinder to be human, and not so fierce.

The girl went on, her voice crackling. "I feel like I'm chasing my tail, only I have three tails and only one jaw. And I try to talk to my friends and they look at me like I'm insane, and give advice that doesn't fit, and all I can do is change and run, and it feels all right for a moment and then I'm back and everything's the same."

She looked at the older woman, despair in her eyes. "Does that make any sense?"

"None at all," Katya said, in the voice that said *Yes, it makes perfect sense, I understand.*

She had not always been an old woman. Once her skin had been dusky-smooth as well. Her eyes had been bright, her heart fierce, and she had loved a man who could not match her, and would not let her go.

You could not choose where your heart went. You could only suffer the consequences.

The girl finished speaking, draining the dregs of her tea and placing it with exaggerated care, as though she were drunk, on the small round table beside her, the glass top perfectly polished, the cast iron legs weather-washed and nicked. Like her, like this girl: a survivor.

"I don't know what to do."

Katya did not give advice. She did not make promises, and she did not lie.

The girl had a faraway look in her eyes, the kind that looked at something distant, invisible. "I don't want to hurt him. But I will. I'll gut him, if I have to, to get away. He doesn't get that."

Katya closed her eyes, the powder-dry skin softening in repose.

They never do. Not until it is too late.

They both heard the howl rising, and both turned to look; a motorcycle, turning down the street, cutting the engine in front of Katya's house, the rumbling echo fading into the sky above the houses. He swung his leg over the beast, removing his helmet and placing it on the handlebar. A handsome creature, as strong and lithe as the girl. Each motion was precise, steady, the moves of a surgeon, or a painter.

"Oh, fuck."

The girl's words were soft, barely whispered, but Katya felt her jaw drop open slightly in sympathetic laughter, a wolf's humor trumping any human shell.

The boy strode up the walk, standing at the base of the stairs, glaring up at them. He was angry, so angry; Katya could feel the heat of his rage simmering above his skin. The girl was angry too, but she controlled it, holding it within. Females have more understanding, they know how to embrace their emotions, offering them up to the Moon, racing them down until they're manageable, shifting them into calories burned, not words said.

An alpha female thinks long-term, survival of the species. Males know only kill, or die.

"Get down here!" His voice was hoarse, his gaze not angry but despairing. He does not understand; he will not leave without her, not willingly.

He is were; he should know better. But they have no choice, none of them.

"Humans are fortunate," Katya says, speaking as much to her own memories as the flesh and blood girl in front of her. Too late, the lesson comes. "They can let go of love. It fades, dims, becomes a pleasant memory. They can choose to part as friends.

They didn't, all too often, but they had that choice.

"We are made from stronger passions, and domestication has neither stripped nor blunted us. We have only two options: turn love to hate, or love until we die."

The words were no comfort. A were who loved was a mighty thing. A were who hated . . .

Freedom, like love, has a price.

"I can't do this."

But the girl stands, her body slim but muscled, her head high and her eyes clear, staring down her fate, and Katya knows that she can.

IN SHEEP'S CLOTHING

MOLLY TANZER

My daughter turned into a lamb and I ate her.

It wasn't my fault—I mean, it was, it is. It is still my fault, but I didn't know what I was doing. *I knew not what I did*, that was an expression, or something similar, at least. I knit the sweater, but how could I know about the other? Times were lean, dire even. We were so *cold*. I should have put two and two together, as the expression used to be. Simple math. In high school I struggled through algebra and geometry, but I dropped trig. I could do the easy stuff, I used that later, keeping the books at the yarn store, but I liked more to work with my hands, cooking, and crafts. Knitting, of course.

Now the school is closed. I mean, no, it is open, but open to the sky; the roof caved in because we stripped the shingles, took everything salvageable, so though it is closed it is still open, empty, like a skin. Like her skin. What was left of it.

Things get worse before they get better, that was another expression, and it was like that for me, for a time, even after the corn-sickness. *Darkest before the dawn.* That was another way they used to say the same thing. Things get worse before they better, it's darkest before the dawn, but now things are just worse, and I don't like daylight very much any more.

The funny thing is, I thought I was safe. I didn't eat anything with corn syrup in it, never-ever, and I never let Elsbet eat it either. I've always been into natural living, now more than ever, I suppose, green, eco-friendly. I'd talk to others about it on internet forums, I once drove down to Boulder to go to a workshop on minimizing my carbon footprint. The news was full of global warming and consumerism, the sheep flu that mutated and mutated, sheep, then people, then cats, ferrets even, spreading, people were dying, it was bad. The government rushed to find a vaccine but I didn't take it. Jimmy did, he said it was all right, said they'd tested it enough. He wanted Elsbet to get it but I wouldn't allow it; there's mercury in vaccines, I read an article about it in *Mother Jones*.

Why they never talked about the dangers of corn we'll never know, but that's what did it. I figured it out for myself, after everything. Not the stuff on the cob, though that was dangerous enough, but the syrup and the derivatives and the isolates and whatever. I always said that stuff would be the death of us, but I was speaking metaphorically. I thought. Just an expression. I was talking about heart disease and cancer, not actually the corn itself, but what it did to your body, spiked your blood sugar, made you fat, rotted your teeth, made kids too hyper to learn. But in the end, it was the actual corn, not just the long-term stuff, and it got all of us, in its own way.

I thought I was doing the right things, and I guess it turns out I was. Maybe. If I think about it, remember, or if I look at old cans when I find them, cat food, even, it all had corn. Animal feed. Envelopes, the sweet taste when you licked them. I knew something would happen, I mean, if you mess with the genetics of something enough, how can you tell what it will do in the real world? It isn't natural. I knew it. I figured it out. For myself.

We had been GMO-free in our house for years, but it didn't save Jimmy. He loved soda, that's how it got him. He had gone to the doctor's office, I remember that, Jimmy got vaccinated that day. It was the first day they had it where we were, *in the boonies* or *the sticks*, as they used to say, before everywhere was the boonies. I stayed at the yarn store while he waited in line for hours to get it, and then he went to the vet to get the vaccine for Smokey, she was his cat from before we were married, and he insisted. I had told him to get gas, and he got a soda while he was there. I saw the cup in the trash. That night we watched the news and heard there had been a rash of hospitalizations, people sick, they didn't know what was wrong. We turned it off. They said to call poison control if you had unexplained abdominal cramping, vomiting, bloody diarrhea.

I fed Smokey. She had a routine, she'd meow and meow when I opened the can, purring around my legs. When she was done she'd lick her whiskers and roll on her back, but that night, she stopped halfway through her dinner, stood up on her hind legs, howled at us, started walking around. Elsbet started crying. We called the all-night vet but they weren't there, just the voice mail. Finally we got Smokey into her carrier, but when we drove by, the place was dark. A lot of places were dark. Houses. Like I said, it all happened so fast, it felt like overnight, now that I think back on it. So we shut Smokey in the basement with some water and a blanket, we didn't know what else to do. Elsbet was so sad, she was three and she loved the kitty so much. We put in a video because nothing any of us liked was on. Most of the stations were just test patterns anyways.

It was a long time before I checked on Smokey. I don't know when she died. I forgot about her, because of Jimmy. At first it seemed like salmonella, he just doubled over while brushing his teeth, shat himself on the bathroom floor. Then he was gone—911 didn't answer when I called. Neither did the police. I was scared, really scared, I slept in Elsbet's bed with her, tried not to cry so she wouldn't be scared too. I wondered if we would die, but we woke up the next morning just fine. I thought we were lucky.

I don't know how many people died. A lot. Maybe most. That shit was in everything. And I don't know either if it built up in the bloodstream or was just a bad batch that poisoned everyone. Probably the latter, Jimmy didn't eat so much of it, and it was just the one Dr Pepper that got him. But Elsbet and I, we were fine. Our town was small, outside of Boulder, and frankly, we weren't doing too well before it happened. Knotty or Knice, my yarn shop, Jimmy and I had sunk a lot of money into it, but before everything, with the way things were, it was more expensive to knit your own scarves and hats and sweaters than to just buy them, even the nice brands. Yarn was pricy. And it still was after the corn-sickness got everyone, you just couldn't buy it with money. Credit cards, and even cash got abandoned pretty quick. You couldn't eat it, you can't really wear it. Most of the bills got stuffed into blankets or hats or shoes as padding, the coins melted down for more useful purposes. Barter economy. It just sort of fell into place. At least it did where I was. I don't know about anywhere else.

There was a lot of theft, in the wake of it all, but at that point we had no choice, it was getting cold already. Another expression: *desperate times lead to desperate measures*, more true than the others. Sometimes two and two don't get put together, and sometimes, as I said, the dawn doesn't break after the darkest part of the night. But desperate times *always* lead to desperate measures.

People stocked up on food and clothing for free, looted, stole. Not as violent as you'd think, and no one stole my yarn. We didn't even have a window broken at Knotty or Knice. Target, Wal-Mart, after the first few weeks no one was taking the TVs and jewelry. When we realized how widespread it was it became about clothing, warm clothing, shoes, and old-fashioned household appliances, the kind you could use without electricity. And food. Nothing with corn syrup. You couldn't be too careful. At least, in my opinion. I saw fools taking soda and Oreos and ketchup, but not me. After we'd cleaned out our local supermarket of meat and produce, and our health food store for cookies and shit that didn't have the killer corn, we went on a raid to Boulder, loaded up in our Subarus and used precious gasoline to drive down and see what we could get. I left Elsbet with a couple of the other kids who survived, some were older and could be trusted.

There was more to eat down there than you'd think, not a lot of people in Boulder were left, even with their ordinances and bike paths and eco-friendly coffee shops and whatever. Most of them drank Coke, ate unsafe candy, got a shot of corn-laced hazelnut syrup in their lattes, and that was all it took. When we walked into Whole Foods there was a gang of ragged-looking folks raiding the meat case, most of it had gone off but some was still all right, we talked with them for a while but when they found out we were out-of-towners it got a little ugly. After it all, my friend Samantha suggested we see if any seeds were left at Home Depot and there were, we took cucumbers and squashes and broccoli and carrots and everything. I don't have a green thumb, I traded most of those for food.

I thought we were set, and we were, at first. Our house was old, we had a wood-burning stove, and I kept Elsbet and I in meals by teaching people to knit. I'd made another stop before I'd driven back up home, Michael's, Jo-Ann Fabrics, took all the yarn they had in stock. There was a lot, people weren't thinking ahead. Most of it was acrylic, I'd never knit with it before, but it was more about keeping warm than anything else.

So finally people were coming to Knotty or Knice, people who never cared to support me before the corn-sickness. The snows started early that year and a few months in, when their stuff wore out or they just needed more scarves and socks to bundle up in at night, they came. They were quick studies. When the needles sold out they made them out of dowels pilfered from the hardware store, sanded down. Elsbet and I were rich, so much food, we put on weight while our neighbors were getting thinner, but with all the factories shut down and no phones I couldn't order more yarn when it ran out. I had to get it from somewhere else. But I'm getting ahead of myself. *Begin at the beginning, and when you get to the end, stop.* Another expression. Or was it a quote? I can't remember now. *Also, if you teach a man to fish.* When my yarn ran out, times got lean again, people were frogging their sweaters and re-knitting them. I'd taught them to fish, but I ended up hungry for it.

Jimmy used to make fun of me for not eating meat. He used to laugh and say that humans hadn't crawled to the top of the food chain just to eat lettuce. But there's a problem with being at the top of the food chain. I had read an article on pesticides killing birds of prey, they were dying because of farmers setting out poisoned grain to kill rats. The rats would eat the poison and die, and then vultures and eagles and owls would eat the poisoned rats, and they'd get poisoned. Same with sharks and mercury-tainted fish. They were at the top of their food chain, I mean, except for humans, but it wasn't doing them any favors. Not in the end.

In the end, it didn't do us any favors, either.

I had started eating meat. I had to. Elsbet too, though she hadn't ever had it before, Jimmy had been all right with us raising her vegetarian, but towards the middle of that first winter, when we ran out of canned beans and damn near everything else, I traded some knitted stuff for some goat meat and we cooked it and ate it. It had been so long I couldn't recall if it tasted strange or not, but we were starving, it wouldn't have mattered. Elsbet hated it, eating animals. I did too. At first. But what can you do? *Desperate times.* Meat was scarce, though, a lot of animals had died, too, corn in their feed. The ones that survived must've been immune, a slight genetic abnormality or something. Recessive traits, I remember doing Mendel's Squares in biology class. Something like that. But thinking about it I also remember reading something about evolutionary defenses, how onions make you cry because they're trying not to get eaten, like poison ivy—*one-two-three, don't touch me,* another expression—or like skunks. Maybe skunks would be a better analogy here because they're animals. But I'm not sure. It's all I've got, my only theory, I figured it out for myself.

The way it started was this: I had seen Fred Jones in town, he traded me some meat for a scarf and a hat, he didn't have time to learn to knit, he was a farmer, his wife had died. Anyways Fred and I got to talking and I told him I was running low on yarn, and he asked if I could spin, he had a bunch of sheepskins and if I wanted to shear off the wool and spin it into yarn I'd be welcome to, as long as he got something out of it. So I went out there.

It should've tipped me off when I saw the flock, standing on their hind legs, huddled together, bleating at one another like it was the most natural thing in the world. But things had gotten so crazy at that point it didn't even occur to me that I should be concerned. I'd seen odder things, everybody had, but the sheep, there they were, standing upright. I wish now I'd asked Fred if that was normal for them. I can't ask anymore, I can't speak, only to myself, so it's too late. I'd ask the sheep, but they shy away from my scent, and rightfully so.

I took the fleece and began to learn to spin it. I had a book in the shop and a few distaffs, spindles, and spinning wheels Jimmy and I had ordered when we thought our shop would be a success. I mean, it was. Briefly. Just not in the way we'd meant. Actually, it wasn't. Isn't. Not anymore. It doesn't matter. I got the hang of it quickly—it wasn't too hard, really, but everything takes time. I finally had enough to knit some long underwear for Fred and a sweater for Elsbet, and I'd just started on the knitting when the wolf attacked us.

I had been cooking up some of the mutton Fred had given me. The wolf must've smelled it, he opened the door with his paw and just walked right in through the kitchen door on his hind legs like something out of a fairy tale, mouth open, tongue lolling, saliva dripping down his chest, I expected there to be a bonnet on his head and glasses perched his muzzle, *the better to see you with, my dear.* Elsbet screamed and ran, but I shot it with Jimmy's shotgun, I kept it close by, everyone did, it was just a good idea. I wasn't a good shot. I clipped its shoulder but it was enough to take it down and then I stabbed it through the heart with my kitchen knife. It was ugly, *eat or be eaten*, or maybe *nature, red in tooth and claw*. I threw the carcass outside and calmed Elsbet down, washed off with some hot water and we ate dinner. Then I put her to bed.

I was knitting her sweater when I had the idea—it was a shaggy wolf, and I could spin fur into yarn as easily as wool. I cut it off with the shears, and when I got bored of knitting, I'd spin it. It was coarse, terrible, oily stuff, more like rope than yarn when it was spun, and I decided to make a belt out of it, mine had snapped a month before and I'd been holding up my pants with rope.

When I put the sweater on Elsbet she complained, said it was itchy. Her cries sounded like bleating. She'd always worn shirts under her sweaters before, but they'd all gotten too tight and she had to wear it against her skin. Over the next few days I noticed her face and her hands and feet got darker, her ears longer. Then one night when I went to put her to bed I couldn't get the sweater off, it had grown into her skin. *Elsbet?* I asked. *Maaaa, Maaaa,* she replied. She couldn't say anything else.

She wouldn't eat mutton after that night, or goat. It made her sick. But she could graze on leaves and dry grass when I raked away the deep, deep snows, cracked the ice. It was so cold.

As for me, I was ravenous for meat.

I'd sold most of the yarn I'd spun from Fred's sheep, and I hadn't much to trade other than that. Times were lean. I was hungry constantly, I even ate the wolf I'd shot, it had frozen solid in the snow and been preserved well enough. When I couldn't stand the hunger any longer I took the axe and chopped it into pieces and fried them up, gnawing them down to the bones after I put Elsbet to bed. The more lamblike she became the more it distressed her to watch me eat, and I admit now, it was probably a pretty grisly sight.

Gradual changes never seem like change at all, which is why I think I didn't notice what was wrong with me until I went next door to my neighbor's house to beg for some hay for Elsbet—they kept horses, and she'd clipped the lawn bare, front and back, and we were friendly, I'd traded them some of the yarn I got from Fred. I knocked, I heard my neighbor come to the door, but he fumbled with the knob for a while before getting it open. When he saw me he screamed and slammed the door in my face. I knocked again but I heard him through the door, *Go awaaaay, go awaaaaaay.* I growled at him, I just wanted some hay. When he didn't respond I stole it, *desperate times*, wondering the whole time if they'd gone crazy, shut up in their house like everyone else, trying to keep the cold at bay. But when I came back to my house I caught sight of myself in the hall mirror and I understood.

The pointy ears and muzzle had grown so slowly I don't think I ever would've noticed them if my neighbor hadn't said something. When I looked down at my hands I realized it hadn't been the cold in my joints that had prevented me from knitting recently, they were little more than paws. I paced back and forth and then unknotted my wolf-fur belt and peed in my favorite corner, thinking hard. Where was Elsbet? I couldn't remember the last time I'd seen her, but I finally remembered tethering her in the yard to graze—had it been this morning, or the morning before, or the morning before that? Her wooly coat made it less important for her to be inside, she seemed to like the cold. I spent most of my hours in front of the wood-burning stove, curled up, always hungry, always sleepy. But that wasn't right, she was my daughter. She should be inside.

Either I don't remember so well what happened next or I've tried to forget for so long that I've convinced myself I don't remember. I know I opened the door to our back yard and saw her, standing in the twilight, shivering, nibbling something. I had hay for her, I remembered then, and I ran and got it from where I'd dumped it in the foyer, and brought it outside. She must have smelled the hay first, *Maaa, Maaa,* she bleated, but then she smelled me and her eyes went wide. I certainly smelled her, the dung smell farm animals have, and also her little-girl smell, plastic dolls, juice. Delicious. I dropped the hay and loped towards her, I was so very hungry, ravenous, I was salivating and she couldn't run away, easy prey, an old dog's collar around her neck, tethered to the tree in our backyard. I had nursed her under that tree when she was an infant, later, tea parties with the My Little Ponies that had been mine when I was a girl. *Maaa, Maaa,* she said, begging me, but then I was curled up by the wood-burning stove again, full, warm, the rich taste of blood and stringy muscle caught in my teeth.

Elsbet. Where was she? I ran upstairs, maybe it was a dream, I remember hoping I had just eaten some more of that old frozen wolf, but she wasn't in her room. At some point my pants tore off of me as I ran, frantic, the tail popped them and they hung in shreds, my crooked legs didn't fit anymore, but the belt stayed on, part of me, that gray belt, gray like my own fur. She wasn't upstairs. I paced her room, back and forth, growling, and hopped up on her bed to look out the window. There she was, what was left of her. The collar was still around her neck, her little mauled head surrounded by stripped bones and pieces of meat, lots of white wooly fluff.

I'd like to say I felt remorse, that I feel it now, but I'm not sure anymore what I make up—what are stories I tell myself as I sleep by the wood-burning stove after I've eaten—and what is real. I'd like to say I howled, mourning for a daughter lost, but I know what I felt was *fullness,* of being sated, not hungry, warm. It is how I feel as I eat Fred's sheep, one by one, sneaking into the barn at night. It's safe against most predators but not against me. I hear them whispering stupid sheepish things to one another as they stand together, huddling for warmth. I have culled the flock, they are fewer now. Some of the females are pregnant, I can smell it on them, and that means lamb in the spring. I like to think I will keep enough alive that I can leave them be through the summer, to breed, to last through the next winter, eating the deer that are too skittish and skinny to bother with now. But if I cannot, if I get too hungry, I saw Fred looking at me through the window, in the long underwear I knitted for him and nothing else. I smiled at him, toothy, and he ducked away from my gaze, but not before I saw him fumble to shut the white curtain, his hands useless, mere cloven hooves.

ROYAL BLOODLINES

(A LUCIFER JONES STORY)

MIKE RESNICK

Back in 1936 I found myself in Hungary, which ain't never gonna provide the Riviera with any serious competition for tourists. Each town I passed through was duller than the last, until I got to Budapest, which was considerably less exciting than Boise, Idaho, on a Tuesday afternoon.

I passed by an old rundown arena that did double duty, hosting hockey games on weeknights and dog shows on Saturdays, then walked by the only nightclub in town, which was featuring one of the more popular lady tuba soloists in the country, and finally I came to the Magyar Hotel and rented me a room. After I'd left my gear there I set out to scout out the city and see if there were enough depraved sinners to warrant building my tabernacle there and setting up shop in the salvation business. My unerring instincts led me right to a batch of them, who were holed up in the men's room of the bus station, playing a game with which I was not entirely unfamiliar, as it consisted of fifty two pasteboards with numbers or pictures on 'em and enough money in the pot to make it interesting.

"Mind if I join you gents?" I asked, walking over to them.

"Either you put your shirt on backward, or else you're a preacher," said one of 'em in an English accent.

"What's that got to do with anything?" I asked.

"We'd feel guilty taking your money," he said.

"You ain't got a thing to worry about," I said, sitting down with them.

"Well," he said with a shrug, "you've been warned."

"I appreciate that, neighbor," I said, "and just to show my good will, I absolve everyone here of any sins they committed between nine o'clock this morning and noon. Now, who deals?"

The game got going hot and heavy, and I had just about broken even, when the British feller dealt a hand of draw, and I picked up my cards and fanned 'em out and suddenly I was looking at four aces and a king, and two of my opponents had great big grins on their faces, the kind of grin you get when you pick up a flush or a full house, and one of 'em opened, and the other raised, and I raised again, and it was like I'd insulted their manhood, because they raised right back, and pretty soon everyone else had dropped out and the three of us were tossing money into the pot like there wasn't no tomorrow, and just about the time we all ran out of money and energy and were about to show our cards, a little Hungarian kid ran into the room and shouted something in a foreign language—probably Hungarian, now as I come to think on it—and suddenly everyone grabbed their money and got up and started making for the exit.

"Hey, what's going on?" I demanded. "Where do you guys think you're going?"

"Away!" said the British feller.

"But we're in the middle of a hand," I protested.

"Lupo is coming!" said the Brit. "The game's over!"

"Who the hell is Lupo?" I demanded.

"He's more of a what. You'll leave too, if you know what's good for you!"

And suddenly, just like that, I was all alone in the men's room of a Hungarian bus station, holding four totally useless aces and a king, and thinking that maybe Hungarians were more in need of a shrink than a preacher. Then the door opened, and in walked this thin guy with grayish skin and hair everywhere—on his head, his lip, his chin, even the backs of his hands.

"Howdy, Brother," I said, and he nodded at me. "You better not plan on lingering too long," I added. "Someone or something called Lupo is on its way here."

He turned to face me and stared at me intently.

"I am Lupo," he said.

"You are?"

"Count Basil de Chenza Lupo," he continued. "Who are you?"

"The Right Reverend Doctor Lucifer Jones at your service," I said.

"Do you see any reason why you should run at the sight of me?" he continued.

"Except for the fact that you got a predatory look about you and probably ain't on speaking terms with your barber, nary a one," I answered.

"They are fools," he said. "Fools and peasants, nothing more."

"Maybe so," I said, "but you could have timed your call of Nature just a mite better, considering I was holding four bullets and the pot had reached a couple of thousand dollars."

"Bullet?" he said, kind of growling deep in his throat. "What kind?"

"Well, when you got four of 'em, there ain't a lot left except clubs, diamonds, hearts, and spades," I said.

"But not silver?" he said.

"Not as I recollect."

"Good," he said, suddenly looking much relieved. "I am sorry I have caused you such distress, Doctor Jones."

"Well, I suppose when push comes to shove, it ain't really your fault, Brother Basil," I said.

"Nevertheless, I insist that you allow me to take you to dinner to make amends."

"That's right cordial of you," I said. "I'm a stranger in town. You got any particular place in mind?"

"We will dine at The Strangled Elk," he said. "It belongs to some Gypsy friends of mine."

"Whatever suits you," I said agreeably.

We walked out of the station, hit the main drag, and turned left.

"By the way, Brother Basil," I said, "why were all them men running away from a nice, friendly gent like you?"

He shrugged. "They are superstitious peasants," he said. "Let us speak no more of them."

"Suits me," I said. "People what entice a man of the cloth into a sinful game like poker and then run off when he's got the high hand ain't headed to no good end anyway."

I noticed as we walked down the street that everyone was giving us a pretty wide berth, and finally we turned down a little alleyway where all the men were dark and swarthy and wearing shirts that could have been took in some at the arms, and the women were sultry and good looking and wearing colorful skirts and blouses, and Basil told me we were now among his Gypsy friends and no one would bother us, not that anyone had been bothering us before, and after a little while we came to a sign that said we'd reached The Strangled Elk, and we went inside.

It wasn't the cleanest place I'd ever seen, but I'd been a couple of weeks between baths myself, so I can't say that I minded it all that much. There was nobody there except one skinny old waiter, and Basil called him over and said something in Gypsy, and the waiter went away and came back a minute later with a bottle of wine and two glasses.

Well, we filled the glasses and chatted about this and that, and then we drank some more and talked some more, and finally the waiter brought out a couple of steaks.

"Brother Basil," I said, looking down at my plate, "I like my meat as rare as the next man, but I don't believe this has been cooked at all."

"I am sorry, my friend," he said. "That is the way I always eat it, and the cook simply assumed you shared my taste." He signaled to the waiter, said something else in Gypsy, and the waiter took my plate away. "It will be back in a few moments, properly cooked."

"You always eat your steak like that?" I asked, pointing to the slab of raw meat in front of him.

"It is the only way," he replied, picking it up with his hands and biting off a goodly chunk of it. He growled and snarled as he chewed it.

"You got a bit of a throat condition?" I asked.

"Something like that," he said. "I apologize if my table manners offend you."

"I've et with worse," I said. In fact, if push came to shove, I couldn't remember having dined with a lot that were much more refined.

Well, my steak came back just then, and after covering it with a pint of ketchup just to bring out the subtle nuances of its flavor, I dug in, and just so Basil wouldn't feel too conspicuous I growled and snarled too, and we spent the next five or ten minutes enjoying the noisiest meal of my experience, after which we polished off a couple of more bottles of wine.

"I have truly enjoyed this evening, my friend," said Basil after we were all done. "So few people will even speak to me, let alone join me in a repast . . . "

"I can't imagine why," I said. "You'd have to search far and wide to find a more hospitable feller."

"Nonetheless," he said, "it is time for you to leave."

"It's only about nine o'clock," I said. "I think I'll just sit here and digest the repast and maybe smoke a cigar or two, that is if you got any to spare, and then I'll mosey on back to my humble dwelling."

"You really must leave now," he said.

"You got a ladyfriend due any minute, right?" I said with a sly smile. "Well, never let it be said that Lucifer Jones ain't the soul of understanding and discretion. Why, I recall one time back in Cairo, or maybe it was Merrakech, that I . . . "

"Hurry!" he shouted. "The moon is rising!"

"Now how could you possibly know that, sitting here in the back of the room?" I asked.

"I know!" he said.

I got up and walked over to the doorway and stuck my head out. "Well, son of a gun, the moon *is* out," I said. "I don't see your ladyfriend nowhere, though."

I turned back to face him, but Count Basil de Chenza Lupo wasn't nowhere to be seen. In fact, there wasn't no one in the room except the old waiter and an enormous wolf that must have wandered in through the kitchen door.

"Well, I've heard of restaurants that got roaches," I said, "and restaurants that got rats, but I do believe this is the first eatery I ever been to that was infested by wolves." I turned to the waiter. "What happened to Basil?" I asked. "Did he go off to the necessary?"

The waiter shook his head.

"Then where is he?"

The waiter pointed to the wolf.

"I don't believe I'm making myself clear," I said. "I ain't interested in no four legged critters with fleas and bad breath. Where is Basil?"

The waiter pointed to the wolf again.

"I don't know why it's so hard to understand," I said. "That there is a wolf. I want to know what became of Basil."

The waiter nodded his head. "Basil," he said, pointing at the wolf again.

"You mean the wolf is named Basil, too?" I asked.

The waiter just threw his hands up and walked out of the room, leaving me alone with the wolf.

Well, I looked at the wolf for a good long while, and he looked right back at me, and as time went by it occurred to me that I hadn't seen no other wolves in all my wanderings through Europe, and that some zoo ought to be happy to pay a healthy price for such a prime specimen, so I walked over kind of gingerly and let him smell the back of my hand, and when I was sure he wasn't viewing me as a potential appetizer, I slipped my belt out of my pants and slid it around his neck and turned it into a leash.

"You come along with me, Basil," I said. "Tonight you can sleep in my hotel room, and tomorrow we'll set about finding a properly generous and appreciative home for you."

I started off toward the door, but he dug his feet in and practically pulled my arm out of the socket.

"Now Basil," I said, jerking on the leash with both hands, "I ain't one to abuse dumb animals, but one way or the other you're coming with me."

He pulled back and whimpered, and then he snarled, and then he just went limp and laid down, but I was determined to get him out of there, and I started dragging him along the floor, and finally he whined one last time and got to his feet and started trotting alongside of me, and fifteen minutes later we reached the door of the Magyar Hotel. I had a feeling they had some policy or other regarding wild critters in the rooms, so I waited until the desk clerk went off to flirt with one of the maids, and then I opened the door and me and Basil made a beeline for the staircase, and reached the second floor without being seen. I walked on down the corridor until I came to my room, unlocked it, and shagged Basil into it. He looked more nervous and bewildered than vicious, and finally he hopped onto the couch and curled up and went to sleep, and I lay back down on the bed and drifted off while I was trying to figure out how many thousands of dollars a real live wolf was worth.

Except that when I woke up, all set to take Basil the wolf off to the zoo, he wasn't there. Instead, laying naked on the couch and snoring up a storm, was Basil the Count, with my belt still around his neck.

I shook him awake, and he sat up, startled, and began blinking his eyes.

"You got something highly personal and just a tad improbable that you want to confide in me, Brother Basil?" I said.

"I tried to warn you," he said plaintively. "I told you to leave, to hurry."

"You considered seeing a doctor about this here condition?" I said. "Or maybe a veterinarian?"

He shook his head miserably. "It is a curse," he said at last. "There is nothing that can be done about it. I am a werewolf, and that's all there is to it."

"And that's why all them guys were running away from you at the station and looking askance at you on the street?"

He nodded. "I am an outcast, a pariah among my own people."

"Yeah, well, I can see how it probably hampers your social life," I opined.

"It has hampered all aspects of my life," he said unhappily. "I have seen so many charlatans and *poseurs* trying to get the curse removed that I am practically destitute. I cannot form a lasting relationship. I dare not be among strangers when the moon comes out. And some of the behavior carries over: you saw me at the dinner table last night."

"Well, it may have been a bit out of the ordinary," I said soothingly, "but as long as you don't lift your leg on the furniture, I don't suppose anyone's gonna object too strenuously. Especially since if they object at the wrong time of day, there's a strong possibility they could wind up getting et."

"You are the most understanding and compassionate man I've ever met, Doctor Jones," he said, "but I am at the end of my tether. I don't know what to do. I have no one to turn to. Only these accursed Gypsies will tolerate my presence, because it amuses them. I think very soon I shall end it all."

At which point the Lord smote me with another of His heavenly revelations.

"Seems to me you're being a mite hasty, Brother Basil," I said.

"What is the use of going on?" he said plaintively. "I will never be able to remove the curse."

"First of all, you got to stop thinking of your condition as a curse," I continued. "What if I was to show you how the werewolf business could be a blessing in disguise?"

"Impossible!"

"You willing to bet five thousand dollars on that?" I asked.

"What are you talking about?" he demanded.

"You see," I said, "the problem is that you ain't never really examined yourself when the moon is out. You ain't simply a werewolf, but you happen to be a damned fine-looking werewolf."

"So what?"

"On my way into town, I passed an arena that holds a dog show every Saturday. The sign said that the prize money was ten thousand dollars."

"You just said five," he pointed out.

"Well, me and the Lord have got to have a little something to live on, too," I said.

"What makes you think a wolf can win a dog show?" he said dubiously.

"Why don't you just concentrate on being a handsome, manly type of critter and let me worry about the rest of it?" I said.

Well, we argued it back and forth for the better part of the morning, but finally he admitted that he didn't see no better alternatives, and he could always commit suicide the next week if things didn't work out, and I went off to buy a leash and some grooming equipment at the local pet store, and then stopped by the arena for an entry form. I didn't know if he had an official werewolf name or not, so I just writ down Grand International Champion Basil on the form, and let it go at that.

The biggest problem I had the next two days was finding a vet who was open at night, so I could get Basil his rabies and distemper shots, but finally I convinced one to work late for an extra fifty dollars, which I planned to deduct from Basil's share of the winnings, since the shots didn't do me no good personally, and then it was Saturday, and we just stuck around the hotel until maybe five in the afternoon, Basil getting more and more nervous, and finally we walked on over to the arena.

Basil's class was scheduled to be judged at seven o'clock, but as the hour approached it began to look like the moon wasn't going to come out in time, and since I didn't want us to forfeit all that money by not showing up on time, I quick ran out into the alley, grabbed the first couple of cats I could find, and set 'em loose in the arena. The newspaper the next morning said that the ruckus was so loud they could hear it all the way over in Szentendre, which was a little town about forty miles up the road, and by the time everything had gone back to normal Basil was about as far from normal as Hungarian counts are prone to get, and I slipped his leash on him and headed for the ring.

There were three other dogs ahead of us, and after we entered the ring the judge came over and look at Basil.

"This is a class for miniature poodles," he said severely. "Just what kind of mongrel is that?"

"You know this guy, Basil?" I asked.

Basil nodded.

"He one of the ones who's mean to you when you walk through town?"

Basil growled an ugly growl.

"Basil?" said the judge, turning white as a sheet.

Basil gave him a toothy grin.

"Now, to answer your question," I said, "this here happens to be a fully growed miniature poodle what takes umbrage when you insult its ancestry."

The judge stared at Basil for another couple of seconds, then disqualified the other three dogs for not looking like him and handed me a blue ribbon.

Well, to make a long story short, old Basil terrorized the judges in the next three classes he was in and won 'em all, and then the ring steward told me that I had five minutes to prepare for the final class of the day, where they would pick the best dog in the show and award the winner the ten thousand dollars.

Suddenly Basil started whining up a storm. I couldn't see no ticks or fleas on him, and he couldn't tell me what was bothering him, but something sure was, and finally I noticed that he was staring intently at something, and I turned to see what it was, and it turned out to be this lovely looking lady who was preparing to judge the Best in Show class.

"What's the problem, Basil?" I asked.

He kept whining and staring.

"Is it her?"

He nodded.

I racked my mind trying to figure out what it was about her that could upset him so much.

"She's been mean to you before?" I asked.

He shook his head.

"She's got something to do with the Gypsies who cursed you?"

He shook his head again.

"I can't figure out what the problem is," I said. "But what the hell, as long as we let her know who you are, it's in the bag."

He pointed his nose at the ceiling and howled mournfully.

"She's from out of town and doesn't know you're a werewolf?" I asked with a sinking feeling in the pit of my stomach.

He whimpered and curled up in a little ball.

"Will the following dogs please enter the ring?" said the announcer. "Champion Blue Boy, Champion Flaming Spear, Champion Gladiator, Champion Jericho, and Grand International Champion Basil."

Well, we didn't have no choice but to follow these four fluffy little dogs into the ring. The judge just stared at us for a minute with her jaw hanging open, and I figured we were about to get booted out, but then she walked over and knelt down and held Basil by the ears and peered into his face, and then she stood up and stepped back a bit and stared at him some more, and finally she walked over to me and said, "This is the most handsome, rugged, masculine dog I have ever seen. I have a female I'd love to breed to him. Is he for sale?"

I told her that I was just showing him for a friend, and that she'd have to speak to the Count de Chenza Lupo about it later. She scribbled down his address, and it turned out that she was staying three rooms down the hall from me at the Hotel Magyar.

Finally she examined the other four dogs briefly and with obvious disinterest, and then she announced that Grand International Champion Basil was the best dog in this or any other show and had won the ten thousand dollars.

Well, Basil and me stuck around long enough to have a bunch of photos taken for the papers and then high tailed it back to the hotel, where we waited until daylight and he became Count Basil again and we divied up the money. Then he walked down the hall to talk to the judge about selling himself to her, and he came back half an hour later with the silliest grin on his face and announced that he was in love and she didn't mind in the least that he was a werewolf and all was right with the world.

I read in the paper that the other dog owners were so outraged about losing to a wolf that they tore the building down, and with the dog shows canceled for the foreseeable future I couldn't see no reason to stick around, so I bid Hungary farewell and decided to try my luck in Paris, where I'd heard tell that the sinners were so thick on the ground you could barely turn around without making the real close acquaintanceship of at least a couple of 'em.

I never saw old Basil again, but a few months later I got a letter from him. He'd married his lady judge and left Budapest for good, and was living on her country estate managing her kennel—and he added a proud little postscript that both his wife and her prize female were expecting.

THE DIRE WOLF

GENEVIEVE VALENTINE

The bone is worrisome.

"It's huge, Lia," says Christopher over the phone. "The guy who found it thought it was a bear jaw."

"What's the quality of the joint?" she asks, like she's stumped.

"Great condition on one side."

She guesses the other side has been broken off. (When werewolves fight, it's almost always a dive for the throat—the skull gets in the way.)

"I'm sorry to call you," he says, "but I figured if anyone would know—"

"I'll come out tomorrow," she says.

She hangs up the phone, her palm pressing flat against the receiver as if she can keep the news from spreading.

Velia doesn't really worry, the whole journey up to Fairbanks. People find bones from time to time. She can find a place somewhere in the Canis family to put almost anything. She's identified the remains of more rare species than any other xenoarchaeologist in the country.

She doesn't worry when Christopher shows her the jawbone and says wonderingly, "I've never seen anything like it—I mean, there's no meat left, but it's so . . . "

"Fresh?" she asks, and Christopher pulls a face that means *Yes*.

"I'll take a look," she says, as if she's planning some tests, but she's already planning the paperwork. It's only a bone fragment. She'd name it a gray wolf already and call it a night, except that it was good to put on a show of working hard.

(The jaw is missing a third of the left mandible, snapped clean away. She had forgotten how powerful a werewolf could be when it was cornered.)

Velia isn't worried at all, until Christopher says, "We called in someone else to help speed up the identification. If there are dangerous animals in the park somewhere, we need to know."

Then she sets down the bone with trembling hands.

She doesn't listen to Christopher after that. No need; she knows who they've called in.

She would have called him in, too, if they were still speaking.

The dire wolf did not survive.

The fossil record says the dire wolf vanished. It wasn't clever enough to live in the age after ice, after the mammoth was gone. It was all force, no cleverness. It was too large to live in the close, tight foliage of the world's new spring.

The skulls line the walls of the Tar Pit Museum, tidy rows of dead.

Velia had spent one summer carefully brushing dust away from the piles of bones in La Brea, picking tar from around the eye sockets and the incisors, edging the little furrow that ran from nose to neck. By the end of August they had eleven skulls.

"God, no wonder they all died," said Alice, holding up a skull with no jaw—the jaws never made it. When Alice held the base, the front teeth pressed into her elbow. "Smallest cranial I've seen on a dog. Poor puppies. Too stupid to get out of the tar." She patted its head. "Adapt or die, right?"

Velia had more pity. She knew what it was like to be blinded by want.

He arrives late.

She's running her fingers over the clean break on the mandible, and when she hears him coming and looks up she sees that the windows have all gone black, and her little lamp is the only thing fighting the dark.

It's almost dark enough to hide his flinch when he sees her. (Almost; not quite.)

She's grateful to have been the one who knew it was coming. She didn't want to think about how she might look if he ever caught her unaware.

"Velia," he says.

He's only ever used her full name. ("If you ever call me Lia, I'll know you're under duress," she said once, and he had looked up for a long moment before he smiled.)

It's been six years. He hasn't aged.

"Mark," she says, the same tone.

Even tired, worn out from travel, his dark eyes are sharp. He glances around the room, leans against the doorway too casually, sets his bag down like it's a trap and he's ready to run. The draft from the outer door hits her; snow, and evergreens.

She can see his fatigue in the slope of his shoulders. She doesn't even know where he came in from; his work takes him all over, and it's not like they're in touch.

After a second he asks, carefully, "Have you been expecting me?"

"Allan told me he'd called you, after I got here."

He looks at the jaw in her hand. She's been playing with it without noticing. Now it's hanging from her wrist; the front of the jaw follows the curve of her hand, the teeth small pressure points against her knuckles. One has cut through the skin, and a little red bead is forming under the white.

(The teeth on a dire wolf are impossibly sharp. If you shove a pipe in its mouth, the wolf will bite clean through it and keep coming.)

She says, "The ones from La Brea are so dark from the tar, you start to think that's just what they look like."

He doesn't answer. When she finally looks up, he's watching her without blinking. He looks torn.

She remembers, too late, what it feels like to have him watching her.

"It's good to see you," he says, and it almost sounds like the truth. (Almost; not quite.)

There was a wolfish quality about him right from the beginning. He had a way of leaning back in a chair, tilting his head down when he was deep in thought, that answered some need she didn't know she had.

They had been in Alaska then, too, studying the migratory patterns of wolves.

(One of the other anthropologists was in love with him; you could see it in the way she half-turned her head when he spoke.)

Halfway through the project, it stormed, and all five of them spent days sitting close together in the main room of the rented house, because it had the only fireplace.

Velia spent most of her time at the kitchen table (she didn't mind the cold). She looked at foliage lists for the Russian and Alaskan sides of the Bering Straight, glancing absently at the sketch of the dire wolf beside the gray wolf, the gray wolf looking spindly and half-grown next to its dead cousin.

From one of the chairs near the fire, Mark asked (his first words to her), "Velia—why would you cross a land bridge when there was sufficient prey where you were?"

"The fever of pursuit," Velia said, absently.

When she looked up, he seemed caught off-guard for the first time since she'd met him. For the rest of the night, he cast long looks her way when he thought she couldn't see him, as if a worthy opponent had walked onto the field and taken him by surprise.

She let it pass. She didn't get involved with people.

He stands in the doorway like he's thinking of something cutting to say, but in the end he leaves his bag behind and approaches with long quiet steps to peer at the jawbone.

He doesn't touch her, but as he lifts and turns the bone she rolls her hand along with it, not letting go, and he looks at her palm before he looks at the bone.

"Whoever won this fight will want to keep this under wraps," he says, after a long examination.

She knows. It's why she was worried about Mark's coming. Werewolf

fights—always to the death—are such a waste. Dire wolves are rare
enough as it is.

She says, "Whoever won this fight woke up with bone in his teeth."

He half-smiles, doesn't look up from the jaw. When he runs his fingers
over the flats of the teeth, the pad of his thumb just brushes her skin.

Her stomach turns over.

She ignores it; it's residual. Old habit.

The dire wolf had a temporal fossa out of proportion to its brain cavity. It
was what made the top of its skull so different from the skull of an Arctic
wolf or a grey wolf; the dire wolf's cranium was low and narrow, the
caved-in temples on either side looking like two kicks from a horse.

For a long time, Velia thought the slender skull meant that the dire
wolf wasn't clever enough to survive the new age without adapting.

After she met Mark, she began to think more about the temporal
fossa, the deep indentations in the skull that housed the jaw muscles.
The skull was narrow because the muscles were large.

When the dire wolf bit down, it held on. That's what it was made to
do.

She sits awake for an hour, imagining she can hear him breathing,
before she gets up the courage to go to sleep. It's her imagination; the
sudden shock of nearness had brought back old caution. That was all.

(It was easier to be lonely. His companionship was dangerous.)

If in the middle of the night he walks back and forth outside her door
like a sentinel, scuffing the carpet just loudly enough to cut through her
dreams—well, maybe she imagines that, too.

If in the dark she bolts awake, listening to an animal breathing warm
and strong in the snow outside—that, she's not imagining.

"Does it frighten you?" he asked.

She said, "Always."

She's been awake for an hour, watching out the window, when he knocks
on her door. It's not quite dawn, but she's not surprised; she knows he's
been awake, too.

"There's another wolf," he says.

In the small room, in the welcome dark, he seems impossibly far away.

She stands up. "I know."

He flushes, goes white. "You haven't—have you been outside? You can't go out there, Velia. It will kill you."

There is a stab in her side, just for a moment, as if he's cut her. She fights to stay calm. There is no safety with him any more.

"I'll be fine," she says.

He takes two steps. They're close enough to kiss. "Velia," he says, his voice rumbling in his chest, "that wolf snapped another's jaw clean off. What is it going to do with you?"

"Talk," she says.

To a dire wolf, the human form is like a paved street; the wolf lives in the tree roots that silently push until the stone swells and cracks and falls apart.

Velia has done better at keeping human than most wolves, but it's hard to ignore another of your kind when it comes calling.

She parks her car close to the trees. (It's a useless human habit; the wolf can run faster than any speeding car can save you.)

When she's far into the forest and can smell she's alone, she folds her shirt and pants and boots under the branches of a fir tree, where the snow has not reached.

(Any dire wolf who lives in human form has had to explain their nakedness. The smart ones learn to leave their clothes where they can be retrieved before people find them naked and start asking questions.)

She proceeds barefoot, wrapped in her coat—waxed cotton, the closest texture she can find to human skin. It's nice to have a human skin that doesn't hurt.

She stops short when she smells the other wolf.

The change surges into her throat like vomit; she swallows and tries to breathe. She won't give in to the wolf unless she has to.

(The pain is worse than the fight.)

She reaches the clearing where the wolf has been—the smell of blood is still strong—and hangs back, waiting.

It's rare for dire wolves of the same form to fight one another. As humans they attract each other, as wolves they form packs. But those who stay in human form often go mad, or fall in love with humans, and the true wolf has no patience for either one. The human wolf must be careful.

It won't be the first time Velia's had to fight for this body.

Her father died of some human cancer. He wouldn't let anyone treat him for it ("What if they find out somehow?"), and as he took his last breaths, a ripple of the wolf's face slid over his features, a last toothsome grin before he was gone. It was how Velia would have wanted to remember him.

Her mother died later that year during a new moon, while her body was trying to make the shift back from the wolf. Velia gathered her mother in her arms and sobbed into the soft gray fur until the form in her arms was human, and Velia could pick her up and carry her home.

(The dire wolf takes human form when it dies; that lets them pass through the world without leaving proof behind.)

It was her mother's broken heart that did it, Velia knew. Her mother could have lived another fifty years, another hundred—their kind was hardy, if they could strike some balance between human and wolf that didn't drive them to the brink. It was a weak heart that had taken her mother.

Velia learned early that it was safer to be alone.

She never told Mark how rare it was for a dire wolf to care for a real human. Even after he knew what she was, how could she explain what even the dire wolves struggled to come to terms with?

She told him, early, "I can't."

Later she told him, "We can't."

Just that word frightened her, the idea that there was danger to more than just herself, that she had to worry for them both.

He fought her on it. They parted badly.

But she was right. Two years after she left him, she had to identify the teeth marks on a human man who had been torn to pieces by a wild beast. A pack of coyotes, she said. The bites looked big because there had been so many of them overlapping, she said.

She never found out if the wolf had killed its own lover, or if it had been punishing another wolf for keeping human company.

Velia spent every new moon that year looking forward to the change. On four legs, at least, she could hunt without thinking.

An hour later, the wolf appears.

Velia tenses, once, just to make sure she hasn't frozen. But her muscles are warm and ready (she's never really been cold), and she's not frightened.

The wolf has never frightened her. It's how she can live as a human without losing her mind; she accepts the shape of the beast.

(In her bones, she knows that sooner or later, she'll give in to the wolf and disappear.)

It pads to the edge of the clearing opposite her and stands in the shadows, waiting. Once, it shifts, and the sun catches its head for a moment—one amber eye, sharp tight muzzle-fur the color of dust.

"I'm here," Velia says. "What do you want?"

When there's no answer, she tries again, in her true language. Silence.

"Why did you kill one of your own?"

It's one of their own—the jaw of one of their own is sitting in the dinky office lab ten miles away—but those who live as wolves don't like hearing solidarity from those on two legs.

The wolf-change claws at Velia's throat; she bites her lips against it until she tastes blood.

"What do you want?" she calls again, finally, but the wolf startles and runs, leaves nothing behind but a maze of prints and a cloud of breath that hangs in the air for a few moments after the wolf has disappeared.

She shivers; pretends it's from the cold.

Velia takes her time putting her clothes back on.

They make her feel more human, a little less afraid.

The wolf, in all things, protects itself.

It's why Velia studied animals. It's why she examines bones and tags them wolf or coyote or some breed long dead. It helps keep them all from being found out.

She fears for her kind. They are fragmented (the human-living and the beasts, taking turns hating one another more), and she knows that even under threat they would not unify. Some humans would submit to the knife rather than give in to the beast, and the true wolf would kill all comers until it died of exhaustion.

So she keeps her human shape, walks through the world, tags her jaws "Canis lupus arctos"; because what else could humans do but wipe them out, if they knew?

Velia and Mark were at the end of the Alaska winter when the thaw came.

They got called away from wrap-up in Alaska to work a dig in Iceland. Spring had come early, and they were summoned to take advantage of the softer ground and dig down another layer.

("What are you really looking for?" he asked, like he already knew why she agreed to come.

She didn't ask why he had come with her. She knew what pursuit looked like.

"I can't explain," she said, as if it answered him.)

For two weeks she scooped mud out of her taped-off square and carved bone after bone in bas relief, and all the while she knew she wasn't alone. The mossy tundra had eyes for her, and whenever she was near Mark, under his wolfish eyes, she felt a beast in the forest hating her.

(A wolf knows a wolf.)

They were done for the night, back at the rickety two-bedroom house near the dig site, when the wolf came.

There was the single howl as it called her to battle (they both stood up so fast the work table skidded), and then nothing but the wind; the dire wolf is silent when it hunts.

"Stay behind me," Mark said.

Then came the thunder of the charging beast.

It was too fast for her to get away, too fast to hide Mark, too fast to explain.

There was only time to throw open the door and leap (Mark shouting at her to stop), force the change between one breath and the next, so that she furled inside-out and the air crackled with the sound of snapping tendons and the grind of bone.

(She won. She doesn't remember how. All the way home she coughed up bits of the other wolf; spat up bone and teeth and fur.)

The fight carried her a quarter-mile from the cabin, and she padded back as the wolf.

There was a chance he hadn't seen her. There was a chance he didn't know.

(No chance.)

When she saw him standing in the doorway, the blanket in his hands, she made a high, keening noise that started as a howl, and became— between one breath and another—a human cry.

(Grief.)

Her bones seemed painfully soft and frail in her human form; she could hardly feel her blood pumping through such long, twisted veins. She set her weakling jaw against the shaking, but her skeleton rattled inside the meat.

It was worse than the new moon, ten times worse. It was the tree roots erupting through the pavement, shattering the stone.

Mark got both arms under her and carried her inside, out of the ice and the dark. He smelled like snow and detergent and fear, and she didn't know why a smell like that would be comforting to a wolf.

(She didn't know much about love, back then.)

He carried her up the stairs and ran a hot shower until the blood and dirt were gone, and his hands were shaking.

(Fear, she thought then. She knows now—desire.)

When she came downstairs again, he was standing outside. There was a wolf's footprint in the snow outside the cabin. It was the same length as Mark's foot, and as wide; her claws had pierced right through the snow and dug up four thin sprays of black dirt across the white as she ran.

He passed his foot over it, smoothing the snow free of the evidence. She waited, wondering what she would do if he threatened to expose her.

(It was a lie. She knew what she would do. On four legs, she could hunt without thinking.)

After a long time, he took a step backwards, closer to her, without turning.

"Does it frighten you?" he asked.

She said, "Always."

When he came at her, the kiss drove her against the door with a thud, and he tore away the blanket as if he wanted some part, any part, of her fight.

She dragged her nails over his back, five thin trails of red against his skin.

The dire wolf that lives in human form spends the day of the new moon curled in a corner, trembling, aching, grinding her teeth as the bones scream for change. The moment of transformation is unbearable (there is always the wrenching cry), but it passes, and the bones and the fur and the teeth of the wolf are her relief.

A dire wolf can turn at will, but it's the last line of defense; between pain and death, some choose death.

Changing at every new moon from human to wolf and back can drive you mad. Most dire wolves eventually give in to their true form, and make their homes in forests, or tundra if arctic wolves are nearby, or desert caves. They can go anywhere once the moon has lost its power over them. What animal would stand up to a beast twice as large as a wolf, twice as fast, twice as cunning?

Legend, which looks for monsters within its own neighbors, claim that werewolves are people who achieve the body of the wolf.

This is untrue.

The dire wolf took on a human form; down at the bone, between every breath, each of them is really the animal. The human shape is a useful trick, that's all.

(Adapt or die.)

Christopher's waiting at the lab when she comes back.

"Mark says it looks like an Arctic wolf that got on the wrong side of a bear attack," he says. "What are you thinking it is?"

"I think that wolf had a pretty sad end," she said. "Did you find anything else of the skeleton?"

Christopher shakes his head. "We don't have the manpower we used to, but as far as we looked, there was nothing to find. Maybe the head got carried over to where our guy found it."

"Was there any skull? Any other bones?" She thinks about the deep, low temporal fossa—a jaw is easy to disguise, but the skull would be hard to explain.

He shakes his head.

"Where's Mark?"

"Went out looking for you," Christopher says. "I'll call him back in on the radio."

When she's alone, she looks at the jaw under the magnifying glass, marks on her report the hundred tiny dents where the birds pecked the flesh away, the smooth expanses where the insects got there at last, carrying away whatever was hanging on.

The bone is cool, and smooth as human skin.

Mark opens the door too fast, gets too close.

"I saw the tracks," he says, quietly, so Christopher won't hear. "It's big."

He means, it's bigger than you. His breath is warm on her scalp.

"I'll win," she says.

After a little silence, he says, "I'd forgotten what it feels like to be close to you."

She doesn't know what he means; doesn't dare ask.

The dire wolf was too slow to evolve, everyone knew.

"Poor guys," Alice said (she pitied all the bones). She waggled the saber-toothed tiger skull she was working on, like it was nodding. "The saber-tooth says nature cuts us all down sooner or later. He should know. Poor kitty."

Alice always got punchy near the end of an excavation.

"Nature might surprise you," Velia said, ran her tongue over her teeth.

"Promise me you won't fight," he says.

They're in his room. He's pacing; she's watching the moonlight play over his face. When he passes back and forth, his shoulder brushes her shoulder.

"It doesn't want to fight," she says.

He stops and looks at her. "What can I do? How can I help you?"

She doesn't know how to explain how he's only ever been a danger. She doesn't know how to tell him how different he is from most of his kind, in loving her.

(Most wolves find a mate in each other, because humans are frail; because when faced with a monster, a normal human senses danger and retreats.)

She says, "Live where there are no wolves."

He frowns like she's cut him. She knows that pain.

She wants to leave here with him and go somewhere where there are no wolves, carve some narrow sliver of love from each of them, see what it can build.

Doesn't dare.

They don't embrace; his hands are shaking, her hands are fists. He kisses her temple, presses his lips to the temporal fossa; she holds her breath, closes her eyes.

At night, the wolf's tracks are easier to follow. There's a better quality of shadow when the moon is out, and in her waxy coat and bare feet, Velia is an extension of the snow; only her dark eyes and black hair give her away.

(They used to be the color of dust, and her face was broad and sharp-mouthed. There's too much human in her face, now.)

The den is in a shallow cave, close to the surface. It's shallow enough that by the time Velia smells decay, she is looking past the narrow entry through the darkness to the wolf and the human body of its dead mate.

Of course there were no wolf bones to find; the human shape is the dire wolf's last defense.

But Velia's eyes have always been sharp, and she can see from where she's standing that there's an empty shadow beneath the torn throat, the wrinkled skin. (She was old, old enough for even the true wolf to die.)

The break in the jaw was a clean one. It must have snapped as he dragged his mate's body to the shadow of the den, before the change, where he could make sure no stranger would find her.

He watches her with gleaming eyes, and she braces herself against his sorrow.

She says, "We found the bone. You're safe. You can find another place."

The head droops, and a huff of breath mists over the black for a moment.

Then the wolf lies down beside its mate and stretches its neck along the ground, waiting for the strike.

Velia hadn't known enough true wolves to know what can happen when a wolf is parted from its mate. She had hoped her parents were the exception, and not the rule. But the dire wolf does what she dreaded; it mates for life.

No, she thinks, I can't, I can't, but the wolf is willing. (The human form is just a trick; at the roots, the wolf is always waiting.)

When the change comes over her, the other wolf whimpers a welcome. She chokes through the pain before the wolf form takes, bites down on her cries.

Old habit. The wolf is silent when it hunts.

According to the fossil record, dire wolves hunted in packs to the exclusion of good sense, leaping into the tar pits by the dozens until every last one of them was drowned.

"Live together, die together, I guess," sighed Alice, cleaning dirt off her chisel. "I mean, what could possibly drive an animal into the tar pits, once you saw what happened to the others? They couldn't *all* be stupid."

Velia blew a layer of dust off the skull at her feet and wondered about that first wolf, the first one who had retreated from the edge of the tar. She wondered how it got desperate enough to turn to humans just to find some pack to live among.

That was the dire wolf that had fathered them all. The true wolf had always been separate; had been always alone.

When Velia can stand on her two feet, she washes the blood off in the river, then pulls on her waxy coat and walks back the way she came.

She scuffs gently over her footsteps on her way, so that no one might find the tracks and disturb the dead.

She leaves that night. She doesn't ask where Mark was going. Doesn't dare.

(When the dire wolf bites down, it holds on. That's what it's made to do.)

TAKE BACK THE NIGHT

LAWRENCE SCHIMEL

Some have said I'm crazy. Well, lots have said that about me, actually.

I run an all-night bookstore. An all-night feminist bookstore.

Take back the night, we'd demanded in all those demonstrations and marches. This is my way of doing just that, claiming the night as my own. I'm making a safe place for women to go to at night, a reason besides the bars for going out—and someplace to stop on the way home from them.

Not that I don't allow men in the store. Their money's just as good as anyone else's, so long as they're respectful, and I certainly need that money to stay open.

And, sure, I get a lot of riffraff coming through, but I'm not the kind of woman to let that stop me. And anyway, the cops know to keep an eye on the place. The new guy especially, Albert, likes to come in every now and then, and I let him take a used mystery novel for free. His taste is for police procedurals, and I never can figure out, if he's dealing with the stuff all day long, why he wants to read about it on his time off, but maybe he's looking for tips and pointers. I just hope he realizes reading is no excuse for experience, especially in his line of work.

One night in mid-summer it was hot as hell and I had the doors open. Around 2:30 AM—late at night or early in the morning depending on your perspective. I was standing on the porch having a cigarette, since I don't allow smoking inside the store. Too much of a fire hazard, what with all those old dry books.

The moon was full and fat and sort of orange as it perched above the sports bar across the street, looking as if it were a basketball teetering on the rim of the hoop. I felt a powerful urge within me to jump up and slam dunk the moon right over into tomorrow, and right as I'm thinking about that metaphor a large dog climbed up the steps and walked into the store, just as casual as can be.

I looked around the street for the owner, but no one was in sight. I stubbed out my cig, and followed the dog inside. She was sitting in front of the cash register, as if waiting for me. I walked around the counter, wondering what to do. Call the cops? Or was it the fire department who handles pets, or only the ones stuck in trees and stuff?

The pooch turned to face me, just siting there, waiting. She wanted something from me, I was certain, but I had no idea what. A doggie treat? She seemed to expect me to recognize her.

I didn't know whose dog she was, and had never seen her around town. She wasn't wearing a collar. But something made me trust the beast.

"Come here, girl," I said, bending down. She eagerly came towards me, and licked my face and sniffed my crotch as I ruffled the scruff of her neck and stroked her back. "Didn't you read the sign on the door? *No Dogs Allowed.*"

I didn't really mind. I like dogs, a lot in fact. I just don't want them in my store. I was losing some customers by not allowing dogs—people out walking their dogs used to stop in and browse when I welcomed pets. But one night a man came in with a doberman and the damned creature lifted his leg on two shelves full of hardcovers. Couple hundred dollars worth of damage, and I didn't even find out until after they'd left the store. Not even an apology. After that, the sign went up on the door. I figure I'm saving money in the long run, and who knows, maybe before I was losing customers who were afraid of dogs, who now felt welcome.

She barked twice, as if to get my attention, and then began to howl. I clapped my hands over my ears and stood up.

"Quiet there, you'll wake the dead with that racket!" I stared down at the beast. "I should change the sign to read: *No Dogs Aloud,* but you couldn't read it anyway."

She shook her head, as if to disagree.

"If you could read it, then why'd you come in?"

She disappeared into the back of the store. Had she come here to get a book to read? I wondered if I should follow her, wondering what damage she might be doing to the stock back there, but just as I was about to set off after her she reappeared. She had a book in her jaws, which she placed at my feet. I picked it up and wiped the slobber off on my jeans. *Women who run with the wolves.*

I looked down at her, and her lips pulled back, revealing her large sharp teeth. She was grinning.

I felt like I was in an *X-Files* episode or some horror movie. She'd run with the wolves, and now was one. I wondered if she were one of my customers. Instinctively I wanted to reach out and pat the top of her head, comfort her by saying "It's all right," but I didn't think it was appropriate.

Instead, I put the book down on the counter and looked out the still-open door at the dark night. "Kansas," I said, "I've a feeling this isn't Toto anymore."

The wolf and I sat on the front steps as I smoked another cig and tried to think of what to do. Or at least, what to do next.

At first I kept trying to think of ways to cure her, since I'd fallen into the kinds of thinking that assumed that was why she had come to me. But as I looked at her, sitting next to me, I got to wondering more. Was there anything wrong with her being a werewolf? Maybe she'd come to me because I knew her, or because she knew I'd understand. I had no idea how it had happened, whether she'd wanted it or not. She didn't seem in any distress or anything, so why fix something that wasn't broken.

Although with canines, one did have them fixed as a preventative measure . . .

I watched the smoke drift upwards. There was just a tiny sliver of moon peeking over the edge of the building, like the slivers of moon on my fingernails. I looked over at Wolf. Would she turn back into a woman as soon as that sliver disappeared? But no—just because we no longer saw the moon didn't mean it had set. Not yet.

I wondered about clothes. Would she have any when she changed?

I couldn't help wondering how long it had been since I'd seen a live naked woman. Not that I don't practice what I preach. It had just been a long time is all. I tried to remember exactly how long and gave up before I became depressed.

I tried to imagine what it would be like if it was me instead of her who'd wound up as a werewolf. And as I tried to figure out how I'd feel, I realized how much I'd changed.

I'd grown older.

I'd become such a goody two shoes. I no longer went to rallies, ACT UP meetings, no longer did any civil disobedience of any sort. I didn't have the time, struggling to keep the bookstore open and alive.

I'd turned into a solid, conservative businesswoman—a model citizen. I was a member of the chamber of commerce. I paid my taxes like a good little girl and didn't even complain all that much about how they were being spent. About the most radical thing I did anymore (besides run an all-night feminist bookstore) was sign petitions.

I felt sick.

I was disgusted with myself.

I'd betrayed all my earlier dreams.

Suddenly, I shoved my hand in her mouth. "Bite me," I said. What was I thinking? Was I even thinking? As the words flew from my mouth I realized I should've had her bite me someplace else, that I'd be crippled with only one hand to use. Still, sometimes sacrifices must be made for the greater good and I didn't pull my hand back.

She waited for me to reconsider, then bit down.

I flinched, but it was only a pinch, and then a prick, like having your blood type tested at the doctor's office, the kind of prick you had to give yourself in biology lab.

And then the world dropped away in a flash of pain as her teeth broke skin.

I howled.

I have no idea what my body did. I think I thrashed about and convulsed. But my mind was numb to anything but pain. That pain was liberating, setting me free from my body. I looked down at myself, sitting on the porch of my bookstore with a wolf biting my hand, and I thought: Well, why don't I do something?

That was when I snapped back into my body. She released my hand and I stared down at the neat puncture points her teeth had made. I was calm and detached about the blood that leaked from them; my mind kept repeating one phrase: Why don't I do something? I'd been feeling this way for a while, I only now realized. Maybe this is why the werewolf was here, to wake me up from this stupor, reclaim me as a lesbian avenger. Not a loup garou but a lesbian garou. My mind began to race through imagined scenes, the power we would have.

I was already beginning to act like a werewolf: the bleeding was slowing as my new super-fast metabolism began to kick in. I figured I could get to liking this. I'd even get a humane fur coat out of it.

Of course, I had still to see how painful the Change would be.

"Watch the store," I told her, then went upstairs to get gauze and neosporin.

When I got downstairs again, the wolf was gone.

In its place was a naked woman. "How do you feel?" she asked.

I looked her over: mid-thirties, dark brown hair that hung to her shoulders, slightly overweight but seemingly unselfconscious about her body. Here she was, buck naked in a used bookstore, and she was able to hold a conversation. I liked that.

My hand throbbed. It felt swollen big as my thigh. "I'll live," was all I said.

And a part of my mind whispered that I would, that I would heal from any ordinary wound, heal from anything but silver.

She smiled and before I could help myself—I generally had more presence of mind, but perhaps I was too flustered at seeing a naked woman again, after so long, or maybe I was just rusty from lack of practice flirting—I blurted out, "Why me?"

She closed the coffee table book she'd been leafing through and put it down on the counter. "It was the wolf. Instinct. My feet just knew where to take me. I guess they knew you'd be able to handle this." She looked away from me, as if suddenly shy, and then added, "The wolf is not a solitary creature."

What was she asking of me? Or had I already decided, when I'd asked her to bite me? Was I now part of her pack?

She looked to me like I was the alpha female. So I took charge.

"Human's aren't either," I said, and reached for her.

I didn't bother to open the store the next day. For one thing, it had been so long since I'd had someone in bed with me, I didn't want to get out of it. And I'd just have to close up at sundown, anyway, which would confuse people. What if I couldn't get rid of all my customers in time, I wondered, if I turned into a snarling bitch right in front of them. Every store needs a gimmick these days, but that just didn't seem right for mine.

The Change began like a severe case of cramps, only it was all over my body at once, not localized to my belly. I wondered briefly if taking Midol or aspirin before the Change would help dull the sensations. I resolved to try it next time, just as my body convulsed and I lost all conscious thought to the pain.

When I uncurled my body from the floor and stretched my limbs, I knew something was different but I couldn't place my finger on what it was. Perhaps it was because I no longer had fingers per se. I yawned, my jaws gaping wide, and I knew suddenly how sharp my teeth had become. I'd felt them, the night before, when Laura bit down on my hand.

And Laura. She, too, would have changed. I could feel her near me, the heat of her body picked up somehow through my new wolf's senses.

I didn't bother to look for her, but nosed open the apartment door we'd left ajar and ran down the steps. I was oddly comfortable in this new body, as if I'd lived in it once before. Perhaps being a werewolf was like riding a bicycle, a skill you didn't forget. I jumped up and pushed open the outer door, which we'd blocked open with a rock, and ran out into the night.

This was nothing like riding a bicycle. This was like riding the wind.

I ran through the city's streets, hearing the click of my nails on pavement, and the echo of Laura's behind me, as we raced.

I remembered how one night a friend and I had gotten dressed in male drag and gone out. We were packing dildos in our jeans, and it gave us a glorious feeling of power. It made us feel cocky, in all sense of the word. We didn't know where else to go, so we went to a gay bar, and we watched the men cruising each other, and were ourselves sometimes cruised, sometimes cruising, wondering what we'd do if one of these big men took us up on our offers, how they would react when they got us home and found out our dicks weren't real. Would they want us to fuck them anyway? We never found out.

I remembered that heady sensation of power I'd felt that night, but compared to this packing was just playing a wolf in cheap clothing.

This was power. I could feel the energy coiled in my limbs as my silvery pelt stretched and moved across my wolf muscles and sinew.

This was taking back the night.

I felt the familiar anger begin to burn in my belly, a hungering for justice and retribution. I wanted a fight, to test my newfound strength, to redress the balance. The night wasn't a safe place, only now it wasn't as safe for the people who made it unsafe.

I could be shot, I realized. I could be knifed.

Only silver can harm a werewolf, a voice inside my head reminded me. Although I didn't doubt that an ordinary bullet or knife would hurt like hell.

I prowled. My ears strained to pick up the sounds of a disturbance of any sort. The city seemed eerily empty of that sort of activity.

How come nobody warns you that being a vigilante is boring as hell most of the time? Where was a rapist when you needed one? Were they all off having a pot luck somewhere?

Laura seemed to know my restlessness and pulled suddenly ahead, leading me off on a new path. Had she heard something I'd missed, more accustomed to discerning stimulus from her lupine senses? Or did she just fear that I would attack some innocent passerby if I didn't find release for this building anger soon? We passed a Dumpster with an enticing smell, but I didn't stop to investigate. I loped after her, anticipation building as we dashed through the alleyways behind buildings. I had no idea where we were, and wondered if I'd even be able to recognize this part of town if I were on the street looking at the fronts of these buildings.

I heard a scream, and all musings ceased as my body took over. I sprinted ahead of Laura and into the alley, my body working on instinct as it leapt. A man crumpled beneath me, and I could sense another body, the screamer, nearby, cowering against the wall. His body collapsed beneath my weight, my jaws gnashing as they closed upon cloth and flesh. Even as I bit I thought of Laura's pale thighs, like an atlas with blue vein roads leading towards the moist center of her sex.

And as my jaws locked on his shoulder and I shook my head back and forth, digging my teeth deeper into his flesh as he screamed, I had an epiphany, in the part of my brain that was still me and not fully animal: I must kill this man, or he, too, would become a werewolf, having been bitten. I must kill him or he would not merely run free, he would have this same power I now felt, use this force to attack others.

It was not hesitation when I released him, let him try to scramble away. I leapt on him again, and he twisted beneath me, rolling onto his back, his arms coming up to cover his face. My muzzle pushed through these weak defenses. My teeth sunk into his throat and tore and blood spurted into my mouth, warm and delicious, and I growled deep in my throat with the sound of the release of pleasure, as if I were coming, or had my face buried in the wetness of a woman who was coming.

There could be no turning back now.

I had tasted of the forbidden fruit, Adam's apple, and I now had knowledge of good and evil.

MONGREL

MARIA V. SNYDER

They call me Mongrel. I don't mind. It's true. My blood is mixed like vegetables in a soup. I've lived in so many different places, and I never belonged to any of them. But the other homeless don't know that when they tease me. Say I waste food on my mutts. That I reek of dog.

So what? I like the smell of dog. Better than people. Better than the others I hang with. Not that I enjoy their company, but they're useful at times. Warned me about the police raid a few months back, let me know when the soup kitchen opened and the women's shelter—not that I would live there without my pups, but a hot shower is a hot shower.

As long as no one messes with my stuff, I don't care what they say. It's mid-January and I need everything I've scrounged to survive. My spot is near perfect. I sleep under the railroad bridge and I share my blanket with five dogs. The term hot dog has a whole new meaning for me.

The others huddle around a campfire on the broken concrete slabs of the abandoned parking lot. We're all trespassing on railroad property, but the owners only send the police about once a year to chase us away. So far, never in the winter. Nice of them. (Yeah, I'm being sarcastic).

That night, snarls and growls wake me. Animals are up on the bridge fighting. My lot is awake with their tails tucked under and their bodies hunched low. A yelp stabs me in the chest and I'm running toward the sound. Something rolls down the side of bridge, crashes into the brush, and lays still. Something large.

A wounded animal can be dangerous, but I'm next to him before my brain can catch up with my body. It's the biggest damn dog I've ever seen. He lifts his head, but the fight is gone. He's panting and bleeding from lots of cuts. I yank off my gloves and run my hands along his legs, searching for broken bones.

He's all black except for the tips of his hair. They shine with silver like he'd been brushed with liquid moonlight. No broken bones, but a knife is buried in his shoulder. Up to the hilt.

I spin around and scan the bridge. Sure enough a figure is standing there, looking down at me. My pups catch the stranger's scent and start barking and baying. I don't hush them, and soon the person leaves.

The noise brings the others. They *tsk* over the injured dog, but will only help me drag him to my spot after I give them cigarettes and booze as payment. They laugh and lay odds on how long the dog will live. People disgust me.

When the others go back to the fire, I open up the good stuff—eighty proof. By now the big brute is shaking and I grab the handle of the knife. He's either going to live or die quicker without it in him. I tug it out, scraping bone. The dog shudders once then stills as blood pours.

Staunching the wound, I use the eighty proof to clean it before stitching him up. He doesn't make a sound as the needle pierces his skin. I count them as I tie the string. Fifteen stitches in all. When I'm done, I lay beside him with the pups nestled around us and cover us all with the blanket.

He's still alive in the morning so I make my daily rounds, searching for food, checking Dumpsters, and my usual haunts. Wearing layers of grimy clothes, I'm invisible to the normals. Slush covers the city's sidewalks and cars zip by, spraying water without care.

A couple businesses are aware of me, and once in a while, they'll add a few extra leftovers to their trash cans. I chuckle as I score a dozen hamburgers still wrapped up like presents in the Dumpster behind Vinny's Burger Joint.

Vinny doesn't like me, wouldn't help me if I was starving to death on his sidewalk, but he's got a soft spot for dogs. People are funny like that.

I don't linger long—Vinny doesn't like that, but I spy a small terrier crouched next to the dumpster. Almost missed the little rat. She is trembling and wet. Dirt stains her white coat gray. I lure her with a bit of burger and have her in my arms in no time.

Back at my spot, I'm greeted with wagging tails and excited mutts that are all happy to see me. Can't get that from people. Not for long. Eventually they ignore you or abuse you, then leave you.

I spilt the burgers among my pups, counting heads. I got to be careful not to keep too many and the ones I keep are the littles who have no homes. The big brute eats half a burger—a good sign. I think he's one of those Irish wolfhounds or Scottish deerhounds I've read about.

The new pup isn't sure what to make of the pack. Doesn't matter. She's wearing a collar and won't be here long. I inspect my trash bags, arranged just so. Funny that foster kids use garbage bags to carry their stuff, too. I don't have much—a few clothes, some toiletries, a propane stove that's a life saver, and cigarettes and booze for paying for favors. Nothing's missing.

Most of the others won't leave anything behind, pushing their belongings around in stolen shopping carts instead. We're not a trust-worthy bunch. But no one's stole from me since I've been sharing my spot with the mutts. I just smile when I sees one of the others limping around with bite marks on his ankles. Serves him right.

However, if the hound recovers, I'm gonna need more food than I can scrounge. So I grab my nicest clothes and head to the women's shelter for a shower.

The lady who answers the door is nervous. She keeps the chain on and looks at me like she wants to call the police.

I hold up the white dog. "Found your dog, ma'am."

And there it is. The woman's face changes as if a button is pressed inside her head. Joy beams from her and I soak in it.

She flings the door wide and presses the pup to her chest, kissing and hugging the little squirming rat. "Thank you so much! We've been so worried. My kids will be thrilled."

She goes on, but I don't listen. It's always the same. What's not the same is what happens next. I'm polite and not demanding as I ask about the reward money. Just a gentle reminder. "Your flyer at the grocery store offered fifty bucks?"

The joy dies and she eyes my best clothes with scorn and suspicion. I smooth my pink sweater and tuck a strand of long brown hair behind an ear.

"Where did you find Sugar?" she asks.

"Behind Vinny's on Sixth Street."

"That's over two miles away. Sugar would never go that far. You took her from our back yard, hoping for reward money. That's why the gate was still locked."

"No, ma'am. I—"

She slams the door in my face. No surprise just disappointment. Sometimes I'll get the money. Not often.

I hurry away before the cops arrive. Since I wore my best clothes, the library staff won't bother me. Pulling my favorite book, *The Complete Dog Encyclopedia* from the shelf, I flip through the pages until I reach the hounds. The big brute is thick in the body and tall legged like the Irish wolfhound, but his long face doesn't match. I scan the various breeds. The Siberian husky has similar eyes and muzzle, but not quite. I guess he's a mongrel like me.

On my way home, I do a sweep of the flyers hanging in the vet's waiting rooms, grocery stores, and churches. Looking at the pictures of lost dogs, I think they're easier to find than missing children.

Halfway home, I remember the knife and rush to get it. The dogs press near me, hoping for supper. I shoo them away, explaining about the ungrateful woman. Yes, I know they don't understand me. I'm not stupid nor am I crazy. It's just nice to talk sometimes. And the big wolfhound (better than calling him a brute) peers at me with his intelligent gray eyes as if he does understand. He's sitting up—another good sign he'll be on his feet soon.

I find the knife, clean the blood off and hurry to the pawn shop before it closes.

"Stolen?" Max asks, examining the weapon. The silver blade gleams in the fluorescent light. The pawn shop smells of engine oil and mold.

"Found it," I say.

"Uh-huh." Max sucks his teeth while he thinks, making slurping sounds that crawl over my skin like lice. "Cheap metal, imitation leather handle . . . I'll give you ten for it."

Never accept the first offer. It's crap.

"It does have a nice design . . . how about fifteen," Max says.

"That blade's got silver in it. A hundred bucks at least."

He gasps and pretends to be horrified. It's all an act and all I want is to go back to my pups. In the end, Max gives me sixty dollars. Enough for a fifty-pound bag of Science Diet and a couple packs of ground beef. I carry the bag over my shoulder. It's getting dark and I'm almost home when I figure I've been followed.

A quick check confirms a man is trailing me, but I keep going. Not that the others will help me. They'll disappear as fast as the ground beef in my bag. Not like this hasn't happened before. I might be invisible to most people. And despite the smell of dog and layers of grim, the strays of society still find me. At eighteen, I'm young for a street person, and high school boys, college boys, and even foster fathers can't resist. My scent attracts them just like a bitch in heat.

The curse of developing early and curvy. My foster father called me beautiful. He named the dog Beauty, but never bothered her the way he did me. Lucky bitch.

I reach my spot and my pups. Too bad the big wolfhound is too weak to stand. Dropping the bag, I grab the metal baseball bat a kid left at the park and wait for the stranger. As long as the guy isn't armed, me and my lot'll do just fine.

Wearing khaki pants, brown loafers, and a long wool coat, the guy resembles a lost professor. As he nears, the wolfhound pokes his head out from under the blanket and growls deep in his chest.

The man takes his hands from his pockets. "Hello?" he calls all friendly like.

But my pups' hackles are up.

"I was hoping you could help me," he says, stepping closer. "I'm looking for my dog. Someone reported seeing him in this area."

Bullshit. I wait as his gaze scans the mutts and lingers on the baseball bat in my hands.

He tries a smile. "He's quite large."

"Haven't seen him," I say. "Go away."

"Are you sure?" He keeps coming.

I raise the bat. "Yep." By now all the dogs are growling.

He is unconcerned. "Settle your dogs."

"No."

He is close enough to see the wolfhound. They exchange a glance and it reminds me of two competitors acting nice until the game starts.

"Settle them or I will." His right hand pulls out a gun. He aims it at me.

A bone chilling cold seizes my heart. "Quiet," I order. They're familiar with this command. It's the first thing I teach a new pup. They sit down on all fours and wait without making a sound.

"Drop the bat," he says.

I let it clang to the ground.

The man tries to comfort me. "I'm just here for my dog."

Yet the wolfhound doesn't seem happy to see him. Go figure. Now the guy is under the bridge and the hound lurches to his feet. The dog's massive jaws are level with my chest. The blanket remains on his back like a superhero's cloak.

The man shakes his head as if he's amazed. "How many near misses, Logan? Four? Five? Only you would find some homeless person to nurse you back to health. Too bad I found you first."

And people call *me* the crazy dog lady.

He turns to me and says, "His injuries are too extensive, I'll have to put him down." He aims the gun at the wolfhound.

The urge to protect one of mine is instant and hot. "Wait," I say. "Can you take the blanket off him? It's my only one and I don't want it full of holes and blood."

The man laughs. "I see your charm with the ladies remains the same," he says to the wolfhound. He's careful to keep the gun out of the dog's reach as he pulls the cover off.

My pups are well trained. And while being quiet is important, I've taught them protecting my stuff is essential. They hop to their feet and attack his ankles and calves with their pointy little teeth. He yells. I scoop up my bat and slam it down on the man's arms. The gun fires, but no yelps so I swing again and again until he drops the gun. Until he rolls on the ground, shielding his body from my bat.

I taste the desire to pound him until he's a pile of broken bones and bloody meat. Coming here and thinking he can just take what he wants. Just like my foster father sneaking into my bedroom. But this stranger isn't him, so I pull myself together and call my dogs off.

"Go away," I say to the man.

The man staggers to his feet, but his gaze is on the wolfhound. Odd, considering *I'm* the one holding the bat.

"Next time I won't come alone," he says to the wolfhound before limping away.

That's bad. I look at the wolfhound. "Does he mean it?"

I swear the dog nods a yes. Okay so maybe I am the crazy dog lady. I pick up the gun and unload it as I think. If I hock it, I'd have money, but no weapon. The bullets are shiny silver. Living on the street, I've seen my fair share of guns and bullets, but these are special. Expensive, too.

We could move before he comes back. But that rankles. Nobody's gonna run me off my spot.

"How many will come with him?" I ask the hound. "Two?"

A shake—no.

"Three? . . . Four? . . . Five?"

Five. Shit. "When? Tomorrow morning? . . . Afternoon? . . . Night?" *Yes* to the night. I've a day to plan, but the wolfhound gives me a decisive nod (yep, this confirms the crazy), and he takes off. Well, he tries. Poor boy stumbles after two strides. The knife damaged his muscles and he's still weak. He also ripped his stitches.

Half carrying him, I bring him back and fix him.

"Look," I say. "I didn't spend all that time and energy on you to see you throw it away, trying to be noble. You're part of mine now and I protect mine."

A day isn't much time so I'm at the Humane Shelter's door as soon as it opens.

"Hey, Mongrel." Lily greets me with a smile. "Find another pup?"

She's filling bowls with generic dog food (such a shame!). I help her feed her charges. Excited barks and yips ring through the metal cages. Lily's the only normal person I talk to on a regular basis.

"Not today."

"Take a look at the flyers. There's a black Lab missing. Owner's are offering a hundred dollar reward."

Lily saw my face. "I can be your go between and make sure you get the money," she says.

"How did you know?"

"Police came yesterday asking questions about you. They thought you have a dognapping scheme going on."

So much for earning money that way. "What did you tell them?"

"The truth. You're better at finding lost dogs than anybody in town. That you're providing a service to this city and should be paid."

Lily is good people. "Thanks. Now I really hate to ask you for a favor."

She straightens and looks at me as if I just told her the sky is orange. "In the two years I've known you, you've never asked for anything. If I can, I will. Ask away."

I blink at her a moment. Didn't she want anything in exchange? She insists not and I make an unusual request which she grants. Did I tell you Lily's good people? Well she is.

After a stop at the pawn shop, I take my littles to Pennypack Park—a tiny snake of green in the middle of the city. I find a nice safe place for them, ordering them to stay quiet. They're handy against one intruder, but against five, one of them is bound to get hurt.

I return to the wolfhound about an hour after sunset. He's alert with his nose sniffing the cold breeze. Somehow, I know the professor and his goons aren't going to arrive with the wind, so I sit close to Logan and keep watch downwind. The others are nowhere in sight. That homeless sixth sense accurate once again.

As I wait, my heart is chasing its tail, running fast and going nowhere. It's not too long before five black shapes break from the shadows and approach. They're easy to see in the bright moonlight.

My insides turn gooey, but I draw in a breath. Nobody messes with mine. Not anymore. I stand as they slink toward me. No, I'm not being dramatic. Slink is the perfect word. Five big brutes just like Logan. Massive jaws and shaggy hair. The professor isn't in sight, but a tawny wolfhound leads the group (give him two pairs of loafer's and he'd fit the part of the professor).

Now you're gonna to tell me something like this just doesn't happen, and I'd agree with you every other night. But not tonight.

The pack fans out, and I've seen enough street fights to know if they surround me I'm dead. I raise the gun, aim, and fire. I'm a pretty good shot. Thanks in part to my foster father. Unlike all the others before him, he'd taught me a few life skills and I'd loved him until . . . well, you know.

The tranquillizer dart hits the shoulder of the far left hound. (If you thought I'd shoot them with bullets, then you haven't been paying attention).

I squeeze off a couple more darts, picking off two more wide receivers before the remaining two catch on and rush me. Dropping the gun, I palm a dart in one hand and pull the silver knife I reclaimed from the pawn shop, exchanging it for the lost professor's gun.

Then it's all hair, claws, and teeth. The wolfhounds are fast and it's like fighting a giant yet silent dust devil. I jab the dart into dog flesh and strike, stab, and slash at anything I can reach with the knife. The tawny grabs my wrist with his teeth while his last goon is overcome by the tranquilizer.

Tawny bites through my skin like it's paper. I yell and drop the weapon. He pushes me over and stands on my chest. Breathing with his weight on me is an effort, and my heart lodges in my throat. He stares at me for a second with regret in his gaze, giving me just enough time to thrust my arm between his sharp teeth and my exposed neck.

A bit of surprise flashes in his black eyes as he latches on. I'd coated my sleeves and pants with Tabasco sauce. Useful for keeping pups from chewing things. In this case, not so smart as the burn makes Tawny angrier. The pressure increases in my forearm and I'm convinced my bone's about to snap in two when the brute is knocked off.

Logan and Tawny roll together. And the fight's no longer silent as they growl and snarl. I worry about Logan's shoulder as I dive for the tranquilizer gun. Lily showed me how to wrap up his leg to support his weight, but it's not much.

I'm outta darts. With Logan injured, the fight isn't fair. Most things aren't. And I guess that's the only way Tawny can win.

I spot a glint just when Tawny pins Logan. Sweeping up the knife, I lunge toward Tawny and bury the blade in his hindquarters. Up to the hilt.

He yelps and bucks. Logan presses his advantage and regains his feet. In a blur, Logan strikes and silences Tawny. Logan's muzzle is dripping with blood. I meet his gaze and can tell by his expression that he's sickened and sad. He's not a killer, but Tawny forced him to be one. Why couldn't he just leave Logan alone?

I'd asked my foster father the same thing. He said I was too irresistible so I ran away when I turned sixteen, removing the temptation. I'd thought I was smart, but no one knows about his inability to resist. It's been two years. What if he has a new foster child? Staring at Tawny's ripped throat, I realize a person has to stay and fight until there's a clear winner and loser or else you're problems don't ever go away.

The burning pain in my arm snaps me back to my current problems. I inspect the damage. Ragged, bleeding flesh too mangled for eighty-proof and Band-Aids, but I don't have another option. Once Logan's cleaned up—his stitches have ripped again—and hidden under the blanket, I hurry to the Humane Shelter.

Lily's working late and I suspect she's there for me. She sends a couple volunteers to pick up the sleeping wolfhounds. I return the tranquilizer gun.

"A pack of wild dogs that are all the same breed is so unusual," she says. "Usually they're a bunch of mongrels." She slaps her hand over her mouth. "I didn't mean—"

I smile. "I know. Nothing wrong with mongrels."

Lily sees my arm and insists I go to the emergency room. I almost laugh. Invisible on the streets, I'm nonexistent in an ER. No money. No insurance. They'd fix a cockroach's broken leg before attending to me. I lie and say I'll go, but she sees right through me. Despite my protests, she escorts me to the ER and stays until I'm seen. The ER doctor gives me thirty-two stitches. Funny how the number of stitches is always reported like it's a source of pride.

By the next day, my life returns to, well, not normal, but back to the same—taking care of the pups. Logan is healing faster than me and eating like a horse. I feed him my share most days. Don't matter to me, my stomach's upset anyways. Tomorrow—one week after I found Logan—I'm gonna tell the authorities about my foster father.

I'd rather face a pack of wild dogs, but I'm determined to grab the man by the throat and not let go, finally doing what I should have done two years ago.

Five days later, Logan takes off and doesn't return. The hurt cuts deep and reminds me of how I'd felt moving from one foster home to another. Crazy lady that I am, I'd been talking to him about the police and the lawyers and the questions. No one is quick to believe me, and I don't have much proof so it's been rougher than I thought. Somehow telling my problems to Logan made the whole ordeal bearable.

But he's gone, and my resolve to go after my foster father wavers. But there is also a tiny bit of relief inside me. Keeping the wolfhound fed was hard. And with one of life's little twists of fate and timing, I find the missing black Lab after Logan left. Lily handles the reward money. Without Logan to feed, there's plenty of money to keep my pups in Science Diet.

Three—maybe four weeks after the night I helped Logan, a stranger enters the parking lot. Wearing blue jeans and a leather motorcycle jacket, he doesn't hesitate, heading right for my bridge. His black hair hangs in layers to his shoulders, and his stride is familiar.

I'm searching my memories to place him when my pups race toward him. Good. Except they don't bite him. They dance around, tails wagging and yipping in excitement. He crouches down and pets them! I grab my bat.

He glances up as I swing and dodges the bat with ease. Strike one. I pull back for another.

"Mongrel, stop," he says. "It's me."

I freeze and study him. He's a few years older than I am, about six feet tall and lean. Good looking enough to attract the girls. His gray eyes don't belong in the face of a man though.

He opens his jacket, and pulls his collar down, showing me an almost healed scar on his right shoulder. "Fifteen stitches."

I lower the bat. "Logan."

"Yep."

He moves closer and I back up. Logan pauses. "You weren't afraid of five werewolves, but you're scared of me?"

Werewolves. Saying the word out loud made it real. Before I could explain them away as really smart mixed breeds.

"Guess I'm better at trusting . . . werewolves than men," I say.

"One man dooms the whole species?"

"What about the guy . . . wolf after you?"

"He wanted to be in charge."

"And that's my point. Dogs . . . or wolves'll fight it out. One dominates and the other slinks away. The human side of him tried to cheat. Right?"

Logan says nothing.

"He used a knife and then returned with a gun. Very un-wolf like behavior."

"Let me prove to you we're not all bastards."

"Why?"

"You saved my life three times."

I tap the bat against my leg. "So buy me a couple bags of Science Diet and we'll call it even."

"No. I owe you much more than that."

He's serious and I suspect stubborn as well. "Go away, Logan. You don't belong here," I say.

"Neither do you."

I huff and squash the sudden desire to take another swing at his head. He thinks my silence is an agreement 'cause he's now standing a foot away. And my heart's acting like it's scared. I expect him to crinkle his nose at the smell of dog on my clothes or for him to try to hide his disgust at my unkempt appearance.

Instead he takes my hand in his and pushes my right sleeve up with his other one, exposing the jagged purple scars on my wrist and forearm. I didn't heal as fast or as well as his did. Logan traces them with a finger.

A strange teeter-totter of emotions fills me. My first impulse is to flinch away from his touch, but his familiar scent triggers fond memories of the big wolfhound I cared for.

Logan taps his thumb on my arm. "You've been bitten by a werewolf deep enough for his saliva to mix with your blood."

"So?"

He quirks a smile. "You accepted our existence with ease, yet you don't know the legends."

I gesture to his shoulder. "I believe what I see."

"You've been infected, but one bite isn't enough to change you into a werewolf." All humor is gone as he stares at me with a sharp intensity. "For you to become one of us, a bite from two different werewolves within a month is required."

He turns my arm over, revealing the light underside. His canines elongate. "I've never offered this to anyone, and it's a hell of a way to repay your kindness, but it seemed . . . right. Interested?"

My mind races. He's giving me a choice. "What about my pups?"

Another smile. "Only you would think of them first. They can stay with you."

"Here?"

"No. My pack has a network of places. We try and keep a low profile, but we'll support you in going after your foster father."

"Why?"

"Because you'll be part of mine and I protect mine."

I grin at the familiar words.

Logan adds, "It's not an easy life, and there is no cure. No going back. We don't belong to the human world or the wolf world."

"So you're a bunch of mongrels?"

"Yep."

"Then I'll fit right in." I raise my arm to his mouth, and he sinks his teeth into my flesh.

DEADFALL

KAREN EVERSON

My name is Olwen Ap Howell, and I am the last of a very old family.

That in itself is nothing special, I know. The American South is full of Old Families. People boast ancestors antebellum, revolutionary, colonial, lineage that traces back to English or European nobility. My family has its roots in legend, but I learned pretty quickly I had to keep quiet about it. Old families have their particular rules and expectations, here where tradition still casts long shadows. My family's traditions are cloaked in secrets, and they throw shadows longer and stranger than most.

Secrets are tough for young kids. Mom drinks, or Dad lost his job. . . . Try "My Dad can turn into a wolf." It gets more entertaining when *you* can turn into a wolf. You can't share that, not even with your Best Friend in the Whole Wide World.

There are variations on the theme. Do not let anyone outside the Family see you Change into a wolf. Before you Change, hide your clothes, so they will still be there when you Change back.

Always remember where you hid your clothes.

Never, ever Run on an empty stomach. You may eat something you'll regret later.

The rule I was thinking of breaking was another important one: The family does *not* deal with its enemies by trying to eat them.

Okay, I wasn't really planning to eat anybody, but I knew that what I did want to do was a Bad Idea. I couldn't bring myself to care. I didn't see any way I could endanger my grandfather with what I was planning, and he was all the Family I had left. There was a limit to how severely I could be disciplined for my actions—after all, I was the Last Ap Howell. I belonged to the land, Blood-Oathed by my ancestors who had founded this town. I was *necessary*.

So was action on my part. Rob Merrow and his two friends had badly hurt someone I cared about, and they had gotten away with it. What went deeper than my sense of outraged justice, and what I would never have admitted to anyone, was that Rob had given me my first taste of true physical fear, and a vision of my future that had left me shaken and sick. I wanted to return the favor.

That night was my chance. Word had come through the high school grapevine that Rob and his crew were laying claim to the Deadfall. With the reputation they had, no one else would venture anywhere near the place. I would have them to myself, in the night and the forest. I would not be a prisoner inside my human skin, the way I had been when Rob and his crew jumped 'Rion and me.

The sun was well down when I crossed my private Rubicon, the dirt lane that separated my Family's safely fenced private acres from the wild forest that still covered so much of our small town's land. I hurried into the protecting shadows, heart thumping. I could already feel the wolf-fire turning my eyes to hot gold, the prick of canines growing longer and sharper in my soft human mouth. I could have held the Change back, but I was eager for my other self, my swift silence and sharp teeth. Sheltered by trees and a dense clump of dogwood I began shedding clothes, stuffing them into the pack I carried. My shoes went in on top and I just had time to hide the pack before the wolf rolled me under.

The world, all sense of time and place, was lost in the roil of the Change. There's no real pain, but there is a moment that feels like drowning, of being lost in an element so foreign that survival seems impossible. From that chaos the Self bursts out like birth, flesh or fur, into a world rendered new. Touch told me less of fine texture, more of substructure that meant silence or sound beneath my paws. Sight told less of color and detail and more of mass and movement. Scent was multiplied and magnified into a revealed language of enormous complexity.

I lifted my nose. The spring breeze brought me the scent of the James River, even though it was ten miles distant. The Deadfall was near the river. A few miles was no matter. I set out in the wolf's easy hunter's lope, the night and vengeance stretched out before me.

The Deadfall was the name given to a forest clearing, older than I was, made when an enormous, ancient oak had been felled by lightning. The clearing had quickly become a beacon for the young. It was an easy hike from the road, but deep enough into the forest that even campfires were not readily visible. Lightning had struck the trunk seven feet from the ground, and the massive, ragged stump formed a kind of shelter, the humped roots a natural cluster of seats and tables, some of which had been whittled and carved to better serve those purposes. The enormous trunk sloped from the top of the stump for yards before coming to rest on the forest floor. A tarp tossed over the trunk and staked on either side made a satisfactory tent. Dogwood, wild rose, and redbud bordered the clearing, beautiful in the spring, but human use had kept the center clear of brush and saplings.

Rumor had it that the Deadfall had been a lovers' trysting place at first, then a camping spot. For my own generation it had a more sinister reputation. Gangs like Rob and his crew gathered there to drink or do drugs or settle disputes with fists or knives. Other people stayed away then, unless they were looking for trouble.

I was looking to make trouble, so that was fine.

Rob and his friends were already drunk and noisy. I was careful anyway, but sneaking up on them was easy. I could have done it even in human shape. All three had their backs against the huge stump of the Deadfall, a good six-to-seven feet tall and at least that wide. The fallen trunk, still hanging from the top of the stump, stretched away like a broken gate to their right. It was easy to angle myself so that I could track them through the gap between the trunk and the ground. Their small fire deepened the shadows for me to hide in while it spoiled their night vision. Their firewood was too green to burn cleanly, putting up thick coils of smoke. My nose sorted the thick, layered scents of their camp: several kinds of burning wood, sharp sap and sharper lighter fluid, Wild Turkey and Budweiser, and the funk of sweat and piss.

The stink of their flesh and the sudden blare of their laughter nearly undid me, flooding me with memories so visceral that I shrank down onto the forest floor, nearly shocked backed into a girl. I bellied into the punk beneath the trunk of the Deadfall, shivering, holding tight to my wolf-shape while human memories rocked me, breathing deep the smell of ancient wood and damp humus while I remembered the stink of blood and violence.

They'd been waiting for us, Rob and his followers Lee and Jeth, hiding in the woods along a lonely stretch of Old Route 15. It was a road we'd walked together since grade school, me and Orion and his older sister Athena. But Athena had graduated and gone north to college to study pre-med. That left just 'Rion and me, a black boy with a white girl, walking and talking alone together.

I didn't see much. There was a rush of motion when they jumped us, a rustle of grass and weeds against jean-clad legs, a muffled pounding of feet against the green verge. I had a glimpse of Rob's face, grotesque with excitement, the bigger forms of Lee and Jeth flashing past, going for 'Rion. Then I was down, my face forced into the dirt and gravel of the road's shoulder. My nose crushed sideways and soaked the dirt with blood. I could barely turn my head enough to get a breath. My right arm was pinned under my ribs, and Rob was gripping my left arm in both fists, using my own arm to hold my face in the dirt. Pain warred with outrage and disbelief. I was Olwen Ap Howell! My grandfather employed half the town. Bullying trash-talk was one thing—that was just high school. But I had never thought anyone would dare touch me, *hurt* me.

Rob had his full weight on me, and I couldn't move. Even through my slacks and his tatty jeans I could feel his erection as he ground his hips against my buttocks. "Did I break your nose, bitch?" he growled in my ear. "Let's see you look down your nose at a real white man with your pretty face all messed up. You Ap Howells, sitting on your pile of money, thinking you're so much better than everybody else. Does the old man know you're screwin' the nigger help?" He pulled back on my arm and smashed it as hard as he could into the back of my head. I screamed and choked against the dirt.

He kept talking, all the things that Rob thought a "man" like him should be teaching me, but what was worse than the filth and pain and the struggle for breath were the sounds and the stink of what Jess and Lee were doing to 'Rion. He'd fought them, probably hurt them some, but they'd taken him down, and I could hear the thud of fists and feet hitting flesh and bone. Even with my own blood filling my nose and mouth with coppery fire, I could still smell my friend's blood. Even with Rob panting in my ear I could hear the grunts and gasps of pain 'Rion tried to hold in. Then there was the crack of bone breaking, and finally, 'Rion screamed. Rob and his friends hooted with laughter, as if that high, helpless noise was the best joke they'd ever heard.

Then I was fighting myself, fighting my wolf, all my training telling me to keep my Family's secret instead of defending myself and 'Rion. I fought, too, because part of me knew, if I loosed my wolf in the midst of all that pain and blood, I would kill all three of them.

A car saved all of us. Rob and the others ran. The driver—a black woman—stopped for 'Rion and me, took us home, where I lived and 'Rion's mother, Iris, worked.

Grandfather took one look at my face, grabbed my nose and pulled it out straight. He didn't say a word, and I bit off my shriek. We heal fast—but that doesn't mean broken bones won't knit crooked if they aren't set straight in time. I had cuts and bruises all over my face and body, but I was what I was, and I as I washed blood and grit from my wounds they were already beginning to heal.

'Rion was the one who had suffered. He was cut and bruised all over, with two black eyes and a split and swollen lip. They'd broken his left arm and cracked some ribs. He gave me one look that told me to keep silent, and refused to say a word about who had hurt him until the doctors at the clinic were done with him and we were all home again.

"We're not pressing charges," he told his mother and my grandfather calmly. They argued, but he held firm. "If we take this to court it will only make things worse. The parents won't think their kids did anything wrong. It'll be like when you promoted Dad." That shut even Grandfather up. Grandfather had promoted 'Rion's dad over several white workers who thought one of them should have had the job. There were mutters of favoritism, among other things, and both our houses had been vandalized. A few months later, at the start of deer hunting season, 'Rion's dad had been found dead in the woods, an "apparent hunting accident."

"It's only a few months until I graduate," 'Rion said. "I'll hang back when we're walking home, so it won't look like Olwen and I are together. I already talked to 'Thena and she says I can move in with her as soon as I'm done with school." He looked down, unable to meet his mother's eyes, or mine. But his voice was hard and bitter, and left no doubt of his intent. "Let the bastards think they've won. Who cares? I'll be out of here, out of this God-forgotten town for good. Them? They're too stupid and too ignorant to even know they're trapped."

His words hit like a blow to the stomach. I wrapped my arms around myself turned away, trying to hide my shaking and the tears that started in my eyes. I don't know why, but I had always though 'Rion would stay, even after 'Thena left. Or maybe he—maybe we—would go away to school, but we'd come back. We'd grown up like brother and sister, but we weren't brother and sister. I'd thought maybe our friendship might grow into something more when we got older. I thought that, no matter what, 'Rion would be one person who would stay here and help me make this town *better*.

It came home to me that I was trapped, too, not because I was stupid or ignorant or poor, but because I was an Ap Howell.

I could never leave. I could travel, even go away for school, at least as long as Grandfather was still alive. But my ancestors had blood-oathed our family to this town, to this land. It was, it always would be, the center of the compass of my life. I didn't blame my many-greats grandparents for what they'd done. I'd read their accounts, knew that most of a Welsh village had followed them here to Virginia. They'd wound up on an uninhabited stretch of the James River, their resources exhausted.

My grandparents went into the forest alone. They begged the spirits to guide them to a place where their folk might take a living from the land. In return, they made an offering of their own blood and the blood of their descendants, pledging that we would watch over the land and the folk they brought to it.

They called it Landfair. It had everything the spirits promised—timber, fertile topsoil, and underground waters that called the dowser's rods and filled wells with deep, cold water. There were beds of a fine clay for pottery, and, at last, on the piece of ground my grandparents had claimed for themselves, the best slate in the county. It had been nearly two hundred years, and the land still gave a living. And we gave it us.

Me.

It must have seemed well worth it, when the place was new, before inbreeding and the ills of time and place ate away at it. It's still a pretty place. But it's become a place where too many people cling to ignorance as though it's something to be proud of, a place those graced with intelligence and ambition only want to *leave*—as Athena had, as 'Rion would.

While people like Rob stayed, to poison what was left.

Rage rose in me like a cleansing wind. I lifted my wolf's head, from the forest floor, my ears flattened to damp the noise of their boasting and laughing. I turned my mind to my purpose.

I wanted to scare them, hurt them, but not at risk to myself. I knew my quarry would not have come to the forest unarmed. There were few local households that did not possess at least one gun. Most boys owned a shotgun or a rifle of their own before they hit puberty, and a gun was a practical precaution against the feral dog packs that roamed the area. Rob was the leader of this pack of thugs. He would have brought a gun as symbol of his status. The other two would have switchblades or hunting knives. I was fast—here, in this forest, supernaturally fast—so the blades did not worry me too much. But the gun had to go. It may be that there are Shifters out there who can only be harmed by silver. I'm not one of them.

I crouched in the shadows and let eyes and nose search, until I was certain there was only one single shotgun, a melange of oil and rust, steel and gunpowder, lying carelessly among the empty beer bottles. It looked old and smelled badly kept, but that didn't mean it wouldn't work.

My mother had never found her wolf, but she had come to us a witch. I had inherited her sensitivities with the stronger gifts of the wolf. The Deadfall whispered to me, heavy with the potential for magic. The ground had been fed with lightning, semen, and blood, and those powers had knotted themselves into the deep, secret history of the ancient roots, the centuries of summer leaves that had fallen and been turned to loam. I called on my blood-bond with the land and took a little of that potency into myself, the raw power stoking the magic that ran ancient and deep in my blood.

I was shadow silent, so swift across the clearing that only Lee startled. Then I was gone, a brindled darkness beneath the heavy branches of a moon-flowered dogwood, the gun in my jaws. I dropped it where the shadows were deepest, buried it with dirt and leaves.

"What was that?" Lee said uneasily. "I saw something."

"Squirrel, or a rabbit, maybe." Rob said. "Nothing that matters. Everybody knew we were gonna be here. Nobody'll mess with us."

"We will fear no evil, 'cause we are the meanest sons-of-bitches in the valley," Jeth laughed. Jeth was smart enough, but he was a follower, a perfect mark for Rob's stronger personality. "Relax, Lee. Have another beer."

"I saw something, and it wasn't no damn squirrel," Lee muttered. He took the beer Jeth tossed him, but his eyes moved uneasily over the shadows. Kinder people in town called Lee "slow." The more sharp-tongued said his mama had dropped him on his head one too many times. But he wasn't too stupid to know when he was the brunt of a joke, and he was big enough and strong enough to ensure that people didn't make fun of him more than once. I thought there was more to him than people gave him credit for. Maybe school gave him trouble, but he trusted his own eyes.

I ghosted around behind them, considering. Maybe I couldn't make them feel the humiliation 'Rion and I had suffered, but I could give them a taste of the terror we had felt, and the pain. My gift did not carry in my bite. Let them feel my teeth.

I lifted my muzzle and howled, putting into the sound all my rage and all my loss.

The night answered.

One of the wild dog packs, I thought—one of the reasons I was forbidden the forest beyond my Family's protection. But my throat was full again even as I thought it, vibrating with the strange double harmony of the wolf, that quality that makes a pack of six sound like a score, and a score like a hundred. And again, I was answered.

The boys were cursing steadily now. Rob was scrambling on hands and knees, searching for the gun among the empties and not finding it. Lee had pulled a branch from their small campfire and was thrusting at the shadows shaped by the jumping flame. Jeth gripped a six-inch hunting knife, trying to look everywhere at once. "Dammit, Rob, get the fucking gun!"

"I can't find it!"

"Rob," Lee hissed, "we got company."

Eyes began to shine in the darkness between the trees.

Instinct carried me, a long leap up onto the highest point of the fallen giant oak. My fur bristled to make me look larger, my tail high and bushed as I growled. *My place. My prey.* Growls answered me, and the pack leaders slipped into the ring of firelight.

There were two of them, Dobermans, tails and ears chopped to stubs. I knew them for dangerous animals. They'd killed pets and food animals, even attacked people, and had evaded several attempts to hunt them down. Once they'd guarded a junkyard. One day the owner had locked the gate and walked away, leaving the two dogs to starve or survive on rats and rainwater. They'd escaped. Half-feral already, before long they led a pack of desperate, discarded hounds and mongrels, turning them as vicious as they were.

The three boys had frozen; if they had run, the feral pack would have given chase. Dogs gone feral are far more dangerous than wild wolves—they've learned that without their weapons, men are easy prey. Rob was crouched in the dirt, his right hand clenched on a beer bottle, his face pale and sweating in the wan light. Lee was crouched so close to the fire he was almost in it, and Jeth and his knife were trying to become one with the tree trunk. They weren't going anywhere.

I jumped down, landing lightly, answering the challenge presented by the Dobermans with a display of size and dominance. They were litter mates who worked as a team, but I was a big wolf, 110 pounds, in good condition and perfect health. They were thin, ridden with parasites and poorly healed wounds.

They were also experienced fighters. They could have torn me to shreds, but they didn't know that.

I was a born Alpha. I had come into my wolf when I was eleven, at the first breath of puberty, without rite or ritual. Maybe I had never fought in earnest, but my father and grandfather had run with wild wolves, and they had taught me how to bluff.

I skinned my lips back from my teeth, subtly longer and sharper than a natural wolf's, stretched toes set with claws more like those of a bear than a wolf. Magic sang in my blood. *See me! I am terrible and beautiful and wise. Accept me, and my power will be added to yours, and all that runs will fall before us.*

The thinner of the Dobermans whined and dropped his head and tail, and then the other. One by one the pack stepped out—bluetick and coonhounds, a shepherd mix, and four of the dingo-like mixes that wild dogs seemed to breed back to—with heads and eyes dropped in submission. A good-sized pack, hunters all—and mine.

I swelled with the knowledge. For tonight, at least, I *did* have a pack, a pack who knew what it was to hunt and to kill. The Dobermans, I knew, would not hesitate at human prey. They had been headed that way on their own.

One of the Dobermans shifted his eyes behind me, and snarled.

I turned faster than the eye could see. I felt, I *knew*, that I was all that I had promised the pack. I was beautiful and terrible, my mane a nimbus, my eyes molten, my white teeth gleaming in that wet snarl that promises mayhem. The sight of me fixed Rob to the earth like a beetle pinned to a board, his eyes wide with terror.

The pack began to move, shadows with firelight gleaming in their eyes, closing ranks around me, asking with each movement, with the lips skinned back from yellow teeth, *Is this the hunt? Is this the kill?*

I stared at Rob, clutching his stupid bottle, and knew he was mine to take.

This is my place! I thought at him. *This is my forest. This is my town! You hurt somebody under my protection, somebody good and kind and intelligent. I think you'll go on hurting people until somebody stops you.*

I can stop you. Here. Tonight.

I think I will.

I took a step, one step, and felt the pack tense around me, as if each hunter was an extension of my will. Was this what it was like, to run with the wild ones, to lead the hunt that was life and death? The three who had hurt Orion, who had driven him away, could die, right here, tonight. My tracks would be lost in the tracks of the pack, the tearing of my teeth and claws lost in so many wounds. Even my grandfather would not know, not for sure.

Rob Merrow looked into my eyes, and pissed himself.

"Oh, God," he moaned. He'd dropped the bottle. His hands were raised in supplication. "Not me. Please. Take them, not me."

He stank of fear. 'Rion had been afraid, too, had screamed when his arm snapped. But he hadn't been afraid like this. Not like this.

Was this the bully on whom I had wasted so much hate? He was not worth hunting. Not worth the kill.

The thought shocked me. I hadn't come here to kill. Had I?

A world without Rob could only be a better place. But Rob and Lee and Jeth were no threat to me, not here and now. It was one thing to kill in immediate defense of myself or of another. But murder was murder, even on four feet.

I couldn't use this pack, *my pack*, to work a vengeance that was entirely my own. Maybe it was only a matter of time before the Dobermans, at least, went after a human being. But if I made them kill for me tonight, every person who could carry a gun would be out here, shooting anything on four legs. The wild dogs, too, were mine, like the forest, like the town, and tonight they had come to me of their own will. I owed them better.

And Rob and Lee and Jeth would become martyrs of a sort, their cruelty and their bigotry whitewashed, buried under flowers and candle wax. I owed Orion better than that. I owed myself better.

Stories and movies about werewolves always make the beast the killer. It kills without reason, without remorse, driven by blood lust.

It's so easy to blame the wolf. But I understood then what the Family chronicles had been trying to teach me. The werewolf is dangerous because the wolf is a *weapon*—murder without apparent motive, the ultimate misdirection.

Bloodlust is *human*, not lupine. A wolf kills for food, for territory, or to protect the pack. I wasn't hungry. The land spoke to me through my flesh and blood, indisputably, forever mine, whether I liked it or not. And murder here would destroy the dog pack, and destroy my grandfather.

The meanest son-of-a-bitch in the school had just wet his pants at the sight of me. It would have to do.

I took a step back and howled. For a moment I felt the pack trembling around me, surprised, perhaps relieved. After a moment I felt them relax. Muzzles lifted, and we sang, voices tumbling over and over the boys who crouched frozen and ignored in the dirt.

Then I turned and lead the pack into the forest, where we ran and hunted the plentiful deer beneath the gibbous moon.

On Monday it seemed at first that the night at the Deadfall had never happened. Rob, Jeth, and Lee were hanging out in the hall as usual, where I'd have to pass them to get to my locker. There was an added opportunity for humiliation because Thomas, a boy I actually *liked*, was just a little down and across the hallway, stacking books for his morning classes.

On the other hand, I'd seen Rob cowering and terrified. I snugged that image up against me like a shield and continued down the hall.

"Who let the dog out," Rob sang, sniggering. He made woofing noises, then gave a poor imitation of a coyote howl.

Normally, I'd have hunched in on myself and scuttled down the hall to my locker. This time I just turned around and stared. I saw that neither Lee nor Jeth were wearing the sly, malicious grin that usually accompanied these little dominance displays. Jeth was looking at the floor. Lee's lip curled in disgust, but he was looking at Rob, not me. And I understood I'd gotten my revenge.

I'd exposed their leader as a coward. And if he was a coward, what were they, who had followed him? I'd broken Rob's hold. He wasn't harmless—no one who will use violence and stealth to make his point is ever harmless. But, here and now, I'd stolen much of his power.

He had been raised to think that being white and male made him better than anyone who wasn't. But even here, in this backwards Southern town, no black folks were going to step out of his path, and no girls of either color were going to want him just because their other options seemed worse.

Hell, he and his little crew had run from the young black woman who had stopped to help 'Rion and me. The thought made me grin.

Rob had noticed Lee and Jeth weren't backing him. His grin went sickly, then turned thin and hard. He glared at me, but his posture was hunched, defensive. "Bitch," he snarled at me, "what are you smiling at?"

Out of the corner of my eye I saw Thomas scowling, pushing his books back onto the shelf while his long hands curled into fists. Part of me really wanted to let him come to my rescue, just so I could smile gratefully up into his beautiful brown eyes. And it would be satisfying to see sweet, bookish Thomas, who was also six-four and ran track, mop the floor with Rob.

But that way lay heartbreak, I reminded myself. Thomas was smart and sweet, which meant in a year he'd be gone, just like 'Rion. So I handled it myself.

I walked up to Rob, still grinning. I pushed into his space, the way an alpha wolf can crowd a subordinate, dominating by the simple act of not being afraid. And even though he was six inches taller than me, he cowered. "I was just thinking," I said. "That if you are going to howl like that, you should at least do it right." And I tilted back my head, and howled.

It wasn't a proper wolf-howl, of course, but it was as close as a human throat can come.

And that whole noisy corridor went completely silent, as that sound rose up from me. Lee and Jeth went dead white, and for a moment I thought Rob was going to wet himself again. When I finished, I gave him a slow, satisfied smile. Then I walked away, feeling his eyes on me.

Just for a moment, I looked back, and let my eyes flash gold.

RED RIDING HOOD'S CHILD

N.K. JEMISIN

If Anrin had not needed to finish the hoeing, all might have gone differently. The blacksmith was a strong man and the walls of the smithy were thick. Not that the smith would have killed him—except perhaps accidentally, if he'd put up too much of a fight—but his future would have been set in the eyes of the villagers. Blood told, and they'd been waiting for Anrin's to tell since his birth. This was what happened instead.

"Come here, boy," said the smith. "I've something special to give you."

Anrin stopped hoeing the tailor's garden and obediently crossed the road to the smithy. "More work, sir?"

"No work," said the smith, turning from the doorway to reach for something out of sight. He returned with a big wooden bowl, which he held out to Anrin. "See."

And Anrin caught his breath, for the bowl held half a dozen strawberries.

"Lovely, aren't they? Got them from a nobleman traveler as payment. Came from the king's own hothouses, he swore. Have one."

They were the most beautiful strawberries Anrin had ever seen: plump, damp from washing, redder than blood. Entranced, he selected a berry—making sure it was small so that he would not seem greedy—and took a careful bite from its tip. To make it last he rolled it about on his tongue and savored the tart-sweet coolness.

"Lovely," the smith said again, and Anrin looked up into his wide smile. "If you come inside, you can have more. I have sugar, and even a bit of cream."

"No, thank you," Anrin said. He gazed wistfully at the strawberries, but then pointed toward the half-hoed garden. "Master Tailor will be angry if I don't finish."

"Ah," said the smith. "A pity. Well, you'd better get on, then."

Anrin bobbed his head in thanks and trotted back across the road to the garden. He'd finished the hoeing before it occurred to him to wonder why the smith, who had never been kind to him before, had suddenly offered him such a delicacy.

No matter, he told himself. The strawberry had been ever so sweet.

Once upon a time in a tiny woodland village there lived an orphan boy. As his mother had been less than proper in her ways—she died unwed, known well to several men—the villagers were not kindly disposed toward the tiny burden she left behind. They were not heartless, however. They reared young Anrin with as much tenderness as a child of low breeding could expect, and they taught him the value of honest labor so that he might repay their kindness before his mother's ways took root.

By the cusp of manhood—that age when worthier lads began to consider a trade and marriage—Anrin had become a youth of fortitude and peculiar innocence. The villagers kept him at arms' length from their homes and their hearts, so he chose instead to dwell within an eccentric world of his own making. The horses and pigs snorted greetings when he came to feed them, and he offered solemn, courtly bows in response. When the villagers sent him unarmed into the forest to fetch wood, he went eagerly. Alone amid the dappled shadows he felt less lonely than usual, and the trees' whispers were never cruel.

Indeed, Anrin's fascination with the forest was a source of great anxiety to the old woodcutter's widow who boarded him at nights. She warned him of the dangers: poison mushrooms and hidden pitfalls and choking, stinging ivies. And wolves, of course; always the wolves. "Stay on the path, and stay close to the village," she cautioned. "The smell of men keeps predators away . . . most of the time."

Old Baba had never lied to Anrin, so he obeyed—but in the evenings after his work was done, he sat atop the small hill near the old widow's cottage. There he could gaze out at the dark, whispering forest until she called him down to bed.

On one of those nights, with a late winter chill making the air brittle and thin, he heard a howl.

The next day began the same as always. At dawn he rose to do chores for Baba, and then he went from house to house within the town to see what needed doing.

But as Anrin came to the smithy, he noticed an odd flutter in his belly. His first thought was that he might've eaten something bad, or perhaps pulled a muscle. After a moment he realized that the sensation was not illness or injury, but dread. So startled was he by this—for he had never feared the villagers; they were too predictable to be dangerous—that he was still there, his hand upraised to knock, when the door opened. The smith's apprentice Duncas stood beyond, escorting another village man who held a new riding-harness. Both of them stopped at the sight of him, their expressions shifting to annoyance.

"Well?" Duncas asked.

"I came to see what chores the smith has," Anrin replied.

"He's busy." Beyond Duncas, Anrin saw the smith talking over a table with another customer.

"I'll come back tomorrow, then." Nodding politely to Duncas and the goodman, Anrin turned away to leave and in that moment felt another strange sensation: relief.

But he had other houses to visit and other work to do, and by sunset he had forgotten all about the moment at the smithy.

That evening Anrin again sat on the hilltop and looked out over the dark expanse of trees. This time he heard nothing but the usual sounds of night, though he found himself listening for the mournful cadence of wolfsong. He heard none—but as the waxing moon rose he thought he saw something move in the distance. He narrowed his eyes and made out a fleet dark form running low to the ground against the tree line.

"Come down, boy," Old Baba called up, and with a sigh Anrin gave up his darkgazing for the night.

Old Baba did not greet Anrin as she usually did when he reached the foot of the hill. Instead she gazed at him long and hard until he began to worry that he had done something to upset her.

"The gossips in the village are all a-whisper, Anrin," she said. "They say the smith offers you gifts."

Unnerved by her stare and the statement, Anrin said, "A strawberry, Baba. I would never have taken it if he hadn't offered."

"Did he ask anything in return?"

"No, Baba. He said I might have more if I came into the smithy, but I had other work. What's wrong? Are you angry with me?"

She sighed. "Not with you, child." After another moment's scrutiny, she took hold of his chin. "You are not quite a boy anymore."

The gesture surprised Anrin, for Baba had never been particularly affectionate with him, though she was never unkind either. He did not resist as she turned his face from side to side. "Such thick dark hair, such deep eyes . . . so like your mother. You've grown beautiful, Anrin, did you know that?"

Anrin shook his head. "The moon is beautiful, Baba. The forest is beautiful. I am neither."

"No, you're the same," she said. "Just as wild, and just as strange—but innocent, at least for now." She sighed almost to herself. "So many things out there would devour that innocence if they could."

"Things . . . in the forest, Baba?" Anrin frowned.

She smiled a little sadly and let him go. "Yes, child. In the forest. Now get to bed."

All through the next day, Anrin pondered the conversation with Old Baba. Should he have refused the smith's gift? Baba had denied being angry with him, but if not him then whom? The smith, perhaps . . . but why?

He had come to no conclusion by the time he finished bringing water to fill the leatherman's curing-cistern, and climbing trees to gather winter nuts for the trapper's wife. At sunset he wandered back to Baba's, intending to climb the hill again. But when the old woman's cottage came into view, the door was open with a familiar man's silhouette blocking the light from within. Voices drifted to him, sharp and angry on the chilly wind.

"—a fair price," the smith was saying. All but shouting, and Anrin saw that his nearby hand gripped the doorjamb so tightly that the wood groaned. "I'm generous even to offer. It's time the boy earned his keep!"

"Not like that," Baba's voice snapped from within. Anrin had never heard her so angry. "And you'll not take him either, not while I still have lungs that can shout and hands that can wield a pitchfork. Now get out!" And her gnarled hand shoved against his chest; when he stumbled back the door slammed in his face.

The peculiar flutter in Anrin's belly returned fourfold. He stepped off the dirt path that led to Baba's farm and crouched in the bushes. A moment later the smith passed by, muttering imprecations and swinging his great clenched fists. When he was gone, Anrin climbed out of the bushes. He considered going to the house to talk to Baba, but already the day had been too strange; he wanted no more of it. He went to the hill, climbed up, and sat there too troubled to find any of his usual comfort in the night.

"Anrin," Baba called after a while, and silently he went down to her.

Her lips were still tight with anger, though she said nothing of the smith's visit and he did not ask. Instead she took him by the shoulder and steered him toward the barn as they walked. "Before you go to work in the morning, Anrin, I want to talk to you. Not now, of course; you've had a long day."

"Yes, Baba," he said uneasily. He suspected she meant to speak of the smith. He would be able to ask her all the questions in his mind at last, he realized, but he was no longer certain he wanted to know the answers.

"Sleep well tonight, Anrin—and be sure to lock the barn door behind you."

Anrin blinked, for he had never locked the barn in all his years of sleeping there.

"Mind me, child," she said, pushing him into the barn. "Bolt it fast, and open it for no one before dawn."

He turned to her on the threshold, all the small disturbances of the past three days welling up inside him. He wanted to somehow vomit the strange feelings forth, expel them from his heart before they could poison him any further, but he could think of no way to do so.

She stood watching him, perhaps getting some inkling of his thoughts from his face; her own was softer than usual. She put a hand on his shoulder and he almost flinched as one more disturbance jarred him, for she had to reach up to touch him. Unnoticed, unmarked, he had grown taller than her.

"In case of wolves, child," Baba said. "Lock the door in case of wolves."

It was a lie, he sensed, but also a gift. Until morning, the lie would give him the comfort he needed.

He nodded and she let him go, turning to go back to her cottage. He watched until she was inside, then closed and locked the barn door.

Beyond them and unseen by either, a shadow crouched at the edge of the forest, only a few yards beyond Anrin's hill.

Late in the night Anrin heard the barn door rattle. He woke right away, for he had slept lightly, his dreams turbulent and incomprehensible. Quickly he climbed down from the barn loft and went to the door. "Is that you, Baba?"

There was a moment's silence from beyond. "It's not Baba, lad," came the smith's voice. "Open the door."

In Anrin's belly the little flutter rose to a steady beat, spreading foreboding through his soul like night-breezes through trees. "You have work for me, sir? So late?"

The smith laughed. "Work? Yes, lad, work. Now let me in."

"Old Baba told me not to."

"As you like," the smith said, but Anrin saw from the shadows under the door that the smith's feet did not move away. Instead the door began to rattle again, and Anrin remembered that the smith carried his tools with him always.

In the back of Anrin's mind, the night breezes rose to a sharp, cold gust.

There was a horse door at the back of the barn. Anrin went there and pushed aside the pickle-barrel that blocked it. If anyone had asked, he could not have told them why he fled. All he could think of was the smith's wide smile, and the sound of groaning wood, and the fear in Old Baba's eyes. These indistinct thoughts lent him strength as he wrestled the heavy, half-rusted latch open.

And then Anrin was free of the barn, running blindly into the bitter night. At his back he heard the smith's curse; the squeal of wood and metal; the querulous voice of Baba from within her cottage calling, "Who's there?" Into the forest, the night breezes whispered, and into the forest he ran.

When the boy fell, too weary and cold to run any further, the shadow closed in.

Anrin awoke in dim smoky warmth and looked about. A fire flickered at his feet; the roof of a cave loomed overhead. He turned and found that his head had been resting on the flank of a great forest wolf. Silently it watched him, with eyes like the winter sun.

Anrin caught his breath and whispered, "Beautiful."

Something changed in the wolf's golden eyes. After a moment, the wolf changed as well, becoming a man.

"You do not fear me," the wolf said.

"Should I?"

"Perhaps. You were nearly meat when I found you in the forest. I might eat you yet." The wolf rose from his sprawl and stretched from fingers to toes. Anrin stared in fascination. The wolf's body was broad and muscled, sleek and powerful, a model of the manhood that Anrin might one day himself attain. He stared also because had never seen a grown man unclothed before, and because Old Baba was not there to tell him to look away.

The wolf noticed Anrin's gaze and lowered his arms. "Do you still find me beautiful?"

"Yes."

The wolf smiled, flashing canines like knives. "Good." He crouched, leaning close to sniff at Anrin. "You are not like other men. They fear the forest and all things beyond their control. They are like two-legged, hairless sheep."

Anrin considered his lifetime among the villagers and found that he agreed. "Perhaps it is because I am a whore's son."

"What is a 'whore'?"

"I have never been certain. The villagers call my mother that when they think I cannot hear them. Old Baba tells me only that my mother was too curious and too free, straying too often from propriety. I don't see how that could be so terrible, since now it seems they want me to be like her."

"Yes," the wolf said. "That is the way of things." He leaned closer, sniffing at Anrin's hair, then his ear, then down the curve of Anrin's neck. Anrin remained submissive when the wolf took hold of his shoulders and pressed him back on the packed earth. He knew that animals often inspected one another on first meeting, checking for health and strength. As a guest in the wolf's den, he wanted to be polite.

"You are on the brink of a change," the wolf said, tugging Anrin's shirt open with his teeth. He sniffed at Anrin's chest, lapped in passing at one of Anrin's nipples. "You have felt it coming for some time now, I think. I have seen you sitting on the hilltop watching for it."

Anrin shivered at the brush of the wolf's nose against his skin. "I have been watching for nothing. Just the moon and the trees."

"In your head, perhaps. But your body has been watching for what will come. It has grown and made itself ready. Are you?"

"I don't know," Anrin said. This troubled him for reasons he could not name.

The wolf sat up on his haunches, straddling him now. Anrin saw that the wolf's skin was heavily furred with down. The wolf reached down to stroke Anrin's chest and Anrin felt the caress of fur on the wolf's palms as well. The sensation stirred yet another strange feeling within Anrin—something powerful for which he had no name. It was like the spike of fear that had shot through him when the smith came, and yet somehow entirely different.

"Others can smell your body's readiness as I can," the wolf said, his eyes gleaming in the dim light. "They will steal the change from you if you do not lay claim to it yourself. That is inevitable."

"But . . . I don't want to change," Anrin said. "Why can't I remain as I am?"

The wolf's hands paused. "Because innocence never lasts." Abruptly the wolf rose and went over to crouch by the fire, apparently losing interest. "But perhaps you are not yet ready."

Anrin sat up and pulled his shirt closed, his hair tumbling disheveled about his face and shoulders. The wolf spoke in riddles, and yet Anrin thought he understood. The answers he wanted were here, if he could only grasp them. If only he dared.

"What should I do?" he asked the wolf.

"That is for you to say—for now," the wolf said. "If you want to return to your village, follow the sun east. Take the bearskin in the corner since you have so little fur of your own."

So Anrin rose, wrapped himself in the bearskin, and went to the thick oiled-hide curtain which served as the cave's door. He paused at the threshold, but the wolf did not turn from the fire, and so Anrin stepped out into the light.

"When you grow tired of playing sheep," the wolf called as the flap closed behind him, "come back to me."

With his mind full of thoughts he had never pondered before, Anrin returned to the village.

But the smell of death was on the wind as Anrin stepped out of the trees.

It came from the barn, where the half-hinged door swayed like a drunkard in the noontime breeze. The creak of the hinge stuttered now and again as the door stopped against something lying across the threshold. A pitchfork, its tines dark and red at the tips. Beyond that lay Old Baba.

After gazing down at her body for a very long while, Anrin left the cottage and went back into the woods.

The sun had just set when Anrin found the wolf's den again. The wolf crouched beside the fire as if he had not moved since Anrin left. Anrin walked up to him and stopped, his fists clenched at his sides.

"Old Baba taught me there are secrets in the forest," Anrin said.

"That has ever been true," the wolf agreed.

"She told me there are things in the forest that eat fools like me."

"There are indeed," the wolf replied.

"Make me one of them," said Anrin, and the wolf turned to him and smiled.

When the wolf stood, Anrin saw that his body was different: still as muscular and powerful as before, but this time a part of the wolf had grown and now stood forth from his body unsupported. It was not the first time Anrin had seen such a thing—for his own body had done the same at times—but now at last he understood the why of the phenomenon, and what it implied for the immediate future. And this understanding in turn clarified the past: the smith's offer of the strawberry, and Old Baba's anger, and even the circumstances of Anrin's birth. Both the villagers and the wolf had been right all along: some things were inevitable, natural. Blood always told.

"You are still beautiful," he told the wolf.

"As are you," said the wolf, who then took Anrin's hand and laid him down on the bearskin and tore his clothing away. He caressed Anrin again with his down-furred palms, and licked Anrin with a long pink tongue, and finally lifted Anrin's legs up and back, bracing them both to proceed.

"You're certain?" the wolf asked. The smoke-hole was above them; a shaft of moonlight shone into Anrin's eyes. In silhouette only the wolf's teeth were visible.

"Of course not," Anrin whispered, shivering with ten thousand fears and desires. "But you must continue anyhow."

At this, the wolf smiled. That smile grew as his mouth opened impossibly wide, the canines flashing. He leaned down and Anrin trembled as those teeth touched the skin of his shoulder, then pressed, warning of what was to come.

Then the teeth pierced Anrin's flesh, hard, burning like fire. In the same moment something else pierced him, just as hard but larger, just as painful but stranger, and Anrin cried out as his body was invaded twice over. The wolf growled and worked his jaws around the wounds, as if to make absolutely certain that the wolf-essence would pass properly. His teeth slid out, then in again—a little deeper, a little harder. And again.

And again. And between Anrin's thighs, the wolf's hips mirrored his jaws.

And then Anrin was writhing as the change began somewhere deep within him, in his belly, in his veins, spreading outward like fire and consuming every part of him. Somewhere amid the searing waves the pain became pleasure and fear turned to savage delight. And as the wolf tore free to turn his bloodied face up to the moonlight, so too Anrin arched with him, and clawed him back down, and howled over and over for more.

In the morning Anrin slept, for it was the nature of wolves to shun the day. Toward evening he awoke hungry, and the wolf took him outside and taught him to read scents and to hunt for good, hot, fresh meat. When night fell the wolves ran together through the forest, traveling east to the edge of the village.

Old Baba had been wrong, Anrin understood now. The forest had its dangers, but so did the paths of men; in the end, it was simply a matter of choice. Sometimes it was better to charge roaring into the shadows than be dragged helpless and broken through the light.

He smiled to himself, wishing Old Baba could see him. What big teeth you have, she would have said.

All the better to eat men, Anrin would have replied.

Then with his packmate at his side, he slipped into the village to do just that.

ARE YOU A VAMPIRE OR A GOBLIN?

GEOFFREY H. GOODWIN

Once again, Yvette startled awake from the nightmare where she was devouring the twelve-year-old boy from down the street. And the day-old daffodils on her nightstand had turned rotten. She checked the small clock above the room's door. She'd been asleep for nineteen minutes.

The first few times, the recurring dream—and how it had the capacity to turn fresh-cut flowers into black lumps of rot in the waking world—freaked her out. The last few times, the dream was becoming a form of personal exploration. Yvette was uncertain whether this was good or not, but the transformation from freaky dream to prismatic memoir was worth noting.

She couldn't shake the belief that if she paid enough attention, was observant and clever enough, she would solve her mysterious recurring nightmare.

The Institute let her stay for longer periods of time and she was grasping the basics of lucid dreaming. Yvette had accepted that controlling these bizarre dreams was the most important facet of her personalized treatment plan. She'd learned how to flip light switches, how to see colors that didn't exist in nature and, a new favorite, she was learning how to cut off the fingers of her right hand, one by one with pruning shears, to prove she was having a dream and that the evil visions—like the boy from down the street, and the fork, knife and dinner napkin—were not real.

Or these events were real, but not occurring the way they did in dreams. Her doctors stressed that she'd make a better decision if she mustered a few granules of serenity and inner peace. Her recurring nightmare got in the way of most forms of mustering.

Yvette was afraid she'd cut off her actual fingers but hoped that the Institute wouldn't leave dangerous shears lying around. Over time, through astute observation, she concluded that pruning shears were rarely found lying around in the waking world's incarnation of the Institute.

The cannibalistic dream didn't happen every night. That was the worst. Before proving that she really needed long-term professional help and thereby earning a free pass to stay in the Institute whenever she wanted, Yvette had tried everything: stuffing her face, exercise regimes, dozing on the couch, drinking a glass of warm milk, drinking seven glasses of ice cold brandy. She'd called psychic hotlines, worn a glowing lightmask over her eyes that was supposed to stabilize her beta waves but was pure quackery, and she'd even tried sleeping every other night to see if that would make her tired enough that she wouldn't dream of eating the boy. It distressed her that she kept dreaming of chewing his flesh and couldn't control her nightmares.

She didn't know him at all well and sometimes couldn't even remember that his name was Timothy.

She was certain that she'd never been particularly drawn to blood-drinking or soul-slurping. So the phenomenon, until these minor breakthroughs, had remained quite a mystery.

The process, of healing or of "learning to embrace her true preponderance of selfhood" or whatever it was she was trying to do—whatever it was she was trying to accept now that she was finally chipping through her grungy patina of self-resignation—began when she consulted the family physician at her yearly checkup.

Yvette hadn't wanted to schedule a special appointment just to discuss her nightmare of devouring Timothy.

Dr. Burningheart squiggled several notes on his clipboard before eventually chuckling and saying, "I've known your parents for almost twenty-six years and we didn't want to pressure you or tell you before you were ready, but you're going to have to choose between being a vampire or a goblin."

Yvette hadn't liked the sound of either choice, but her dreams had cost her several jobs—including hostessing at a lovely supper club—so she asked, "Will that make the nightmare go away?"

"Probably not, but finding your true incarnation might help you learn to enjoy the nightmare . . . "

"I'm not very familiar with all this."

"None of us are. The last thing my patients want to find out is that we're all responsible for our own wellness and that wellness has a rather healthy time commitment. Few, at first, are comfortable with the idea of killing in order to live. It takes time to make a thorough adjustment."

"What's the difference between vampires and goblins?"

"That reminds me of a joke that gets me slapped. We used to think they were quite similar, but recent research believes that the distinction is decided by motive: vampires eat people because they want darkness while goblins eat people because they want souls."

"So I have to figure out why I want to eat people? That's gross."

"*Everyone* has to figure out what they want, not just you. It's tough but that's how it is. Anyone who says that life is easy is lying through their teeth."

Yvette was certain she didn't want to eat people for any reason, so she started screaming uncontrollably.

The police were kind. They took Yvette to the gothic halls of the Willis & Rothgate Institute, inaugurating her visits.

Yvette was getting used to visiting Willis & Rothgate too. Further episodes of uncontrollable screaming were why she was no longer hostessing at the supper club and why she'd lost most of her other jobs. She'd even been fired from a tobacconist's shop. They hadn't minded the screaming but—no matter how hard she tried—she couldn't smoke enough to be a convincing saleswoman. Even hardcore tobacco fiends are put off by a saleswoman who coughs and gags frequently.

Because of her nightmare, the Willis & Rothgate Institution became her second home. She learned to adore how the orange gelatin tasted spicy like Mexico and the blue gelatin tasted like the planet Earth looked in satellite photos.

And the staff was carefully trained in non-confrontation. Non-confrontation, Drs. Willis and Rothgate believed, was the most caring approach for helping the clients they called bispecials. Yvette liked the idea of being special, just hated the consequences that came with it.

Her room at the Institute had a machine that could read her thoughts and play music that fit her mood. And they brought her fresh flowers every night. The methods of non-confrontation believed that the pleasant stimuli of flowers led to purer dreams.

The staff was exceedingly nice—even when they took away the horridly nasty flowers every morning—though, once, a few candystripers held their noses and commented that no one had ever blackened so many flowers.

Bispecials, she learned early on, in classroom sessions called Chalk Talks, were exceedingly rare. Most people were just people. They could no more become a vampire or a goblin than they could become a time-traveling wombat or an Oriental rug, but some people did become vampires—no need to bite the neck, you could bite the big toe or solar plexus if you preferred—and some people wanted to drink blood so badly that a stray force, unknown powers with an electric crackle of menace, just let them turn into a vampire.

Other people, for equally nebulous reasons, became goblins, and a truly rare minority manifested slight signs in both directions and then had to consciously decide whether they wanted to be a vampire or a goblin. Bispecials had to choose which characteristics they wanted to embrace, as difficult as the decision could be for more sensitive individuals.

The signs were sometimes so minor that they were overlooked. A penchant for doing a bad Transylvanian accent at parties or obsessing over the poems of Christina Rosetti and paintings by Pre-Raphaelites were classic indicators of impending transgressions.

Yvette learned that a bit of dander could be all it took to tilt a person's scale. It amazed her that as little as a drop of blood could make a person irrevocably sick.

It wasn't something people would volunteer for or want, more like being conscripted. Yvette detached from the process, understanding that purer brainwaves led to purer dreams, as if they were an attempt to get back to cleaner living. But she didn't want this mission: the mood-reading music machine, going beyond flipping light switches in dreams to controlling the actual gradation of light, the sensory deprivation tank, orgone box, and vegan raw food diet.

Yes, Yvette saw the irony in avoiding meat and animal byproducts even though cannibalism was her likely end. She saw the irony and it made things worse. Veganism meant she had to give up the flavored gelatins that she'd liked.

Dozens of Chalk Talk sessions, some even led by the illustrious Drs. Willis and Rothgate, helped Yvette gain a greater understanding of her condition, but they never—because of their belief in non-confrontation—urged her to come to her decision hastily. She was encouraged to take the time she needed to make up her mind.

Mutual-help groups had people who'd chosen to be goblins come in and talk about how they learned to enjoy soul-slurping. Some kept regular jobs and tried to keep their species a secret. An engaging presentation was given by a radical sect of attractive young women who were professional roller-skaters known, before an incident, as *The Groovy Goblin Girls*. Now, sadly, they were wanted by the police for eating audience members. Even the youngest one, who'd always been friendly and respectful, had stopped returning Yvette's text messages.

A wealthy vampire from New Hampshire offered Yvette infinitely free room and board if she'd stay with him while she thought things over. Her various counselors and social worker considered it a dangerous idea and discouraged her from following up.

For Yvette, the hardest part was watching people from her various groups come to their deeply personal decisions, fill out the special permission slip and leave the Institute. She understood the loops of logic that people applied to their choices. She knew it wasn't like Halloween. Being a vampire or a goblin wasn't a vinyl mask you decided to don one day and could change later. Once you embraced a choice, actually sat down, drew the *G* or *V* at the bottom right-hand corner of the permission slip and signed it, that was it. The incarnation couldn't be shucked or chucked; most people started to mutate, often first noticeable by elongating fangs or bulging forearms, within twenty-four hours.

You were stuck with your new incarnation, until undeath did you part.

One girl, Larissa Blackweight, had signed out from Willis & Rothgate on a day pass and leaped off a high bridge. She'd brought an indestructible cassette recorder with her to record her last thoughts and they'd been transcribed and posted all over the Net, but most bispecials ignored "The Gospels of Larissa the Leaper" claiming they were fraudulent and insane rantings. The gist was that everything in the world was a sham and that people blossom their own destinies, that nothing in life was a clear-cut binary choice. Dr. Willis told Yvette, privately, that he felt Larissa the Leaper's issues were not related to her being bispecial. He told Yvette's parents, at the last encounter group they attended before telling Yvette that they loved her but didn't want to hear any more from her until she'd made up her mind, that Larissa had been a troubled girl who enacted a permanent solution to a temporary problem.

Yvette could relate, maybe even see suicide as the appropriate sacrifice. Sometimes, to herself when no one was around, she'd kneel in one of the showers on a vacant men's floor. She'd surmised that men, especially older ones, made their decisions hastily. Either that or the Institute had multiple men's floors and this one was used less often. Gut instinct told her that men were macho about life and death, less interested in personal fulfillment.

She understood how Larissa could jump, how a conflicted young woman could crunch the variables and decide to plummet. Even though Larissa had been a brilliant painter. Even though they'd had one late-night chat where they'd considered becoming the same monster so they'd never be a species of one.

Friends made in institutions, Yvette realized, were different from other friends. Wishing she could talk to Larissa, in effort to sort everything out and resume some semblance of camaraderie, she kneeled in the shower, trying to hallucinate a conversation with the only kindred spirit she'd ever found.

"Larissa, I know you're dead and that puts a damper on conversation, but I thought maybe I could pretend . . . ask myself questions, then imagine your answers . . . "

At first, nothing happened.

"Seriously, I'm desperate."

"Yeah, I know. But this is lame. Can't you use a Magic Eight Ball or something?" said a ghostly voice that was barely audible over the shower's hissing water.

"Just let me rant to myself, maybe interject a joke or a platitude near the end. I need room to talk to myself without thinking I'm crazy," Yvette said.

"Okay," the voice answered, noncommittally.

"See, red hot poker an inch from my left eye, I'm still unsure. I mean, Larissa, I know the distinctions as well as you did. And I understand how you could leap. With a goblin, you know where you stand—somewhere after nightfall, you're going to be cuisine. They sup on people's sins: no hand behind the curtain, no pretense or performance. Vampires, well, everyone knows that vampires drink their fill of sins early on, then become laconic and overly chatty. Their strength is kept up by the totality, like how a seasoned blood-drinker can chug a priest or a prostitute and barely taste the difference, finding a palatable measure of darkness in either . . . "

"They both minister to the sick . . . "

"Goblins and vampires?" Yvette asked.

"No, prostitutes and priests. I'd even hazard that they're equally likely to endure distasteful things by squeezing their eyes shut and thinking about the good they'll do with the money."

"Zowie, self-induced hallucinations are confusing."

Yvette splashed hot water on her face, trying to make sense of the situation.

"If you're going to talk to me, please don't do it in exclamatory asides."

"I wanted this to help. None of this offers a doorway out."

"You're right."

"Plus, and I know I'm whining, they go and call it bispecial, but there's no way to combine them. I'm so fed up with this externally-imposed inertia that I'd consider the willowy grace of a vampire if it was coupled with the low center of gravity and brute strength of a goblin . . . "

"No, you wouldn't. You'd still have to kill to live and you'd rather go splat from great heights than succumb to murdering innocent people. By the way, from two dozen stories, water does as much damage as concrete."

"That's not comforting."

"You're not locked here in the name of comfort."

"They know I'm having trouble deciding. I can leave whenever I want."

"Stuck in neutral isn't a decision. And you can't *live* whenever you want, so what's the difference?"

The hot water suddenly went cold and Yvette mumbled about how much she disliked the bind she was in, how she'd rather be a prostitute or a priest, but the ghostly voice was gone. She was afraid her hallucination had gotten bored and decided to ignore her. Sometimes it felt that way with dead friends too.

Yvette wasn't sure why her dreams were always about Timothy. No amount of pondering got things to make sense.

She barely knew the boy. Originally, the dreams had been about strangers she'd met during the day: someone who came by the supper club on a tall ladder to change the dead light bulbs in the ceiling, an elderly woman who played chess in the park, a stockbroker who fed pigeons on her break.

Timothy, she presumed but didn't tell anyone, symbolized innocence. He was twelve, with longish hair and a quick wince of a smile. They'd had two conversations of less than three minutes but she considered him a good kid. A kid who shouldn't be eaten by vampires or goblins, even if they were fastidious, using a silk napkin, fine china and antique flatware.

In short, problems filled her head by the cartload.

Yvette wondered if vampires or goblins could reproduce. The answer had to be no, because no one had photographed a vampling or a gobblekin, but there were rumors. Couldn't there be a way to get darkness or souls without having to eat people? Even in her dreams, even with the decorum of napkins and cutlery, it was horrid to imagine. No amount of imaginary black pepper or imaginary hot sauce made the idea even remotely palatable or digestible.

Shivering, Yvette turned the water off and dressed in the shower stall just in case someone else entered the bathroom, putting her baby blue robe and matching flip-flops back on. Quietly, she went to her room and locked the door.

Her music machine read her mood and played a cacophony that sounded like she was smashing every smashable object in the room: mirror, bed, the clock above the door. Yvette heard the sound of her clothes being torn apart and then the sound of the music machine being destroyed.

Then the machine played silence.

A few hours later, Dr. Rothgate shook her awake and dragged her to his office.

Something was very wrong with Dr. Rothgate and it took Yvette a while to figure it out.

She was so sleepy, as the wild-eyed psychiatrist bade her rest on his couch, it seemed like she woke up mid-conversation:

" . . . but I have no desire to eat people . . . "

"Appetites grow over time, like tumors or allergies. Existence, be it breathing or pogosticking or wandering around trying to remember where you've lost your keys, requires extremely complicated machinery. Taken as a vast enough ecosystem, every sprig of existence needs predation. Everyone needs a twinge of *momento mori*, a reminder that we'll eventually die."

"Even monsters? I thought monsters lived forever."

"Oh, well," Dr. Rothgate said while adjusting the strap holding a strange pair of goggles to his face, "it's one of those conundrums of negative capability. You have to keep two conflicting ideas in your head at the same time. My research suggests that the best results come from a simultaneous belief that you'll live forever and that you could die at any moment. It reinforces the Zen koan where you attempt to have both complete commitment and complete detachment. Then again, that's only useful if you care about outcomes . . . "

The sun coming through the shaded window seemed to grow brighter, forcing Yvette to squint her eyes.

" . . . my dear, these conditions aren't brought on by loveless marriages, solipsism, drug addiction or manic-depressive paranoia.

Early on, before she freaked out, back when she babbled more and shrieked less, my first patient told me that, 'Anguish was her prey.' Now I know what she meant."

"Was it Larissa?"

"Don't say her name. It was far before her."

"How long have you treated bispecials?"

"Since the beginning, quite a long and desiccated span of time." Dr. Rothgate cleared his throat. "It was her mother. She was the first of the goblins."

They both turned away from the bright window shade. Dr. Rothgate had a long draught from his brandy bottle, then handed it to Yvette.

"I thought it couldn't pass to kids. And why didn't Larissa choose goblin like her mom?"

"It can't. Anastasia Blackweight birthed Larissa before she was afflicted."

"Remember when we met? You wouldn't have called it an affliction . . . "

"I say many things."

"What did she mean, 'Anguish is our prey?' Larissa said the same thing to me. Skip the hemming and hawing about how she was a suicidal lunatic. I know you want answers."

"I want to help you, Yvette. It's all I want, I think."

He took the brandy bottle back.

"I'm the only way you can save yourself," Yvette said.

"I'm beyond saving. Anyway, she hated her mother. I shouldn't tell because you're still trying to sort things out—we don't believe in shock or confrontation here—but the anguish that twisted and tortured me has vanished now that I've succumbed, er, finally decided."

"Yeah, you were like me, but I can't figure out which way you've gone."

"Good. I don't want you to know."

"This process has taken quite a toll on me. I just want to do what's right."

"In France, a sixteenth century judge sentenced six hundred shape-shifters to death. The *Malleus Maleficarum* has a section on how people change and that was written in 1484."

"I've changed my mind again. I'm going to leap off a bridge if that's the only way to keep from hurting people."

"You know she talked like that, don't you? Are my notes right, did you know her?"

"We talked a few times. Only one conversation stands out. I didn't realize how momentous it would seem in retrospect. I try to hallucinate semi-lucid conversations with the imaginary version of her that I remember, but she's dead."

"If you only sleep once or twice a week for long enough, everything's dead."

"Dr. Rothgate, you're freaking me out."

"I'm sorry. We theorists aren't good at forcing outcomes," the doctor said, before thanking Yvette for her time and encouraging her to rest. He stumbled out the door, leaving her alone in his office. Yvette couldn't tell if he was having difficulty walking because of drunkenness or because his back was changing shape.

Amidst shelves warped with arcane books, two paintings dominated the walls. One was an abstract and roiling sea of red purples and purple reds. A three-dimensional claw, presumably sculpted from modeling paste, reached out from the bloody waters, reaching out to grab the painting's viewer.

The other showed a young goblin girl staring at a storefront window. The window displayed a pink chiffon dress fit for a fairy princess. Tears rimmed the eyes of the girl with pointy ears and green skin.

Rising from the couch, Yvette resolved to delay her decision until she liked one of the options before her. It seemed better to suffer and try to talk to the dead than become an evil creature. In the past, she'd chosen deadlines like Arbor Day or Oscar Night, but her self-imposed deadlines had come and gone, just excuses.

Conversely, Yvette had accepted that she and the rest of the world were going crazy and getting worse.

Over the next two days, she felt like she was sleepwalking. Dr. Rothgate didn't come to find her, preferring to stay in hiding. She understood. Their talk had left her even more fragmented than she'd been before. If Yvette had possessed a belfry, it would've been overflowing with bats.

Another day passed, lethargic and soggy. Yvette dreamed of being a mother, envisioning her children as a bouncing brood of vamplings or gobblekins. The consequences were so dire. Why did it have to be binary? She imagined how pussy willows wiggled in the wind so they wouldn't break. Was the process like having a totem animal? Perhaps body modification would help with her transition. Whiskers implanted, stripes tattooed and teeth filed to little points. And, suddenly, her nightmares weren't always about being a vampire or a goblin. She felt less weird, occasionally picturing her dream self as a wolf-creature. She would need surgery to make her outsides as freaky as her insides, but it struck her as a splendid compromise. She fell back asleep, briefly.

When Yvette woke, she was licking her lips and horrified to be doing it. White roses had been delivered. And they were turned inside out, puckered by the rapid advance of her sorrowful condition.

It was still called Willis & Rothgate, even though Dr. Rothgate's presence was barely felt. New crops of bispecials meandered in and crept out. Yvette stood still while the world of sickness, wellness and horrible compromises scrolled past her. Over time, it felt less and less natural, more and more artificial.

Even though they'd said they weren't coming back until she'd made up her mind, Yvette's parents did finally return. They spoke in harsh but hushed tones.

"We heard you're considering vampire," her father said.

"I'd rather die."

"Then perhaps you've decided on goblin," her mother said.

"Have I mentioned that it's not like a costume party? I don't know who I want to be. The whole thing's permanent, you know. The last thing I want is to despise myself for choosing to be someone I shouldn't be."

"Permanency's better than trickery. You're going to have to live your consequences," her parents said in unison.

Yvette called several candystripers and demanded that they show her mother and father out. Yvette pretended that her parents would've apologized if she'd given them enough time. But she knew it was pretense. She invented people inside her head because it was better than being let down, continuously, by everyone she'd ever met.

The flat sterility of the halls and walls had greater echoes of life than Yvette did. Every breath was drudgery. She shambled to her room. The mood music played one of the Berlioz symphonies about getting hanged then some mopey darkwave ballad that Yvette kind of liked. She thought she'd smashed the machine. For now it was okay, but she'd imagine smashing the stupid thing again if she had to, in dreams or reality or somewhere in between, whatever it took to scrabble together a half-pretty sense of place . . .

Yvette resolved to stay institutionalized, as long as it took. Anything to prevent herself from eating people.

What was there to do?

Tired, always sleepy, Yvette went back to bed. Dr. Rothgate came in the night and took her to his office again. He had trouble walking, his shuffling gait making double-footfall patters in the hallway. He'd lost the distinctive goggles of his last visit and seemed to be having problems with his vision.

"I'm here to warn you."

"You sound like everyone else."

"You haven't been out of the Institute's walls for quite some time. Things have gotten eerie and ridiculous out there. Don't fool yourself into thinking that days are still their normal lengths or that maps lead people where they're going . . ."

A gooey dollop of blood was clinging to Dr. Rothgate's forehead. She still couldn't tell which way he'd gone. She wanted to clarify or crystallize her decision but wasn't sure how knowing Dr. Rothgate's choice would help. Yvette still hated both her options.

"You're summing it up perfectly. I want to be a person who rescues people when they're lost in those dark nights you described. I want to bring them a warm blanket and a candle, maybe a backup snack if they've been foolish enough to get lost without one. When the world goes creepy, everyone needs comfort and snacks."

"Wait. What do you want?" Dr. Rothgate asked, his face gnashing and sliding sideways like he'd become a demon or something far worse than a vampire or goblin.

Yvette didn't see any pruning shears anywhere. She decided she was awake, not having another nightmare.

"I want to be a giving and noble werewolf who wanders late nights when the walls between the worlds are thin. I'll have a large framepack with lots of helpful supplies like: needle-nosed pliers, bandages, protein shakes, safety pins, extra batteries. You know, I could walk the night and have a ready array of supplies to give fellow travelers: new, accurate maps, clean, dry socks, small musical instruments, aspirin . . . "

Dr. Rothgate interrupted, talking into an indestructible tape recorder, "I'm afraid the patient is not responding to treatment. Her politics are the politics of madness."

Dr. Willis appeared from nowhere, head lolling from side-to-side like a weary jack-in-the-box. Dr. Willis shouted, "This isn't about getting to do whatever you want. Life is a brutal, complicated, and messy adventure . . . "

"Right! And I want to a be a considerate and helpful werewolf . . . "

Now Yvette was of the opinion that she was dreaming after all. She used her hands to stop her chin from trembling.

"It's understandable that you identify with victims. It was very hard for us to turn our backs on the Hippocratic oath and learn to stalk the humans. We were forced to choose a side. There is no such thing as a werewolf . . . " Dr. Rothgate began. He grabbed his partner's hand and raised their arms in a victory salute.

"But maybe there is! And maybe they don't want darkness or souls. Maybe werewolves exist and they don't eat people at all."

Saliva oozed from Dr. Willis's bottom lip and his lips were swelling. Dr. Rothgate shouted how Yvette would be sorry if she let her malarkey continue, how the monsters of the world were going to cause her never-ending torment if she didn't surrender her malarkey.

With his green, liver-spotted forearms bulging and raised high in the air, Dr. Rothgate tore out into the hall so fast he could've been a punctured balloon and Dr. Willis snuck his pale, manicured fingers into the breast pocket of his pinstriped suit and, deftly, whipped out a syringe and poked Yvette's arm.

She hoped this meant she'd wake up.

As she blacked out, she thought of how his pointy fangs were too big for his mouth. Dr. Willis had always enunciated well. Now he would be in trouble.

It hurt for Yvette to come to. She was down in the basement, where the strangest experiments had occurred. This was the room with the sensory deprivation tank and the orgone box.

"We have ways of making you talk," Dr. Willis said.

"I thought you didn't believe in confrontation."

"No, our new tactics are all about confrontation. We've done a 180-degree turn. Now we hurt people for fun. It's delightful and I'm willing to remove pieces of you to change your mind," Dr. Willis said, picking up a scalpel.

"I haven't signed my permission slip," Yvette said, realizing she was bound to the operating table by some sort of nylon harness.

"It's a symbolic technicality," Dr. Willis said, waving the scalpel as if conducting an atonal overture.

Yvette set her jaw, her every fiber wanting to flee. Instead, she remembered what she'd learned about granules of serenity and whispered, "We've known each other a long time. How's about you untie me from this bed and give me twenty minutes alone with the form and I fill it out?"

"I will find my partner and consult with him," Dr. Willis said as he locked the door on his way out. Whatever he'd injected into her was having its effect. The room darkened and Larissa appeared in another visitation or dream.

"Yvette, may I call you Evie? I've always contracted your name in my mind."

"No. Are you here to rescue me or are you just pretending to be nice?"

"I'm *your* stupid hallucination. I can babble with you—but I don't think I can interact with the material world, it'd spoil the illusion and I'd vanish."

"Okay. That's not worth the risks. Tell me about your mom."

"Freud's a joke. Remember that scene in *Blade Runner*? Scope out Jung if you want real insight into consciousness."

"No, I just want to understand you."

"And biography's a good place to start? My mom turned into a goblin. Never met my dad. It sucked. I swore it'd never happen to me. End of story."

"Listen, please. I think you're special, Larissa. And I believe in you, but you only got close. I think there's another way out—one that's tailored to me."

"I'm not here to mislead you, you know. Everyone else has lost it. You need to cling to something or the world mutates into nothing but mischief and swerving alleys. Make your call, Evie. Maybe I was wrong to bail . . . "

Yvette realized that the drugs were rearranging her thoughts so severely that she might be seeing things that weren't there.

Drs. Willis and Rothgate charged back into the basement. Dr. Willis' face was covered with blood-flecked saliva and Dr. Rothgate's hair had turned ghostly white, but both were in better moods than when they'd left.

"We, silly little girl who doesn't know what she wants, have brought you your permission slip," Dr. Willis said, grabbing a lab coat off a wall hook and using it to wipe the bubbly blood from his cheeks and chin.

"But we don't want you to be a baby about this. You draw a fancy-schmancy, stylized *G* or *V* and you're gone within twenty-four hours. Vampires are snappy dressers and good with money. Goblins make great demo tapes for reality TV shows and leave riotous messages on your voicemail but have a tendency to become pear-shaped at middle age," Dr. Rothgate said.

"Is it really that tough a choice? You've gone over and over it. Once you accept the change, you'll love it like a new fetish, like psychic incisions have implanted an iguana under your skin. Sure, it'll make you do things you don't want, like controlling your eye and muscle movements even when you think you're too tired to drink blood or slurp souls and would rather put your feet up, read from your antiquarian library, maybe puff a cigar—but, eventually, you'll learn to pretend it's a form of symbiosis, even though you'll know deep down inside that it's really a parasite." By now, Dr. Willis had managed to get the blood off his face, except for a small spot on his neck.

Yvette fought the nylon straps. Why were these two going on and on about this? She didn't want anything that either of their species were offering.

Dr. Rothgate tried a different angle, pulling up a chair and speaking slowly, "We've made our decisions. And, yep, we both eat people, even nice ones like that Timothy you used to dream about, but the rest of the world has crept right over the shadowy brink . . . "

" . . . everyone knows who you are now, Yvette. And they know that you've been here forever. You're famous, on the news twice a day, revered just like their precious, dead Larissa . . . " Dr. Willis said, joining in.

Yvette interrupted them with a quick but loud shriek.

"Have we all inhaled a truckload of ether? Is that it? Let's stop monkeying around. You both idolize her. You have her paintings on your office walls and carry around indestructible cassette recorders because she was braver than you'll ever be. I've figured out my middle path, something that keeps me alive and keeps me from turning out like you—but let's not fool ourselves, okay? A truly brave person is willing to die for what they believe in, even if nobody's looking. So here's the gig: I read your musty edition of *Malleus Maleficarum* and it has a ton about werewolves. So that's what I'm going with. I'm going to be a helpful werewolf, even if it kills me."

Both doctors began to beat her, pelting her with various objects from the room. Eventually they used the orgone box, but the sensory deprivation tank proved too heavy, even with grunting.

Yvette lost consciousness or fell through another layer cake of dreams and alternate realities, one or the other. She wasn't sleeping or dreaming or awake and her body hurt like she'd been beaten with a roomful of heavy objects. It took her twenty minutes to figure out who she was and where she was.

Much to her surprise, Yvette was on the floor of her room and still alive. The vase by the bed overflowed with pink carnations. They smelled like a ballerina's smile.

Yvette grimaced and decided that she didn't believe a word the doctors had said. The lights flickered and she screamed with all the pain her battered body was able to muster. The doctors were the ones who were full of malarkey, inmates in their own asylum, pervy lunatic fringers who demanded certainty because they vanished if they stopped claiming that they had everything sorted out and clearly defined . . . paranoia proven true, every stitch of inner peace unraveled . . .

Lumpy, swollen bruises coated her flesh. It was extraordinary that she could even rise from the bed, a painful challenge to crane her neck far enough backward to see the furry tuft in the rinky-dink institutional mirror. The tail she'd dreamed of was starting to form beneath the clustered bruises at the base of her spine.

Yvette thought she was mutating into what she wanted to be and it was enough to help her forget ninety percent of the heartache she'd been through. She wondered how hard it would be to get stainless steel whiskers implanted.

Lost and startled, the wolf coming to life under her skin, Yvette stumbled through the gothic hallways, finally finding metal double doors and exiting through them. She didn't recognize the foggy and rain-slicked street. She had never been to this place before.

For the first time in a long time, she wanted a cigarette or two.

With grit and maybe blood in her mouth, she discovered a backpack on her shoulders and opened it. Several pairs of recently-sharpened pruning shears tumbled to the cobblestones. Eventually, she might take a moment to pack the bundle of supplies that she'd planned on preparing. At least she was a werewolf and not a vampire or a goblin.

Crawling deeper into the night, Yvette wanted to growl and make further use of her new teeth. She sniffed delicacies in the air and hoped she would never have to sleep again.

When she wasn't gnawing people, prying their skulls open and drowning in the sustenance of their frail, futile and thwarted memories, she might attempt to help the endangered. Maybe, someday, she could spare someone as innocent as Timothy.

But for now, Yvette was too famished. If she had understood how hungry the transformation would make her, her choice wouldn't have ever mattered. She was too ravenous to waste time wishing there had ever been another way.

THE PACK AND THE PICK-UP ARTIST

MIKE BROTHERTON

Prime had barely taken two steps into the dark club before one of his students accosted him.

"Sage just struck out twice," the excited guy said. "He said he's going back in."

"Cool." Sage was Prime's co-instructor at the weekend boot camp. Guys would fly into San Francisco and plunk down three thousand dollars for pick-up instruction and supervised nighttime field work. Out sarging in the evenings, the students were supposed to be the ones approaching the sets while the instructors gave advice and debriefed. Still, it was normal for the guys to want to see their instructors demonstrate their prowess, which normally wasn't a problem.

Apparently tonight it was, for Sage.

Prime looked beyond the student to a hot babe, a seven, no, seven-and-a-half, standing with a couple of guys further into the Den. He smiled and waved in the direction of HB7.5 and pushed past his student.

She smiled and half raised her hand, a little uncertain. It was a standard trick to force a show of interest. She thought she knew him, or that he at least knew her, and didn't want to look like she didn't remember.

Still smiling, Prime eased through the clumps of people, lightly touched her shoulder, and settled in next to her. "Hey, how's it going?"

The guys she was with turned toward him, expressions blank.

The girl still had a half smile on her face and gave an unsurprising response. "It's going okay. What about you?"

The guys turned away to talk to each other, assuming that she knew him, just like they were supposed to.

He wasn't particularly interested in HB7.5, but it was better to be in set than not, and it would build his social proof while he checked out how Sage was doing.

Prime's partner got laid like a rock star, but beyond that similarity, he was not at all like Prime. Sage peacocked, wearing outrageous fancy clothes and even make-up (always accompanied by the perfect cologne), while Prime threw on the same jeans, leather jacket, and cowboy boots night after night. Sage worked and taught pick-up using a very mechanical system and was a great believer in the concept of "fake it till you make it" while Prime often improvised his pick-ups, and believed that if you made yourself into a quality guy the women would follow naturally. To top it off, Sage was a sushi-eating vegaquarian to Prime's carnivorous ways.

HB7.5 was prattling on in response to a question he'd asked her about whether it was infidelity for a girlfriend to make out with a girl, and normally he would have cut her off, but he had just spotted Sage.

His partner, sporting a white suit and hat tonight, was approaching a large group, a mixed seven set, lounging around a fireplace at back. From a technical point of view, Sage looked good at first. He went right in and engaged the whole group, drawing everyone's attention. Nice body language, good kino, touching three of the group within the first fifteen seconds. Still it was all for naught. Prime saw that the attempt was doomed, as the group's body language shifted to lock him out.

Engaging a group of seven people all at once in a noisy club was not an easy thing to do, but a task well within Sage's capabilities. Sometimes failure wasn't your fault—you engaged particular individuals or sets who were not open to being approached by strangers—but this was rare. Almost everyone liked to talk with the coolest guy in the place, the life of the party. Almost everyone.

The girl he had just met continued to jabber on like they were old friends, allowing Prime to take a closer look at the set. Three men, four women, all attractive, both older and younger than him. He paired off the couples based on their seating arrangement and body language. The single girl in the group, well, she was breathtaking when he focused on her. Perfect cheekbones, beautiful smile, and huge eyes. Superhot babe, an eleven on the ten-point scale. SHB11 possessed a raw sexuality dancing in her model-quality features.

SHB11 was worth the risk of failure.

Failure was only certain when you didn't try.

As Sage was patting one of the guy's shoulders on the way out and trying to make his failure to hook the set inconspicuous to observers, Prime was telling HB7.5 that he'd needed to go say hi to a friend and was making his own departure.

As Prime made his own approach he passed by Sage. He smiled at his friend and gave him a quick high-five.

"Impossible set, man," said Sage.

"Nothing's impossible," said Prime.

"Then show me how it's done, Professor Prime."

Prime just grinned at him and moved toward the fireplace.

He didn't bother to open the set properly, the way Sage had done. Prime just bulled his way through to the fireplace and said, "Excuse me," as he squeezed in to sit down on the bricks between SHB11 and one of her friends. "This fire looks awesome."

It wasn't exactly textbook. As an approach, he deserved points for placing himself next to his target, but that was about it. He had no doubt that Sage had tried three variations on textbook approaches and had failed with all of them, so why not?

"Chilly out there tonight," he said, leaning back toward the fire.

There was an awkward moment as they evaluated him. He'd just invaded their space with a barely plausible excuse and they were trying to figure out if they were cool with that or not.

Prime gave them the moment, soaking in the heat. It was a little chilly outside tonight, that was the truth, and he felt no shame in taking the seat he had now.

He was a bold man who broke the rules and rarely felt fear, but at that moment, suddenly and surprisingly, despite the heat, the hairs on the back of his neck rose up. He felt . . . vulnerable.

That was odd. He'd set aside his approach anxiety years ago and just didn't give a crap anymore how anyone received him.

There was something different about this group.

SHB11 leaned in his direction, a little, tilting her head down. His heart picked up its pace as she surreptitiously sniffed him.

Well, that was different. He didn't move and held his position.

Everything relaxed then and his hairs settled back into place.

"I like your T-shirt, man," said one of the guys in the group. Prime pegged him as the alpha member of the group. He was the oldest and the biggest guy there, and it seemed that he had now won the AMOG over without much effort. How had he done that? His shirt?

What shirt had he thrown on today? Oh, yeah. The one that said *Meat is murder . . . tasty, tasty murder*. It was Gaucho Grill day.

"Thanks," Prime said automatically, using it to launch into one of his set stories. He raised his voice and engaged the whole group. "Tonight I hit my favorite restaurant, a Brazilian churrascaria. When the Brazilians barbeque they don't slather on that goopy sauce like they do in the midwest. It's just salt and meat, you know? Natural and honest, and tasty as hell. My place here is awesome, and they have everything. Every cut of beef all served on swords, pork, sausage, sometimes even ostrich. Oh, and chicken hearts, done the way I used to enjoy them in Rio."

"You were in Rio? What were you doing there?" SHB11 asked.

"Yeah. I was there studying jujitsu, but I probably spent more time on the beach." He went on about the views from Copacabana Beach, and the time used his martial arts training to rescue cute Israeli tourists from a mugger. It wasn't his best story, not by a long shot, but it let him drop some interesting displays of higher value without too much bragging, and he could feel out a group with this stuff. Sometimes he turned off the hippy types, way too common in San Francisco, but pick-up wasn't about scoring with every girl you met. It was about finding out who you were and what you wanted and being able to get it when you found it. Hippy chicks were not for him, SHB11 or not. Sage could take those.

"Chicken hearts?" SHB11 said, licking her lips. "Love them."

A show of interest. Excellent. Prime smiled and gave her a quick hug. "You're my kind of girl, aren't you. Wait a second," he said, pushing her away, "can you cook?"

"No," she answered, giggling. "But I can eat."

Hook point. He was in.

Her name was Anastasia, and she was not only a hot girl, she was a cool girl. Her group was . . . odd. The AMOG, it turned out, was her father, Yuri, and her mother was there, too, Elena. The others were an aunt and uncle and her older sister and husband. Not your usual clubbing set, but when you found a SHB11, you didn't question the circumstances. Many of the hottest girls didn't go out to bars at all and you had to find them at supermarkets or the gym.

And if they went out with their family and that was how he found them, that was how he would game them. Romancing a girl in front of her parents was not something he was afraid to attempt.

Prime chatted them all up and everyone was smiling and feeling good and comfortable with him. Time to isolate and escalate, or he'd just be that friendly guy they met that time. He also realized that he felt a bit strange. Not drunk—he didn't drink when he was working or sarging—but warm and light headed, and the air was pregnant with a musky scent.

"I was cold when I came over, but now I'm more on the toasty side," he said, standing up. He held his hand out to Anastasia. "Catch some air with me."

She glanced away from him, a nonverbal check with the parents, and then took his hand and let him lead her out.

They got looks not only from Sage and the boot camp students, but quite a few other envious guys in there.

It didn't bother Prime one bit.

Outside there were a few clusters of smokers lingering about, which gave Prime a bit of an excuse to maneuver them into even a bit more isolation.

"I like it that you don't smoke," he said. "Makes a woman's mouth taste like an ashtray."

"I could never," she said, smiling. Her green eyes glinted in the moonlight. "Hurts your sense of smell."

"You smell good," said Prime. He leaned in, brushed her hair aside, and sniffed her slowly from shoulder to ear. "Mmmmm, really good."

She smiled and made no effort to stop him.

"Smokers or not, so many people have lost their sense of smell in this modern world," he said. "We're so artificial now, like machines, not the animals we really are. Animals, you'll notice before they mate, will always smell each other. We're hardwired by evolution to respond to certain, fundamental things, in the nose and in the gut. Our noses know, so to speak, and tell us things we need to know about the world."

"That's so true," she said. She started to say something else, but stopped as his hand slid up the back of the neck into her hair.

"There are a lot of things like that that we humans have forgotten. You'll notice how lions, when they mate, bite and pull and claw at each other. Here," he said, pulling her hair downward so her face was tilted up toward his. "Like this."

"Yes," she whispered.

"The best, most sensitive places on the body are hidden places, like the nape of the neck where your hair starts, and like the inside of the elbow, the back of the knee . . . "

Prime traced his fingers along some of those places as he spoke. "Places like those have millions of little nerve endings, sensitive little guys, all signaling for the release of endorphins when properly stimulated."

Anastasia seemed entranced, giving him what the community called *doggy dinner bowl eyes*, just the way she was supposed to be at this stage in the game.

He took her arm, bent it a little, and erotically bit Anastasia on the inside of her elbow, slowly closing his mouth and bringing his teeth together.

She shivered.

"Right?"

"Yes," she said. "You understand very well."

"But do you know what I love best?" Prime asked. He pointed at the side of his neck. "A bite right here. This is where the jugular vein is most exposed, and since so many sexual fantasies involve submission and vulnerability, it just floods the brain with endorphins."

He waited. About half the time the girls didn't do anything and he would have to instigate. The other half of the time they were game, but usually the first attempt was lame and he would insist on showing them how it was done.

In either case, a passionate make-out usually ensued with minimal effort.

Anastasia reacted more positively than most.

She jumped him, wrapping her legs around his waist, grabbing his hair, and devouring his lips and neck with her hungry mouth.

Prime staggered back a step against the brick wall, pleasantly overwhelmed.

And then there was no thought, only lust and passion.

Eventually Prime realized that they weren't kissing or biting each other any more, that he was thinking again. At least a little. In the cool night air their breath formed little wisps of mist around their faces. Hell, Anastasia's upper chest was flat out steaming.

"Anastasia!" came a voice calling from the front door of the Den. Her family was leaving.

It took Prime a moment to process that something was going on, so lost in the moment he had been.

That hadn't happened in a while.

"I must go now," she said to him. "Meet me at Muir Woods tomorrow at 1 PM. We will have a picnic, yes?"

Prime tried to re-engage his brain to think through the logistics. Logistics could always ruin the most perfect pick up. He fumbled for his cell phone so she could put her number in.

"No, no, no," she said. "I don't have a phone. Just meet me tomorrow. You will be there, yes? Tell me."

"Yes," he said to her as she backed away from him, his head full of the raw feelings of passion of the last few minutes. "Yes."

"Good," she said.

Prime stood there steaming in the moonlight as Anastasia and her family walked away together.

His mind eventually fully kicked in and he remembered that he had students to supervise. Time to go to work.

Work . . . workshop . . . tomorrow . . . shit.

Prime looked at himself in the bathroom mirror the next morning.

Jesus Christ, he thought.

Most of his neck was a bruised mess and where he didn't have bruises he had scratches.

Anastasia had done a real number on him. How had she done that?

The thing was, he hadn't had feelings like this for a girl in years. Rationally he knew he was thinking like your average frustrated chump. AFCs put pussy on a pedestal and gave women all the power in relationships, and ironically, while women liked that they did not find it attractive in a man.

Prime checked his watch and decided he didn't have time to shave properly or do anything about the superhickeys. He didn't even own a turtleneck.

So be it.

He finished dressing and went downstairs to eat breakfast before the boot camp recommenced at 10 AM in the mansion's living room.

Sage was already there, working on a bowl of Fruit Loops. "Wow, dude! She chewed you up, didn't she?"

"I guess she did," he said, smiling, as he went to make some bacon and eggs. "Not an impossible set, just a dangerous one."

"Yeah, well, I guess so. The crazy chicks, you can have them. You should have at least gotten laid for your trouble."

"I will," said Prime.

"No way. You're going to see a crazy chick like that again?"

Prime cracked a couple of eggs into a pan and started scrambling. "Sure. She's super hot."

"She was hot, but she wasn't *that* hot. And did you see the guys in that group? I haven't seen that many monobrows in the same place, ever. You said they were all family. She's probably got it, too, and plucks daily."

"So what? You get your chest waxed," Prime said.

"Touche."

What was real, what was fake, it all got blurry. Was Sage a hairy-chested man hiding, or a smooth-chested man making himself over to reflect his true self-image? Almost every pick-up artist made themselves over, down to going by names that were really just reworked CB handles. Sage was wise, spicy. Prime was number one. Go by a name for enough time and it becomes part of you.

Prime had been born Jonathan, but hadn't ever seen himself as a Jonathan. Another artificial label, a name. Animals didn't give themselves names. They knew what they were.

Prime carried his food over to the table and joined his friend. "I'm going to have to miss a few hours this afternoon."

"Got a doctor who will see you on a Saturday?" asked Sage.

"No. I'm going to a picnic."

Sage noisily crunched on his cereal for a moment. "I don't think so, Jon. This is a business. These guys aren't paying for you to screw around with crazy chicks on their time."

"It isn't that big a deal. We move my sessions to late afternoon. Move the story telling stuff first."

"We have it in the order we have it for a reason. The British guy, Nigel, he flew over here from London because he wanted body language lessons from the famous Prime. They pay us thousands of dollars because they want us, the Better Man Program, to give them our undivided attention for a few hours. There are a hundred other guys as good as us, just without the rep, ready to take our place if our graduates leave here without real changes in their lives."

"I know."

"So, be professional."

It was his own damn fault, Prime knew. He'd double booked. He hated making promises he couldn't keep, and if he hadn't been so pussy-drunk he wouldn't have done it in the first place.

"If I skip meeting Anastasia," said Prime, "I may never see her again. I didn't get her number."

"Cripes, Jon. You got oneitis already? Go out and fuck ten other girls and you won't remember this one at all. There's always another girl."

Too true, and that was their code. There's more fish in the sea. No need to get needy. No need to compromise to score with any one particular girl. No need . . .

Prime took a bite of bacon. This girl had unleashed something inside him in a way no girl ever had. He knew not only what we wanted to do, he knew what his gut insisted that he do.

"There's a difference between you and me, partner," Prime said. "You make up your rules and follow them to the letter, like a computer, and I admire that. It makes you successful, and it has helped us develop our boot camps. You're the brains here, no doubt, and you define professionalism."

"Thanks, but you're a professional, too," said Sage.

"I am, but I'm not perfect. I have to listen to my heart, my gut. That's who I am. That's what I have to do."

Sage finished his bowl, carried it to the kitchen, and tossed it into the sink with loud clanking. He gave Prime a look, but didn't say anything.

Prime hated the passive aggressive shit. He could read Sage's thoughts and his friend was just too chicken to voice them.

"I have a case of oneitis," Prime said. "So what? That's my problem. The students won't even miss me. If they do, promise them I'll give them each a free follow-up coaching call in a couple of weeks, Okay?"

Sage's posture shifted ever so slightly. That was it. He really wasn't worried about Prime. He was worried about the business.

"Okay. But just be careful out there and remember that she's just a girl."

Prime rubbed at his raw neck. Was she?

Muir Woods not only sported some giant wood, it wasn't the smallest park in the world. Prime wondered how he was going to find Anastasia. Logistics could kill the best pick-up, and he didn't even have a phone number for her.

He'd only been wandering around for a few minutes when *she* found *him*.

"Jon? I knew you wouldn't disappoint us."

Us? He turned and there she was, with her whole entire family.

Well. He only wanted to sleep with her, not the whole pack of them. Still, he had enjoyed their company and if that was how it was going to be, that was how it was going to be.

He walked over to her smiling and gave her a hug and peck on the cheek, then shook her dad's hand and said hello to everyone else.

Sage was right. The guys did come awfully close to sporting monobrows. If he and Anastasia had kids, he'd have to worry about that.

Prime stopped himself. Kids? Where were these thoughts coming from? He'd experienced an overwhelming physical attraction and connection with this girl, but that was not the stuff to make a pick-up artist marry. That was just an everyday occurrence in his life these days.

But he knew that the raw, instinctual feelings he'd had the night before ran deep in his hindbrain.

Normally on a day two meeting like this he'd plan to be alone with his girl and build comfort, rapport. The real thing, too. There was nothing fake about this part of pick-up. The artist just knew how to do it fast.

"Let's go for a walk," Anastasia said. "They can do without us for a while, don't you think?"

"Is that all right with you guys?" Prime asked Yuri and Elena.

"Sure," Yuri said. "You kids have fun."

"And I'll take that," said Elena, reaching for the bottle of wine Prime had brought.

"Thanks," he said, and off they went.

As soon as they were out of sight of the rest of her family, she jumped him again, and it was all he could do to make her stop.

"I don't understand," she said. "Don't you feel what I feel?"

Oh Lord, how he did. There was a palpable, raw lust arcing between them every time they touched.

"Yes," he said. The first instant they'd touched again there was no doubt that they'd sleep together the moment the logistics allowed. The thing was he wanted more, some kind of relationship.

Most master pick-up artists managed a small and revolving harem of girls in non-exclusive relationships. There was always a girl available when he wanted, or new ones to hunt. Prime had three women in multiple long-term relationships at the moment. He just couldn't envision Anastasia as one of these, assuming he could even see her without her extended family tagging along.

He wanted more. He wanted to consume her.

This was all irrational he knew, intellectually. He didn't know this girl at all beyond the facts that she was hot and cool and liked him. That and the fact that the pure physical lust had been overpowering.

"There are a lot of pretty girls in the world," he said. "Other than your looks, what are three things that make you special?"

She took hold of his face between her hands and looked deep in his eyes. "You're still thinking too much, but I will humor you my Jon."

Prime looked right back at her, triangular gazing, moving his focus between her two eyes and mouth.

"First, I am free. I see what I want and I take it, and I am responsible for my freedom.

"Second, I understand the natural order of things and accept it.

"Third," and she paused to smile, showing her perfect teeth, "I can recognize a strong man when I find him, a man with potential to be more."

Wow, what an answer. Most hot girls had to stop and think hard about that question. He'd once seen a pick-up artist on a talk show leave Jessica Alba initially flummoxed, as the question alone had removed her beauty from the attraction question.

Anastasia's response made him think of something that had happened to him. It was not a story he shared often, although it was a true story and important to him.

"I went hunting once, when I was a teenager. I wanted to know what it was like to be responsible for killing one's own food. I'm a carnivore, as you already know, and anyone who eats meat should know first hand what that means."

He paused, thinking about how to articulate the next part, then stopped worrying. It would come out.

"My dad had a friend who hunted, who taught me about guns, and took me. He told me about buck fever, how he'd get so excited before shooting a deer that he almost couldn't pick up his rifle let alone aim it. It made me imagine a housewife at the grocery store pissing herself with excitement as she reached for a pound of ground beef."

He was quiet again, remembering that daydream and the first time.

Anastasia rested her head in the nape of his neck, listening.

"When I had the deer in my sights," he continued, "it wasn't like I was shopping at a grocery store, but it wasn't like I had buck fever either. I'm not religious especially, but it was a holy thing. A beautiful and natural thing that I'd been too ignorant to realize existed every day, everywhere around the world. It wasn't just about eating, and it wasn't just about dying. It was about being part of the world, and understanding you place.

"After I shot the deer and it went down, I cried."

"Why?" she whispered.

Maybe she did understand. The other times he'd tried to tell girls this story they had been near crying themselves and the obvious explanation was not what had moved him. He wasn't sorry he had taken the animal's life or that he found Bambi's mother delicious.

"It was the first time I ever felt truly alive, and glimpsed the responsibility."

She said something then that surprised him with its depth of insight. "That was because you saw the world as it is, but not yet fully your own place in it."

Or was it insightful? Maybe she was just spouting bullshit the way schools trained kids to do.

He held her tighter as he realized it wasn't bullshit. She wasn't a bullshitter, and he was ashamed there was as much bullshit in his life as there was.

Because of the rain they had their picnic in the family's RVs, with Prime, Anastasia, and her parents in one and the rest in the second. The group had two and were touring the west coast on vacation.

The logistics suddenly seemed nearly impossible, but Prime was committed to making more of this strange, blossoming relationship.

"And what do you do for a living?" Yuri asked over a bite of chicken leg.

"Yes," said Anastasia's mother. "Last night you told us you repaired disposable lighters, and while that was a very funny answer, I don't think it is true."

There was a short answer to the question, and a long answer that was more obscure but no less true. Unlike some pick-up artists, he was not shy or ashamed about how he made his very good living. He told it the way he saw it.

"I take nerds," he began, "and guys broken by divorce, and socially stunted Silicon Valley executives, and fellows whose fathers were either clueless in the first place or failed to pass on their wisdom, I take them all, and I help them make themselves better men."

"Sounds like the army," Yuri said.

Prime grinned. "We do call our workshops 'boot camps,' and some of the same principles apply. Men are resistant to change, even when the change is good for them. Even when it is about them realizing their every dream and becoming responsible for their own power."

This was the long answer, and truer, at least to him, than any trite answer about teaching guys to get laid. The term pick-up artist conjured up negative connotations to so many who thought the trade was all a bag of tricks about how to manipulate women out of their panties. Well, he admitted, some of it was. But the core of it to Prime had always been about helping men realize themselves and their personal power. He liked the army analogy better than the self-help guru image that he knew Sage preferred.

"That sounds like a fine thing," Yuri said. "Is that what you always want to do with your life?"

He didn't know if Anastasia's father realized it, but that was a loaded question. To Prime, it sounded like he was asking if he intended to spend the rest of his life fucking around. Well . . . did he? Was there the immediate alternative of cruising around the country with this girl and her family?

"I'm happy for the moment, although I do understand that the nature of life is change," Prime replied. "What do you all do?"

"We do," said Yuri, "exactly as we please. We have a little money, and we do not have complicated needs. We have the world, and family. We have simple pleasures. Eating, breathing, enjoying nature. It is a good life."

They kept chatting and Prime had a good time. These were good people. A little weird, but who wasn't? He was happy with who he was, but he wasn't normal by any means. At one point he asked about Sage.

"My friend tried to talk to you last night," he said. "The guy in the white suit. Remember him?"

"Oh yes," said Elena, a subliminal "tsk, tsk" in her voice. "Poor boy."

Poor boy? Sage? The man had picked up twins at the Playboy Mansion and had a threesome in the grotto. That was no poor boy.

"Yes," said Anastasia. "He is sad, isn't he?"

Sad?

"He smelled of rabbit food," said Yuri, authoritatively. "I hope your friend does better in the future. Maybe you can help him. I trust you are good to your friends."

Okay, some people were weirder than others.

"You're being ridiculous," Sage said. He turned away from Prime dismissively and bent to turn on the gas fireplace.

Prime steamed. "No. I feel like I'm finally waking up. You're not jealous, are you? Maybe I shouldn't have told you they thought you smelled weak."

"Look," said Sage, standing back up, "I've got Sally coming over soon, so I don't have time for this nonsense. Isn't tonight your night with Brenda?"

"I cancelled," said Prime.

Sage rolled his eyes. *Oneitis*, said that look.

"Don't you want me to be happy?" he asked his friend.

"God, yes!" roared Sage. "And that is why you need to get back on track."

"Are you happy with this lifestyle?"

"Of course. What more could I want? I sleep with beautiful women, live in a mansion in San Francisco, wear the finest clothes and eat the finest foods."

Prime smiled, remembering it had been called "rabbit food." Still, he couldn't help but feel that he had had a peek into a simpler, more natural, and more honest life. A life with Anastasia. And he was going to take up the invitation he'd been offered.

"Well, let's just wait until after tonight, okay?"

"More hanging out with the Monobrows? Jeez, man, it's like a bad *Saturday Night Live* skit, and you're living it."

"I'm living life," Prime replied, simply. "Respect that."

Sage sighed audibly. "Fine. I do respect you, you know that. I just don't like to see you regressing into some kind of AFC. You'll end up broken."

"Or changed."

Sage nodded.

Prime met up with Anastasia and her family out at Yosemite.

They already had a more than respectable fire blazing at their campsite and were working on a small keg. Camping, fire, beer . . . not a bad start. As Prime looked at his woman, he knew what a perfect night like this also needed: sex. And it was there.

Out came a boom box. Out loud came classic rock, Creedence Clearwater Revival's "Bad Moon Rising."

Okay, everything wasn't pure and natural, but music was good to have. Primal.

Anastasia danced with joy, tilting her head up toward the night above, the firelight dancing across her features.

Prime finished his beer and rose to join her in the stepless dance of life.

Together, they moved.

The night faded. Her family faded. Together they were only two, under the stars and the rising full moon.

His arms over her shoulders, her green eyes locked onto his.

A voice. Yuri's.

"You want to chase real tail? You want the real thing?"

Dancing. Intoxicating smell of woman.

Yuri's voice, still calling, but more . . . howling than calling.

"You want to live life? Howl at the moon, man!"

At least that's how it seemed, as he spun with Anastasia.

"You want it?" she asked. "You want a natural life? A simple, honest life? A free life?"

He didn't think too hard about that? Why should he? The answer had been hidden in his heart for years.

"For a real man, this life is the best," she said, grabbing his head, pulling his hair. "For you, my mate."

Who was picking up who?

Did it matter?

They danced and Prime opened his senses while turning down his analysis.

At some point the physical urges became too much and he had to have her. Damn the lack of privacy. Damn the family. Damn the world.

They ripped their clothing. Their own. Each others. It was all the same.

Words became sounds.

Smells.

Tastes.

Pull hair.

Lick skin.

Bite.

Feel the air, the moving air, the wind.

Feel the real.

Howl!

Wait, what was he doing? What was Anastasia becoming? What was the biting doing to—stop!

Stop thinking. Feel. Go with it, truth, life.

Howl!

Time for Prime to become Primeval.

Hair, sprouting. Fangs, growing. Claws, extending. Nose, blossoming. Eyes, sharpening. Ears, encompassing. Body, transforming. Becoming a better . . . being.

Time for Primeval to take his mate.

On all fours, hunching, biting, howling, coming, with the scent of blood spilled from the sex for the first time. An honest mating. The best.

Running through the night, howling again, with wind, with his true family, his pack.

He belonged. He had his place.

He had his mate.

He had his pack.

It was going to be a long-term relationship.

Primeval howled with satisfaction.

He'd been picked up.

THE GARDEN, THE MOON, THE WALL

AMANDA DOWNUM

The ghosts follow Sephie to work again that day.

They stand outside the windows of the bookstore, staring in with hollow eyes—more of them now than a few days ago. She tries to ignore them. At least they never come inside.

Most of them, anyway.

The light dims as she's shelving books, and Sephie turns to find her ex-boyfriend grinning down at her, pink filming his long ivory teeth. He tilts his head, shows her the still-wet ruin a bullet made of the left side of his skull.

Her hands tingle with adrenaline shock as the smell of his blood coats her tongue—copper sweetness, and beneath that the familiar salt-musk of his skin.

A wink and he's gone, and the air smells like books and dust and air freshener again. Sephie wobbles, and the stack of books in her arms teeters and falls, hardbacks and trades thumping and thwapping one by one, echoing in the afternoon quiet. No blood stains the worn green carpet.

The third time this week. Cursing, she crouches to pick up the books, and pauses as she reads the nearest title.

Lycanthropy: An Encyclopedia

Caleb always was a smart-ass—she shouldn't expect that to change because he's dead.

"Are you okay?" Anna calls from across the store.

No, she thinks. *Not even a little.*

The sky darkens as they close, October nearly over and autumn chewing the days shorter and shorter. Purple eases into charcoal, and the grinning jack-o'-lantern moon rises over the jagged Dallas skyline.

The moon doesn't bother her, never mind Caleb and his lousy jokes.

Sephie lights a cigarette as Anna sets the alarm and locks the back door. Her hands shake, the itch in her veins more than nicotine can ease.

"You want to get some coffee?" Anna asks, pocketing her keys and pulling out her own cigarettes. Her nails are orange and black to match her Halloween hair. Her lighter rasps, and the smell of cloves drifts through the air.

Sephie swallows, her mouth gone dry. The shakes are coming on for real, her stomach cramping. "That'd be nice, but I need to run some errands. Maybe some other time." She likes the bookstore better than any of the other jobs she's had, and doesn't want to get fired because someone thinks she's a junkie.

It's not like she can tell them the truth.

"Sure," Anna says, waving as she turns toward her car. "See you tomorrow."

"Yeah. 'Night." Sephie ducks down the alley toward the street, trying not to think about Anna's bemused little smile.

Tonight will be bad—she hears it in the hollow roar of traffic, sees it in the halos bleeding off the street lamps. But cold sweat prickles her scalp, her neck, and chills crawl up and down her back; she can't wait another day.

Hunching her shoulders, she slides into the ebb and flow of downtown streets.

For a few blocks everything's okay. The night hums and chatters, traffic and voices, the cacophony of city-noises. The air tastes of exhaust and asphalt, the sewer-stench of the Trinity fading now that summer's passed. She catches a whiff of decay, of meat, and saliva pools on her tongue. But it's only a dead dog, not what she needs.

Then it happens, that sideways lurch in the pit of her stomach, and she's alone on the sidewalk. No more neon and shining glass, no more noise. Dusty brick and stone instead, grime-blind windows and the moon grinning overhead.

And the ghosts.

She's learned not to stop, not to listen to their whispers. Keep walking, eyes on the sidewalk—don't look at those pale faces peering out of the shadows, bruised and bloody or just empty, eyes burning with a junkie's aching need.

She knows the feeling, all too well, but she can't help them. She can barely help herself.

Her nose wrinkles against the smell of this place. The city stinks, but at least it's a living stench. This is dry bones and dust, old tombs.

The wind that sighs from black alley-mouths is worse—sulfur and ammonia, sickness and pain. It aches like a bruise when it touches her, makes her eyes water.

Her footfalls echo as she lengthens her stride. It will pass. It always does. She has to keep moving, out of the between-places.

But she's a between-thing now, and she may never leave this place behind.

A breeze eddies past her, and Sephie stumbles to a halt. Rose gardens and evergreen, the smell of evenings as summer melts into autumn. The smell of her dreams.

The scent leaks from under the door of a narrow shop, its windows curtained and dull. She reaches for the knob with a trembling hand.

But her stomach cramps again, and already the braver ghosts are moving toward her, murmuring, pleading.

She turns and runs, and doesn't stop until the world slips back to normal.

Bobet & Cask Funeral Services is long closed, but a light burns in the back. Sephie crouches in the shadow of a hedge, holly pricking her back as she finishes her last cigarette and tries to slow her breathing. Her legs cramp from exercise, but that's nothing to the pain in her gut. She wipes clammy sweat from her face and drags her fingers through the curling cowlicked mess of her hair.

Peter waits by the back door, even though she's early. Hands in his pockets, shoulders hunched, eyes flitting back and forth—he looks like a really bad spy.

"You should start smoking," she says, moving out of the dark. "It'd look more natural."

He jerks, presses his back to the door. The smell of his fear cuts through the muggy night and Sephie's stomach growls.

"I—" He swallows, Adam's apple bobbing. "Come inside."

He always invites her in; he's read too many books. She follows him down the corridor, down the stairs to the morgue.

The air smells of chemicals and death, and she rubs her arms against crawling goosebumps. Her sweat gels in the cold, sticking her shirt to her back. A body lies on a metal table, and her stomach clenches again. Peter glances at her, blue eyes narrowing, like he thinks she'll start gnawing on an arm.

She's not sure what would happen if he weren't here.

He opens a refrigerator, takes out a lidded plastic bowl. "It's heart, and liver, and some other things . . . A car crash, so I could take a little more than usual."

"This guy?" She nods toward the corpse in his funeral suit, wrinkled face coated in makeup that can't simulate living color, no matter how skillfully it's applied.

"No, he had a heart attack. The accident was a few days ago."

Sephie smiles, close-lipped. "Thank you." She tugs a roll of bills out of her pocket, trades it for the container. He tried to give the money back, once, but she makes him keep it. She's afraid he'll ask for something else if she doesn't.

He stands there watching her, gangly and awkward, while her fingers tighten on the plastic and she swallows hungry spit. Finally he ducks his head and retreats. "I'll be outside if you need me."

When his footsteps recede, Sephie sinks onto the cold tile floor and opens the container. Thin slices of organs—pomegranate heart and pinky-brown liver-and slivers and cubes of fat-marbled flesh. Once he gave her an eyeball, but it was salty and bitter and too gross even for her.

She saves the heart for last, chews it slowly, sucking bloody juice out of the muscle. Shudders ride her, and she closes her eyes against a flood of scattered images and sensations. She doesn't want to know about the person whose heart this was.

"This is what you left me for?"

She opens her eyes to find Caleb crouching in front of her, long hands dangling between his knees. Blood and brains drip onto the floor, vanishing when they hit the tile.

"Leave me alone!" Her voice cracks. The empty bowl falls from her hand and rolls in a lazy spiral.

"Tell me this is what you want. Tell me you don't miss me."

She closes her eyes, pulls her knees tight against her chest.

"Tell me you wouldn't rather eat that boy of yours. He might like it."

A hand touches her knee and Sephie gasps, but it's only Peter. "Are you all right?"

Caleb's vanished again.

She stares up at Peter—she feels his pulse through her jeans, hears the nervous rhythm of his heart. He wants her. He's afraid of her. He smells like food.

Caleb knows her too well, damn him. She's had more than one daydream about fucking Peter on a cold steel embalming table. Some of those fantasies end with her tearing the poor boy's throat out. The smell of warm flesh fills her nose.

She pulls away, crab-crawls across the floor and stumbles to her feet. Peter gapes; she's getting faster.

"I'm fine." She nibbles a drop of coagulated blood from under her nail and straightens her blouse. "I need to go."

Peter frowns, and she can see him searching for the nerve to ask her to stay. He's like the ghosts, needing, wanting. Whether he wants a girlfriend or a pet monster, she's not sure, but she can't offer him either.

"Thank you," she says again, cutting him off. "I'll be back next month, okay?"

He nods, shoulders sagging. "Yeah. I'll see you then."

And Sephie flees up the stairs, into the dark, and hurries for home.

The apartment is empty. Seth's gone a lot lately, looking for work—jobs that pay cash and don't run background checks. Sometimes, like this week, it's out-of-town work, leaving her alone. Hard enough to sleep most nights, even with his steady snoring drifting down the hall. When it's her and the echoing silence, it's nearly impossible.

The ghosts never come too close when he's here. This week she's seen a few lingering near the stairs.

Even if the ghosts don't find her, the dreams always do.

She slips one of Seth's cassettes into the old tape deck by her mattress. Sephie teases him about his music, sad bluesy stuff a few generations before her time, but some of it's pretty. Billie Holiday's husky-soft voice chases away the silence, wraps around her like a blanket.

Her gun is a hard lump under the pillow; she always sleeps with it when she's alone.

Tell me this is what you want.

She thought she was rid of Caleb six months ago, when she left him sprawled in a cooling pool of blood on a dusty Oklahoma street. Not that she could even do that herself—she had to find someone else to pull the trigger for her.

His words echo in her head. Is this what she wants? The cramped apartment, the string of lousy jobs. Gravemeat and ghosts. Seth is gone half the time, and she doesn't dare make other friends, not even something as simple as getting coffee with Anna.

She's wanted lots of things over the years—travel, excitement, glamorous jobs that turned out to be too little glamour and too much work. But the one thing she's always wanted, as long as she can remember, is to not be afraid anymore.

"I've done a great job of that, haven't I?" she whispers to her pillow, to the gun beneath it.

The tape clicks over to the B-side before she finally drifts off. Lady Day's voice follows her into the dark.

She dreams of the wall again. A wall in a dark forest, stones pitted and pocked with age, veined with moss and ivy. Too high and sheer to climb, so she follows it on and on, searching for a door. Her fingers bruise the green, filling the air with its musty-damp scent, and sap clings sticky as blood on her skin. Yellow eyes gleam in the shadows around her.

The werewolves.

Tall spindly beasts, long-armed and stilt-legged, tongues lolling amid bone-needle fangs. They never approach, never touch her, only stare and follow, muttering and laughing to themselves, singing to the swollen orange moon.

Maybe there's no door, no opening, and she'll circle the wall forever. But Sephie's smelled the wind from the other side, a wind that smells like forests and gardens, like heaven. Roses and evergreen, ripe peaches and fresh bright blood.

And she knows, with the certainty of dreams, that the garden is a place for her. An Eden for ghouls and monsters, where the trees pump blood instead of sap and hearts grow ripe and beating on the vine. A place where she'll never have to eat cold meat, never have to kill. Where she won't be afraid.

It's enough to keep her walking the wall, night after night, ignoring the werewolves' snuffling laughter.

She doesn't find the door tonight. Instead the dream splinters and she falls through the cracks, falls back onto her sagging mattress. The shadowed bedroom ceiling stares her down while Billie Holiday sings about the moonlight.

Something woke her, but she's not sure what, until the mattress creaks and a warm weight settles over her. Familiar scratch of stubble, the salt-sweet taste of Caleb's skin.

He shouldn't be here, but his hands are sliding under her shirt, callused fingers kneading her ribs, and her body still remembers him, remembers when she didn't spend the nights trembling and alone. She arches against him as his tongue traces the angle of her jaw; her fingers tangle in his wet hair.

"Tell me you don't miss me." His breath tickles her sternum as his fingers slip beneath the elastic of her underwear. She bites her lip and doesn't answer.

His hair trails over her stomach, leaving warm wet streaks behind.

"I would have taken care of you." He tugs her underwear over her hips and her breath hitches. "I still need you, Sephie." Lips press warm and rough below her navel, the pressure of teeth.

"Caleb—" And she shrieks as he bites. Light flashes in the window and she sees her blood on his mouth, his blood smeared over her breasts and belly and hands, his eyes gleaming yellow in the glare.

And she wakes with a gasp. She's alone again, with the music and the soft sounds of traffic beyond the window, and only sweat slicks her skin.

Sephie can't sleep again that night, and when dawnlight creeps through the blinds she's aching and groggy. She wants to call in sick, but she gave Peter the last of her cash and the electricity's due soon, so she drags herself into the shower when the alarm shrieks.

She searches the foggy mirror for changes, like she does every time she eats. Maybe her teeth are a hint longer, a little sharper. Her nails have thickened, so thick now she can't chew them like she used to, has to worry her cuticles instead.

She thinks of Caleb's bloody grin, the dark half-circles under his nails. She's not like him, no matter what she's becoming.

Not yet, at least.

Another day of ignoring ghosts, of dodging Anna's questions and invitations. She aches with tension and fatigue by the time she gets home.

Caleb is waiting for her, bleeding on her dumpster-rescue couch. Sephie pauses on the threshold, nearly turns and runs.

But she's too tired, and running hasn't worked so far. She locks the door behind her.

"What do you want?"

"Your help." It's not what she expected. He's too serious; it looks strange on him.

"My help? Maybe you should have asked for that before you started stalking me. And anyway, you're dead."

His eyes narrow. "Whose fault is that?"

"You should have let me walk away." But it's hard to stay angry with a ghost. Arguing with Caleb is familiar, almost domestic, and better than being alone.

"You weren't walking—you were running. You wanted me to be strong. You wanted me to be scary. And then you couldn't handle it."

"I didn't want you to kill people."

"You wanted a pet monster, a killer on a leash."

She closes her eyes. "I wanted to feel safe."

"If I could have done that, I would have." She feels him in front of her, though she never heard him move. His hand cups her cheek, cool and rough, his touch lighter than it ever was. If she pushes, she might pass right through him.

"How did you find me, anyway?"

"I can feel you, everywhere I go. We're still all tangled up together."

"I'm trying to cut myself loose." She reaches up, not quite touching his bloody face. "I am sorry, though, about how things ended."

"Then help me. I can't stay here, Sephie, even for you. It's getting harder and harder. It hurts. But the other place—the badlands—are worse."

In spite of everything, in spite of the blood, the too-sharp teeth and gleaming eyes, he's still Caleb. Still the boy she fell in love with. She was always a little afraid of him, but it was a safer fear than others.

"What can I do?"

"You've seen it—the garden, the wall. I need to go there. I need to get inside."

"I can't find the way in. And it's only a dream." But she remembers the door downtown, the smell of roses and summer.

They just have to get there, past the ghosts, through the empty places. The thought makes her stomach lurch.

But if it weren't for her, for her fear, Caleb wouldn't be dead. Wouldn't need her now.

"Come on." She touches his cold hand. "I think I know the way."

The moon watches them as they cross the hollow city, spilling light the color of rust. In the distance something howls, like no dog Sephie's ever heard.

The dead follow in their wake, nearly a dozen ghosts now, watching with hungry eyes.

"Have you talked to them?" Sophie asks, trying not to glance back at their silent shadows.

"No. I think they're scared of me." He pauses. "We're scared of each other."

The shop is still there—she was afraid it would vanish, that she imagined it to begin with. This time she sees the sign: *The Dream Merchant.* As Caleb tries the door, she turns to face the ghosts.

She swallows, her throat dust-dry. "What do you want?"

Caleb catches her arm. "Sophie, don't—"

"We want out of here," the nearest answers. A woman, her bone-white face mottled with bruises, hair pale as cobwebs tangling over her shoulders.

"I don't know what to do. I don't know how to help you."

"Take us with you." She nods toward the shop. "Whatever's in there, it can't be worse than this place."

"It's locked," Caleb says, slamming his hand against a pane; it doesn't even rattle. "I can't break it."

Sophie touches the door. It feels real enough, peeling paint and dry wood, cold dirty glass. She can't see through the windows. Before she can think too long, she punches the glass.

She gasps as it shatters and pain spills hot up her arm.

The blood that blossoms on her knuckles is definitely real. The smell fills the air, bright and rich against so much nothing. The ghosts sigh like wind in the grass, and sway forward. Caleb swallows, and Sophie pulls her hand away.

Careful of the glass, she slides her good hand through the broken window, fumbling till she finds the lock. The door opens inward with a hollow rattle of bells. She listens for an alarm, but hears nothing.

The howl echoes again, closer now.

"Come on." Caleb steers her through the door, but Sophie turns to face the ghosts.

"Follow us if you want to, but I don't know where we're going."

One by one they trickle over the threshold, into the darkness of the shop. Sophie shuts the door behind them, and turns the lock. Blood drips off her fingers.

Caleb's hand tightens on her arm. "There it is."

She sniffs, catches the smell again, from somewhere in the darkness across the room.

"And what exactly are you looking for?"

Sephie spins, heart leaping in her chest, as a light blossoms on the stairs. Her eyes water at the sudden brightness, and she raises a hand against the glare.

"Who are you?" Sephie asks. The light is wrong, milk-blue and cold, its glare obscuring the man who holds it.

He chuckles dryly. "I'm the owner of the building you've broken into, the floor you're bleeding on. So I'll ask again—what is it that you want?"

She swallows. "We're looking for the garden."

The light dims enough for her to catch his puzzled frown. His black hair is tousled, shirt hanging open, and stubble darkens his jaw. "The— Ah." His eyes flicker toward the other side of the room. "I see. And who are you, young lady? The Pied Piper? The dead are much more nuisance than rats."

All the ghosts huddle behind her, even Caleb, shielding their eyes from the pale lantern.

"Please." The word catches in her throat. "I'm sorry about the window. But I have to take them to the garden."

"I run a business, not an underground railroad for the dead. Such services aren't free."

"I don't have any money. But I can get some—"

He studies her for a moment, his eyes cast in shadow. "I'm sure you can. And what surety will you give me, if I let you pass tonight?"

She opens her mouth, closes it again. "What do you want?"

His smile turned her stomach to ice. "I'll have your name, as a down payment."

"No," Caleb whispers.

"It's Sephie."

"No, my dear. Your whole name. And I'll know if you lie."

"Don't," Caleb says, louder. He moves toward the stairs. "Leave her alone."

The man raises the lantern higher. The light blazes, and Caleb falls back with a groan. "The name, if you please. Or I can send your friends back to the ground where they belong."

"Sephronia Anne Matthews."

"Excellent. Very well, Sephronia—" She winces at the sound of her name in his mouth. "—you and your friends may go down."

He descends the rest of the stairs and the ghosts flinch from the light as he passes. He unlocks a door in the far wall; it looks like a closet, but when it opens a shiver runs through Sephie's bones. His lantern can't touch the blackness inside. One of the ghosts moans.

"This is it?" But she can smell it, warm and summer-sweet.

"That is the way."

She glances at the man, her eyes narrowing. "And we can come back this way?"

"You can. We still have your debt to settle."

"What now?" Caleb murmurs.

"We go down." The steadiness of her voice amazes her. Her good hand gropes for Caleb's as they step into the dark.

Down and down and down. Caleb's hand tightens painfully on hers, and she remembers the last time they went below, the trip into the darkness that started all of this. The gravemeat, the secrets of the dead. When they first became monsters, between-things.

But this road doesn't smell like death.

The ghosts make no sound behind them; Sephie doesn't look back.

She brushes her wounded hand against the wall, leaving a trail of blood—better than breadcrumbs. It feels like cement at first, cold and rough, but the texture changes, becomes sleeker, slicker, ridged and curving.

She doesn't know how long they walk, or how far. Step after step, one foot after another. The dark swallows sound, swallows time.

Eventually the wall falls away, and the smothering sensation eases. A moment later the stairs end, become a gentle slope; earth and rocks skitter beneath her boots. The air warms, and a humid breeze carries the smell of green things. The ghosts whisper among themselves. Sephie's hand is falling asleep in Caleb's, but she doesn't let go.

The darkness changes ahead, lessens. The mouth of a cave—they're almost out.

Something moves in the shadows, rasping breath and scraping claws. Three pairs of eyes burn against the black.

"What's this now?" A rough guttural voice. Nothing that comes from a human mouth.

"Little feet trip-trapping down our stairs," another hisses. "Is that you, merchant?"

"No, sisters. It's the little dreamer." And this a woman's voice, deep and rich.

"Ahh, so it is. I knew she'd find the way eventually."

"And she brought her friends."

"What do you want, little ghoul?"

Sephie swallows, trying to moisten her tongue. "We want to find the garden."

"Well, that's easy, isn't it sisters?"

"All you do is follow the path."

"But you must pay the toll, to leave the cavern."

"Yes. Passage is not free."

"Not again." Sephie tugs her hand free of Caleb's, flexes tingling fingers. "What do *you* want?"

Even as her eyes adjust, she can't make out the speakers. Only vague shadows and glowing eyes, gold and silver and poison green. They smell like fur, like musk and blood and autumn leaves.

One of them laughs, a chuffing animal noise. "Come closer, child."

Caleb tries to hold her back, but she shakes off his grip and steps forward. Shadows lap over her, thicker and cooler than the air, and she shivers. Something crunches under her foot, dry and hollow; she doesn't look down.

"What's the price?" She searches her pockets. Coins on the eyes of the dead, but she can't remember where she read that.

"Not that," says one of the women—or whatever they are—as change rattles in Sephie's pocket. "We have no use for money."

"And I doubt you have enough for everyone you've brought."

The sisters move closer, surrounding her. Hot breath tickles the back of her neck.

"Orpheus sang his way in," hisses the shadow on her left, the green-eyed. "Do you have a song for us?"

Sephie shakes her head. Even if she could carry a tune, her voice is caught in her throat and she can't remember the words to any song she knows.

"She's bleeding," the golden-eyed beast whispers.

Sephie flexes her right hand; crusted blood cracks on her skin.

"So she is." The silver eyes lean in. "Living blood. It's been a long time since we've tasted that."

She holds up her hand. "Is this enough? Will this pay our way?"

The green-eyed sister hisses. "Ghoul blood is cold and dusty. I want something sweeter. Perhaps . . . " Something cool and scaly touches Sephie's cheek and she fights a flinch. "A young girl's tears. Yes."

"Sephie—" Caleb's voice drifts through the dark.

"Be silent, little ghost. This is her bargain to make."

Long clawed fingers catch her right hand, pull it down. Hot breath stings the cuts. She clenches her fist, reopening the wounds. The pain of tearing scabs makes her gasp, makes her eyes water.

"Blood and tears, fine. Take them."

Serpents writhe against her face, tongues flickering toward her eyes.

"If we all may name a price," the silver-eyed woman says, "then I want a kiss."

Sephie closes her eyes. Moisture beads on her lashes, and the snakes lick it away. The beast's tongue laps her hand, hot and rough, rasping against the cuts. "Fine," she whispers. "Just do it."

A hand cups her cheek, cold and lifeless, tilts her chin up. The woman's mouth closes on hers. Silk-dry lips, icy tongue, teeth like icicles. She tries to breathe, but the kiss steals the air from her lungs, steals the heat from her veins.

We can take it all, the woman's voice whispers deep in the whorls of her brain. *All your pain, all your fear. Even your debt. We can take everything, and you'll be free.*

She's truly crying now, crying and bleeding and gasping for air. Snakes in her eyes, teeth piercing her hand, and that tongue in her mouth, leeching her dry.

What does that leave for me?

Nothing. You'll have nothing, be nothing, want nothing. And nothing will ever hurt you again.

She can't answer, can't feel her limbs or her tongue. Caleb is shouting somewhere far away, calling her name. But she can't answer, because she's falling into the dark.

But the dark doesn't want her, spits her out again, and she wakes with a gasp. Cold, so cold, and she can't stop shivering. Caleb holds her; he's warmer than she is.

"What happened?" she whispers.

"They're gone. I thought you were, too."

She sits up, rubs her stinging eyes. Her right hand is shredded, like she was mauled by a dog, but none of the wounds are bleeding. Her chest aches, and it's hard to get enough breath.

"Where are the ghosts?" she asks, glancing around the empty cavern.

"They went on, into the forest."

Carefully she stands, leaning on Caleb. He feels more solid now, more real. Or maybe she's less.

"Come on. Let's find the garden."

A path leads into the trees, like the sisters promised. Birds and insects sing in the darkness, and animals move through the underbrush. The peach-golden moon is high overhead, dripping light through the canopy, turning all the leaves to amber and jade.

The trail takes them straight to the garden wall, and this time, the gate is easy to find. Curling iron, the bars wrapped thick with vines and flowers. One side stands open, and the werewolves are waiting for them.

This time, Sephie isn't afraid.

"Hello, children," one beast says. After the guardians in the cave, its growling voice is welcoming, kind. "We wondered when you would find the way."

The wind drifts past them, flutters Sephie's hair. The smell of the garden eases some of the aching cold inside her.

She turns to Caleb. His color is better, and as she watches, the constant dripping blood slows, dries. An instant later the wound is healed, leaving nothing but tangled dark curls.

Her wounds are still there.

"Come with me," he says, stroking her hair. "Stay with me. We'll be all right here."

She leans against him, hears the whisper of a heartbeat in his chest. So tired. Not scared anymore—now she's just numb. It would be so nice to rest.

Caleb bends down and she lifts her head for a kiss, a kiss to warm her frozen lips, to ease the memory of the cave. It could be like this here, like it was before things went so wrong.

Will Seth wonder what happened to her? Will Anna? Will they worry? She won't be hungry here, won't owe anything to anyone.

Nothing.

"I'll take care of you," Caleb whispers, his stubble scratching her lips.

She stiffens, turns her head aside. "You never could do that."

"I tried to be what you wanted . . . "

"I never should have asked." She pulls away, runs her fingers over his cheek. "I'm sorry."

"What's up there for you? What's worth going back to?"

"I don't know. But it's something. It's my life."

"Sephie—"

"Goodbye, Caleb."

She tilts her head toward the gate, and the waiting monsters. "Go on."

He takes a hesitant step toward the garden. She waves once in farewell, then turns away. She doesn't look back.

The cavern is empty. No one challenges her as she climbs the black and winding stair.

Halfway up, her hand starts to hurt again, and then to bleed. Not long after, she begins to cry. When she reaches the top of the steps, her chest burns, and all her weary muscles ache. But she's not afraid.

As Sephie opens the door, the weight of her debt settles heavy on her shoulders. She pauses on the threshold, breathes in the garden's scent again. Then she steps into the light and noise and stink of the world.

BLAMED FOR TRYING TO LIVE

JESSE BULLINGTON

—◆—

The summer after Charles's mother died he decided to become a werewolf. Not really, of course, he wasn't crazy, even after the murder and moving to a city that was as hot and wet as the inside of a mouth, every breeze like warm breath in his face, every afternoon the clouds sneezing warm rain; he wasn't crazy and he wasn't a kid who believed everything he read or saw in a movie. He was really, really bored, though, and he didn't have any friends, and one of his library books on werewolves had a six page chapter on how people turned into them, and with the start of tenth grade still a month away Charles figured in the name of science he should put the book to the test. He knew nothing would come of it, not really, but he'd never drunk water from a wolf's pawprint or dealt with the Devil, either, so who knew?

If he had hit on the plan back when they were making him see the two psychologists he wouldn't have mentioned it, obviously, but he knew what the shrinks would probably have said. The older one would think that Charles's ambition came from an urge to protect himself and his remaining family, and the younger one would have told him that lycanthropy was his way of metaphorically dealing with his post-puberty anxiety. They were both, in Charles' estimation, dumb as balls.

"Mr. Jenkins said Rickards is an urban high school," Charles had told Mr. Matherne, his A.P. history teacher and an old friend of his mother's.

"Jenkins dropped the U on you, huh?" Mr. Matherne shook his head the way he always did when Mr. Jenkins came up, as though the principal's name was a fly buzzing around his ears. "You know what that means, right?"

"Ghetto," Charles and Mr. Matherne said in unison.

"It won't be easy, being the only vegan in the ghetto," said Mr. Matherne, and that was the double truth, Ruth. Charles's dad didn't buy that shit, and his gramma, while she tried, didn't understand, and so the only people he knew who really understood what the V-word meant were back in Baltimore. Person, Charles would correct himself, *person*, because even back home he'd never told his friends when he restarted his vegan clock, and while Mr. Matherne was still embedded in 4A waging his one man war against ignorance, Charles's mom was gone, even if her bones weren't going anywhere.

Southside was *the* ghetto, too, Charles soon realized, even worse than the Frenchtown neighborhood that lay bunched up on the far side of the public library. *Lie-berry*, his gramma pronounced it, and Charles winced every time. For an "urban" area there were a lot of dirt roads linking the narrow paved streets, actual dirt roads shaded by the huge live oaks that peppered Tallahassee, as if the rednecks who had built the place didn't know the meaning of the word city. The shotgun shack Charles moved into with his dad and gramma was over a mile from the library but three blocks from the nearest liquor store, two if you took the path through the kudzu-smothered vacant lot next door. That's a ghetto, all right, Mr. Matherne had agreed in his last email to Charles, watch out for drive-bys.

Except Tallahassee wasn't enough of a city to have drive-bys, at least not real ones. A silver hatchback full of white kids would occasionally prowl down the narrow streets to shout or throw trash at the crack-veterans who patrolled Southside like the world's shadiest neighborhood watch. They had pegged Charles with a McDonald's bag when he was returning from a library trip, the car's bass almost-but-not-quite muffling the sound of laughter. Looking down at the class-trash they had nailed him with Charles felt the old sting in his eyes and the shaking in his legs, then let out a long sigh and kicked the bag away.

At least they hadn't jumped him like the crew of Southside locals that took umbrage to a cheeseduplittlebitchsteppinout, or whatever they had said.

"They just think you're a faggot cause of your glasses," Charles's dad had told him knowingly, his sour breath reeking like whatever was on sale at the ABC. "Next time clock'em in the face."

"I can't fight them all," Charles had said, instantly regretting having told his father. "And don't say faggot. The community's ignorance about homosexuality—"

"*Are* you a faggot?" Charles couldn't tell if his dad was messing with him or not but the way he recoiled reminded the boy uncomfortably of his own reaction when Mr. Matherne had casually mentioned his orientation during one of their first lunches together.

"No," said Charles, his heart picking up like it did when other kids focused their attentions on him. "But so what? As black males it's our responsibility to cut out the bullshit homophobia—"

"Don't take that high tone with me," his dad scowled. "This ain't that dumb comic strip, and this community don't care about hurting your feelers. Fifteen years old and already talkin like her. Comin down here'll do a world of good for you."

Her. Charles went inside and his dad stayed on the porch, reflecting through his buzz that it was maybe still a little soon to discuss the problematic rearing his ex-girlfriend had given their only child. He had reason enough to be bitter with her, and once the kid got himself together he'd set'em straight. She'd cut north after graduation, not even telling him about the boy until Charles was five, for christsake, and then refused to take the boy to visit, making him fly up instead, and by then Charles was ten or eleven, already looking like that Urkel kid with those glasses and pressed clothes, so it's not like he could be blamed for being a deadbeat dad or whatever—he didn't even know about the kid for years, so how the hell was that his fault?

"These are good," Charles said as he chewed the turnip greens and surreptitiously pushed the ham further away from his oasis of watery vegetation.

"Long's you're in my house you'll have vegtables," his gramma said, patting his knee.

"Next time let me know before you cook," said Charles. "I'd like to learn to cook southern like you, ma'am."

"Cookin's good work," his gramma said, giving Charles's snickering father a reproachful glance. Since moving down Charles had found himself cooking far more than he ever had at home. There was a hippy grocery store an hour walk or so down Magnolia so he'd been able to spend what little allowance his dad gave him on actual safe food. That, and plain bean burritos at the Taco Bell. Once he had started public school Charles had covertly revolted against his mother's diet, but ever since the funeral he couldn't look at meat or smell eggs without getting queasy. He knew it would make her happy if he—

"Jus put the hamhock in with the greens, so they soak the flavor and—" His gramma went on, making Charles' dad howl with laughter as the boy put down his fork. She broke off, confused. "What? What's funny, Douglas?"

"Nuthin," Charles's dad said, spearing a piece of the pink meat and waggling it at his crestfallen son. "Nuthin at all. Clean your plate, Charlie, or no allowance this week. Serious, now, you need meat."

Reset vegan clock to zero, Charles thought glumly as he picked up his fork. The longest he had made it so far was four days. By the time he had worked his way through the greens his dad was back on the couch and his gramma took the ham off his plate, winking at him. "Tonight you don't gotta, but you'll get sick if you don't start eatin right, Charlie."

Charles went to his room and looked at his twin stacks of books. The pile that was on semi-permanent loan from the Matherne Collection consisted of the poetry of Langston Hughes, the fiction of Ernest Gaines, and the autobiographies of Olaudah Equiano and Malcolm X. The other stack came from his most recent trek to the library—non-fiction on werewolves, bigfoot, and more werewolves. Not even losing the only real parent he had ever known had dampened his interest in horror movies and books, although of late his predilections had shifted to what his gramma dubbed "things comin out the woods people never heard of," instead of more mundane slashers and thrillers. Charles had already worked his way through vampires, and avoided the subject of ghosts as carefully as he tried to eschew meat and dairy.

After a while he put the Dead Prez CD Mr. Matherne had given him into the dusty jambox his dad had left him upon moving out to the living room. Since the self-proclaimed Holten Street Clique had liberated Charles of his iPod, the *Let's Get Free* album was the only music not trapped inside his mom's laptop that he was now only allowed to use for an hour a day.

"They're from Tallahassee," Mr. Matherne had told him. "Rickards alumni, even; knew that name was familiar. Pro-veg, pro-active."

"Really?" Charles accepted the compact disc with the reverence of a relic.

"For real, like Sarandon in *Fright Night*," said Mr. Matherne. "I also tried to find *The Beast Must Die* but it's out of print. So keep your eyes peeled for that down in the dirty dirty."

"Are they also positive?"

"Who? Oh, no, it's a movie. Great white hunter has a dinner party."

"Except?" Charles smiled.

Mr. Matherne smiled back. "Except all the guests are suspected werewolves. And the great white hunter's a black guy."

"Cool."

"Very."

"I'm not a hunter, but I'm told . . . that, uh, in places like the arctic where indigenous people, uh, sometime might, might hunt a wolf." A man lecturing over the sound of howling wolves opened the album, a chairman of some group or movement. *"They'll, they'll take a double-edged blade, and they'll put blood on the blade, and they'll melt the ice and stick the handle in the ice so that only the, the blade is protruding. And that a wolf will smell the blood and wants to eat, and it'll come and lick the blade, tryin to eat. And what happens is, when the, when the wolf licks the blade, of course, ah, he cuts his tongue and he bleeds and he thinks he's really havin a good—and he drinks, and he licks, and he licks and of course he's drinkin his own blood, and he kills himself. That's what the imperialists did to us with crack cocaine . . . ".*

That was when Charles always pressed the skip button. The first time he had put the CD in and heard that bullshit he had turned it off, and it was several weeks before he gave it another chance. That Mr. Matherne would give him something like that right after what had happened to his mother was crazy and stupid, and he had hated his teacher for a few days afterwards.

"*And they actually think that there is somethin that is bringin resources to them but they're killing themselves just like the wolf was lickin the blade, and they're slowly dying without knowing it. That's what's happening to the community, you with me on that? That's exactly and precisely what happens to the community. And instead of blaming the hunter who put the damn handle and the blade in the ice for the wolf then what happens is the wolf gets blame, the wolf gets blamed for trying to live. That's what happens in our community. You don't blame the person, the victim, you blame the oppressor. Imperialism, white power is the enemy, was the enemy when they first came to Africa—*"

"Bullshit," Charles whispered, the word a mantra he recited whenever he heard those lies. Maybe some of it was sort of true on some other, higher level, but the crackhead who had knifed his mom wasn't a victim, he was a wolf, a hunter, and he didn't deserve any sympathy or justification. He was a beast, and he should die. She had fed him, fed all of them in that slouching brick building the color of old blood that she had single-handedly turned from a crackhouse into a shelter, she was there six days a week and even brought her son along, made him come along if he wanted the allowance he spent on pizza and beef jerky and chocolate milk and everything else he guiltily wolfed down in the cafeteria after throwing away the tempeh sandwiches she made him, the salads and fruit. The junkie wasn't the victim of white oppression and imperialism, he was a drug addict and he tried to jack her car right there in the fucking parking lot, and Charles knew she couldn't have, wouldn't have fought him over it, probably tried to talk him down like she talked everyone down, but instead of getting talked down he stabbed her twenty-eight times and then crashed her car into a parked police cruiser two blocks away.

Charles had to think about something else, so he turned the music off and picked up the second werewolf book. He opened it and saw the chapter was simply titled "Becoming a Werewolf." Twenty minutes later he knew how he would be spending the rest of his summer.

The simplest method for a young man trapped in a sweltering southern city distinctly lacking in werewolves to coerce into biting one's arm seemed to be the herbal recipes the book listed, complex combinations of various dried plants brewed in this tea or bound in that poultice, whatever a poultice was. The bulk bins of New Leaf Market were, to Charles's disappointment, void of wolfsbane, hemlock, and just about everything else but a few of the more common dried flowers. Day One was a bust but Charles was not in a hurry to return home, so after eating a rare, hot vegan lunch he walked in the grass bordering the big road down to the tower of the capital and the two smaller, domed buildings abutting it, the architecture resembling a dude's junk even to non-teenaged viewers.

The downtown was nothing but offices, banks, and government buildings, and finally Charles marched south. He had no way of knowing he passed within a block of a local vegan soulfood cart, or four blocks of a twenty-four hour veg-friendly coffee shop, just as he had no way of knowing that there were dozens of non-asshole kids in his neighborhood, kids who preferred reading and riding bikes and playing video games to terrorizing their peers and getting fucked up. The sun was setting as Charles reached Holten Street but he walked around the block a few times before going inside the dilapidated house where his gramma was already cooking something he didn't want to eat.

There was a bike in his room. It didn't have gears and was a little small but it was, undeniably, a bicycle. Charles felt a lump in his throat, and then felt stupid for feeling it.

"Gotcha bike," his father said over the hoppin john that Charles could barely taste the fatback in.

"I really appreciate it," Charles said. "Thanks."

"Can't be walkin everywhere lookin like such a target," his dad went on, a strange expression on his ashy cheeks. "Gotta be able to dip out quick next time them toughs come atcha. Fight's out, so that leaves you with flight. What?"

Charles realized he must be looking pretty confused himself, his gramma looking back and forth between her son and grandson with a beatific smile on her pinched face.

"I went to school, boy," his dad shook his head and set back to his meal. "Maybe not as much's *some* but I went, and that's how I got the state job. Rickards is hard but it'll be good, toughen you up, and then you can head over to Fam like your mom and me. That's the last thing the government wants, us simple coloreds getting degrees."

Florida Agricultural and Mechanical College wasn't exactly Ivy League, and Charles knew his father had only received an AA, but it was the closest thing to a good night he had enjoyed since arriving. It only got better—after dinner his dad took him out to the video store and let him pick out a movie. When his gramma went to sleep they settled in on the couch his dad slept on with a battered VHS tape called *Black Werewolf*. About halfway through the film Charles realized it had to be the same movie Mr. Matherne had recommended, *The Beast Must Die*, just with a different title for some reason. Not even his dad offering him a hit on the acrid joint he puffed and cutting up with "Werewolf my ass, that's a damn dog leapin all over the place. More like leap-wolf, you ask me" could diminish Charles's pleasure. That night he dreamed of being a real werewolf, and not like the obvious German shepherd in the movie but the real deal, a beast both ferocious and fair, a cross between a superhero and a monster. Then he dreamed about his mom and woke up feeling sick and scared.

The next morning Charles pored over his book and realized he was rapidly running out of means of becoming a werewolf, given the short supply of rare herbs and the continued absence of the Devil offering up magic ointments. One method the book listed was to sleep outside under a full moon on a Friday, but who knew when the next one of those would be, and if that actually worked, the world would have been long overrun in lycanthrope winos and boy scouts. Just about everything else involved werewolves or, failing that, normal wolves, and so Charles had almost given up hope when he re-read the paragraph about being cursed.

There weren't a lot of Gypsies in the ghetto, but if Hollywood had taught Charles one thing it was that the South was brimming over with magical black people. Of course, they always appeared whenever white people needed them so Charles was at a marked disadvantage there, but he *did* know an old black lady, and if she didn't know voodoo or whatever she could at least point him in the right direction. His gramma spent most of any given day in the community center a few blocks away, and Charles was halfway there before he remembered his bike and trotted back home to get it.

It lacked a kickstand and he had to peddle backwards to brake but the feel of the wind on his face was a welcome one. Leaning the bike against a handicapped parking sign, Charles walked up the cracked concrete walkway and pushed open the tinted glass doors. He felt like he had jumped into the neighborhood pool back home, the AC burning his sweaty skin. Taking off his glasses and wiping them on his shirt, Charles realized at once why his gramma spent so much time there.

"Charlie!" she cried, and putting his glasses back on he saw he had walked in on an impressively stereotypical game of bingo. His gramma waved him over and he moved between the tables crowded with old men and women, most of whom seemed put out by the distraction. The tables were obviously from a school cafeteria, and his gramma scooted down the bench to make room for him, the older gentleman beside her smiling at Charles as he squeezed between them.

"This is Charlie," she said proudly.

"E-nine," announced the portly man at the front of the room, causing a flurry of groans, mutterings, and laughter. "E-nine."

"Charlie, that's Mr. Johnson next to you, and this is Ms. Hattie, and she's Mrs. Leacraft, and—" a half-dozen more introductions were made, to the consternation of those who actually treated the game with the severity it deserved. Finally Charles's gramma finished up and seemed ready to turn her attention back to the game but Charles realized he had hit the jackpot and acted quickly before the attentions of the seniors could return to their bingo cards.

"Ma'am, I came here to ask you something," said Charles, pleased to see Mr. Johnson and a few of the others were watching him curiously.

"Well go on then," she said, her eyes flitting back to the front of the room where the announcer sifted out the next ball.

"Is there anyone around here who knows about voodoo and cursing people and all that?" Charles asked.

"What?" His gramma frowned at him, her voice nearly drowned out by the laughter of some of her neighbors and the disapproving voices of others.

"We're Christians, boy."

"Don't go messin with rootwork."

"You think you're funny?"

"Charlie's dad's been showin him movies bout, whatsit, werewolfs," his gramma said defensively, though she had every intention of bawling him out once they were alone. "He's just got himself curious."

"Ware woofs?" Ms. Hattie said, peering at Charles. "Takem on ta the juneya moosam, they got ware woofs there."

"They do?" Charles couldn't believe what he was hearing.

"Red'uns," Ms. Hattie nodded, the thick patch of hair on her neck making Charles wonder if a bite from her would be sufficient. "Ma Davie liked'um."

"Don't you get her started on her boy," Charles's gramma hissed. "Go on home and don't come back in here less you behave, Charlie. I swear—"

Charles didn't wait to see what she swore, instead thanking Ms. Hattie and booking it. Back at the house he dug through the phonebook, and in five minutes he had directions to the Tallahassee "Junior" Museum. He considered asking them about werewolves but it wasn't like he had a lot else to do if Ms. Hattie was as crazy as she sounded, and so he set off down Orange Avenue.

The neighborhoods thinned out as he peddled and it took him over an hour before he even reached the turn-off. Regular as locker searches at Rickards High School the afternoon rain came down and soaked him as he rode, but finally he hit the hilly stretch of gravelly road. He was out in the woods now, poison ivy and brambles filling in the gaps between the scrub pines, the sounds of the highway he had foolishly ridden on fading as he rolled into the parking lot. The wooden building looked awfully small and wanting in spooky architecture for a place purported to hold some variety of werewolf but in he went, drenched from sneaker to snout.

The Junior Museum was more or less a zoo for local animals. Beyond the building lay a re-creation of an old farm, and trails wound through the woods and over long boardwalks near a lake. There were supposedly alligators and a panther but they must have been hiding in their large enclosures, everything green palmettos and brown leaves and reddish cypress and gray oak. There were hardly any other people on the grounds as he wound through the maze of paths and walkways, and then he arrived. Charles grinned, the plaque on the raised boardwalk overlooking the pen clarifying Ms. Hattie's rambling.

Red Wolf. Endangered. Rare wolves, indeed.

They looked like dogs, lanky and brown and lolling in the shade of the underbrush at the mouth of their den—two wolves. Charles wondered just what in hell was wrong with him, coming to a zoo. He supposed the patch of woodland was their natural habitat but still, locking up intelligent animals was unfair. That was why he didn't eat them, after all, because they were smart and felt pain and rejection and the sting of confinement, because they were just as real as he was and deserved to live for themselves instead of being locked up.

Looking down at the bored wolves Charles couldn't believe what a kid he had been. Even if werewolves were real, which they weren't, why would he want to be one? He didn't even eat cheese anymore so why would he want to gnaw bones and rend flesh? Would he scare the Holten Street Clique straight, or fix the crackhead who had killed his mom? What he was doing was daydreaming about violence, no different than some fool thinking a heater or a knife would even the score or keep him safe. What did violence beget? Again, what in hell, Charles? The Vegan Werewolf sounded like a pretty dumb premise for a children's book, not a mature plan for fixing himself and helping his community, like his mom had—

They came up behind him, braying in their exaggerated dialect, and somehow he knew, as if even then his nose were keener, his ears sharper.

"—bwah, that shit is r-tarded," one of them hooted.

"See one fight a red-nose pit, that'd be tight," said another, and Charles turned around and looked at the three white kids from the silver hatchback that had pelted him with garbage his first week on the Southside. There was a fat one with a kango hat, a bulky but strong looking dude, and a wiry little one in a wife beater. None of them looked older than Charles but clearly one of them had a license.

"Hey," the smallest nodded at Charles and they moved a little way down the boardwalk.

"Nuthin here, either." The ripped guy said. "Bunk as fuck."

"My moms'll go to work in another hour," the skinny one said. "Try out that gravity B I built?"

"Go ghetto-callin later," the fat one said in a low voice, glancing over his shoulder at Charles as they turned and went back down the walkway, away from the pen. "My cousin showed me how to get piss into a water balloon."

Then they were gone around the bend of the wooden boardwalk, and Charles exhaled, light headed and nauseated. Looking down into the enclosure his eyes focused immediately on a small puddle, probably rainwater, and the footprints around it. What else was he going to do that summer? The chain-link fence went right up to the railing of the boardwalk and Charles went over before he chickened out.

Halfway down he realized what he was doing and froze. It took more strength than he knew he had to turn his head, knowing they must be about to pounce and drag him down to a bloody, painful death. Instead he saw the two wolves watching him lazily from their shady lookout. He scrambled the rest of the way down, painfully aware of the noise the metal fence made as he descended into the pen.

Fingers still biting into the fence, he glanced away from the wolves to the muddy earth at his feet. Dry pawprints speckled the ground but a few feet away one was filled with blackish water. Squatting down, he moved like a nervous crab over to the print, the wolves still motionless but watching. Then Charles giggled at how stupid he was being and, dropping onto all fours, stuck his mouth in the pawprint and slurped up a mouthful of muck-water. He coughed on it but stood triumphantly, which was when he saw that only one of the wolves was still lying in the shade watching him.

Charles turned back to the fence, knowing what he would see. The boy had suffered nightmares before, had seen a horror flick or two, and knew what came next. Sure enough, the red wolf stood between him and the fence, its teeth bared, its hackles raised, a low growl bubbling out of its throat. Bullshit, thought Charles, and then it lunged forward.

Charles kept his bloody hand in his pocket as he passed through the museum building and out into the parking lot, dusk creeping down from the dirty clouds. The white kids must still be on the grounds somewhere, the silver hatchback one of the only cars in the lot, and after looking around Charles took his damp shirt off and wrapped his hand in it before getting on his bike. He had only peddled halfway to the main road before he had to ditch his bike and throw up, still terrified and confused.

It knew what he wanted and was helping him, a part of Charles told himself, but the rest of him was certain the wolf had been just as scared as he was, territorial but scared, and that's why it had fled back to its mate after nipping his hand instead of dragging him down and ripping out his throat. Charles didn't know how he had made it up the fence afterwards, his bound hand already dying the shirt an impossibly bright red. The silver hatchback passed him as he got back on his bike but none of the kids seemed to notice him, and Charles rode as fast as he could, his stomach twisting, his head pounding, his hand itching.

The setting sun at his back, Charles peddled harder and harder, his bike whining, traffic content to cruise behind him instead of passing the crazy-looking kid flying down the road on a tiny bike. Then the bike was too slow, and in the deepening twilight he left Orange Ave and skidded his bike to a stop on a side road by one of the FAMU gardens. When the last car passed him he hurled the bike down into the gully that ran parallel to Orange and scrambled down the steep bank after it, foam flecking his lips, a fever working its heat from his spinning head down his parched throat and into a ball of fire in his belly. He fell the last few feet down the overgrown slope, kudzu tangling his legs, and lay beside his bike in the shallow, mucky stream at the mouth of the culvert that dipped under the side road. Charles guzzled the water until he vomited, and then he drank more.

The creek had to be toxic, what in hell, Charles, his skin burning and his limbs aching and his bowels pinching, and he scrambled into the wide culvert, away from the headlights shining at the top of the deep ditch. Then all of his bones broke, every single one, and Charles couldn't even scream from the agony of it, just the sound of the splintering bones making him throw up, except instead of ditchwater a long, dripping tongue spilled out of his mouth, dangling by his chin. Charles tried to stop himself from shitting his pants, as if that were somehow the worst part about dying, as if embarrassment hurt worse than real pain, but he couldn't even scream so holding it in was futile. Then it *was* real pain, it *was* the worst part, and he managed to make his twisting, warping arms get his pants down to relieve the pressure.

The length of spine that had split out of the skin beneath his tailbone extended further without the jeans to constrain it, and that freedom was when the pain turned to pleasure, when Charles finally let himself acknowledge and believe what was happening to him. Not bad water, not exhaustion, not craziness—he was a werewolf, a real werewolf, and he could no longer control himself. He was going to forget himself, he was going to be a deadly beast hunting the crackheads and wannabe gangbangers and ghetto-callers, he would rip them apart and he would lick and he would drink and he would drink and he would lick and when he came back to himself the next morning he would be covered in scratches and bruises and no memory of what had happened, but when he saw a human finger or some bling in the toilet bowl he would realize that it was time to reset the old vegan clock, yes indeed, and every full moon it would happen and—

Charles realized it had finished, his body trembling but again complete and static, yet he was still himself. Mentally, at least—his eyes were sharper, as were his nose and ears and, flexing his paws in the drainage pipe, his claws. Trying to get up, Charles felt the faintest tinge of disappointment that children do when things do not go exactly as they expect—he was not some hulking, half-human lupine monster who could walk on his hind-legs, he was a wolf, and not even a very large one. Nevertheless, moving on all fours felt so natural and cool that Charles laughed, a raspy, alien growl. Standing at the mouth of the pipe, he licked his chops and looked up at the full moon, wondering if it had been the water in the footprint or the bite or simply his desire. Then he tried howling, and it came as naturally as walking had, and dogs took up the cry all over Tallahassee.

Staying to the channel, Charles marveled at how stunning the night was, the smells and sounds so rich he felt like he was gobbling them up, and he only left the wild of the filthy brook when streetlights began spilling down into the dark ravine. He waited until the sounds of cars were a safe distance off and scrambled up the side, the trickiest maneuver thus far. Then he crossed Orange and headed home by way of the FAMU campus, smelling and hearing any would-be witnesses long before they caught a glimpse of him, and if anyone working late at the university saw a large dog loping across the parking lots it did not make the paper the next day.

Southside was beautiful under the full moon, Charles realized, beautiful but sad. The scarcity of streetlights in this particular urban area allowed him to walk right up the middle of the street, his nails clicking on the rough pavement, and whenever headlights rounded a corner he cut into a backyard or under a house, most of them raised shotgun houses like his with plenty of room for a beast to hide until the car passed.

A silver hatchback was parked in front of one of the houses Charles ducked under, and he waited there until the trio of white kids came down the stairs, their fear stinking more than the dried-up pot in their pockets or the cigarettes in their hands. Charles kind of wanted the beast to take over then, at least to scare them, but one of the Holten Street Clique who had jacked Charles was with them, and even bristling with teeth and claws Charles was scared of the big thug—he had a funky, metallic smell about him that might well have been a gun. Otherwise the kids smelled the same, more or less, which meant something, Charles supposed.

Charles moved on as they jawed in front of the hatchback, and in a vacant lot he rested by a worn fence and watched three men pass around a glass pipe, their fingers the only parts of their bodies not shaking as they smoked the stinking, sour lumps. Charles realized with a single sniff that one of them was the father of the Holten Street bully who was with the white kids two blocks over, and he wondered if the boy knew his dad was a junkie. The kid certainly had nicer clothes than his father, but that wasn't saying much.

Deeper in the night and the Southside he found a group of men and women enjoying a midnight grillout in a backyard, and further on a fenced-off yard where several pitbulls woke up growling at his approach, the dogs ripe with anger, their throats scarred from fighting, the stink of their dead fellows rising out of shallow graves beside the fence. Charles checked the address of the house to report them to the police in the morning. By then he was starting to fade, his tongue panting, his limbs sore, and he followed his own scent back to Holten Street, toward his bed.

His father was asleep on the front porch, an ashtray and the cordless phone on a stool beside him. Charles nosed the screen door open and padded inside the dark house. Hopping onto his bed, he curled up and fell into a deep and dreamless sleep.

"Boy, don't you sleep naked in your gramma's house!" Charles sat up in bed at his father's voice, his head pounding, his whole body sore and scratched and bruised and his eyes watering from the ruthless sunlight. "Charlie, I don't wanna call the police on you but you *cannot* be stayin out all night, not callin or nuthin. You don't wanna go where I've been, Charlie, *trust me*. What's wrong with you?"

"Sorry," Charles blinked away the tears and saw his father had turned away from him in the doorway. "I was—"

"I don't wanna hear it," his father shook his head. "But this is it, understand? No more. One free get-out-of-shit card and you just used it, son—no more. I lied to my mom for you, Charlie, I told her you got in right after she went to sleep. How do you think that made me feel? I rented us another wolfman movie and you make me stay up all night thinkin you run off or got yourself killed with that smart mouth of yours. Where you get off . . . "

Charles wondered if he would transform the next time the moon swelled. His father droned on, clearly taking satisfaction in the lecture, and Charles realized that he had been wrong about a whole hell of a lot of things. He was actually relieved that he had woken up human, and more than even knowing how the night-air of Tallahassee tasted or what the full moon smelled like, that was the most surprising thing about the summer that Charles became a werewolf.

THE BARONY AT RØDAL

PETER BELL

⮕

> In Norway and Iceland certain men were said to be
> *eigieinhameer,* not of one skin .... The full form of this
> superstition was, that men could take upon them other
> bodies, and the natures of those beings whose bodies
> they assumed ... and a man thus invigorated was called
> *hamrammr.*
>
> —Sabine Baring-Gould, 1865

The excursion to Norway was something of a new departure for Fraser, who had previously rarely travelled abroad.

It had long been his habit to spend his holidays visiting botanic gardens. Powerscourt beneath the Wicklow Mountains, storm-lashed Tresco Abbey in the Scillies, the Hebridean splendours of Achamore, Arduaine and Inverewe—Fraser had visited them all; as well as countless others, by no means all of which were open, officially at least, to the public; but, by fair means or foul—for he was not averse to trespass—he had ticked them off his list.

Now, with the broad plain of retirement extending before him, he was exploring pastures new: a cruise of the Norwegian fjords, courtesy of his daughter, Eloise. The stark northern climes of Scandinavia had never previously struck him as a likely hunting ground for exotic flora; but Eloise, who had worked for a time at Kristiansand University, assured him that the cherry trees bloomed prodigiously all along the grey banks of the fjords, hinting at treasure troves as wonderful as Kew, trees mightier than anywhere back home in Argyll. Fraser was not convinced.

As the coach traversed the mountains, they listened with exasperation to their prattling Norwegian tour guide, Inge, a rotund, rosy-cheeked, middle-aged woman, with curiously idiomatic English, whose appearance reminded Fraser of a garden gnome.

"To your right you see the Grønnfjell." She gesticulated towards the wooded slopes, adopting a melodramatic tone. "And here, in the forests, long ago there lived man-wolves and bears, and things that are drinking blood, including the terrible bloody fox . . . "

"Like something out of Bergman!" Eloise exclaimed.

"Bergman is Swedish, my dear. I wouldn't let our guide hear that, it's like saying the Welsh are Scottish! . . . "

"Well, a lot of the old Norwegian noble families have Danish or Swedish blood in their veins. They've all been united one time or another."

Still the guide droned on: now it was trolls.

" . . . and these trolls, they lived in caves up on the hillside, and hidden away in dark dells, and on a lonely dark night, if a traveller he meet a troll, then he might not live to see the day, or will go mad with fear . . . "

There was something about the guide's jolly, lilting Scandinavian vowels that, to an English ear, sounded vaguely comic, curiously and uneasily framing the horrors.

"This is as bad as Scotland!" declared Fraser. "Nothing but ghosts and legends! Where are all these wonderful gardens?"

"Stop complaining! You're the one who's always telling people Grandmother Campbell had second sight!"

They were entering a tunnel.

" . . . and above here, in a high pass, there was a slaughter in the olden days, very bloody . . . "

"She'll be blaming the Campbells next!" he said.

"Not unless she's a MacDonald!"

"Aye, they get everywhere!"

The guide's history lesson continued, of questionable accuracy.

"Notice how she glosses over the War," whispered Eloise. "Nothing but heroics. They've buried the past here, alright."

Eloise was a historical researcher, her specialism Norwegian resistance in the Second World War. Indeed, her scholarship had won her the fellowship at Kristiansand, a post she had been reluctant to vacate, having unearthed previously unstudied material in the National Archives that shed new light on the Nazi occupation. It involved some of Norway's most respected families. The picture was, however, incomplete; further research was needed, not to speak of circumnavigating the suddenly disobliging attitude of the university authorities. Fraser got the impression she had left under a cloud. The present trip, he suspected, was as much inspired by his daughter's scholarly agenda as by a desire to indulge him in the botanical wonders of the North.

Eloise had arranged things so she would have time at the end of the trip to revisit the Archives in Oslo; and, beforehand, to network with colleagues from Kristiansand. Fraser had been left to wander the old university town alone, which had not been without its rewards. Meanwhile, Eloise had not wasted her time: an interview with a surviving member of the Norwegian Resistance, Evald Akerø, great-uncle of a former colleague, had left her quite excited.

"Akerø told me about a Resistance operation to help refugees escape to Sweden that ended in a massacre," she explained over supper in the sterile luxuriance of the Bergen Radisson, "It involved one of Norway's oldest families, the von Merkens. This ties in with hints in my own research. Some of these nobles were only too glad to sell out their people for the sake of a quiet life! Akerø gave me the name of an old servant who's apparently still on the estate. Said he could tell a few tales about goings-on during the War when a certain Anders von Merkens was in residence."

"Where's that?"

"The *Baroniet Rødal*!" Eloise declared, smiling.

"That's on our itinerary, isn't it?" he responded. "You knew that all along! I thought this was a holiday!"

"Let's call it a mix of business and pleasure!"

"So what's this place, Rødal?"

"Oh, you'll love it! An old Norwegian manor house with landscaped gardens. Over a hundred species of rhododendron—they should be at their best now—and ten thousand English roses! Rødal—the Red Vale! So called for its brilliant autumns."

Later, in bed, Fraser studied the glossy brochure. Rødal was on the final day. Intervening visits were less alluring, though this was perhaps unfair: had his interests not been so obsessively botanical, there was much of promise, including a visit to Edvard Grieg's house, complete with special piano recital; and a trip to the "magnificent island home" of another nineteenth century composer he had never heard of, Øle Bull, described as Hardangerfjord's "best kept secret."

He must have dozed, for he was awoken from a fearful dream which had seemed to be happening outside the window, as if something were scrabbling at the pane. It felt sufficiently disquieting and real for him to get up and check. Drawing back the curtains from the half-open window, he was startled by a fluttering commotion: a large bird, a raven maybe, flapped up into his face, its beady eyes glinting in the moonlight. He recoiled in loathing. It was some time before he could catch sleep again.

Next day began with a tour of Bergen, the most interesting feature being the Mariakirken, with a fine medieval triptych and a set of exquisitely carved wooden statues of Christ and his disciples. There was John, the only beardless one, denoting youth and not, as crackpot theorists claimed, Mary Magdalene. A model of a wooden sailing ship hung suspended above the nave, a routine feature of Norwegian churches, indicative of the country's intimate connection with the sea; as were sarcophagi shaped like upturned boats. In the Museum of Modern Art they joined the gaping crowds before *The Scream*, Edvard Munch's dreadful paean to human angst.

The highlight of the day, however, was Grieg's villa, a few miles out of town. The great composer had chosen his domain well: the elegant wood-framed house was set in spacious grounds, with stunning views to the hills and across Lake Nordås. Everywhere there were trees. Inge was gathering them outside, like a fussing mother hen.

"Shortly, we are going into Grieg's fine house, to hear his piano played. He lived here for twenty-two years with his wife, Nina. It was Nina who named the house *Troldhaugen*, the Troll Hill, for it is up here in the mountains that the trolls lived, where the ashes of Grieg and his wife now lie in the cliff above the fjord. You have heard *Peer Gynt*, which, of course, is about Norway's legends? Peer, you know, is taken by troll maiden to the Hall of the Mountain King, where there is an orgy and, then, these troll girls, they want to kill him, for he is a Christian, but he is being too clever, and so escapes the terrible trolls."

"There's no end to them!" whispered Eloise.

"I think we've got one conducting the tour," he remarked, too loudly.

The guide paused, thinking Fraser was asking a question, then proceeded, "Grieg's grandfather, he came from Aberdeen in Scotland. And so, there are many saying his music is very Scottish, but it is the Norwegian inspiration really, all the hills and the forests. Many Scots they are descended of the Vikings, from when Norway was powerful. Nowadays, we are a peace loving people."

The cruise around Hardangerfjord proved more rewarding than expected. At Bakke there were Bronze Age carvings, depicting fertility rites, the rocks hollowed out to catch the blood of sacrifice. At Eidfjord was Norway's largest Viking graveyard, and a fourteenth century church built by one Ragna Asulfdatter to atone, so legend told, for the slitting of her husband's throat. At Espevær they visited the *Baadehuset*, a stately residence of 1810, said to be haunted by the ghost of its creator, a conscience-stricken naval captain. Best was Øle Bull's eccentric retreat on the wooded islet of Lysøen. The flamboyant, blue and white wooden villa, with its ornate fretwork and onion dome, was according to their ever-cheery guide the scene, on Bull's death, of the most magnificent funeral ever witnessed in Norway. It was, nevertheless, with the satisfaction of reaching a long-awaited goal that they arrived, finally, at Rødal.

As they waited in the fine morning rain to be taken to the Barony, Eloise was like a racehorse stamping at the starting tape, keen to find her wartime witness.

"What are you going to say?" Fraser asked. "People are funny about the War, you know, here on the continent. It's not like in Britain—all those jolly memories of the Blitz! . . . What did you say this bloke's name was?"

"I didn't. But it's Jonas Nielsen . . . Must be well into his eighties.'"

"The family's still here then?"

"The von Merkens?" Eloise gave him a thoughtful look. "No, no, not anymore. Anders disappeared after the War. No-one ever found out what happened to him. The Barony passed to a distant member of the family in Denmark—an absentee landlord, a playboy. A hideout for his mistresses, basically! After that, it's the usual story. It fell into disuse, conservationists got going about national heritage, the government stepped in, and now it's run jointly with the University of Oslo. Everyone who lived and worked on the estate had the option to stay including, presumably, Nielsen."

The party was chauffeured up to the Barony through rolling park-land by minibus. The house stood in brilliant formal gardens; built of stone, painted white, with grey-tiled roof and mullioned windows; plain, unassuming, functional, yet with an elegant solemnity. It spoke of tradition, stability, of all that was fine and ordered, of continental gravitas; and, whilst calling to mind a baronial house of Scotland, was quintessentially Scandinavian. A park and lake stretched beyond, enclosed by woods. A stark mountain skyline completed the view. Fraser could hardly wait to explore.

First, however, there would be the conducted tour of the house. This he would have been happy to miss; they only had a few hours, and the last thing he felt like was listening to any more babble from the guide.

"It'll probably only take half an hour," Eloise protested. "Then you can wander round, and I'll see if I can find Nielsen."

The tour lengthened beyond the half hour, beyond three-quarters, beyond an hour. Thankfully, it was not conducted by Inge, who grinned and nodded throughout like a toyshop doll, but by an attractive young woman in her twenties, with brown, intelligent eyes and long blond hair, Solvejg, a heritage student from Oslo University.

"Keep your eyes off, she's too young for you!" Eloise cautioned, as Fraser smilingly signalled approval of their new chaperone.

Solvejg spoke with an American twang, blending curiously with the

Norwegian vowels. Though her command of English was occasionally eccentric, she gave a professional account of herself, and was remarkably knowledgeable, even when asked questions.

Except in one respect: her detailed history of Rødal's owners, delivered outside in the courtyard, skated hazily over the War, leaving unmentioned its last and most controversial master; though the family's earlier tenure was lengthily described, and much made of the rakish playboy and the conservation story. All attempts by the inquisitive Eloise to coax her were politely sidestepped behind a bland public relations smile; and by this process of attrition, as the party became increasingly impatient, not helped by Eloise's insistent donnish manner, the matter dropped.

"Well, what do you expect?" he whispered. "Going on like an intellectual. People hate that! And I told you, continentals don't like the War!"

Rødal dated from 1665 and was granted the status of barony, the only one in Norway, by King Christian V in 1675. The house itself was extensively rebuilt in 1745 following a terrible fire, attributed by local lore to an ill-advised marriage. The gardens and park were laid out in the 1840s, amidst inhospitable wilderness. The first owner, Ludwig von Merkens, scion of a Danish aristocratic family, had been awarded Rødal for ridding the area of brigands, associated with an ill-reputed nobleman of Swedish ancestry, ousted amidst great bloodshed in 1664. The name of this renegade was Cornelius Lindhorst, descendant of a family going back centuries, linked with all sorts of primitive superstition and atrocious violence. Here their young chaperone had lapsed into a dramatic manner worthy of the garden gnome.

"In the twelfth century, they say, one of Lindhorst's most evil ancestors lived here in an old castle, which was destroyed. His name was Björn, which means the bear. Björn, well, he was *berserkr*. You know, a man of unnatural strength and diabolical fury? And so you have in English "going berserk?" Well, it is said, he was often changing form. Sometimes appearing as an awful bear, or a wolverine, sometimes as a running dog, or a wolf, or a bloody snarling fox, sometimes as a cruel bird with terrible beak, or a bat, or even, they say, a spider or bloodsucker insect—for always he is sucking the blood—and that the form you see him in, well, it is the form you most fear in the creatures.

"Of course, what we are remembering, actually, is a very bloody landlord who killed and tortured his people. And so, they translate this into superstition and tales of horror. For, these *berserkrs*, they clothed themselves in the hides of bears, and so you have your horrid legends! But, perhaps, in olden days they really believed? As you see, the windows of this house, they have glass that you cannot see through, only the light. Well, that was to keep out the wild beasts, the monsters, who they hoped are not existing if they do not see them!"

Solvejg was now leading them upstairs to a long corridor lit by stained glass windows, where family portraits were displayed. Portraits were not an art form Fraser appreciated; they seemed to speak more of the vanity and egotism of the subjects than the talent of the artists. The assembled sombre visages of the von Merkens, sternly looking down from the huge gilt frames in dour Lutheran self-righteousness, did not break the mould; though, if Solvejg was to be believed, some were masterpieces by esteemed Norwegian artists whose grandeur, alas, had thus far been overlooked by the outside world. They were disconcertingly numerous and the meticulous guide was determined to say something about each in turn, working her way along from the founder, Ludwig. She paused before the picture of an effete, overweight youth in a feathered cap.

"And so, here we have a ghost story! Like in all your country houses!" She put on a hushed voice. "Well, the ghost of Augustus von Merkens, who you see here, who died of a consumption, it is said he walks at midnight . . . but he never passes the turning to the stairs . . . and, you know why? . . . Well, look!"

Heads turned in unison towards a portrait at the top of the stairs: it depicted a grim, humourless, middle-aged woman.

"Well, you know who we have here? . . . It is, of course, Birgitta Lindhorst, his wife's mother . . . And so, he is too frightened to go past the mother-in-law, and so, he goes back to bed!" The party laughed uproariously.

"I thought these Nordic folk were supposed to be liberated!" whispered Fraser.

"A concession, I would think, to the plebeian sense of humour! . . .
They're a lot more liberated actually!"

"So I've heard!" he said, grinning.

"I've told you! She's too young for you!"

Relentlessly enthusiastic, Solvejg reached, finally, a portrait of a
red-haired woman of uncertain age. An oddity about her face, with
its high cheek bones and prognathous jaw, crimson lips half-smiling,
was that it just stopped short of being ugly, yet resulting in a striking,
if somewhat sinister, beauty. Her prominent grey eyes appeared to
scrutinise the viewer with rapacious curiosity. Her cheeks and brow
were pale, as if the paint were fading, her throat long and white. Furs
draped her broad shoulders. Her garments were voluminous, the
shade of ruby wine. The painting seemed to occupy more space than
necessary, as if positioned where once two had hung.

"And here," declared the guide, "we have the last of the line, Sophia
von Merkens, who died in 1945. A very beautiful woman, who tempted
men to their fates. It was said of her that even when she was coming as
an angel, she was walking as a demon!"

"Aha!" laughed Fraser, "Very liberated! A *femme fatale!*"

"It's a form of empowerment!" hissed Eloise.

The guide was elaborating on Sophia's dubious charms. "She was a
Swede," she concluded, as if that explained many things.

"What about *Anders* von Merkens?" interrupted Eloise, somewhat
haughtily. "He was here in the War? . . . That makes *him* last of the line,
surely? . . . I'm talking about her husband."

"Ah, yes!" The guide put on her professional smile. "She was married to
Anders, her cousin, the Baron. His portrait, it is being restored in Oslo."

"Leave it!" whispered Fraser, nudging her. "Don't start accusing the
Norwegians of war crimes! That'll go down really well!"

Their companions, mostly elderly Americans, were regarding her
impatiently, anxious to terminate the interminable tour. Eloise made
to speak, then stopped. Solvejg's smile remained impregnable.

"So, our tour, it is over. The upstairs rooms are private offices for
the university. Thank you very much, ladies and gentlemen. Now we
are going down to the restaurant for a cup of coffee. And, perhaps, a
delicious cake of Norway?'

"Funny, that," said Fraser, as they sat down with their espressos. "The name, I mean. Lindhorst?"

Eloise eyed him quizzically. "What?"

"Well, here's an ancient rogue, banished in the seventeenth century by the family, and then the name comes back through intermarriage?"

"Yes," replied Eloise, looking somewhat nonplussed. "But you know how it is with names! How many MacDonalds are there in Scotland?"

"Too many!"

They both laughed.

Eloise looked serious for a moment, as if to say something, then drained her cup. "I must find the curator, or whoever's in charge. See if they can direct me to our friend. Finish your coffee."

The minutes lengthened.

Fraser eventually located his daughter in the courtyard with a matronly woman, whose smart two-piece suit loudly proclaimed her custodian of the Barony. She appeared to be remonstrating, shaking her head, keen to terminate the conversation, his arrival prompting her departure.

"Meet our friendly curator," said Eloise. "She didn't seem keen on me meeting Nielsen. He lives in a cottage just on the other side of the park. I got the impression they'd like to see the back of him. He's an alcoholic, by the way. It's a problem here, you know? That's why there's so much tax on booze. Blame the long dark winter nights! And all the rain!"

"The more like Scotland, the more I hear!" groaned Fraser.

"Anyway," Eloise continued, "I'm going to see if I can find him. We'll meet up later."

"No problem," said Fraser, his spirits rising at the prospect of unalloyed solitude. "Let's say back at the boat about five-thirty. We're not sailing until nine."

Fraser studied the map Solvejg had provided. The grounds were vast, rising to a narrowing valley, with high peaks beyond; much of it was pasture, with belts of woodland. The map was colour-coded, denoting public and private areas. Though the park and gardens, shown in green, were freely open, intriguing pathways tailed into the encircling forests—into the red zone. Fraser noticed a small church on the edge of the estate, separated from the house by a swath of red; it could not be far from where he now stood. Solvejg had mentioned the medieval stave church, St. Olaf's, the oldest in Norway. The first priority, however, was botanical exploration.

The way to the lake led through a glade of rare trees, all neatly labelled in Latin. A bewildering profusion of flowering shrubs fringed its shores. There were sculptures and pergolas, a classical temple on an island. Fraser wandered randomly, defiantly treading the lawns, ignoring notices—*Tråkk ikke på gresset*—he could always say he didn't know the language. No one was about, not even members of the tour party; the rose garden would be their limit.

Eventually he found himself on the threshold of a pine woods; a wooden gate marked the public boundary. He clambered over, into the red zone. The conifers thinned into a dreary glade, interspersed with scrub hazel and birch, like a recently felled area reclaimed by nature, rampant with nettles. The pines loomed, dark, dense, forbidding, their intoxicating resin scent suffocating in the airless wood. Sunshine flickered harshly through the dismal soughing trees, circled by restless fluttering rooks, their harsh caws unsettling. The place exuded a disquieting ambience, difficult to define, but dreadful . . .

Fraser was besieged by an unutterable desolation, an anxiety bordering on terror; a feeling, almost, of physical malaise. He glanced into the brooding gloom of the encroaching forest, imagining voracious eyes . . . What a terrible place to die! . . .

Rapidly, he retreated—out of the glade, over the gate, back to the sanctuary of the gardens. He found himself on an elevated path, lined by a laurel hedge. The path was veering right, away from the direction of the lake, back into the woods; the direction did not feel right. The red-circled notice confronting him was unambiguous: *Adgang Forbudt!*

The map confirmed matters: here the path entered the red zone; he should have been lower down. It looked quicker, though, to proceed now straight ahead, through the wood, and pick up an alternative track that would bring him to the front of the house, to its courtyard.

In less than a quarter of a mile the trees thinned. The way back to the house, however, was less obvious than the map suggested. To his right was an ascending path; ahead, on a natural elevation, partly obscured by bushes, was an intriguing structure. He hesitated, then curiosity triumphed over caution. Curving steps led up through straggling shrubbery to a high stone wall, inset by an ornate metal gate. Another sign confronted him: *Gravelund. Privat! Adgang Forbudt!*

Fraser stepped up towards the gate.

Two luxuriant shrubs, of an exquisitely ghastly beauty, overhung it, forcing him to stoop. They were of a species he could not identify. Twisting copper boles with striated bark rose up into olive-shaded evergreen foliage. The blossom was remarkable, as if illumined from within. The thickly-bunched outsize scarlet flowers had splayed-back petals and prominent stamens. The blooms were exotic, outré, almost horrible; they exuded a pungent aroma, swiftly transforming from the delightful to the disagreeable. Most disgusting were the strange appendages that hung from the lower branches, two on one shrub, one on the other, like cocoons of thickly-matted straw.

The graveyard, evidently a family burial ground, resembled nothing so much as a walled garden run to seed. Wisteria and ivy clambered riotously up the walls, choking bedraggled fruit trees. Most of the graves were flat slabs, tangled with briars, weathered, neglected. There was no funerary ornamentation, not even so much as a simple cross; doubtless, the Norwegians took all this business more soberly. Fraser perambulated idly, casting his eye over the inscriptions.

The graves were arranged in strict order of decease. The name Lindhorst, he noticed, featured on quite a few. Here at the very end of the line was the resting place of Sophia von Merkens: it, too, bore above her married title the name Lindhorst. Though his knowledge of the language was limited, he guessed the lengthy dedication on her stone outlined her lineage. Inscribed also was, presumably, her place of birth—somewhere in "Sverige;" the slab was badly chipped, the exact location obscure, except for the initial letter "R."

It was a cheerless place, even in the bright sunshine. Fraser, moreover, could not shake off a sensation of being observed, which he could only put down to his act of trespass. On the rising slopes above, dark spruces loomed. The way back to the house, he recalled uneasily, had yet to be discovered. Time was already short. Hurriedly, he departed.

Brushing past the outlandish shrubs, he was distracted by a surreptitious movement in the densely tangled branches; something glittered in the shadows. The wings of whatever it was he had aroused whirred disagreeably towards him, and, in the seconds that it took him to think the bird extraordinarily large, he felt its beak slashing at his face. He fell back, protecting his eyes. The bird soared up above the graveyard wall with an eldritch cry, vast as an eagle. As he left, he saw to his distaste that in the fracas one of the cocoons had burst; perhaps the creature had been feeding. Whatever was teeming in the yawning crannies, he didn't wait to look.

It took a disconcertingly long time to find his way back to the house, and he could not shake of an irrational fear that the bird might reappear. It had drawn blood, but only slightly so, beneath the left ear. By the time he reached the courtyard, the last of the party had gone. There was no minibus. It was almost an hour before he got back to the boat. There was no sign of Eloise.

Guests were already at the tables before his daughter arrived. She looked pale and perplexed.

"Sorry about this, I . . . " Eloise gave a mirthless laugh. "Well . . . I got lost!"

"Lost?" replied Fraser, incredulous. "Anyway, any luck?"

"Well, yes and no," she said uncertainly. "Look, let's have dinner, and we'll talk about it later." She was trembling.

"Are you all right?" he asked, concerned.

She gave another hollow laugh. "I had a bit of a fright, that's all. I wasn't going to tell you."

"You mean because of Nielsen?"

"No, no!" she said. "It was after I left Nielsen . . . "

She hesitated, as if still weighing up whether to say more, then proceeded, very deliberately, as if retracing the memory in her own mind.

"By the time I got away it was getting late. I took a shortcut across the park, instead of going all the way back round. I was glancing up towards the house, thinking how lovely it looked in the evening sun. Then I saw something . . . An animal . . . Running down from the direction of those woods. I thought for a minute it was a fox—from the colour—but it was too big. As it got closer I decided it was some kind of a dog—but an unusually large one. There were sheep grazing—maybe it was rounding them up, or worrying them, or something. But it ran right past! . . . It must've been only a few hundred yards away before it dawned on me that it was *coming for me*! . . . Its eyes! They seemed to be blazing in the sunlight! . . . I don't think I've ever been so terrified in my life! . . . It was a bit like one of those huge German shepherds—you know the type, all shoulders and no neck, shaggy fur—but that's *not* what it was!"

She shuddered.

"To be honest, I've no idea *what* it was! . . . I just went into a panic and ran, no idea where I was going. I ended up on a driveway coming down from that old wooden church . . . Luckily, there was a car passing—the minister actually—and he offered me a lift."

"Did he see it?" exclaimed Fraser. "Didn't you tell him what you saw?"

"I began to, but, I don't know, I suddenly didn't want to, it sounded silly. Anyway, it had disappeared . . . I know this sounds ridiculous, but the last time I looked back I could have sworn it was running on hind legs!"

"Nonsense! It was probably just a farm dog loose, that's all," he said, dismissively. "Some kind of Scandinavian breed."

"Dog loose or not," she snapped, still trembling. "You know I can't stand the damned things! . . . This was no bloody farm dog!"

Over dinner their conversation avoided matters unpleasant. Fraser enthused about the afternoon's botanical treasures, saying nothing about his own encounter with the bird. The business of the dog was dropped. His daughter, he noticed, ate with little relish and drank considerably more wine than was her wont.

Fortified by coffee and cognac, as the *Edvard Grieg* bore them down the silent fjord, they relaxed at last in the bar. Eloise returned to her tale.

"Nielsen was a servant in the von Merkens household during the War. A lot of what he said I couldn't quite get—he spoke in a curious dialect, and it was all very rambling. I'd like to think what he said was the ravings of senility, or alcohol. But there were too many plausible details. Anders von Merkens, as I've long suspected, was a collaborator. Quisling and other leading Nazis were frequent house guests at Rødal, where Sophia was famous for hosting lavish parties. One night there was a terrible massacre, exactly as Akerø said."

"What, here at Rødal?"

"Somewhere in those woods. Nearby, there's a track into the mountains that leads eventually to a remote stretch of the Swedish frontier. The *Milorg*—the Resistance—were helping a party of Bergen Jews, mainly women and children, to escape to Sweden. But they were found out about it. They were rounded up and, well, they put them to death."

Eloise hesitated, as if hesitating to go on.

"It was worse than a massacre," she continued. "It was some kind of blood sacrifice . . . The victims were strung from the trees, their throats cut and bled dry . . . Sophia von Merkens, if Nielsen is to be believed, drank of the blood . . . It was June 1942, second anniversary of the German invasion—there was a great banquet in full sway. There was a Swede, a businessman, a brother of Sophia's. An important man, Nielsen thought, from the way he was treated, the one behind it all . . . and there was more . . . "

She regarded her Rémy-Martin. "I've suddenly gone off this." White-faced, she left the bar. Thoughtfully, Fraser pushed his own glass away. Other guests looked askance.

By the time they reached Oslo Eloise had recovered her insouciance; and her ardour for research had certainly not abated. Fraser was not at all sure that digging over war crimes was good for anyone, and he told her so.

"You said the authorities weren't keen on your inquiries. I'd keep out of it. You never know what might happen! I've told you, it's a sensitive topic."

"I can't leave it now. There's a file in the Archives I must get back to."

"What file? What about it?"

"Oh, it's a bit complicated. Remember I told you I'd discovered a misplaced file? I didn't have time to go through it properly before the university froze me out. You see, there's a correspondence file in the Ministry of Finance, its economic intelligence section, and it's to do with Quisling and the Nazis, but it's marked as a top secret file from the Ministry of Internal Security—all their records were destroyed at the end of the War, so it's priceless . . . "

"So?"

"Well," she sighed. "It's this name Lindhorst . . . it's bothered me from the beginning . . . it rings a bell . . . I think I may have seen the name somewhere in that file."

"I thought you said it was just like MacDonald?" he said wearily.

"I know," she said, "But the more I thought about it . . . And I think Nielsen mentioned the name too—it was all a bit garbled . . . There's some funny connection between the Lindhorsts and the von Merkens."

"Well, we know that," said Fraser. "A historical one. The portraits . . . And the graves."

"Graves?" Eloise eyed him curiously.

"Didn't I mention it?—we were too busy talking about Nielsen!"

Fraser summarised his findings.

Eloise raised her eyebrows when he told her that Sophia von Merkens was a Lindhorst. "Curiouser and curiouser!"

"It's just a case of persistent intermarriage, that's all!" he said, shrugging. "Common amongst the upper classes . . . Listen, I'm not really sure where all this is going?"

She frowned. "Nor am I. But I've got to go back to that file . . . Look, you'll enjoy the day exploring Oslo! Enjoy it while it lasts!"

Fraser was, in truth, not in the mood for sightseeing; he felt rather under the weather. It was inflamed where the bird had pecked; perhaps he should have sought first aid. And his nerves were bad; for reasons he could not explain he felt anxious about Eloise, though she was patently capable of looking after herself. He passed a depressing, desultory day, flitting from one attraction to another, unable to focus upon any, even the splendid municipal gardens. The final hour he whiled away in a bar, sipping an outrageously priced lager, awaiting five o'clock, when he had arranged to meet his daughter outside the National Archives Office.

A commotion of some kind surrounded the elegant nineteenth century building, set back in leafy grounds. Traffic was being diverted, blue lights flashing, the sound of police klaxons. The oscillating wail of an approaching ambulance charged the crisis atmosphere. Fraser's pulse quickened. A large crowd had gathered outside. Yellow-jacketed police bunched around the shrubberies in front of the building. His way was barred by a burly officer, shooing voyeurs away.

"An English girl, some kind of attack," declared a large American woman, catching his mute entreaties. "I thought it was safe to walk the streets here! I'm from Atlantic City!"

Fraser moved too quickly for the officer, who shouted after him as he ran to the rescue scrum in the bushes.

Eloise was lying in a gathering pool of blood with half her face missing.

Once his identity had been established, the police began asking questions. The ambulance had arrived too late to be of use, if it ever could have been. A doctor at the morgue assured him the severed jugular would have been sufficient to kill outright, quite apart from other ravages; it must be the work of a maniac, someone gone berserk. Nevertheless, Fraser's every movement that day, every detail of their trip, were checked and double-checked; and the detectives were very inquisitive about Eloise's purpose in the Archives. A silver-haired, distinguished-looking man in his sixties was introduced to him: Dr. Olaf Müller, Curator of the National Archives. He had questions too.

"Your daughter, Mr. Campbell, it appears, stole something from the Archives, though if this has anything to do with her killing, we are not sure."

A senior officer, of pale blue eyes and unsmiling face, continued to stare right at Fraser, a radar ready to detect every wayward blip.

"Do you know anything about your daughter's work, Mr. Campbell?"

continued Müller, "She was a professor once at Kristiansand? . . . For example, does this document have any sense to you?" He extracted from a briefcase several sheets of mottled paper printed in old-fashioned type.

Fraser stared blankly at the Norwegian text. The thick type swirled before his eyes like arcane hieroglyphics.

"Sorry, Mr. Campbell, I will try to summarise . . .

"These papers were found concealed on your daughter's body at the scene. They were clearly hidden to get past our rather poor security . . . This document, it is from 1942, the War? . . . It has the name of a big Swedish arms manufacturer . . . The Swedes, you know, were neutral in the War? This was, what is the phrase—? A double-edged sword! This firm, you see, Mr. Campbell, it traded weapons to the Nazis . . . and, I'm afraid, much, much worse . . . "

He tapped the papers before him.

"The company," he went on, "it still exists today, it is multinational now, very famous, though under a different name . . . and it is not good news, this document, for their reputation . . . for international relations . . . or some politicians in Norway and Sweden . . . So we wonder what your daughter was doing, Mr. Campbell? Maybe working for a newspaper?"

Fraser had ceased to listen; a faded photograph had slipped from within the pages of the document in Müller's hand. It showed top-hatted dignitaries celebrating. There was one face he had seen before—or something very similar. It was remarkable how the same grotesque features reconfigured: as arcane beauty in the female, phenomenal ugliness in the male . . .

"The signature here, Mr. Campbell," continued Müller, glancing over his gold bifocals, "is the head of the family firm in those days, who you see there in the company photograph with Nazi businessmen in Munich . . . " He was pointing to a man with formidably high cheek bones and an ugly jutting jaw. "Cornelius Lindhorst, Managing Director of Råbäck Chemicals. A powerful man!"

"Are you feeling alright, Mr. Campbell?" exclaimed Müller, dropping his papers. The silent officer moved forward to steady him as he swayed.

Fraser had arisen from his chair in a great agitation. He was staring behind them, beyond the desk at which they sat, towards the tall third-floor windows.

His interrogators didn't seem to be aware of the frightful fluttering outside, the scratching at the panes, the darkening of dreadful wings.

INSIDE OUT

ERZEBET YELLOWBOY

Gretchen's dreams were drenched in forests, luminous and thick. In them she ran until she faded and dissolved, a spill of black ink ever thinning on the surface of a bright moon. That moon, which also shone in her dreams, was fading now as the sun slowly burnished the landscape beyond her open window. Sheer curtains wavered as the day's first breeze touched them. The hem of one caressed Gretchen's face as she slept. She pushed it away and watched as mist was swept from the field by a broom made of eldritch light. She did not need an ephemeris. Her blood knew what this night would bring.

She had the day, she thought. Might as well make the most of it; her sisters would insist. They shared an old farmhouse on the far edge of town, rented it from the owners who gave up their crops many years ago. The house was run down, the shingled roof sagged and paint flaked from the wooden siding. Behind it, unkempt fields spread out, sometimes spitting up stalks of corn in late summer. Gretchen's older sister, May, had her own small garden where lettuce, onions, tomatoes, beans and other greens Gretchen cared nothing for grew wild, almost, for May was a lazy mistress to her own crop. She worked hard, she said, at the grocer's in town, and besides, rain and sun did most of the growing for her.

Gretchen twisted her black hair in a knot, wishing for the thousandth time for the courage to cut it all off. Her sisters would murder her and she knew it, especially Molly, youngest of the three women. Molly's hair had never known scissors; she abhorred them. Her hair hung to her thighs in a thin wash of amber, straight as a carpenter's line. Molly worked at the bar serving drinks to the locals, a perfect job for a pinched and unpleasant young woman. The men respected her, the women ignored her, and Molly was fine with that. There were few enough jobs to be had in this small, nowhere town, and Molly didn't care who thought what as long as she was employed. The clients tipped her well, no doubt for her loyalty. When strangers came in for a night on the drink, she made certain they knew their place and she kept them in it.

Gretchen did not have a job and resented her sisters for theirs. If ever she could work, it wouldn't be in this town. People asked too many questions in a place like this and she and her sisters were already considered a bit strange. What kind of women would live on their own? What sort did not entertain men? May swore she had no time for such things, while Molly kept her dalliances far away from home. As for living alone, they simply said they preferred it that way.

"Morning," May said as Gretchen wandered into the kitchen. There was bacon on the stove and coffee in the pot, but Gretchen could not eat today.

"How do you feel?" May asked, as usual.

"I'm fine."

"You sure you won't eat something? I made enough for all of us."

Every month, the same. Gretchen sighed. Good-hearted, frumpy May meant well—both of her sisters did. Still, Gretchen felt stifled by their overbearing care. Trapped, she was, no better than an animal in a cage, unable to fend to for herself.

"Thanks, but no. You know how it is." Gretchen shrugged and sat at the table, unable to pretend she led a normal life.

"Have you seen Molly yet this morning?" May said.

"No. She worked late last night, didn't she?"

"Yeah, traded shifts with Paul so she could have today off. She'll sleep in, I guess."

Molly and May both always made certain they were home on this day and the next. They did whatever they must to protect Gretchen. She should be grateful for that, but instead it made her more aware of the freak she was.

Gretchen watched May eat jealously. The scent of meat made her mouth water, but if she gave in to hunger now, it would not go well this night. She rose and pushed open the screen door leading out to the back, where bindweed covered the remains of an old stone step. In the sky, barely visible, she could see the moon outlined by the light of the sun. It would glow, fully rounded, when night fell. Her hair felt heavy and thick, it bristled along her arms and behind her neck. Her skin tightened, grew uncomfortable. She scratched at her calves with her foot.

May watched—Gretchen could feel her sister's eyes on her. By the end of the day, she would feel everything.

Momma always said, "Beware the wolfweed, it will change you," but Momma said many odd things. It was ten years too late to wonder at what else Momma knew. When Gretchen was fifteen years old, Momma died. May, eighteen then, took over the care of her sisters. They had been together ever since. Where their father was, no one knew.

If only Momma could see me now, Gretchen thought. She'd never say *I warned you* or *I told you so*. No, Momma would have held Gretchen as she cried, and as she changed.

Momma knew every herb in the field, every tree in the forest and every flower that bloomed by the road. Wolfweed grew wild in the woods near the house where the four of them lived, when they were a happier family. The plant was dense, dark and beneath wide, purple leaves there were thorns as long as fingers.

"This one, we can eat. This one here," she would say, "we must avoid."

She was soft-spoken and gentle, and stronger than anyone Gretchen knew. She must have been, to raise three daughters alone. The night she died none of them heard a thing. Momma, too proud and perhaps too strong, never once called for their help. May found their mother the next morning, sideways in her bed. Gretchen ran. Into the woods, heedless of danger, she fled from the blood-stained sheets upon which her mother had vomited up her life.

It was dark in the trees. Gretchen tripped over a root and fell. She hit the thorns before she saw them, felt the welt raise on her shoulder when she landed in the patch of wolfweed. She thought nothing of the plant, but the pain brought her back to her senses. Slowly, brushing leaves and needles from her hands, she rose and looked back toward home.

May wrapped her arms around Gretchen as she entered, put salve on the wound and said nothing of her flight. They each had to deal with Momma's death in their own way. Molly, thirteen then, had curled into a ball on the sofa and was crying.

Two weeks later it began to happen. The moon, bloated with their grief, hung low in the sky. They were packing; May was moving them. They could not live in that house, she said. Not where Momma died. It was late, the three were tired. Molly was rubbing her eyes.

Gretchen, wrapping dishes in newspaper, suddenly felt her skin begin to burn. It started at her shoulder where the wound, red still but nearly healed, raised up, incredibly inflamed. Gretchen yelped, attracting the attention of her sisters, whose eyes widened as they turned to her.

"Gretchen, what is it?" May said as she rose from the floor and ran to her sister's side.

"It burns," Gretchen whimpered, her hands clutching her arms.

She began to rock back and forth as May held her. Molly crept over to her side. Huddled there, on the floor of the old kitchen, Gretchen learned the language of pain and her sisters, that of fear.

Gretchen didn't know how they'd managed to get from there to here, but here they were, in another old house, near woods with no sign of wolfweed. Ten years gone, and it never got any easier. May and Molly still held her as it happened, still stroked her hair and whispered in her ear, *we love you, Gretchen*, speaking her name over and over as though to help her remember who she was. They accepted, now, there was no cure.

May put her plate in the sink as Molly staggered into the room. Gretchen turned from the door to greet her, but all she received in response was a savage grunt. Molly was no morning person, that was sure.

"Coffee," she said, and May obliged.

"Rough night?" Gretchen asked when the cup was empty.

"Hell yeah. The Bailey boys were at it again, had Tucker pinned to the wall and would have beat him senseless if John hadn't of walked in."

May rolled her eyes. "John's after you, you know."

"I know it," Molly said. "I'm not messing with a cop, no way."

Gretchen and May exchanged a glance. They both knew Molly fancied him, but didn't want to risk the law getting too close.

"I don't see how it could hurt," May said.

"I do."

Gretchen turned away from them. "I'm going for a walk."

"You're in a mood," Molly said.

"Yeah."

"She's hungry, leave her alone." May put her hands on her wide hips and tried to stare Molly down.

"She shouldn't be out there alone today, you know." Molly stared back.

"She knows what she's doing."

Molly raised an eyebrow, but said nothing more.

Gretchen left them to their bickering. She wouldn't be gone long, she knew the dangers and the risks. She was restless; she only wanted a little time alone. It happened this way, sometimes. The morning would call her out, as though the monster in her was willing to greet the sun, if only it was able.

She no longer knew who was the monster and who was not. She, Gretchen, walking upright, dressed in ordinary jeans and a shirt, brown eyes and black hair, could pass through any town without notice. No one would ever guess, much less believe, what she was. She carried her terrible secret and knew, as she passed bland strangers on the street, she would sink her teeth into any one of them if she must. She, it, hunting on all fours, sniffing the air, saliva dropping from her jaws, knew nothing about secrets. She, it, was a pure thing, run on instinct. It knew nothing but scent and sound. Gretchen hated the monster. She hated the unholy charade her life had become.

Her sisters were waiting for her when she returned to the house. They worried too much about the wrong things, Gretchen thought, but she smiled at them anyway.

"It's a beautiful day. You want some help out in the garden?"

"Sure," May replied to Gretchen's offer with a smile. "The weeds must be taking over by now."

"They are. Molly, you coming?"

"Why not," Molly said. "There's nothing else to do."

The three sisters spent several hours beneath the sun, sharing gossip and a jug of water and laughing as though it was any other day. For a time, the specter of the evening was vanquished.

"I'm starved," Molly finally said, and then glanced at Gretchen, who had suddenly become very still. "Sorry."

Gretchen shook her head. "It's okay. I'm not that hungry now."

She lied. Her belly growled, but not with a hunger her sisters could ever feed. Unless she ate them, she thought.

It was a fear they had, early on, before they realized their scent scared her off. They would not be pleased to find Gretchen contemplating it now. Gretchen stifled a cruel laugh. It was the monster, easing its way out.

She showered as they ate their supper and cleaned up after them when they were done. They worked, she tended the house. It seemed an unfair trade, but fair had nothing to do with this life they lived.

Afterward, they all became restless. These last hours were the worst as they waited for a thing that would give them little warning when it finally appeared.

They never, ever used the word *werewolf*. Gretchen was not some figment of myth or superstition. But they knew, sure as they knew the sun would rise in the morning, that's exactly what their sister was.

Wolfweed: rare, mysterious, grown out of the book of legend. They would never have believed it, had they not seen firsthand what it could do. When they finally made the connection, they went back to the old woods and burned every inch of it out. Only one thorn survived and this, Gretchen kept, as a reminder to heed Momma's words.

They had no idea how it worked. Years of their own research had not offered a clue and a medical assessment was entirely out of the question. Even to ask that the thorn be examined was too dangerous. May had visions of her sister being used in weird genetic experiments. She imagined the military becoming involved. No sister of hers would be treated like an animal, even if animal she was.

At dusk, Gretchen stripped off her clothes, right there in front of her sisters. They watched as she wrapped a sheet loosely around her lithe body. They would reach out to her then, if they could, but Gretchen was tense and closed in. Her long night was already beginning as she prepared for transformation.

As the sun touched the ground, they filed out of the house. Somberly they sat on the earth behind the garden, where laughter echoed from only a few hours ago. The moon was still pale, but as night crept in around them it pulled shadows along the ground. Gretchen began to shiver and her eyes rolled.

May gently unwound the sheet from Gretchen's shoulders and pulled her into her arms. Molly, close behind, leaned against her.

"We're right here," they said. "Gretchen, we'll be right here."

Gretchen could no longer hear them. Her body was aflame and her sinews tense as her bones reconfigured themselves. She growled and groaned as fine hairs thickened in their follicles. She arched her back and flung out her arms. Her sisters ducked, but did not leave her side. Gretchen wept and she screamed as though touched by a thousand suns.

They clung to her as long as they could, until—for their own safety and hers—they had to back away. Squatting, they watched as their sister transfigured from young, lovely woman to wolf.

It rose on trembling legs, shook itself and loped away, bristling. It would have run if it were not so weak; the scent of humans terrified it. The woods called, the moon shone down and behind it, two sisters put their heads in their hands and cried.

The wolf stopped at the tree line, sniffed the air and padded its way into the brush at the edge of the field. Its fur condensed the heat still wafting up from the mulched leaves below. Pines, a few twisting maples, an oak here and there: these were the wolf's landmarks, scented time and again as it made its way down the familiar trail.

It reveled, one could say, in the freedom of movement. Limbs stretching as blood pumped through its veins, it ran, dodging fallen limbs, leaping through bracken, careless, for a little while, of the sound it made as it traveled.

Soon, the wolf slowed. The trees were thick in this part of the forest, close and tall. Moonlight trickled over the uppermost leaves, but close to the ground light was scarce. The wolf did not steady its pace because of this, however. It knew, as wolves do, that it must attend to its surroundings. Each scent and sound meant something. The wolf translated; its ears flicked back and forth, its nose pointed north.

Hunger moved it. She knew, by the hollow of her belly, that it was long since she'd eaten. She smelled prey, but it was distant. Water was close. A stream that wound its way over a rock-strewn bed, once much wider, ran just west of where the wolf was standing. She picked her way between the trees until she reached it. A dam, abandoned last season, was slowly being dismembered by the current. She had feasted here, before the beavers left for less dangerous turf.

She followed the water upstream, northward, toward food. The soft earth of its bank absorbed her prints. After several miles, she stopped. She raised her nose. Some unfamiliar odor stretched her out; her hackles raised and a low growl began in her throat.

Ahead was a place she knew well. Knew to avoid, not from any recent danger, but because of a lingering scent. Man-scent. A dwelling, an old cabin—though she could not name it as such—nestled in a clearing near the stream. It had grown, over time, into the trees, or the trees had grown back into it, reclaiming it as part of their wooded tribe. The roof was all but gone. What slats remained were leaf- and lichen-thick, barely visible to the eye. The door hung open, the cupboards were home to mice and the rafters to birds.

There was a tang in the air, the taste of iron, that was not there before. And, entwined within it, the raw stink of human activity. Something else tinged the place, a musk that covered the wolf in a cloud of memory. She knew that scent, somehow, and though she feared it, the flavor it of spoke to her of home. She shivered as she crouched beside the water, tail flat on the ground.

She knew not to approach the cabin. Her usual detour took her far around the clearing, but something about these new, disturbing smells drew her in. She circled cautiously, creeping ever closer, all senses alert. The air was close and still; the strange odor remained.

The wolf had never known another of her kind. The land was emptied out. Any pack that may have once claimed this territory had been hunted to its end. She ruled by default, killed as she pleased and knew to avoid the places of men. She knew, as wolves know things, that she was now breaking survival's rules.

The scent that teased her on was foul. Feces, blood, urine: it was the stench of pain endured too long. No fresh kill was this she trailed, nor healthy flesh for the taking. It was human, but it was also more. For the first time, she caught the whiff of wolf in the forest. She was compelled to follow. It seemed to her that she, forever so alone, had been somehow divided.

Close now, near enough to see the outline of the cabin, she came to a full stop and crouched again. Dragging her belly along the ground, she inched forward. Leaves rustled, though what sound was night and what was wolf could not be distinguished. She was a shadow, black as the sky, sleek and cautious. The wolf knew fear, but she crept onwards until instinct told her *this is close enough*.

The clearing was just there, beyond the thicket in which the wolf lay, ears alert for danger. The cabin sat on the far side and before it, some thing the wolf could not decipher enclosed a figure stretched out prone on the ground. The wolf exhaled a sharp burst of air and suddenly, the figure rose. The wolf bristled, but did not back away. Information cluttered her brain; there was no way to make sense of the mingling of scent. Matted hair, half-crusted wounds, wolf and woman combined. The figure turned. Eyes met eyes in the still night. The wolf, overwhelmed, stood and ran.

To the stream and through it she rushed, feet finding and following a path between trees and shrubs, until finally, confusion was behind her. She halted, panting, and put her nose in the air and howled. Every hair on her body stood erect as, for the first time ever, she was answered.

The night, half gone, pulled the wolf back into it. Hunger moved her now, and a sense of hurriedness. She must hunt and eat before the dawn. She did not know the source of her impatience, only that these things must be done. North again, she found her prey. A raccoon, rifling through a rotted log, was eventually devoured. Back now to the stream, which she followed, circling wide of the clearing, ignoring the scents and sounds, pacing herself so as to reach her destination in time.

As the moon dipped low and dark began to fade toward morning, she found herself at the edge of the wood. Across the field the house lay quiet. She knew this place, was drawn to it though the wolf would never comprehend why. In her mind it was den and desperation.

At dawn, the wolf began to writhe. A cacophony of growls and yelps ensued as muscles tore and bones bent under the force of change. The wolf, lost in this transfusion of blood to blood and genes gone awry, was captive in a human mind until, as the sun erased the moon, it disappeared.

May and Molly left the house at dawn. They carried two jugs of water, a bundle of washcloths, a towel, bandages of assorted sizes and a soft blanket in which to swaddle their sister. They knew she would be close, but not exactly where. It was always the same. The wolf came, by some intangible understanding, as close to its human home as it could bear.

They didn't speak until they found her.

"Gretchen," they said. "Gretchen, we're here."

They sat her up, pulled leaves from her hair. Later Molly would wash and comb it. They checked her hands and feet for wounds. Often, they would find scrapes and bruises. This morning there were none. May dampened a washcloth and wiped vomit from her sister's chin. Her body, a merciless thing, regurgitated food as it shifted. While Gretchen knew this, the wolf would never learn. May gently scrubbed at Gretchen's cheek where blood had dried in dark smudge. May did not think about how it might have got there. It was not her business to judge the wolf.

"Come on," they said when they were done.

They stood her up between them and wrapped the blanket around her naked body, allowing her to lean on each as they slowly made their way across the field.

Inside the house, they steered Gretchen into bed, pulled the curtains and left the door ajar. She would sleep for hours and when she woke, she would still be somewhat confused. The sisters were used to it now, they carried on with their day as Gretchen dreamed of running, running, and following scents to their end.

The phone rang not long after. Molly answered with a groan.

"Shit," she said as she hung up the receiver a few moments later. "I have to go in tonight. Ryan is sick."

"I bet he is," May said. "Sick of working at Rudy's."

"Whatever. If you can't take the boozers, you shouldn't work in a bar. I'm in at eight. Will you be okay with Gretchen?"

"I don't see why not. She'll be almost herself by then. We'll be fine."

"It'll be a late one."

"I know."

Molly fiddled with her mug of coffee, turning it round and round.

"What's up? You seem awfully quiet this morning." May knew her sister well enough to sense that something was on her mind.

"I don't know." Molly paused, and then continued. "Do you ever think about the future?"

"Not if I can help it."

"I mean, do you ever wish . . . "

May cut her off. "Stop right there. No, I don't wish."

Molly sighed. "I don't know what's wrong with me."

"I do. You're getting old." May laughed, hoping Molly would join her.

Molly did laugh, though it was not quite the joyous sound May wanted.

"Let's fix something nice for lunch," May finally said. "Something Gretchen will like."

It was the scent of a roast stewing in the pot that pulled Gretchen of out her slumber. She woke in a daze of half-remembered moonlight. It took her several minutes to assess her surroundings. White walls, wooden bedposts, ancient dresser with two handles missing: finally she recalled her whereabouts. Safe, she exhaled relief. Shakily, she pulled loose trousers to her hips and tied them. She lifted a worn shirt from the back of a chair and buttoned it, though her fingers clumsily left half of it undone. Warily, still sensing her environment more than seeing it, she slipped out of the bedroom and made her way down the stairs.

Her sisters greeted her as usual.

"Good morning, Gretchen. How do you feel?" May was always the first to question her well-being.

"Hey, sis," Molly said.

"What do I smell?" Gretchen asked in response.

Her sisters were never quite sure if they were talking to wolf or woman on this, the day after the full of the moon. Appearances were deceptive, and May more than Molly understood that the wolf often lingered much longer in spirit than it did in body.

"Meat. I made stew for lunch," May said as she watched Gretchen's nostrils flare.

The wolf had left its mark as time passed by. After ten years of this, Gretchen no longer had a taste for much fruit, nor certain vegetables. Leafy salads were fine most of the time, and certain berries, but beans, tomatoes, and onions were out of the question. She drank water, milk, and occasionally coffee, but not tea and never soda. Meat was the staple of her diet, but May could live with that as long as Gretchen didn't start asking for it raw.

As she ate, Gretchen's thoughts slowly settled into more familiar patterns. Something was different this morning, however. Some memory, some unfamiliar disturbance tugged at her. She touched it, circled it as the wolf would, tried to catch the scent of it, but to no avail. What happened last night? She felt an ache she did not recognize.

"What is it?" May asked when she noticed Gretchen staring absently at the window.

Gretchen blinked her eyes. "Nothing. Something. I don't know. Last night. I don't know."

She never spoke of the night. May, concerned, put a hand on her sister's forehead. "Nothing seemed amiss when we found you. You sure you're okay?"

"Yeah. I'm fine. Don't worry," Gretchen smiled, a bit more like her usual self.

"Well, let me know if you need anything," May said.

"I will."

After she finished, Molly washed her hair and helped her dress in more reasonable clothes. By then, Gretchen felt almost human. Molly nattered on about nothing while May swept the floors. Gretchen caught herself gazing toward the dark forest and shook her head. Whatever was haunting her must not be brought into the light.

What the wolf knew as it ran through the forest was like a distant dream to Gretchen, one that she always gladly let fade the following day. She despised everything about the wolf and what it had done to her. She separated it, culled it from the experience of her own life, pretended that she and it were two distinct beings. They would never meet, nor know of each other's cares. Yet, that night, as she curled up in her bed, images passed behind her closed eyes: a cabin, a cage, a shape inside it. Scent returned, new blood on old, musk, hair, and fear.

Gretchen sat upright in horror as it came to her. The wolf had seen a ravaged woman in a cage, and she was alive.

"Holy shit," Gretchen whispered into the room.

Sleep did not come easily that night and wouldn't have at all had she not still been exhausted from the night before. Dreams stirred like leaves on the forest floor, but she could not catch them. They passed, like summer does into autumn.

For days she was restless. Alone when her sisters worked, she paced the halls, ate little and worried at the wolf's memory. There was no way to know what was real and what was not. The human mind must categorize, put color to objects, know distance in feet and yards. The wolf-mind knew shapes, sensations, the taste of air. She felt dirty, touching these things. Shame at what she was overpowered her at times, bending her knees, crawling along her skin like an insect. She rubbed at her arms, shivering, and tried to brush it off. She almost did cut off her hair, as though by doing so it would distance her from the wolf. She warred with it, she did not want to know the wolf's mind, and yet she must comprehend these visions. If this thing she thought she'd seen was real, if there was a woman in a cage, she must do something. She could not leave her out there alone.

There was something else come through from that eerie night. A longing, a connection almost, that Gretchen could not name.

"That's it," she said at last to no one. "I've got to go back."

The next day her sisters both worked early. May's shift began at nine, Molly's at one. When they were gone, Gretchen left a note on the table, packed food and water into a bag and left. She did not know when she would be home; she could not guess how far away the cabin was. Her sisters would worry if she did not return before them, but she could not bring herself to tell them of her plan. There was no way to explain it, this thing she saw out of the wolf's eyes.

In the woods, she stopped. Each direction seemed as viable as the other. Gretchen realized with a slow burn of horror that she would never navigate this place on her own. But for the image of that woman, she would have turned away then and given up, gone back to the house, done anything but what she must do now.

Gretchen breathed deeply and focused, trying to invoke the monster that slept inside her. Down deep she went into the primal source of mind, where flesh means less and instinct is all. She moved, step by step, until her feet became sure and led her onwards toward the stream. Gnats flew into her eyes, things scurried in the brush and overhead, a bird called out in warning. She grew hungry, she gnawed on bread and chicken left over from the last evening's meal. Hours passed and she barely noticed. She was only half-human now. The wolf led her through the wood.

She stopped in a copse as fear gripped her. Gretchen neither saw nor heard anything unusual, but she heeded the feeling and kept still for several long moments. In the quiet, a faint whimpering and whining—the sound a dog would make if it were pleading—became audible through the trees.

Gretchen pressed on, urgency driving her steps. Fully herself now, she was less cautious than she should have been; sticks snapped underfoot and branches cracked as she pushed them out of her way.

She tracked the sound of the weeping animal to the clearing. She stopped at its edge and ducked down behind a young maple surrounded by brush. Twigs caught in her hair and snagged on her shirt; she ignored them. From behind the tangle of branches she saw the cabin, forlorn and yet obviously tenanted, for there was freshly cut wood stacked beside it and litter strewn around the door. She registered the dwelling, but it was not this that held her attention. In the scuffed and flattened ground before it, she saw what had been making the noise.

Silent now, hackles raised, a crushingly pathetic wolf was held in a cage. It was an ancient construction of black iron, much like those used in old traveling circus shows. In the advertisements, they rose up from the backs of colorful wagons in a merry display meant to arouse excitement and draw unwary customers in. The reality of the device repulsed her. The wolf, sensing her presence, turned toward her. Eyes met eyes. Gretchen's breath caught in her throat.

Before she had time to process the vision, as if any sense could be made of it, the door to the cabin was kicked open and a man stood in its frame. He was as rotted as the wood surrounding him. Thin, knotted hair topped a skeletal face. Two narrow eyes glared out at the wolf as, from behind the door, the man pulled a rifle.

"Whatsa matter," he called out to the wolf. "Ain't you had enough?"

Gretchen held her breath as he approached the cage, gun held over his shoulder. The wolf and Gretchen cringed as one as he swung his weapon, clanging the butt against the bars.

"Cry, you freak. Cry, or I'll give you something real to cry about."

The wolf began to whine and writhe on its belly, opening wounds on its legs that would never have a chance to fully heal if this was their treatment. The man grinned and looked out into the forest before turning away. As the cabin door slammed shut behind him, dislodging debris from the roof which fell in a soft rain to the ground, Gretchen felt her skin begin to burn.

The monster was close. Wolf called to wolf and the strange ache blossomed in her chest. Rage consumed her; she tried to tamp it down, aware of the danger she was in. Slowly and ever so silently, she backed out of the thicket and, still on all fours, crept away from the clearing. When she could no longer see the cabin, she rose, but she kept to the trees, moving swiftly from one to the other until she reached the stream.

Home never looked so sweet as it did when she finally left the woods. Running, she crossed the field, only slowing as she reached May's garden. May was home by now and Gretchen did not want to rush in and alarm her.

"You've been gone for hours!" May said when Gretchen entered the kitchen. "Where have you been?"

"Didn't you see my note?"

"Yeah, but 'gone for a walk' could mean anything." May peered at her sister. "Are you okay?"

Gretchen knew better than to lie to her sister, but she wouldn't give her the whole truth. How could she? "Not really, no. I got a little creeped out in the woods, that's all. I don't even know why I went out there."

May inspected her sister's face. "Yes, you do."

Yes, Gretchen did, but she wasn't prepared to admit it. There was no woman out there; it was just a wolf. Sad, yes, but just a wolf. It had nothing to do with her. She'd been tricked by her own imagination. She wouldn't let it happen again.

"Well, you just take it easy, okay?"

"Promise. I'm going to get cleaned up and then I'll help you with supper."

"Good. There was a sale on ribs and I grabbed a few packs. We're having those."

In the shower, Gretchen scrubbed her body until her flesh glowed a pale red. No matter how she tried, the wolf would not wash away. She wept, quietly so May wouldn't hear her, unable to contain the emotions that wanted to pull her to the tiled floor.

The monster had been so close. Too close. She still felt it lurking now, just there where she could almost touch it, if she reached a hand into herself. It, she, was howling in frustration. It felt terror and again that same rage. Gretchen was overcome with a scent she couldn't possibly, as a human, comprehend. As the hot water finally wore away her confusion, a clear thought evolved in her mind.

I was certain there was a woman in that cage.

But it was the wolf's foul memory describing that figure, not hers. Gretchen shook the water from her hair. There was not much difference remaining between them, and she was terrified.

The two conflicting memories tortured her throughout the evening. Both Gretchen and May were relieved when Molly walked through the door.

"How'd it go?" May asked as Gretchen smiled a greeting.

Molly blushed and May's eyebrows raised.

"Fine," Molly said.

"Just fine? Come on, something happened. You're red as an apple."

"John asked me out," Molly said in a small voice very much unlike her.

"And?" May would not give up.

"I agreed."

"I knew it!" May grinned and swatted her sister on the arm. "It's about time."

"But . . . "

"No *but*. I know what you're thinking. Don't worry about it. When's your hot date?"

"Tomorrow night. I'm meeting him in town. He's a cop, he's going to ask questions, you know." Molly insisted on airing her fears.

"Tell him we're weird," Gretchen said. "Just enjoy yourself, for god's sake." An unbidden harshness edged her voice.

Molly stared, and then finally said, "All right."

Three sisters did not sleep well that night.

Molly did something the next evening that left both Gretchen and May dumbfounded. Her hair was piled on top of her head and her eyes were lined with black kohl. Their younger sister was transformed, but this was no monster that greeted them at the stair.

"You look lovely!" May said as she hugged her.

Eyes downcast, Molly said, "Thank you."

"It's true. You must really like this guy," Gretchen teased.

"I just felt like doing something different," Molly said, but her sisters were not fooled.

After she'd gone to meet John at the diner, May slipped off to read in her room. Gretchen, left with her thoughts, began pacing again.

Molly seemed so happy tonight, Gretchen mused. It was the first time she'd seen her make an effort with her appearance. Gretchen frowned. There was no reason for either of her sisters to become spinsters on her behalf. Molly—though she hid it well—was a joyous soul who would do well with a family of her own. May might, in time, find someone, though Gretchen doubted it. May seemed content to follow Momma's lead. These troubles seemed far removed from Gretchen's own muddled reality, but they were closer than she realized.

Gretchen now felt a fool for ever imagining her own life as a cage. She was fortunate, she finally realized, to have such sisters as hers. Anyone else would have put a bullet in her, or worse. She could not stop thinking about the wolf, battered and starved. That, she thought, could have been me. Still, it was just a wolf, unless what she saw beneath the moon was true? Could it be? She put her hands to her head to still the pictures that passed in a blur before her closed eyes.

They were interchangeable, wolf and woman. Wolf saw one thing, woman another. Gretchen thought she'd explode from the contradiction and she let a small cry escape from her throat. She sank into the sofa in the living room, huddled over and wrapped her arms around herself. The ache returned, an incredible longing. She understood, at long last, how very lonely she was.

Gretchen never shared Molly's interest in boys—not in school, when the possibility still existed, nor as as a young woman, when because of the wolf a lover was out of the question. Before the change, she often wondered if there was something wrong with her. Even May had the occasional weekend foray into the strange world of men. Not so, Gretchen. There was once, just before Momma died, when a girl in her class made her young heart flutter. The way she felt when this girl entered the room scared Gretchen. When Gretchen changed, it was almost too easy to accept that love was not for her. Better that than face this other thing.

Now, wolf scented wolf and the woman Gretchen had become was in turmoil as she was slowly forced to recognize an affinity. Cotton curtains fluttered in a breeze, drawing Gretchen out of herself. She would have to go back. There was nothing else she could do.

"You've been spending a lot of time in the woods lately."

May could no longer hide her concern. Gretchen had been irritable and distracted for days, but that was understandable. The moon was rounding and would be full in less than a week's time. But this strange mood of her sister's began when she returned from that first trek in the forest, and only increased every time she went there. Daily now, Gretchen left the house while her sisters were at work. Molly, who came in late most nights, was unaware of Gretchen's habits, but May had been watching and finally she demanded an answer.

"I know. It's okay, really it is."

"You're lying to me. You're a mess every time you come home. What's going on?"

Gretchen turned her face away from her sister. How to explain the horror she witnessed daily? She had honed the skill of silent stalking, she had inspected the cabin from all sides and the cage next to it. She knew the habits of the man who kept the wolf in such horrific conditions. She knew how purely awful he was. She saw the locks, too, that kept the cage sealed, and the keys hanging from his leather belt. She knew the wolf now. Ragged and broken in body, its spirit remained intact though as far as Gretchen could tell, it wouldn't for much longer.

The man was brutal. She saw what and how he fed the creature, rotted meat dangled over the cage, withheld until the creature crawled, begging, toward him. Her ribs pushed through her sides and her coat hung in patches over scabbed flesh. Her eyes wept dark matter down over her nose. Gretchen felt the monster in her shift and slither, struggling to surface. She fought to keep it down.

"If you must know," she finally spoke, "it's the wolf."

There. Not a lie, but not exactly true, Gretchen offered this to her sister in appeasement. She also knew that to mention the wolf was to draw a line neither of her sisters would cross.

"Oh Gretchen, I'm so sorry. I wish I could do more to help."

"Well, you can't."

May sagged and Gretchen, contrite, hugged her.

"I'm sorry," she said. "Don't mind me."

"What are you two fussing about?" Molly said as she swung in, a pleasant smile on her face.

Molly was going through a change of her own. Under John's attention, at first reluctantly accepted, she was softening. An inner beauty once known only to her sisters was transforming the shape of her face, so much so that even the patrons at the bar had commented.

Gretchen wanted to say *wolves*, but she didn't. There was no reason to deflate her sister's good mood.

"The usual. Gretchen wants a whole cow for supper and I've only got three steaks thawed out," May said.

They shared a laugh, but Gretchen's was false and both sisters knew it.

Still troubled by her initial memory of a woman in the cage, she agonized over it until the night of the full moon. There had to be way, she thought, to be certain of what the wolf saw. She and the monster shared the same brain, didn't they? Somehow the wolf knew to go home when the night was gone. Somehow she must be able to connect with the beast and remember, more clearly, what it would see. Gretchen soured at the thought, but it was the only way she knew to solve this puzzle.

That night, as her sisters held her, Gretchen fought for control. Pain, she could almost endure. It was the sensation of every cell dislocating from the others that was impossible to bear. Her consciousness separated as her tendons burned. Her vision blurred and shifted, condensed and expanded with her skin. *Remember*, she thought, *my name is Gretchen.* She screamed with the effort, but as her sisters moved away, all that was Gretchen was gone.

The wolf hunted. A young fawn, unattended for one moment too long by its mother, went down easily under her strong jaws. She shredded it, burying what she didn't eat well away from the scene of its demise. In ever tightening circles she coursed through the forest, avoiding the outlying fields. Shortly after midnight, she found herself beside the stream. The running water triggered an echo of remembrance; she put her nose in the air and waited, for what she did not know. The wind stirred the upper leaves of the trees, bringing with it the taste of metal. The wolf shuddered and, as wolves do, it recalled. It turned and ambled along the bank, snuffling as it went, and then stopped as a cry pierced the night.

She would have run, but something held the wolf back. She knew that sound, it resonated and called her out, back to the clearing. Wolf eyes watched; she scented present danger but saw nothing. The cage stood empty. The cries came from within the shuttered cabin. The wolf crouched low and waited again, alert and still.

In time, the wolf's patience was rewarded. The cabin door opened and the man emerged, dragging someone behind him by the arm. The wolf tensed; the stink was incredible. She watched as he approached the cage, kicked it open with his foot and heaved his baggage inside. The wolf saw the way his hands moved on the iron and heard the locks click into place. The figure inside did not move as the man walked away, but it wept with a most pitiful sound. The wolf recognized the song of sorrow. The place reeked of fresh blood and pain.

The wolf waited still. Night settled softly around her. It would be dawn soon and as the sun drew nigh, she felt her usual compulsion to return home. She did not. She was held as captive by the cage as the figure inside it. The scintillating scent of wolf buried within woman held her there.

Finally, at long last, the figure moved. It rolled onto its side and heaved itself up with a bruised arm. One hand wrapped around a bar of the cage. She leaned her head against it and sighed. The wolf, watching this, must have disturbed a leaf with its breath. The woman turned and met the wolf's eyes.

Something was exchanged between them, some plea in a coded language only those two could understand. It lasted for but a moment, and then the woman lost her grip and slid back to the bottom of the cage.

The wolf was done here. She retreated through the forest, breaking into a trot only when the clearing was left far behind. Home called, dawn was coloring the horizon. She was running out of time.

She had not yet reached the boundary where wood met field when it came upon her. The wolf, mid-stride, twisted and fell. Leaves scattered in her wake as she slid for a few paces in the dirt. Tortured by her own mutation, she choked on vomit and released a burbling half-howl. When it ended, several endless minutes later, Gretchen lay motionless on the ground.

She did not respond to her sisters' calls. They, trampling through the brush at the edge of the wood, were almost frantic.

"Where could she be?" Molly said, her eyes wide with fear.

"I don't know." May's brows drew in. "She must be close. She knows to come home."

"She's been acting funny lately. I hope she's okay."

May was surprised Molly had noticed. "Has she said anything to you?"

"No, not really. She just seems so withdrawn." Molly kicked a pile of damp leaves out of her way.

"It's hard on her. She needs us, Molly, maybe more now than she ever has."

"I know." Molly hung her head. "I've been away too often. I'm sorry."

"Oh, no, that's not what I meant." May was overjoyed at Molly's newfound romance and did not want it to stop. Molly deserved all the goodness she could get.

"We just . . . " May hesitated. There was nothing they could do for Gretchen that they weren't already doing. "Never mind. Let's keep looking."

They were close to panic when they finally found her, stretched out in a copse of trees. She sat upright as May's hand touched her, startling her sisters who gasped and jumped back.

"It was a woman," Gretchen said. Her voice was hoarse, not yet acclimated to human vocal cords.

May recovered and wrapped Gretchen in the blanket. "We're here, Gretchen," she said. "We're right here."

Gretchen sagged into her arms. May and Molly said nothing as they tended her and half-carried her back to the house. Once she was in bed, they met in the kitchen.

"What was she talking about?" Molly asked.

"I've got no idea, but we're going to find out. She needs to talk about whatever has been bothering her and we've got to make her do it. Tonight."

"She'll be a mess!"

"I know it. She may actually open up."

Gretchen did, and it was not what her sisters expected.

"I'm telling you, I know what I saw."

"You can't possibly expect us to believe you know what you saw out there as a . . . a wolf. You've said yourself you don't remember anything. And what you have seen is bad enough."

"You've got to tell someone, Gretchen." Molly was terrified that the someone would be John. They were getting along so well; the last thing she wanted was for him to discover just how weird her family was. And yet, what Gretchen described was a matter for the authorities. John was sure to learn of it, one way or another.

"It's no ordinary wolf. Under the full moon, it is a *woman*. We can't bring in the law. What do you think they'll do with her? And how long do you think it will be before they look at me?"

Perhaps now had not been a good time to speak to Gretchen after all,

May thought. Yet, she had a point. If, and that was a large *if*, Gretchen had seen another of her kind as she so astonishingly suggested, they could not risk anyone else becoming involved.

"Okay. You're tired. Why don't we call it a night and see what tomorrow brings."

Relieved, Gretchen nodded. "Fine. But I know what I saw."

After she'd staggered off to bed, Molly and May sat in silence.

"Do you think it's true?" Molly finally asked.

May reached across the table and took her hands. "I don't know. I think she's just had a bad dream. But don't worry. We'll make sure John stays out of it, whatever it is."

"Thank you," Molly said, holding on tight. "Thank you."

Gretchen rose the next morning in a stupor. The walls of her bedroom were close and confining. Her legs were weak and she clung to the back of a chair until she found her balance. Shadows seemed superimposed on the window frame: dark limbs of trees, scuttling creatures, the outline of a wolf somehow standing upright.

She was more certain than ever that what the wolf saw was accurate. Her sisters might not believe it, but she knew. She could not leave it alone. Gretchen gathered her wits. Both sisters were awake before her. She cornered them in the kitchen before either could wish her good day.

"I can't leave her out there. Don't argue. This is none of your business."

Shocked, the sisters turned as one. Gretchen's eyes were black, feral. They felt the monster there in the kitchen where no monster belonged. Fear tainted Molly's belly, but May held firm.

"Let us know what you need."

"I need time. Alone," Gretchen said.

Molly drew in her breath, but said nothing as Gretchen sat at the table and put her head in her hands.

"It hurts," she said and Molly went to her side.

"You need to eat."

May heaped a plate with bacon, sausage and eggs. Gretchen ate with her fingers as Molly stroked her hair. It was an uncomfortable morning, but it passed and by noon the eerie light had dimmed in Gretchen's eyes.

"Will you see John tonight?" Gretchen asked as Molly dressed for work.

"No," Molly said with a frown.

"Why not?"

"I don't think I should see him again."

Gretchen took her by the shoulder. "I know what you're thinking, Molly. Don't. You really like this guy, I can tell. Promise me you won't give him up because of me."

Molly wiped a tear from her eye. "But it's too dangerous. What if he finds out?"

"You and May can't protect me for the rest of my life. You need to have a life, too. Look at me."

Gretchen turned Molly toward her. Molly saw her sister, as familiar as her own skin. She also saw, very close to the surface, the wolf. They clung to each other for a moment before Molly stepped away.

"Okay. I won't stop seeing him."

"Good," Gretchen smiled.

"Be careful, will you?" Molly said quietly.

"As careful as I can."

Gretchen cornered May in the living room that night, before she could turn on the television to watch her favorite show.

"I've got to set that woman free."

"What?" May said, startled. "What do you mean?"

"Just what I said. I can't leave her out there to die."

"But what about that man? You said he had a gun." May's flesh grew cold. She rubbed her arms, suddenly very afraid.

"I don't know. I'll think of something."

"It's too dangerous. You could be killed." May grabbed her sister's hand.

"Better that than live like this!" Gretchen shouted and snatched her arm away.

May realized then just how deeply Gretchen's loathing of herself ran.

"And what of the wolf?" she asked quietly. "Would you leave it out there if you didn't have these crazy dreams?"

"They aren't dreams!" Gretchen said, eyes wild, but something in her sister's voice reached her. Would she do such a thing? It was true, it was not the plight of the wolf that moved her, pitiful as it was. Only the thought of the woman drew her back, again and again.

"Gretchen," May said softly, "if what you've seen is to be believed, that thing out there is somehow one of your kind."

"I am not a wolf!" Gretchen bared her teeth.

May sighed. Gretchen had to face this thing she was, but she was clearly not yet ready.

"What can I do to help?"

"Nothing. Do as you've always done. Do what makes you happy," Gretchen said and leaned into her sister. "Just once, May, do what makes you happy."

"*You* make me happy," May said as she left the room.

Gretchen watched the wolf, now almost too weak to stand. She watched the man until she knew his daily routine as well as she knew her own. She came to know the forest as only a wolf could, each tree, rock and thicket became her own. She practiced silence, she stopped wearing shoes. She almost thought the man had become aware of her presence, or a presence in the nearby wood. He came out of the cabin, gun in hand, and stood still, as though listening for some sound. This happened several times, but he never detected the shadow that was Gretchen.

Drop by painful drop, Gretchen came to love the creature in the cage. She wished, still, for her vision to clear, for she could not think of it as a wolf. She saw only the woman she was sure the wolf became beneath the moon. She wanted to see her face, she wanted to wash the sores on her body and comb out her hair. She wanted to hold her, to offer safety and to keep her from further harm. Drop by drop, Gretchen understood. She was going to kill the man.

At home, she thought of nothing else. May absorbed her silent sister into her routine as Molly's romance flourished. Neither were aware that Gretchen intended an action which would have at one time been unthinkable to her. It was the wolf within and the wolf without that forged this thing she had become. She considered weapons, poisons, traps and at last, she considered her own bare hands. She could think of no sure way to see the job done. Two weeks passed, then three and she was no closer to a solution. Her bed was unmade, her laundry piled up, she ate as though she starved.

On the morning before September's full moon, she was rummaging through her closet in search of a clean shirt when she found her answer. Forgotten amidst the dust on the top shelf was a small shoe box. She pulled it down as though it was lost treasure and carefully removed the lid. Inside, wrapped in tissue, was the thorn she had plucked from the wolfweed just before they burned it. She lifted it out reverently, between two fingers. It had not withered in all the last ten years. The outline of an idea, cruel and terrible, formed in her mind.

"You're going into the forest at night?" May asked, home from work early in the evening.

"Yeah. I'll be fine." Gretchen was tired of repeating herself. She knew May would never stop worrying, but she also knew this thing had to be done.

At dusk, she left a pensive May in the kitchen and made her way into the woods. She and the wolf stalked as one. She felt its raw presence within her, she spoke to it, drew it forth, allowed it to breathe in the still air. Her eyes could not see as well in the night as the wolf's and so she let her knowledge of the wood be her guide. She heard the stream before she reached it; the water rushed lightly over rocks and limbs. She followed it until, at a tall oak, she branched off toward the clearing. Gretchen knelt behind her usual tree and was overcome by the eternal patience of the wolf.

She had no way to know if her plan would work. She had only her own experience to go by. Gretchen did not even know if the thorn retained its potency. All she had was hope, and though she tried not to think of how that hope lay in the thing she most hated, it had become too obvious to ignore. Gretchen relied on that which had changed her to change him.

The wolf was sprawled on the bottom of the cage, sides faintly rising and falling with its breath. An air of resignation emanated from the sad thing. At least she's still alive, Gretchen thought. I'm not too late.

Gretchen had never spent a night in the forest, but she had watched the man inebriate himself day after day and knew he would drink himself to sleep. Beer cans and bottles littered the clearing. Where he found the funds for his habit she could only guess. As she lay there, he staggered out once to relieve himself. She was grateful to see him so far gone.

At least an hour had passed with no sound from him before Gretchen dared to move. She knew she should hurry, but when she reached the cage, she paused. The wolf, scenting her approach, raised it ragged head. Gretchen grasped the bars with her hands and looked into its eyes. Had the wolf not been subjected to such excruciating cruelty, this closeness may not have been achieved. But close they were, faces two feet apart, and in other, less obvious ways. The wolf made no sound as Gretchen tried to convey her compassion and her love. She allowed herself to believe, for just a moment, that the woman inside the wolf understood.

The cabin loomed in the moonlight. She crept quietly to the door and pushed it open, holding her breath and listening for any motion from within. There was none. She entered slowly and saw the man sprawled across a rotted cot, his pants and his shirt all undone. Gretchen grimaced at the thought of touching him, but anger drove her on. She peered around, noted the location of the gun. It was propped against the wall beside him and was probably loaded. She gently lifted it and was surprised by how heavy it was. What to do with the thing? She placed it under the cot and, with her foot, slid it as far back toward the wall as she could. Fear raised the hair on her neck, but before she could reconsider she took the thorn from her pocket and jammed it in.

He rose with a roar as Gretchen ran from the cabin as fast as the dim light would allow. The man, confused, did not at first follow, but soon enough Gretchen heard his drunken shouting from the clearing. She, by the stream, stopped to listen. His voice was slurred, his curses struck out at the night, at demons invisible and at the helpless wolf. Gretchen feared he would take his rage out on her, but she could not linger.

Back home in her bed, adrenaline kept her awake for hours more. When she finally did sleep, her dreams were blood-soaked. When she woke, she was ravenous.

She had one last concern. Would she, the wolf, go to the cabin that night? Gretchen kept her mind fixed on it throughout the day, hoping to convey to the wolf the necessity of it, since the knowledge of what she had done would disappear. That night, as her sisters held her, Gretchen gave in to all of her fury as she changed.

The night swallowed the wolf. Never had the two sisters seen it run so quickly from them. They feared for Gretchen, always, but now they also feared for whatever or whoever was out there.

In the wolf's mind, confusion reigned. It wanted to hunt, it wanted to feast, it wanted to sprint through the trees, chasing down its unwary prey. It did none of these things. As though directed by forgotten instinct, it ran toward the stream. Northward it went by the bank, feet splashing in mud, body weaving between the reeds. It was stopped by a sudden awful scream. Nose raised, it smelled all of those things it had come to associate with the cabin: old blood, iron, and pain.

The wolf growled; it did not like these things. And yet again it caught the scent of itself in the air: wolf, woman, and wolf again. There was danger and there was fear, but the wolf shook them off. Something moved it toward the clearing, some taint of another half-scented life. It had a purpose now and suddenly the wolf almost remembered.

Wolves do feel rage. They know the sudden anger of a hunt gone wrong, or of a mate killed by a farmer's bullet. They feel these things, not as a human would, but solidly in their bones. The wolf's eyes gleamed like stars at what it saw there by the cabin.

A grey and mangy wolf was throwing itself at the bars of the cage in which the woman who had so confused Gretchen was crouching. Gretchen, her sleek fur a testament to her fine health, leapt into the clearing and closed her jaws on the rival wolf's exposed throat. They spun, his hind legs flailing at her underbelly, and landed with a crack in the dirt. He broke free, they circled each other, hackles raised and open mouths drooling. Gretchen tensed and lunged at him again.

At that moment she was neither wolf nor woman. Some hybrid, a strange cross-breed, her agile body seemed to inherit all of her disparate elements as she launched at the male with her teeth fully bared. This was not a hunt; it was murder. The male went down.

Though he kicked and scrabbled, Gretchen pinned him with her bulk and he could not loosen her grip on his throat. He writhed and gurgled, he shuddered and bled, but her jaws clenched all the tighter. With one last jerk of his leg, he finally lay still.

Gretchen backed away from the carcass, raised her head and let forth a slow howl. As she did so, the woman in the cage looked skyward. Two cries filled the night in unison, one of victory and one of relief.

When the chorus was over, the wolf snuffled around the clearing but was hesitant to leave it behind. Hunger was assuaged with a haunch of venison found beside the cabin. The wolf ate, tearing flesh from the bone, as the woman reached her arm out through the bars.

The man must have changed there at the cage. His clothes were in tatters on the ground not a foot away. The woman fumbled with his trousers, using fingers unsure of their function, until she was able to pluck out the set of keys. She mimicked his earlier movements of inserting key into lock. The wolf cocked its head as it watched the woman struggle. The top lock took the most effort, for she hardly had the strength to stand, but at last even that came undone. She fell to the floor as the door swung open and there she remained.

Dawn was coloring the horizon by the time the wolf had finished eating. It felt the urge to travel home, but a different need, one unfamiliar and yet somehow expected, kept it there. It sniffed at fallen limbs and drifts of leaves in the clearing as it slowly approached the cage. Warily, unsure of the creature inside, it touched its nose to her foot. She held out her hand and the wolf's breath came hot on her palm. At that moment the sun tipped the trees in golden daylight and the wolf changed.

Gretchen came to her senses and *remembered*. She pushed her aching body up from the ground and looked around her. Her eyes squinted at the body of the dead wolf, now a feast for ants and beetles. She saw the man's clothes, torn and wrinkled, by the cage. And then, as light filled the clearing, she saw the woman silently watching. Gretchen pulled her weary body close and wrapped her arms her. For one, sweet moment they embraced before the woman also changed.

Gretchen pulled away and watched the transformation. This must be what my sisters see, she thought. It was incredible, the woman stretched and bled, but Gretchen knew there was nothing she could do ease her. She watched with a sense of shared agony until the change was complete. Gretchen reached out a cautious hand and stroked the wolf as it lay with its sides heaving. She wanted to label her feelings for the creature unnatural, but so, she knew, was she. As she watched the animal breathe, wolf called to wolf. Her longing for the comfort of a kindred spirit proved too much.

Gretchen stretched out next to it and looked into its eyes, noting no difference between it and her. As morning broke fully around them, Gretchen curled up beside the warm body of the wolf. She relaxed as the animal gently washed blood from her face with its rough tongue. She threaded her fingers into the wolf's fur, mindful of wounds, both old and new.

"I won't leave you," she said, and the wolf lay her head down and sighed.

When they were unable to find their sister, May and Molly made the difficult decision to involve John. He knew the area and was as close to the authorities as the sisters were willing to get. Molly called him that morning, after they'd spent two hours calling for Gretchen in the woods with no response. She said only said it was a family emergency and asked him to please come. He was there within the hour, his maroon car easing neatly into the drive.

"What is it?" he said as they ushered him in, all business.

"Our sister is missing, but sit down. We have to explain something first," Molly said.

"When did you last see her?" he asked as he made himself comfortable, accepting May's offer of a cup of coffee, black.

"Last night, but listen. She's not . . . " Molly looked to May for assistance.

"She's a wolf." May didn't see the need to delay the issue. "She'll be a woman by now, but she's gone."

John eyed the two sisters oddly, but kept quiet. They were obviously stressed and he was used to unusual situations. As a police officer, he thought he'd seen it all.

"Look, I know it sounds crazy, but our sister is a werewolf. She changes during the full moon," Molly hoped he wouldn't end it with her right there.

He did something far worse. He laughed.

As Molly turned away, disgusted, he pulled himself together and apologized. "I'm sorry. It's just so unlike you to tease me this way."

"I'm not joking."

The look in Molly's eyes warned him that this was not a matter she took lightly. May's face was stern and her arms were crossed at her chest.

"This is not a game, John," May said. "We need your help. Last night, Gretchen went into the woods. She does it every full moon. Normally she comes back in the morning and we get her at the edge of the trees. She's not there and we need your help to find her. You know those woods, we don't."

Okay, John thought. I'll go along with this. I'll treat it as any other case. "What do you mean, *get her*?"

Molly rolled her eyes. "She can't walk very well after changing. We have to help her home."

"Changing."

"Yes, changing. You don't have to believe us about the wolf, but if we do find her, you must promise not to say anything about her condition. Just do that much, will you? Now, can we go?" May was anxious. Perhaps they shouldn't have told him, but they didn't know what else to do.

John gathered up some gear from his car as the sisters bundled their usual assortment of bandages and cloths in a blanket. When he asked them what the items were for, they explained. As they made their way into the woods, the sisters attempted to describe what had happened to their sister. They told him of the wolfweed, the long years of watching their sister become something other than human and finally, they told him of what she had seen in the forest.

It upset him that they hadn't mentioned this before they left—he would have brought his gun. Off duty that day, he hadn't even considered it. The sisters made him promise again and again that he would let them handle whatever it was they found. He was there only to lead them through the forest, not to rush in and be an unwanted hero on their behalf.

He almost believed them by the time they reached the stream. "Would she have come here for water?"

The sisters looked at each other. Did the wolf drink? They didn't know.

"Wait a minute, look here," John suddenly said, pointing at the ground. There, at his feet, was the clear track of an animal. He gazed at them, astounded. "That's a wolf."

"And?"

"There hasn't been a wolf seen around here for twenty years."

"There was a wolf around here last night, we told you," Molly said. "Can we follow the tracks?"

"We can try," he said. "There used to be an old hunters' cabin nearby. The tracks are headed that way. We'll check it out."

It was after noon when they reached the clearing. Molly saw them first. "Oh my God, look."

May put a hand on John's chest before he could react as Molly grabbed her arm. "Don't scare them."

It was too late. The wolf raised its head and in doing so, woke Gretchen. She stared out at her sisters as though she didn't recognize them.

"Gretchen, we're here," May said. She slowly knelt on the ground, pulling John and Molly down with her.

Gretchen focused her eyes on the three of them. The wolf didn't move.

"She's hurt. We have to help her. I'm not leaving her here." Gretchen finally responded.

"Gretchen," May spoke slowly, as though to a child, "that's a wolf."

"Yeah," Gretchen said. "So am I."

GESTELLA

SUSAN PALWICK

Time's the problem. Time and arithmetic. You've known from the beginning that the numbers would cause trouble, but you were much younger then—much, much younger—and far less wise. And there's culture shock, too. Where you come from, it's okay for women to have wrinkles. Where you come from, youth's not the only commodity.

You met Jonathan back home. Call it a forest somewhere, near an Alp. Call it a village on the edge of the woods. Call it old. You weren't old, then: you were fourteen on two feet and a mere two years old on four, although already fully grown. Your kind are fully grown at two years, on four feet. And experienced: oh, yes. You knew how to howl at the moon. You knew what to do when somebody howled back. If your four-footed form hadn't been sterile, you'd have had litters by then—but it was, and on two feet, you'd been just smart enough, or lucky enough, to avoid continuing your line.

But it wasn't as if you hadn't had plenty of opportunities, enthusiastically taken. Jonathan liked that. A lot. Jonathan was older than you were: thirty-five, then. Jonathan loved fucking a girl who looked fourteen and acted older, who acted feral, who was feral for three to five days a month, centered on the full moon. Jonathan didn't mind the mess that went with it, either: all that fur, say, sprouting at one end of the process and shedding on the other, or the aches and pains from various joints pivoting, changing shape, redistributing weight, or your poor gums bleeding all the time from the monthly growth and recession of your fangs. "At least that's the only blood," he told you, sometime during that first year.

You remember this very clearly: you were roughly halfway through the four-to-two transition, and Jonathan was sitting next to you in bed, massaging your sore shoulderblades as you sipped mint tea with hands still nearly as clumsy as paws, hands like mittens. Jonathan had just filled two hot water bottles, one for your aching tailbone and one for your aching knees. Now you know he wanted to get you in shape for a major sportfuck—he loved sex even more than usual, after you'd just changed back—but at the time, you thought he was a real prince, the kind of prince girls like you weren't supposed to be allowed to get, and a stab of pain shot through you at his words. "I didn't kill anything," you told him, your lower lip trembling. "I didn't even hunt."

"Gestella, darling, I know. That wasn't what I meant." He stroked your hair. He'd been feeding you raw meat during the four-foot phase, but not anything you'd killed yourself. He'd taught you to eat little pieces out of his hand, gently, without biting him. He'd taught you to wag your tail, and he was teaching you to chase a ball, because that's what good four-foots did where he came from. "I was talking about—"

"Normal women," you told him. "The ones who bleed so they can have babies. You shouldn't make fun of them. They're lucky." You like children and puppies; you're good with them, gentle. You know it's unwise for you to have any of your own, but you can't help but watch them, wistfully.

"I don't want kids," he says. "I had that operation. I told you."

"Are you sure it took?" you ask. You're still very young. You've never known anyone who's had an operation like that, and you're worried about whether Jonathan really understands your condition. Most people don't. Most people think all kinds of crazy things. Your condition isn't communicable, for instance, by biting or any other way, but it is hereditary, which is why it's good that you've been so smart and lucky, even if you're just fourteen.

Well, no, not fourteen anymore. It's about halfway through Jonathan's year of folklore research—he's already promised not to write you up for any of the journals, and keeps assuring you he won't tell anybody, although later you'll realize that's for his protection, not yours—so that would make you, oh, seventeen or eighteen. Jonathan's still thirty-five. At the end of the year, when he flies you back to the United States with him so the two of you can get married, he'll be thirty-six. You'll be twenty-one on two feet, three years old on four.

Seven-to-one. That's the ratio. You've made sure Jonathan understands this. "Oh, sure," he says. "Just like for dogs. One year is seven human years. Everybody knows that. But how can it be a problem, darling, when we love each other so much?" And even though you aren't fourteen anymore, you're still young enough to believe him.

At first it's fun. The secret's a bond between you, a game. You speak in code. Jonathan splits your name in half, calling you Jessie on four feet and Stella on two. You're Stella to all his friends, and most of them don't even know that he has a dog one week a month. The two of you scrupulously avoid scheduling social commitments for the week of the full moon, but no one seems to notice the pattern, and if anyone does notice, no one cares. Occasionally someone you know sees Jessie, when you and Jonathan are out in the park playing with balls, and Jonathan always says that he's taking care of his sister's dog while she's away on business. His sister travels a lot, he explains. Oh, no, Stella doesn't mind, but she's always been a bit nervous around dogs—even though Jessie's such a good dog—so she stays home during the walks.

Sometimes strangers come up, shyly. "What a beautiful dog!" they say. "What a big dog! What kind of dog is that?"

"Husky-wolfhound cross," Jonathan says airily. Most people accept this. Most people know as much about dogs as dogs know about the space shuttle.

Some people know better, though. Some people look at you, and frown a little, and say, "Looks like a wolf to me. Is she part wolf?"

"Could be," Jonathan always says with a shrug, his tone as breezy as ever. And he spins a little story about how his sister adopted you from the pound because you were the runt of the litter and no one else wanted you, and now look at you! No one would ever take you for a runt now! And the strangers smile and look encouraged and pat you on the head, because they like stories about dogs being rescued from the pound.

You sit and down and stay during these conversations; you do whatever Jonathan says. You wag your tail and cock your head and act charming. You let people scratch you behind the ears. You're a good dog. The other dogs in the park, who know more about their own species than most people do, aren't fooled by any of this; you make them nervous, and they tend to avoid you, or to act supremely submissive if avoidance isn't possible. They grovel on their bellies, on their backs; they crawl away backwards, whining.

Jonathan loves this. Jonathan loves it that you're the alpha with the other dogs—and, of course, he loves it that he's your alpha. Because that's another thing people don't understand about your condition: they think you're vicious, a ravening beast, a fanged monster from hell. In fact, you're no more bloodthirsty than any dog not trained to mayhem. You haven't been trained to mayhem: you've been trained to chase balls. You're a pack animal, an animal who craves hierarchy, and you, Jessie, are a one-man dog. Your man's Jonathan. You adore him. You'd do anything for him, even let strangers who wouldn't know a wolf from a wolfhound scratch you behind the ears.

The only fight you and Jonathan have, that first year in the States, is about the collar. Jonathan insists that Jessie wear a collar. Otherwise, he says, he could be fined. There are policemen in the park. Jessie needs a collar and an ID tag and rabies shots.

Jessie, you say on two feet, needs so such thing. You, Stella, are bristling as you say this, even though you don't have fur at the moment. "Jonathan," you tell him, "ID tags are for dogs who wander. Jessie will never leave your side, unless you throw a ball for her. And I'm not going to get rabies. All I eat is Alpo, not dead raccoons: how am I going to get rabies?"

"It's the law," he says gently. "It's not worth the risk, Stella."

And then he comes and rubs your head and shoulders that way, the way you've never been able to resist, and soon the two of you are in bed having a lovely sportfuck, and somehow by the end of the evening, Jonathan's won. Well, of course he has: he's the alpha.

So the next time you're on four feet, Jonathan puts a strong chain choke collar and an ID tag around your neck, and then you go to the vet and get your shots. You don't like the vet's office much, because it smells of too much fear and pain, but the people there pat you and give you milk bones and tell you how beautiful you are, and the vet's hands are gentle and kind.

The vet likes dogs. She also knows wolves from wolfhounds. She looks at you, hard, and then looks at Jonathan. "Gray wolf?" she asks.

"I don't know," says Jonathan. "She could be a hybrid."

"She doesn't look like a hybrid to me." So Jonathan launches into his breezy story about how you were the runt of the litter at the pound: you wag your tail and lick the vet's hand and act utterly adoring.

The vet's not having any of it. She strokes your head; her hands are kind, but she smells disgusted. "Mr. Argent, gray wolves are endangered."

"At least one of her parents was a dog," Jonathan says. He's starting to sweat. "Now, she doesn't look endangered, does she?"

"There are laws about keeping exotics as pets," the vet says. She's still stroking your head; you're still wagging your tail, but now you start to whine, because the vet smells angry and Jonathan smells afraid. "Especially endangered exotics."

"She's a dog," Jonathan says.

"If she's a dog," the vet says, "may I ask why you haven't had her spayed?"

Jonathan splutters. "Ex*cuse* me?"

"You got her from the pound. Do you know how animals wind up at the pound, Mr. Argent? They land there because people breed them and then don't want to take care of all those puppies or kittens. They land there—"

"We're here for a rabies shot," Jonathan says. "Can we get our rabies shot, please?"

"Mr. Argent, there are regulations about breeding endangered species—"

"I understand that," Jonathan says. "There are also regulations about rabies shots. If you don't give my *dog* her rabies shot—"

The vet shakes her head, but she gives you the rabies shot, and then Jonathan gets you out of there, fast. "Bitch," he says on the way home. He's shaking. "Animal-rights fascist bitch! Who the hell does she think she is?"

She thinks she's a vet. She thinks she's somebody who's supposed to take care of animals. You can't say any of this, because you're on four legs. You lie in the back seat of the car, on the special sheepskin cover Jonathan bought to protect the upholstery from your fur, and whine. You're scared. You liked the vet, but you're afraid of what she might do. She doesn't understand your condition; how could she?

The following week, after you're fully changed back, there's a knock at the door while Jonathan's at work. You put down your copy of Elle and pad, bare-footed, over to the door. You open it to find a woman in uniform; a white truck with "Animal Control" written on it is parked in the driveway.

"Good morning," the officer says. "We've received a report that there may be an exotic animal on this property. May I come in, please?"

"Of course," you tell her. You let her in. You offer her coffee, which she doesn't want, and you tell her that there aren't any exotic animals here. You invite her to look around and see for herself.

Of course there's no sign of a dog, but she's not satisfied. "According to our records, Jonathan Argent of this address had a dog vaccinated last Saturday. We've been told that the dog looked very much like a wolf. Can you tell me where that dog is now?"

"We don't have her anymore," you say. "She got loose and jumped the fence on Monday. It's a shame: she was a lovely animal."

The animal-control lady scowls. "Did she have ID?"

"Of course," you say. "A collar with tags. If you find her, you'll call us, won't you?"

She's looking at you, hard, as hard as the vet did. "Of course. We recommend that you check the pound at least every few days, too. And you might want to put up flyers, put an ad in the paper."

"Thank you," you tell her. "We'll do that." She leaves; you go back to reading Elle, secure in the knowledge that your collar's tucked into your underwear drawer upstairs and that Jessie will never show up at the pound.

Jonathan's incensed when he hears about this. He reels off a string of curses about the vet. "Do you think you could rip her throat out?" he asks.

"No," you say, annoyed. "I don't want to, Jonathan. I liked her. She's doing her job. Wolves don't just attack people: you know better than that. And it wouldn't be smart even if I wanted to: it would just mean people would have to track me down and kill me. Now look, relax. We'll go to a different vet next time, that's all."

"We'll do better than that," Jonathan says. "We'll move."

So you move to the next county over, to a larger house with a larger yard. There's even some wild land nearby, forest and meadows, and that's where you and Jonathan go for walks now. When it's time for your rabies shot the following year, you go to a male vet, an older man who's been recommended by some friends of friends of Jonathan's, people who do a lot of hunting. This vet raises his eyebrows when he sees you. "She's quite large," he says pleasantly. "Fish and Wildlife might be interested in such a large dog. Her size will add another oh, hundred dollars to the bill, Johnny."

"I see." Jonathan's voice is icy. You growl, and the vet laughs.

"Loyal, isn't she? You're planning to breed her, of course."

"Of course," Jonathan snaps.

"Lucrative business, that. Her pups will pay for her rabies shot, believe me. Do you have a sire lined up?"

"Not yet." Jonathan sounds like he's strangling.

The vet strokes your shoulders. You don't like his hands. You don't like the way he touches you. You growl again, and again the vet laughs. "Well, give me a call when she goes into heat. I know some people who might be interested."

"Slimy bastard," Jonathan says when you're back home again. "You didn't like him, Jessie, did you? I'm sorry."

You lick his hand. The important thing is that you have your rabies shot, that your license is up to date, that this vet won't be reporting you to Animal Control. You're legal. You're a good dog.

You're a good wife, too. As Stella, you cook for Jonathan, clean for him, shop. You practice your English while devouring *Cosmopolitan* and *Martha Stewart Living*, in addition to *Elle*. You can't work or go to school, because the week of the full moon would keep getting in the way, but you keep yourself busy. You learn to drive and you learn to entertain; you learn to shave your legs and pluck your eyebrows, to mask your natural odor with harsh chemicals, to walk in high heels. You learn the artful uses of cosmetics and clothing, so that you'll be even more beautiful than you are *au naturel*. You're stunning: everyone says so, tall and slim with long silver hair and pale, piercing blue eyes. Your skin's smooth, your complexion flawless, your muscles lean and taut: you're a good cook, a great fuck, the perfect trophy wife. But of course, during that first year, while Jonathan's thirty-six going on thirty-seven, you're only twenty-one going on twenty-eight. You can keep the accelerated aging from showing: you eat right, get plenty of exercise, become even more skillful with the cosmetics. You and Jonathan are blissfully happy, and his colleagues, the old fogies in the Anthropology Department, are jealous. They stare at you when they think no one's looking. "They'd all love to fuck you," Jonathan gloats after every party, and after every party, he does just that.

Most of Jonathan's colleagues are men. Most of their wives don't like you, although a few make resolute efforts to be friendly, to ask you to lunch. Twenty-one going on twenty-eight, you wonder if they somehow sense that you aren't one of them, that there's another side to you, one with four feet. Later you'll realize that even if they knew about Jessie, they couldn't hate and fear you any more than they already do. They fear you because you're young, because you're beautiful and speak English with an exotic accent, because their husbands can't stop staring at you. They know their husbands want to fuck you. The wives may not be young and beautiful any more, but they're no fools. They lost the luxury of innocence when they lost their smooth skin and flawless complexions.

The only person who asks you to lunch and seems to mean it is Diane Harvey. She's forty-five, with thin gray hair and a wide face that's always smiling. She runs her own computer repair business, and she doesn't hate you. This may be related to the fact that her husband Glen never stares at you, never gets too close to you during conversation; he seems to have no desire to fuck you at all. He looks at Diane the way all the other men look at you: as if she's the most desirable creature on earth, as if just being in the same room with her renders him scarcely able to breathe. He adores his wife, even though they've been married for fifteen years, even though he's five years younger than she is and handsome enough to seduce a younger, more beautiful woman. Jonathan says that Glen must stay with Diane for her salary, which is considerably more than his. You think Jonathan's wrong; you think Glen stays with Diane for herself.

Over lunch, as you gnaw an overcooked steak in a bland fern bar, all glass and wood, Diane asks you kindly when you last saw your family, if you're homesick, whether you and Jonathan have any plans to visit Europe again soon. These questions bring a lump to your throat, because Diane's the only one who's ever asked them. You don't, in fact, miss your family—the parents who taught you to hunt, who taught you the dangers of continuing the line, or the siblings with whom you tussled and fought over scraps of meat—because you've transferred all your loyalty to Jonathan. But two is an awfully small pack, and you're starting to wish Jonathan hadn't had that operation. You're starting to wish you could continue the line, even though you know it would be a foolish thing to do. You wonder if that's why your parents mated, even though they knew the dangers.

"I miss the smells back home," you tell Diane, and immediately you blush, because it seems like such a strange thing to say, and you desperately want this kind woman to like you. As much as you love Jonathan, you yearn for someone else to talk to.

But Diane doesn't think it's strange. "Yes," she says, nodding, and tells you about how homesick she still gets for her grandmother's kitchen, which had a signature smell for each season: basil and tomatoes in the summer, apples in the fall, nutmeg and cinnamon in winter, thyme and lavender in the spring. She tells you that she's growing thyme and lavender in her own garden; she tells you about her tomatoes.

She asks you if you garden. You say no. In truth, you're not a big fan of vegetables, although you enjoy the smell of flowers, because you enjoy the smell of almost anything. Even on two legs, you have a far better sense of smell than most people do; you live in a world rich with aroma, and even the scents most people consider noxious are interesting to you. As you sit in the sterile fern bar, which smells only of burned meat and rancid grease and the harsh chemicals the people around you have put on their skin and hair, you realize that you really do miss the smells of home, where even the gardens smell older and wilder than the woods and meadows here.

You tell Diane, shyly, that you'd like to learn to garden. Could she teach you?

So she does. One Saturday afternoon, much to Jonathan's bemusement, Diane comes over with topsoil and trowels and flower seeds, and the two of you measure out a plot in the backyard, and plant and water and get dirt under your nails, and it's quite wonderful, really, about the best fun you've had on two legs, aside from sportfucks with Jonathan. Over dinner, after Diane's left, you try to tell Jonathan how much fun it was, but he doesn't seem particularly interested. He's glad you had a good time, but really, he doesn't want to hear about seeds. He wants to go upstairs and have sex.

So you do.

Afterwards, you go through all of your old issues of *Martha Stewart Living*, looking for gardening tips.

You're ecstatic. You have a hobby now, something you can talk to the other wives about. Surely some of them garden. Maybe, now, they won't hate you. So at the next party, you chatter brightly about gardening, but somehow all the wives are still across the room, huddled around a table, occasionally glaring in your direction, while the men cluster around you, their eyes bright, nodding eagerly at your descriptions of weeds and aphids.

You know something's wrong here. Men don't like gardening, do they? Jonathan certainly doesn't. Finally one of the wives, a tall blonde with a tennis tan and good bones, stalks over and pulls her husband away by the sleeve. "Time to go home now," she tells him, and curls her lip at you.

You know that look. You know a snarl when you see it, even if the wife's too civilized to produce an actual growl.

You ask Diane about this the following week, while you're in her garden, admiring her tomato plants. "Why do they hate me?" you ask Diane.

"Oh, Stella," she says, and sighs. "You really don't know, do you?" You shake your head, and she goes on. "They hate you because you're young and beautiful, even though that's not your fault. The ones who have to work hate you because you don't, and the ones who don't have to work, whose husbands support them, hate you because they're afraid their husbands will leave them for younger, more beautiful women. Do you understand?"

You don't, not really, even though you're now twenty-eight going on thirty-five. "Their husbands can't leave them for me," you tell Diane. "I'm married to Jonathan. I don't want any of their husbands." But even as you say it, you know that's not the point.

A few weeks later, you learn that the tall blonde's husband has indeed left her, for an aerobics instructor twenty years his junior. "He showed me a picture," Jonathan says, laughing. "She's a big-hair bimbo. She's not half as beautiful as you are."

"What does that have to do with it?" you ask him. You're angry, and you aren't sure why. You barely know the blonde, and it's not as if she's been nice to you. "His poor wife! That was a terrible thing for him to do!"

"Of course it was," Jonathan says soothingly.

"Would you leave me if I wasn't beautiful anymore?" you ask him.

"Nonsense, Stella. You'll always be beautiful."

But that's when Jonathan's going on thirty-eight and you're going on thirty-five. The following year, the balance begins to shift. He's going on thirty-nine; you're going on forty-two. You take exquisite care of yourself, and really, you're as beautiful as ever, but there are a few wrinkles now, and it takes hours of crunches to keep your stomach as flat as it used to be.

Doing crunches, weeding in the garden, you have plenty of time to think. In a year, two at the most, you'll be old enough to be Jonathan's mother, and you're starting to think he might not like that. And you've already gotten wind of catty faculty-wife gossip about how quickly you're showing your age. The faculty wives see every wrinkle, even through artfully applied cosmetics.

During that thirty-five to forty-two year, Diane and her husband move away, so now you have no one with whom to discuss your wrinkles or the catty faculty wives. You don't want to talk to Jonathan about any of it. He still tells you how beautiful you are, and you still have satisfying sportfucks. You don't want to give him any ideas about declining desirability.

You do a lot of gardening that year: flowers—especially roses—and herbs, and some tomatoes in honor of Diane, and because Jonathan likes them. Your best times are the two-foot times in the garden and the four-foot times in the forest, and you think it's no coincidence that both of these involve digging around in the dirt. You write long letters to Diane, on e-mail or, sometimes, when you're saying something you don't want Jonathan to find on the computer, on old-fashioned paper. Diane doesn't have much time to write back, but does send the occasional e-mail note, the even rarer postcard. You read a lot, too, everything you can find: newspapers and novels and political analysis, literary criticism, true crime, ethnographic studies. You startle some of Jonathan's colleagues by casually dropping odd bits of information about their field, about other fields, about fields they've never heard of: forensic geography, agricultural ethics, poststructuralist mining. You think it's no coincidence that the obscure disciplines you're most interested in involve digging around in the dirt.

Some of Jonathan's colleagues begin to comment not only on your beauty, but on your intelligence. Some of them back away a little bit. Some of the wives, although not many, become a little friendlier, and you start going out to lunch again, although not with anyone you like as much as Diane.

The following year, the trouble starts. Jonathan's going on forty; you're going on forty-nine. You both work out a lot; you both eat right. But Jonathan's hardly wrinkled at all yet, and your wrinkles are getting harder to hide. Your stomach refuses to stay completely flat no matter how many crunches you do; you've developed the merest hint of cottage-cheese thighs. You forego your old look, the slinky, skin-tight look, for long flowing skirts and dresses, accented with plenty of silver. You're going for exotic, elegant, and you're getting there just fine; heads still turn to follow you in the supermarket. But the sportfucks are less frequent, and you don't know how much of this is normal aging and how much is lack of interest on Jonathan's part. He doesn't seem quite as enthusiastic as he once did. He no longer brings you herbal tea and hot water bottles during your transitions; the walks in the woods are a little shorter than they used to be, the ball-throwing sessions in the meadows more perfunctory.

And then one of your new friends, over lunch, asks you tactfully if anything's wrong, if you're ill, because, well, you don't look quite yourself. Even as you assure her that you're fine, you know she means that you look a lot older than you did last year.

At home, you try to discuss this with Jonathan. "We knew it would be a problem eventually," you tell him. "I'm afraid that other people are going to notice, that someone's going to figure it out—"

"Stella, sweetheart, no one's going to figure it out." He's annoyed, impatient. "Even if they think you're aging unusually quickly, they won't make the leap to Jessie. It's not in their worldview. It wouldn't occur to them even if you were aging a hundred years for every one of theirs. They'd just think you had some unfortunate metabolic condition, that's all."

Which, in a manner of speaking, you do. You wince. It's been five weeks since the last sportfuck. "Does it bother you that I look older?" you ask Jonathan.

"Of course not, Stella!" But since he rolls his eyes when he says this, you're not reassured. You can tell from his voice that he doesn't want to be having this conversation, that he wants to be somewhere else, maybe watching TV. You recognize that tone. You've heard Jonathan's colleagues use it on their wives, usually while staring at you.

You get through the year. You increase your workout schedule, mine *Cosmo* for bedroom tricks to pique Jonathan's flagging interest, consider and reject liposuction for your thighs. You wish you could have a facelift, but the recovery period's a bit too long, and you're not sure how it would work with your transitions. You read and read and read, and command an increasingly subtle grasp of the implications of, the interconnections between, different areas of knowledge: eco-tourism, Third World famine relief, art history, automobile design.

Your lunchtime conversations become richer, your friendships with the faculty wives more genuine.

You know that your growing wisdom is the benefit of aging, the compensation for your wrinkles and for your fading—although fading slowly, as yet—beauty.

You also know that Jonathan didn't marry you for wisdom.

And now it's the following year, the year you're old enough to be Jonathan's mother, although an unwed teenage one: you're going on fifty-six while he's going on forty-one. Your silver hair's losing its luster, becoming merely gray. Sportfucks coincide, more or less, with major national holidays. Your thighs begin to jiggle when you walk, so you go ahead and have the liposuction, but Jonathan doesn't seem to notice anything but the outrageous cost of the procedure.

You redecorate the house. You take up painting, with enough success to sell some pieces in a local gallery. You start writing a book about gardening as a cure for ecotourism and agricultural abuses, and you negotiate a contract with a prestigious university press. Jonathan doesn't pay much attention to any of this. You're starting to think that Jonathan would only pay attention to a full-fledged Lon Chaney imitation, complete with bloody fangs, but if that was ever in your nature, it certainly isn't now. Jonathan and Martha Stewart have civilized you.

On four legs, you're still magnificent, eliciting exclamations of wonder from other pet owners when you meet them in the woods. But Jonathan hardly ever plays ball in the meadow with you anymore; sometimes he doesn't even take you to the forest. Your walks, once measured in hours and miles, now clock in at minutes and suburban blocks. Sometimes Jonathan doesn't even walk you. Sometimes he just shoos you out into the backyard to do your business. He never cleans up after you, either. You have to do that yourself, scooping old poop after you've returned to two legs.

A few times you yell at Jonathan about this, but he just walks away, even more annoyed than usual. You know you have to do something to remind him that he loves you, or loved you once; you know you have to do something to reinsert yourself into his field of vision. But you can't imagine what. You've already tried everything you can think of.

There are nights when you cry yourself to sleep. Once, Jonathan would have held you; now he rolls over, turning his back to you, and scoots to the farthest edge of the mattress.

During that terrible time, the two of you go to a faculty party. There's a new professor there, a female professor, the first one the Anthropology Department has hired in ten years. She's in her twenties, with long black hair and perfect skin, and the men cluster around her the way they used to cluster around you.

Jonathan's one of them.

Standing with the other wives, pretending to talk about new films, you watch Jonathan's face. He's rapt, attentive, totally focused on the lovely young woman, who's talking about her research into ritual scarification in New Guinea. You see Jonathan's eyes stray surreptitiously, when he thinks no one will notice, to her breasts, her thighs, her ass.

You know Jonathan wants to fuck her. And you know it's not her fault, any more than it was ever yours. She can't help being young and pretty. But you hate her anyway. Over the next few days, you discover that what you hate most, hate even more than Jonathan wanting to fuck this young woman, is what your hate is doing to you: to your dreams, to your insides. The hate's your problem, you know; it's not Jonathan's fault, any more than his lust for the young professor is hers. But you can't seem to get rid of it, and you can sense it making your wrinkles deeper, shriveling you as if you're a piece of newspaper thrown into a fire.

You write Diane a long, anguished letter about as much of this as you can safely tell her. Of course, since she hasn't been around for a few years, she doesn't know how much older you look, so you simply say that you think Jonathan's fallen out of love with you since you're over forty now. You write the letter on paper, and send it through the mail.

Diane writes back, and not a postcard this time: she sends five single-spaced pages. She says that Jonathan's probably going through a mid-life crisis. She agrees that his treatment of you is, in her words, "barbaric." "Stella, you're a beautiful, brilliant, accomplished woman. I've never known anyone who's grown so much, or in such interesting ways, in such a short time. If Jonathan doesn't appreciate that, then he's an ass, and maybe it's time to ask yourself if you'd be happier elsewhere. I hate to recommend divorce, but I also hate to see you suffering so much. The problem, of course, is economic: can you support yourself if you leave? Is Jonathan likely to be reliable with alimony? At least—small comfort, I know—there are no children who need to be considered in all this. I'm assuming that you've already tried couples therapy. If you haven't, you should."

This letter plunges you into despair. No, Jonathan isn't likely to be reliable with alimony. Jonathan isn't likely to agree to couples therapy, either. Some of your lunchtime friends have gone that route, and the only way they ever got their husbands into the therapist's office was by threatening divorce on the spot. If you tried this, it would be a hollow threat. Your unfortunate metabolic condition won't allow you to hold any kind of normal job, and your writing and painting income won't support you, and Jonathan knows all that as well as you do. And your continued safety's in his hands. If he exposed you—

You shudder. In the old country, the stories ran to peasants with torches. Here, you know, laboratories and scalpels would be more likely. Neither option's attractive.

You go to the art museum, because the bright, high, echoing rooms have always made it easier for you to think. You wander among abstract sculpture and impressionist paintings, among still-lifes and landscapes, among portraits. One of the portraits is of an old woman. She has white hair and many wrinkles; her shoulders stoop as she pours a cup of tea. The flowers on the china are the same pale, luminous blue as her eyes, which are, you realize, the same blue as your own.

The painting takes your breath away. This old woman is beautiful. You know the painter, a nineteenth-century English duke, thought so too.

You know Jonathan wouldn't.

You decide, once again, to try to talk to Jonathan. You make him his favorite meal, serve him his favorite wine, wear your most becoming outfit, gray silk with heavy silver jewelry. Your silver hair and blue eyes gleam in the candlelight, and the candlelight, you know, hides your wrinkles.

This kind of production, at least, Jonathan still notices. When he comes into the dining room for dinner, he looks at you and raises his eyebrows. "What's the occasion?"

"The occasion's that I'm worried," you tell him. You tell him how much it hurts you when he turns away from your tears. You tell him how much you miss the sportfucks. You tell him that since you clean up his messes more than three weeks out of every month, he can damn well clean up yours when you're on four legs. And you tell him that if he doesn't love you any more, doesn't want you any more, you'll leave. You'll go back home, to the village on the edge of the forest near an Alp, and try to make a life for yourself.

"Oh, Stella," he says. "Of course I still love you!" You can't tell if he sounds impatient or contrite, and it terrifies you that you might not know the difference. "How could you even *think* of leaving me? After everything I've given you, everything I've done for you—"

"That's been changing," you tell him, your throat raw. "The changes are the problem. Jonathan—"

"I can't believe you'd try to hurt me like this! I can't believe—"

"Jonathan, I'm *not* trying to hurt you! I'm reacting to the fact that you're hurting me! Are you going to stop hurting me, or not?"

He glares at you, pouting, and it strikes you that after all, he's very young, much younger than you are. "Do you have any idea how ungrateful you're being? Not many men would put up with a woman like you!"

"*Jonathan!*"

"I mean, do you have any idea how hard it's been for me? All the secrecy, all the lying, having to walk the damn dog—"

"You used to enjoy walking the damn dog." You struggle to control your breathing, struggle not to cry. "All right, look, you've made yourself clear. I'll leave. I'll go home."

"You'll do no such thing!"

You close your eyes. "Then what do you want me to do? Stay here, knowing you hate me?"

"I don't hate you! You hate me! If you didn't hate me, you wouldn't be threatening to leave!" He gets up and throws his napkin down on the table; it lands in the gravy boat. Before leaving the room, he turns and says, "I'm sleeping in the guestroom tonight."

"Fine," you tell him dully. He leaves, and you discover that you're trembling, shaking the way a terrier would, or a poodle. Not a wolf.

Well. He's made himself very plain. You get up, clear away the uneaten dinner you spent all afternoon cooking, and go upstairs to your bedroom. Yours, now: not Jonathan's anymore. You change into jeans and a sweatshirt. You think about taking a hot bath, because all your bones ache, but if you allow yourself to relax into warm water, you'll fall apart; you'll dissolve into tears, and there are things you have to do. Your bones aren't aching just because your marriage has ended; they're aching because the transition is coming up, and you need to make plans before it starts.

So you go into your study, turn on the computer, call up an internet travel agency. You book a flight back home for ten days from today, when you'll definitely be back on two feet again. You charge the ticket to your credit card. The bill will arrive here in another month, but by then you'll be long gone. Let Jonathan pay it.

Money. You have to think about how you'll make money, how much money you'll take with you—but you can't think about it now. Booking the flight has hit you like a blow. Tomorrow, when Jonathan's at work, you'll call Diane and ask her advice on all of this. You'll tell her you're going home. She'll probably ask you to come stay with her, but you can't, because of the transitions. Diane, of all the people you know, might understand, but you can't imagine summoning the energy to explain.

It takes all the energy you have to get yourself out of the study, back into your bedroom. You cry yourself to sleep, and this time Jonathan's not even across the mattress from you. You find yourself wondering if you should have handled the dinner conversation differently, if you should have kept yourself from yelling at him about the turds in the yard, if you should have tried to seduce him first, if—

The ifs could go on forever. You know that. You think about going home. You wonder if you'll still know anyone there. You realize how much you'll miss your garden, and you start crying again.

Tomorrow, first thing, you'll call Diane.

But when tomorrow comes, you can barely get out of bed. The transition has arrived early, and it's a horrible one, the worst ever.

You're in so much pain you can hardly move. You're in so much pain that you moan aloud, but if Jonathan hears, he doesn't come in. During the brief pain-free intervals when you can think lucidly, you're grateful that you booked your flight as soon as you did. And then you realize that the bedroom door is closed, and that Jessie won't be able to open it herself. You need to get out of bed. You need to open the door.

You can't. The transition's too far advanced. It's never been this fast; that must be why it hurts so much. But the pain, paradoxically, makes the transition seem longer than a normal one, rather than shorter. You moan, and whimper, and lose all track of time, and finally howl, and then, blessedly, the transition's over. You're on four feet.

You can get out of bed now, and you do, but you can't leave the room. You howl, but if Jonathan's here, if he hears you, he doesn't come.

There's no food in the room. You left the master bathroom toilet seat up, by chance, so there's water, full of interesting smells. That's good. And there are shoes to chew on, but they offer neither nourishment nor any real comfort. You're hungry. You're lonely. You're afraid. You can smell Jonathan in the room—in the shoes, in the sheets, in the clothing in the closet—but Jonathan himself won't come, no matter how much you howl.

And then, finally, the door opens. It's Jonathan. "Jessie," he says. "Poor Jessie. You must be so hungry; I'm sorry." He's carrying your leash; he takes your collar out of your underwear drawer and puts it on you and attaches the leash, and you think you're going for a walk now. You're ecstatic. Jonathan's going to walk you again. Jonathan still loves you.

"Let's go outside, Jess," he says, and you dutifully trot down the stairs to the front door. But instead he says, "Jessie, this way. Come on, girl," and leads you on your leash to the family room at the back of the house, to the sliding glass doors that open onto the back yard. You're confused, but you do what Jonathan says. You're desperate to please him. Even if he's no longer quite Stella's husband, he's still Jessie's alpha.

He leads you into the backyard. There's a metal pole in the middle of the backyard. That didn't used to be there. Your canine mind wonders if it's a new toy. You trot up and sniff it, cautiously, and as you do, Jonathan clips one end of your leash onto a ring in the top of the pole.

You yip in alarm. You can't move far; it's not that long a leash. You strain against the pole, the leash, the collar, but none of them give; the harder you pull, the harder the choke collar makes it for you to breathe. Jonathan's still next to you, stroking you, calm, reassuring. "It's okay, Jess. I'll bring you food and water, all right? You'll be fine out here. It's just for tonight. Tomorrow we'll go for a nice long walk, I promise."

Your ears perk up at "walk," but you still whimper. Jonathan brings your food and water bowls outside and puts them within reach.

You're so glad to have the food that you can't think about being lonely or afraid. You gobble your Alpo, and Jonathan strokes your fur and tells you what a good dog you are, what a beautiful dog, and you think maybe everything's going to be all right, because he hasn't stroked you this much in months, hasn't spent so much time talking to you, admiring you.

Then he goes inside again. You strain towards the house, as much as the choke collar will let you. You catch occasional glimpses of Jonathan, who seems to be cleaning. Here he is dusting the picture frames: here he is running the vacuum cleaner. Now he's cooking— beef stroganoff, you can smell it—and now he's lighting candles in the dining room.

You start to whimper. You whimper even more loudly when a car pulls into the driveway on the other side of the house, but you stop when you hear a female voice, because you want to hear what it says.

"So terrible that your wife left you. You must be devastated."

"Yes, I am. But I'm sure she's back in Europe now, with her family. Here, let me show you the house." And when he shows her the family room, you see her: in her twenties, with long black hair and perfect skin. And you see how Jonathan looks at her, and you start to howl in earnest.

"Jesus," Jonathan's guest says, peering out at you through the dusk. "What the hell is that? A wolf?"

"My sister's dog," Jonathan says. "Husky-wolfhound mix. I'm taking care of her while my sister's away on business. She can't hurt you: don't be afraid." And he touches the woman's shoulder to silence her fear, and she turns towards him, and they walk into the dining room. And then, after a while, the bedroom light flicks on, and you hear laughter and other noises, and you start to howl again.

You howl all night, but Jonathan doesn't come outside. The neighbors yell at Jonathan a few times—*Shut that dog up, goddammit!*—but Jonathan will never come outside again. You're going to die here, tethered to this stake.

But you don't. Towards dawn you finally stop howling; you curl up and sleep, exhausted, and when you wake up the sun's higher and Jonathan's coming through the open glass doors. He's carrying another dish of Alpo, and he smells of soap and shampoo. You can't smell the woman on him.

You growl anyway, because you're hurt and confused. "Jessie," he says. "Jessie, it's all right. Poor beautiful Jessie. I've been mean to you, haven't I? I'm so sorry."

He does sound sorry, truly sorry. You eat the Alpo, and he strokes you, the same way he did last night, and then he unsnaps your leash from the pole and says, "Okay, Jess, through the gate into the driveway, okay? We're going for a ride."

You don't want to go for a ride. You want to go for a walk. Jonathan promised you a walk. You growl.

"Jessie! Into the car, now! We're going to another meadow, Jess. It's farther away than our old one, but someone told me he saw rabbits there, and he said it's really big. You'd like to explore a new place, wouldn't you?"

You don't want to go to a new meadow. You want to go to the old meadow, the one where you know the smell of every tree and rock. You growl again.

"Jessie, you're being a *very bad dog*! Now get in the car. Don't make me call Animal Control."

You whine. You're scared of Animal Control, the people who wanted to take you away so long ago, when you lived in that other county. You know that Animal Control kills a lot of animals, in that county and in this one, and if you die as a wolf, you'll stay a wolf. They'd never know about Stella. As Jessie, you'd have no way to protect yourself except your teeth, and that would only get you killed faster.

So you get into the car, although you're trembling.

In the car, Jonathan seems more cheerful. "Good Jessie. Good girl. We'll go to the new meadow and chase balls now, eh? It's a big meadow. You'll be able to run a long way." And he tosses a new tennis ball into the backseat, and you chew on it, happily, and the car drives along, traffic whizzing past it. When you lift your head from chewing on the ball, you can see trees, so you put your head back down, satisfied, and resume chewing. And then the car stops, and Jonathan opens the door for you, and you hop out, holding your ball in your mouth.

This isn't a meadow. You're in the parking lot of a low concrete building that reeks of excrement and disinfectant and fear, fear, and from the building you hear barking and howling, screams of misery, and in the parking lot are parked two white Animal Control trucks.

You panic. You drop your tennis ball and try to run, but Jonathan has the leash, and he starts dragging you inside the building, and you can't breathe because of the choke collar. You cough, gasping, trying to howl. "Don't fight, Jessie. Don't fight me. Everything's all right."

Everything's not all right. You can smell Jonathan's desperation, can taste your own, and you should be stronger than he is but you can't breathe, and he's saying "Jessie, don't bite me, it will be worse if you bite me, Jessie," and the screams of horror still swirl from the building and you're at the door now, someone's opened the door for Jonathan, someone says, "Let me help you with that dog," and you're scrabbling on the concrete, trying to dig your claws into the sidewalk just outside the door, but there's no purchase, and they've dragged you inside, onto the linoleum, and everywhere are the smells and sounds of terror. Above your own whimpering you hear Jonathan saying, "She jumped the fence and threatened my girlfriend, and then she tried to bite me, so I have no choice, it's such a shame, she's always been such a good dog, but in good conscience I can't—"

You start to howl, because he's lying, *lying*, you never did any of that!

Now you're surrounded by people, a man and two women, all wearing colorful cotton smocks that smell, although faintly, of dog shit and cat pee. They're putting a muzzle on you, and even though you can hardly think through your fear—and your pain, because Jonathan's walked back out the door, gotten into the car and driven away, Jonathan's left you here—even with all of that, you know you don't dare bite or snap. You know your only hope is in being a good dog, in acting as submissive as possible. So you whimper, crawl along on your stomach, try to roll over on your back to show your belly, but you can't, because of the leash.

"Hey," one of the women says. The man's left. She bends down to stroke you. "Oh, God, she's so scared. Look at her."

"Poor thing," the other woman says. "She's *beautiful*."

"I know."

"Looks like a wolf mix."

"I know." The first woman sighs and scratches your ears, and you whimper and wag your tail and try to lick her hand through the muzzle. Take me home, you'd tell her if you could talk. Take me home with you. You'll be my alpha, and I'll love you forever. I'm a *good* dog.

The woman who's scratching you says wistfully, "We could adopt her out in a minute, I bet."

"Not with that history. Not if she's a biter. Not even if we had room. You know that."

"I know." The voice is very quiet. "Wish I could take her myself, though."

"Take home a biter? Lily, you have kids!"

Lily sighs. "Yeah, I know. Makes me sick, that's all."

"You don't need to tell me that. Come on, let's get this over with. Did Mark go to get the room ready?"

"Yeah."

"Okay. What'd the owner say her name was?"

"Stella."

"Okay. Here, give me the leash. Stella, come. Come on, Stella."

The voice is sad, gentle, loving, and you want to follow it, but you fight every step, anyway, until Lily and her friend have to drag you past the cages of other dogs, who start barking and howling again, whose cries are pure terror, pure loss. You can hear cats grieving, somewhere else in the building, and you can smell the room at the end of the hall, the room to which you're getting inexorably closer. You smell the man named Mark behind the door, and you smell medicine, and you smell the fear of the animals who've been taken to that room before you. But overpowering everything else is the worst smell, the smell that makes you bare your teeth in the muzzle and pull against the choke collar and scrabble again, helplessly, for a purchase you can't get on the concrete floor: the pervasive, metallic stench of death.

ABOUT THE AUTHORS

PETER BELL is a historian, living in York, England. He is a member of the Friends of Arthur Machen and the Ghost Story Society. He writes for *The Ghosts & Scholars M.R. James Newsletter*, and the magazines *Wormwood* and *Faunus*. His stories have appeared in *All Hallows*; *Supernatural Tales*; Swan River Press's *Haunted Histories* series; the Ash-Tree Press anthologies, *Acquainted with the Night, At Ease with the Dead, Shades of Darkness*, and *Exotic Gothic II*; and in the Ex-Occidente Press anthology *Cinnabar's Gnosis; a Homage to Gustav Meyrink*. A collection of his stories *The Light of the World & Other Strange Tales* is to be published in 2010 by Ex-Occidente Press. An article on *Beasts* by Joyce Carol Oates is in the forthcoming *Twenty-First Century Gothic: Great Gothic Novels since 2000*.

MARIE BRENNAN is the author of the Onyx Court series of London-based historical faerie fantasies: *Midnight Never Come, In Ashes Lie*, and the upcoming *A Star Shall Fall*, as well as the Doppelgänger duology of *Warrior* and *Witch*. She has published nearly thirty short stories in venues such as *On Spec, Beneath Ceaseless Skies*, and the acclaimed anthology series *Clockwork Phoenix*. More information can be found on her web site: www.swantower.com.

MIKE BROTHERTON is the author of the science fiction novels *Spider Star* (2008) and *Star Dragon* (2003), the latter being a finalist for the Campbell award. He's also a professor of astronomy at the University of Wyoming, a Clarion West graduate, and founder of the Launch Pad

Astronomy Workshop for Writers (www.launchpadworkshop.org). He blogs at www.mikebrotherton.com.

JESSE BULLINGTON is the author of *The Sad Tale of the Brothers Grossbart* and the upcoming *The Enterprise of Death*, as well as several short stories and articles. He lives in Colorado and can be found online at www.jessebullington.com.

STEPHANIE BURGIS is an American writer who lives in Wales with her husband, fellow writer Patrick Samphire, their son, and their dog. Her YA Regency fantasy novel *The Unladylike Adventures of Kat Stephenson, Book One: A Most Improper Magick* will be published in 2010. Her short fiction has appeared in several magazines, including *Strange Horizons, Beneath Ceaseless Skies*, and *Fantasy Magazine*. To find out more, please visit her web site: www.stephanieburgis.com

AMANDA DOWNUM lives near Austin, Texas, in a house with a spooky attic, and works at a bookstore in addition to writing, cat-herding, and falling off rocks. Her short fiction has appeared in *Strange Horizons, Realms of Fantasy*, and *Weird Tales. The Drowning City*, first of the Necromancer Chronicles, is available from Orbit Books; the second volume, *The Bone Palace*, is forthcoming in 2010. For more information on Amanda or her writing, visit www.amandadownum.com.

STEVE DUFFY's stories have appeared in numerous magazines and anthologies in Europe and North America. Two new collections of his short fiction, *The Moment of Panic* (which includes the International Horror Guild award-winning tale, "The Rag-and-Bone Men") and *Tragic Life Stories,* will be published in 2010. He lives in North Wales.

KAREN EVERSON is a jack-of-all-arts. She has published fiction, non-fiction and poetry. Recent publications include "Support You Local Werewolf," another Olwen story, in Esther Friesner's anthology *Strip Mauled*. Her current writing projects include a fantasy novel, *Crown of Shadows*, and a paranormal romance centered on Olwen and her family. In addition to her writing, Karen runs Moongate Designs, a small business showcasing her art and needlework designs. She lives in Michigan with her other great passions: her husband Mark, her daughter Caitlyn, and numerous pets.

JEFFREY FORD is the author of the novels, *The Physiognomy, Memoranda, The Beyond, The Portrait of Mrs. Charbuque, The Girl in the Glass,* and *The Shadow Year.* His short stories have been collected into three books—*The Fantasy Writer's Assistant, The Empire of Ice Cream,* and *The Drowned Life.* He lives in South Jersey and teaches Writing and Literature at Brookdale Community College.

LAURA ANNE GILMAN started out on the editorial side of publishing, but went freelance in 2003. Her urban fantasy *Staying Dead* (Luna) came out in 2004, followed by *Curse The Dark, Bring It On, Burning Bridges, Free Fall,* and *Blood From Stone.* The first in a spinoff series, *Hard Magic,* was published in May 2010. The first book in The Vineart War trilogy, *Flesh and Fire* (Pocket), was published in October 2009. The second book, *Weight of Stone,* will be available October 2010. She is also the author of the Grail Quest YA trilogy for HarperCollins (2006), and as "Anna Leonard" writes paranormal romances (*The Night Serpent* and the forthcoming *The Hunted*). She also writes short fiction, and as part of Book View Café (www.bookviewcafe.com), is involved in expanding the definition of publishing beyond traditional models. More information available at lauraannegilman.net

GEOFFREY H. GOODWIN is a writer who lives near Boston, Massachusetts. He has two degrees in literature and has spent most of his life working in bookstores and comic book shops. Geoffrey's fiction has appeared in *Lady Churchill's Rosebud Wristlet, Rabid Transit,* and Prime's *Phantom* anthology, among others. He has also contributed nonfiction to *Bookslut, Weird Tales,* and *Tor.com.*

After traveling the world in search of the perfect Bunco group, **SAMANTHA HENDERSON** settled down in Southern California. Her short fiction has been published in *Realms of Fantasy, Strange Horizons, Fantasy,* and *Chizine,* and her 2008 dark Victorian fantasy

Heaven's Bones was nominated for the Scribe Award. She is currently the treasurer of the Science Fiction Poetry Association.

N.K. Jemisin's work has appeared in *Clarkesworld*, *Strange Horizons*, and *Postscripts*, and ranges across science fiction, fantasy, erotica, and sometimes a bit of all three. Her first novel, *The Hundred Thousand Kingdoms*, first of the Inheritance Trilogy, is out now from Orbit Books. She lives and writes in Brooklyn, NY.

C.E. Murphy is a writer, mostly of novels, but sometimes of comic books and short stories. Born and raised in Alaska, she now lives with her family in her ancestral homeland of Ireland, a magical land where winter never arrives. More information about her writing and witty banter with the author are available at her web site, www.cemurphy.net.

Susan Palwick is an Associate Professor of English at the University of Nevada, Reno, where she teaches literature and writing. She has published three novels, all with Tor, and a story collection with Tachyon Publications. She is currently working on a mainstream novel under contract with Tor. Susan's writing has been honored with the Crawford Award from the International Association for the Fantastic in the Arts, with an Alex Award from the American Library Association, and with a Silver Pen Award from the Nevada Writers Hall of Fame. She has also been a finalist for the World Fantasy Award and the Mythopoeic Award.

Mike Resnick is, according to *Locus*, the all-time leading award winner, living or dead, for short science fiction. He has won five Hugos, a Nebula, and other major awards in the USA, France, Spain, Poland, Croatia, and Japan, and has been short-listed in England, Italy and Australia. He is the author of sixty-one novels, over 250 short stories, and two screenplays, and has edited more than forty anthologies. His work has been translated into twenty-three languages. In his spare time, he sleeps.

Lawrence Schimel has published over one hundred books as author or anthologist, including *The Drag Queen of Elfland* (Circlet), *The Future* *is Queer* (Arsenal Pulp), *Things Invisible to See: Lesbian and Gay Tales of Magic Realism* (Circlet), *Two Boys in Love* (Seventh Window), and *Fairy Tales for Writers* (A Midsummer Night's Press). He has twice won the Lambda Literary Award, for *First Person Queer* (Arsenal Pulp) and *PoMoSexuals* (Cleis), and has also won the Spectrum, the Independent Publisher Book Award, the Rhysling, and other awards. He lives in Madrid, Spain, where he works as a Spanish-to-English translator.

MARIA V. SNYDER switched careers from meteorologist to novelist when she began writing the New York Times best-selling Study Series (*Poison Study, Magic Study* and *Fire Study*) about a young woman who becomes a poison taster. Born and raised in Philadelphia, Pennsylvania, Maria dreamed of chasing tornados, but lacked the skills to forecast their location. Writing, however, lets Maria control the weather. Her new Glass Series (*Storm Glass, Sea Glass*, and *Spy Glass*) combines two out of the three things Maria loves: the weather and glass. The third is dogs. Readers are invited to read more of Maria's short stories on her web site at www.MariaVSnyder.com.

MOLLY TANZER is the assistant editor of *Fantasy Magazine*. Her interview with Garth Nix appeared on the *Fantasy Magazine* site, and her nonfiction article "On Books and Animals" appeared in *Herbivore Magazine*. You are always welcome to visit her at www.mollytanzer. com. She knits, but never with wool.

GENEVIEVE VALENTINE's fiction has appeared or is forthcoming in *Clarkesworld Magazine, Strange Horizons, Fantasy Magazine*, and in anthologies *Federations, The Living Dead II*, and *Teeth*. Her first novel, about a mechanical circus troupe, is coming in 2011 from Prime. She has an insatiable appetite for bad movies, a tragedy she tracks on her blog at www.genevievevalentine.com.

CARRIE VAUGHN is the bestselling author of a series of novels about a werewolf named Kitty who hosts a talk radio advice show for the supernaturally disadvantaged. The seventh installment, *Kitty's House of Horrors*, was released in 2010. T.J. in "Wild Ride" is a character from the series. Carrie's first young adult novel, *Voices of Dragons*, is also due to be released in 2010. An Air Force brat, she grew up all over the U.S. but has managed to put down roots in Boulder, Colorado. Please visit her at www.carrievaughn.com for more information.

ERZEBET YELLOWBOY is the editor of *Cabinet des Fées*, a journal of fairy tale fiction, and the founder of Papaveria Press, a private press specializing in handbound limited editions of mythic poetry and prose. Her stories and poems have appeared in *Fantasy Magazine*, *Jabberwocky*, *Goblin Fruit*, *Mythic Delirium*, *Electric Velocipede* and others. Her second novel, *Sleeping Helena*, is scheduled for release in 2010. Visit her web site at www.erzebet.com.

PUBLICATION HISTORY